The Case of
Comrade Tulayev

The Case of Comrade Tulayev

Victor Serge

Translated from the French by
Roger Trask with a new preface
by Gareth Jenkins

A joint edition
published by
Bookmarks and Journeyman

The Case of Comrade Tulayev / *Victor Serge*
This edition published 1993
Bookmarks, 265 Seven Sisters Road, London N4 2DE
Journeyman, 345 Archway Road, London N6 5AA
© the estate of Victor Serge
English translation first published in 1951

ISBN 1 85172 0529 paperback
ISBN 1 85172 0510 hardback
CIP data: A catalogue record of this book is available from the
British Library

Bookmarks is linked to an international grouping of socialist
organisations:
AUSTRALIA: **International Socialists,**
GPO Box 1473N, Melbourne 3001
BELGIUM: **Socialisme International,**
Rue Lovinfosse 60, 4030, Grevignée
BRITAIN: **Socialist Workers Party,**
PO Box 82, London E3 3LH
CANADA: **International Socialists,**
PO Box 339, Station E, Toronto, Ontario M6H 4E3
CYPRUS: **Workers Democracy,**
PO Box 7280, Nicosia, Cyprus
DENMARK: **Internationale Socialister,**
Ryesgade 8, 3, 8000 Århus C
FRANCE: **Socialisme International,**
BP 189, 75926 Paris, Cedex 19
GERMANY: **Sozialistische Arbeitersgruppe,**
Wolfsgangstrasse 81, W-6000, Frankfurt 1
GREECE: **Organosi Sosialistiki Epanastasi,**
PO Box 8161, 10010, Omonia, Athens
HOLLAND: **Groep Internationale Socialisten,**
PO Box 9720, 3506 GR Utrecht
IRELAND: **Socialist Workers Movement,**
PO Box 1648, Dublin 8
NORWAY: **Internasjonale Sosialister,**
Postboks 9226, Gronland 0134, Oslo
POLAND: **Solidarnosc Socjalistyczna,**
PO Box 12, 01-900 Warszawa 118
SOUTH AFRICA: **International Socialists of South Africa,**
PO Box 18530, Hillbrow 2038
UNITED STATES: **International Socialist Organisation,**
PO Box 16085, Chicago, Il. 60616

Printed in Finland by WSOY

'I have undergone a little over ten years of various forms of captivity, agitated in seven countries and written 20 books. I own nothing, on several occasions a press with a vast circulation has thrown filth at me because I spoke the truth. Behind us lies a victorious revolution gone astray, several abortive attempts at revolution, and massacres in so great a number as to inspire a certain dizziness. And to think that it is not over yet. Let me be done with this digression; those were the only roads possible for us. I have more confidence in mankind and in the future than ever before.'

Victor Serge, 1943

Introduction

WHY HAS this, the best novel ever written on the show trials and purges in Stalin's Russia, been out of print in English translation ever since 1951, except for a paperback edition that appeared nearly a quarter of a century ago?

No doubt it has something to do with Cold War politics. Other novels on the same theme, such as George Orwell's *Nineteen Eighty-Four* and Arthur Koestler's *Darkness at Noon* (both continuously in print throughout the post-war period), suited Western propaganda much better. Their terrifying picture of totalitarianism points to the apparently inescapable conclusion that revolutions always end in a worse tyranny than the ones they overthrow. *The Case of Comrade Tulayev*, on the other hand, does not.

The Cold War is now over. But the need for Serge's masterpiece has not lessened. The spectacular collapse of Stalinism has demoralised many on the left, leading them to accept that what the 1917 Russian revolution stood for, the hope of emancipation from below, can only end in the nightmare of the Gulag.

Serge lived through both. From his own experience he knew that Bolshevism, despite the harshness of the regime under conditions of civil war and imperialist intervention, was qualitatively different from Stalinism, with its system of bureaucratic privilege and power. This is what gave him the strength to fight as part of Trotsky's Left Opposition and to survive arrest and deportation to Central Asia between 1933 and 1936—just as the Great Terror got under way.

Serge continued that struggle after exile to France. Life in the West was not easy for Oppositionists. Persecuted by the Stalinist press,

1

which repeated the slanders of the show trials, and worn down by defeat in the Spanish Civil War, many lost their bearings. Serge did not, though his disagreements with Trotsky in the late 1930s over the Kronstadt mutiny of 1921 showed the pressure of those who questioned whether totalitarianism was not implicit in Bolshevism itself.

Serge began writing *The Case of Comrade Tulayev* in 1940, the year in which he was forced to flee the advancing Nazis and find refuge in Mexico. To write a novel which presented the show trials and purges from a perspective of undimmed confidence in revolutionary socialism was an extraordinary commitment on Serge's part—especially as he knew that there was little likelihood of its being published.

Serge's novel is more easily approached with some knowledge of the historical record, though not knowing does not diminish its brilliance. In December 1934, the Leningrad party chief, Kirov (Tulayev in the novel) was murdered. His assassination unleashed mass terror. It coincided with growing dislocation caused by the forced collectivisation of the peasantry and the dizzying pace of industrialisation under the first Five Year Plan. Even sections of the Stalinist bureaucracy, which had defeated all opposition in the party by 1928, urged a slowing down of the frantic tempo of change. Kirov was part of this 'moderate' grouping and his popularity in the apparatus was a challenge to Stalin's authority.

Though a culprit was found, much of the precise responsibility remains obscure (Serge created his own explanation). But even if Stalin was not responsible the assassination suited his purposes. With a rival out of the way, he could use it as a pretext to root out 'enemies' that were supposedly preventing Russia from catching up with the West. A series of increasingly monstrous show trials accompanied the purges, the most spectacular of which were the trials of Zinoviev and Kamenev (two of Lenin's most trusted companions) in August 1936 on charges of treason, and that of Bukharin, another old Bolshevik leader, in March 1938. All three were executed. What riveted the world's attention was the sight of Bolshevik leaders, who had long since capitulated to Stalin, confessing to terrible crimes of treachery plotted over many years across the whole of Europe, in inherently unlikely alliance with Trotsky and the Gestapo. Moreover, their confessions in open court had all the appearance of being unforced.

These trials, reminiscent of witch trials of the seventeenth century, strained rational explanation to breaking point. But there was a rationality to it which Serge well understood. The terror—with its purges of 'enemies of the people' in staged show trials—served a number of purposes. The bureaucracy could hope to deflect popular wrath from itself. It could also eliminate the last of the Old Bolsheviks (that link with 1917), whose continuing existence served as a constant reproach to the lies and crimes committed in the name of the working class. (That many of these Old Bolsheviks had sided, like Bukharin and the Right Opposition, with Stalin against Trotsky or had now capitulated, in order to survive and be 'useful', mattered little: it made the extraction of confessions easier.) Finally, it could discipline the ruling bureaucracy, even at a cost to itself, into a forced consciousness of its common interests as an exploiter of the mass of the population over which it ruled.

Why, though, choose a fictional form in which to explore all this? As Serge put it in his *Memoirs*:

> Historical work did not satisfy me entirely;... it does not allow enough scope for showing men as they really live, dismantling their inner workings and penetrating deep into their souls. A certain degree of light can only be cast on history, I am convinced, by literary creation which is free and disinterested... My conception of writing was and is that [its justification is] as a means of expressing to men what most of them live inwardly without being able to express, as a means of communion, a testimony to the vast flow of life through us, whose essential aspects we must try to fix for the benefit of those who will come after us.[1]

In wanting to bear witness to the truth—and truth is a term that reverberates throughout the novel's thickening web of lies, slanders, distortions and plots—Serge also wanted to penetrate the inner motivation of those caught up in the purges, both executioners and victims. In showing human motivation rooted in material factors, he also demonstrated the 'guilty conscience' of the bureaucracy which could not 'but feel that its roots [were] in a temporary and transient concatenation of national and international circumstances.'[2] Like the Western ruling classes it competed with, every step it took to consolidate its power called into existence the very forces that undermined it.

Serge uses a fragmentary method of narrative to make his point. There appears to be no central character—only a series of overlapping stories. But the narrative's randomness is only apparent. Serge slowly uncovers a 'plot' (in the form of a conspiracy), which pulls his apparently unconnected characters tightly together into a totalitarian order. But he also uses the 'plot' (in the fictional sense) to undercut this 'order': the unexpected consequences of individual interaction give rise to a different vision of order, one based on ties of human solidarity. Seldom has fictional form been used to greater effect.

The way in which Serge's method works can be seen in the opening of the novel. We are presented with an apparent irrelevance: on a 'sudden impulse' a young man called Kostia buys a little ebony-framed portrait of a woman instead of the boots he desperately requires. As the chapter proceeds it becomes clear that the impulse purchase is no accident: it expresses the frustrations in his personal life produced by the imposition of bureaucratic commands on social life. A tiny detail reveals much larger forces at work.

But these frustrations lead in turn to other 'accidents'; almost by chance Kostia kills Comrade Tulayev, an act which sets in motion a series of events with a destabilising momentum of their own that can be traced back to the Chief's (Stalin's) impossible-to-fulfil instructions. In the end nothing can be controlled—the smallest 'mistake' undermines the plot. Serge shows this repeatedly in the way characters interact. In unguarded gestures, slips of the tongue, a sudden recognition that the official line is a lie, the different bureaucrats cannot help betraying themselves.

How right Serge was to be confident about a future for revolutionary socialism:

> The future seems to me full of possibilities greater than any we have glimpsed throughout the past. May the passion, the experience and even the faults of my fighting generation have some small power to illuminate the way forward![3]

Gareth Jenkins
September 1992

Notes
1. Victor Serge, *Memoirs of a Revolutionary 1901-1941*, London 1967, p. 262.
2. Tony Cliff, *State Capitalism in Russia*, London 1988, p. 266.
3. Serge, p. 382.

CONTENTS

THE CASE OF COMRADE TULAYEV

I

COMETS ARE BORN AT NIGHT

FOR SEVERAL weeks Kostia had been thinking about buying a pair of shoes. But then a sudden impulse, which surprised even himself, upset all his calculations. By going without cigarettes, films, and lunch every other day, he would need six weeks to save up the one hundred and forty roubles which was the price of a fairly good pair of shoes that the salesgirl in a second-hand shop had kindly promised to set aside for him 'on the q.t.' Meanwhile, he walked cheerfully on cardboard soles, which he replaced every evening. Fortunately the weather remained fair. When Kostia had accumulated seventy roubles he gave himself the pleasure of going to see the shoes that would one day be his. He found them half hidden on a dark shelf, behind several old copper samovars, a pile of opera-glass cases, a Chinese teapot, and a shell box with a sky-blue Bay of Naples. A magnificent pair of boots, of the softest leather, had the place of honour on the shelf—four hundred roubles, imagine! Men in threadbare overcoats licked their lips over them. 'Don't worry,' the little salesgirl said to him. 'Your boots are still here, don't worry . . .' She smiled at him, and again he noticed her brown hair, her deep-set eyes, her irregular but pretty teeth, her lips— but what was the right adjective for her lips? 'Your lips are enchanted,' he thought and looked straight into her face, but never, never would he dare to say what he was thinking! For a moment her deep-set eyes held him, with their colour between green and blue—just the colour of those Chinese jades he had noticed under the glass top of the counter! Then his eyes wandered on over the jewels, the paper cutters, the watches, the snuffboxes, until, quite by chance, they fell on a little ebony-framed portrait of a woman, so small that he could have held it in his hand . . .

'How much is that?' Kostia asked in a startled voice.

'Sixty roubles—it's expensive, you know,' said the enchanted lips.

Hands that were no less enchanted dropped a piece of red-and-gold brocade, reached under the counter, brought out the miniature. Kostia took it. It was a shock to find his big, grimy fingers holding the little portrait. How alive it was! And how strange! It was the strangeness of it that he felt the most. The little black rectangle framed a blonde head crowned with a tiara; alert yet sweet, penetrating yet mild, the eyes were an unfathomable mystery . . .

'I'll take it,' Kostia said, to his own surprise.

He had spoken so quietly, the voice had seemed to come from such depths of his being, that the salesgirl did not dare to protest. She looked furtively to right and left, then murmured:

'Don't say anything . . . I'll make out the slip for fifty roubles. Just don't let the cashier see what it is when you pay for it.'

Kostia thanked her. But he hardly saw her. 'Fifty or seventy—what do I care, girl? The price has nothing to do with it—can't you see that?' A fire burned in him. As he walked homeward he felt the little ebony rectangle in his inside coat pocket cling gently to his breast; and from the contact there radiated a growing joy. He walked faster and faster, ran up a dark flight of stairs, hurried down the hall of the collective apartment—to-day it smelled rankly of naphthalene and cabbage soup—entered his room, switched on the light, looked ecstatically at his cot bed, the old illustrated magazines piled on the table, the window with the three broken panes replaced by cardboard—and felt embarrassed to hear himself murmur: 'What luck!' Now the little black frame stood on the table, tilted against the wall, and the blonde woman saw only him, as he saw only her. The room filled with an indefinable brightness. Kostia walked aimlessly from the window to the door—suddenly he felt imprisoned. On the other side of the partition Romachkin coughed softly.

'What a man!' Kostia thought, suddenly amused by the recollection of the bilious little fellow. He never went out, he was so neat and clean —a real *petit bourgeois*, living there alone with his geraniums, his grey-paper-bound books, his portraits of great men: Ibsen, who said that the solitary man is the strongest man; Metchnikov, who enlarged the boundaries of life; Darwin, who proved that animals of the same species do not eat each other; Knut Hamsun, because he spoke for the hungry and loved the forest. Romachkin still wore old coats made in the days of the war that preceded the Revolution that preceded the Civil War—in the days when the world swarmed with inoffensive and frightened Romachkins. Kostia gave a little smile as he turned towards his half-a-fireplace—because the partition which separated his room from Assistant Clerk Romachkin's room exactly divided the handsome marble fireplace of what had once been a drawing-room.

Poor old Romachkin! you'll never have any more than half a room, half a fireplace, half a life—and not even half of a face like that . . .

(The face in the miniature, the intoxicating blue light of those eyes.)

'Your half of life is the dark half, poor old Romachkin.'

Two strides took Kostia into the hall and to his neighbour's door, on which he rapped the customary three little knocks. A stale odour of fried food, mingled with talk and quarrelling voices, wafted from the other end of the apartment. An angry woman—who was certainly thin, embittered, and unhappy—was clattering pots and saying: 'So he said, "Very well, citizen, I'll tell the manager." And I said, "Very well, citizen, I'll——" ' A door opened, then instantly slammed shut, letting a burst of childish sobs escape. The telephone rang furiously. Romachkin came to the door. 'Hello, Kostia.'

Romachkin's domain was nine feet long by eight feet wide, just like Kostia's. Paper flowers, carefully dusted, decorated the half-a-mantelpiece. His geraniums bordered the window sill with reddish purple. A glass of cold tea stood on the table, which was neatly covered with white paper. 'I'm not interrupting, I hope? Were you reading?' The thirty books stood ranged on the double shelf over the bed.

'No, Kostia, I wasn't reading. I was thinking.'

The faded wall, the portraits of the four great men, the glass of tea, and Romachkin sitting there thinking with his coat buttoned. 'What,' Kostia wondered, 'does he do with his hands?' Romachkin never put his elbows on the table; when he spoke, his hands usually lay spread flat on his knees; he walked with his hands behind his back; he sometimes folded his arms over his chest, timidly raising his shoulders. His shoulders suggested the humble patience of a beast of burden.

'What were you thinking about, Romachkin?'

'Injustice.'

A vast subject, you certainly didn't exhaust it, my friend. Odd—it was chillier here than in his own room. 'I came to borrow some books,' said Kostia. Romachkin's hair was neatly brushed, his face was sallow and ageing, his lips were thin, his eyes fastened on you, yet they looked afraid. What colour were they? They didn't seem to have any colour. No more, indeed, did Romachkin—at first you thought grey, and then not even that. He studied his shelves for a moment, then took down an old paper-bound volume. 'Read that, Kostia. It's the stories of brave men.' It was issue Number 9 of *Prison*, 'official organ of the Association of Former Convicts and Life-Exiles.' Thank you, good-bye. Good-bye, my friend. Would he go back to his thinking now, the poor creature?

Their two tables exactly faced each other on the two sides of the partition. Kostia sat down, opened the magazine, and tried to read. Now and again he looked up at the miniature, each time with the happy certainty that he would find the greenish-blue eyes fixed on his. Spring skies, pale above the snow, had that light when the river ice went out and the earth began to live again. Romachkin, in his private desert on the other side of the partition, had sat down again with his head in his hands—solitary, absorbed, convinced that he was thinking. Perhaps he really was thinking.

For a long time Romachkin had been living in solitary communion with a depressing thought. His job as assistant clerk in the wages department of the Moscow Clothing Trust would never be made permanent, since he was not a member of the Party. On the other hand, unless he should be arrested or die, he would never be replaced be-cause, of all the 117 employees of the central office who, from nine to six, filled forty rooms under the Alcohol Trust and over the Karelian Furs Syndicate and next door to the Uzbekistan Cottons Agency, he alone knew every detail of the seventeen categories of wages and salaries, in addition to the seven types of remuneration for piecework, the possible combinations of basic wages with production bonuses, the art of reclassifications and paper raises which had no upsetting effect on the total salary budget. 'Romachkin,' the order would come, 'the director wants you to prepare the application of the new circular from the Plan Committee in conformity with the Central Committee's circular of January 6, of course taking into consideration the decision of the Conference of Textile Trusts—you know the one?' He knew. The head of his office, former capmaker and member of the Party since last spring, knew nothing—he couldn't even add. But he was said to be connected with the secret service (supervision of technical personnel and manual labour). He spoke with the voice of authority: 'Understand, Romachkin? Have it ready by five o'clock to-morrow. I am going to the board meeting.' The office was in the third court of a brick building in St. Barnaby Alley; a few sickly trees, half killed by rubble from a demolished building, made a touching spot of green under his window.

Romachkin immersed himself in his calculations. And after a time it appeared that the 5 per cent increase in the basic wage published by the Central Committee, combined with the reclassifications whereby certain workers in Category 11 were transferred to Category 10, and certain workers in Category 10 to Category 9, thus improving the condition of the lowest wage groups (as not only justice but also the directive of the Council of Syndicates demanded), resulted in a 0.5 per cent reduction in the total wage budget if the regulations were applied with the utmost strictness. Now, the workmen in the two mills earned between 110 and 120 roubles, and the new rent increase became effective at the end of the month. Romachkin sadly turned his conclusions over to be typed. Every month he went through some similar operation (though the pretext for it was always new), brought his explanatory tables for the accounting office up to date, waited until quarter to five before he went to wash his hands, which he did slowly, humming 'tra-la-la, tra-la-la' or 'mmmm-mmmmm' like a melancholy bee . . . He dined hurriedly in the office restaurant, reading the leading article in the paper, which always announced, in the same tone of authority, that the country was progressing, was making rapid strides, that there had never been anything to compare with it, that despite all opposition history was being made for the glory of the Republic, the happiness of the working masses—witness the 210 factories opened during the year, the brilliant success in creating a grain reserve, and . . .

'But I,' Romachkin said to himself one day as he swallowed his last spoonful of cold semolina, 'am squeezing the poor.'

The figures proved it. He lost his peace of mind. 'The trouble is that I think . . . or rather, there is a being in me that thinks without my being aware of it, and then suddenly raises its voice in the silence of my brain and utters some short, acid, intolerable sentence. And after that, life can't be the same.' Romachkin was terrified by his twofold discovery—that he thought, and that the papers lied. He spent evenings at home, making complex calculations, comparing millions in goods roubles with millions in nominal roubles, tons of wheat with masses of human beings. He went to libraries and opened dictionaries and encyclopædias to *Obsession, Mania, Insanity, Mental Diseases, Paranoia, Schizophrenia*, and concluded that he was neither paranoid nor cyclothymic nor schizophrenic nor neurotic, but at most suffering from a slight degree of hysteromaniacal depression. Symptoms: an obsession with figures, a propensity to find falsehood everywhere, and an idea which was almost an obsession, an idea which was so sacred that he feared to name it, an idea which solved all intellectual problems, which put all falsehood to flight, an idea which a man must keep perpetually in his consciousness or he would cease to be more than a miserable wretch, a sub-human paid to nibble at other men's bread, a cockroach snug in the brick building of the Trusts . . . Justice was in the Gospels, but the Gospels were feudal and pre-feudal superstition; surely Justice was in Marx, though Romachkin could not find it there; it was in the Revolution, it watched in Lenin's tomb, it illuminated the embalmed brow of a pink and pallid Lenin who lay under crystal, guarded by motionless sentries; in reality they were guarding eternal Justice.

The doctor whom Romachkin consulted at the neuropsychiatric clinic at Khamovniki said: 'Reflexes excellent, nothing to worry about, citizen. Sex life?' 'Not much, only occasionally,' Romachkin answered blushing. 'I recommend intercourse twice a month,' said the doctor dryly. 'As to the idea of justice, don't let it worry you. It is a positive social idea resulting from the sublimation of the primitive ego and the suppression of individualistic instincts; it is called upon to play a great role in the period of transition to Socialism . . . Macha, call in the next patient. Your number, citizen?' The next patient was already in the room, his number in his fingers—fingers of paper, shaken by an inner storm. A being disfigured by an animal laugh. The man in the white blouse, the doctor, disappeared behind his screen. What did he look like? Romachkin had forgotten his face already. Satisfied with his consultation, Romachkin was in a mood to joke: 'The patient is yourself, Citizen Doctor. Primitive sublimation—what nonsense! You have never had the least notion of justice, citizen.'

He emerged from the crisis strengthened and illuminated. As a result of the doctor's advice on sexual hygiene he found himself, one cloudy evening, on a bench on the Boulevard Trubnoy, haunt of painted girls who ask you, in soft, alcoholic voices, for a cigarette . . . Romachkin did not smoke. 'I am very sorry, mam'selle,' he said, trying to sound lewd. The prostitute took a cigarette from her pocket, lit it slowly to display her painted nails and her charming profile—then crushed her body against his: 'Looking for something?' He nodded. 'Come over on the other bench, it's farther from the light. You'll see what I can do . . . Three roubles, right?' Romachkin was overwhelmed by the thought of poverty and injustice; yet what connection was there between such thoughts and this prostitute, and himself, and sexual hygiene? He said nothing. Yet he was half aware of a connection, as tenuous as the silvery rays that on clear nights link star to star. 'For five roubles, I'll take you home,' said the girl. 'You pay in advance, darling—that's the rule.' He was glad that there was a rule for this sort of transaction. The girl led him through the moonlight to a hovel almost indistinguishable in the shadow of an eight-story office building. Discreet knocking on a window-pane brought out a poverty-stricken woman clutching a shawl over her sunken chest. 'It's comfortable inside,' she said, 'there's a little fire. Don't hurry, Katiuchenka, I'll be all right here smoking a butt while I wait. Don't wake the baby —she's asleep on the far side of the bed.' In order not to wake the baby, they lay down on the floor on a quilt which they took from the bed, in which a little dark-haired girl lay sleeping with her mouth open. A single candle gave the only light. Everything, from the dirty ceiling to the cluttered corners, was sordid. The iniquity of it went through Romachkin like a cold that freezes to the bone. He too was iniquitous, an iniquitous brute. In his person, iniquity itself writhed on the body of a miserable, anæmic girl. Iniquity filled the huge silence into which he plunged with bestial fury. At that instant, another idea was born in him. Feeble, faraway, hesitant, not wanting to live, it yet was born. Thus from volcanic soil rises a tiny flame, which, small though it be, yet reveals that the earth will quake and crack and burst with flowing lava.

Afterwards, they walked back to the boulevard together. She chattered contentedly: 'Still got to find one more to-night. It's not easy. Yesterday I hung around till dawn, and then didn't get anyone but a drunk who didn't have quite three roubles left. What do you think of that? Cholera! People are too hungry, men don't think about making love these days.' Romachkin politely agreed, preoccupied with watching the struggles of the new little flame: 'Of course. Sexual needs are influenced by diet . . .' Thus encouraged, the girl talked of what was happening in the country. 'I just got back from my village, oh cholera!' Cholera must be her favourite word, he thought. She said it charmingly, now blowing out a straight stream of cigarette smoke, now spitting sidewise. 'The horses are all gone, cholera! What will people do now? First they took the best horses for the collective, then the township co-operative refused to furnish fodder for the ones the peasants had been left or had refused to give up. Anyway, there wasn't any more fodder because the army requisitioned the last of it. The old people, who remembered the last famine, fed them roof thatch—imagine what fodder that makes for the poor beasts after it's been out under rain and sun for years! Cholera! It made you weep to see them, with their sad eyes and their tongues hanging out and their ribs sticking through their sides—I swear they really came through the hide!—and their swollen joints and little boils all over their bellies and their backs full of pus and blood and worms eating right into the raw flesh—the poor creatures were rotting alive—we had to put bands under their bellies to hold them up at night or they'd never have been able to get back on their legs in the morning. We let them wander around the yards and they licked the fence palings and chewed the ground to find a scrap of grass. Where I come from, horses are more precious than children. There are always too many children to feed, they come when nobody wants them —do you think there was any need for *me* to come into the world? But there are never enough horses to do the farm work with. With a horse, your children can grow up; without a horse a man is not a man any more, is he? No more home—nothing but hunger, nothing but death. . . . Well, the horses were done for—there was no way out. The elders met. I was in the corner by the stove. There was a little lamp on the table, and I had to keep trimming the wick—it smoked. What was to be done to save the horses? The elders couldn't even speak, they were so sunk. Finally my father—he looked terrible, his mouth was all black —said: "There's nothing to be done. We'll have to kill them. Then they won't suffer any more. There's always the leather. As for us, we will die or not, as God pleases." Nobody said anything after that, it was so quiet that I could hear the roaches crawling under the stove bricks. My old man got up slowly. "I'll do it," says he. He took the axe from under the bench. My mother threw herself on him: "Nikon Nikonich, pity . . ." He looked as if he needed pity himself, with his face all screwed up like a murderer. "Silence, woman," says he. "You, girl, come and hold a light for us." I brought the lamp. The stable was against the house; when the mare moved at night we heard her. It was comforting. She saw us come in with the light, and she looked at us sadly, like a sick man, there were tears in her eyes. She hardly turned her head because her strength was nearly gone. Father kept the axe hidden, because the mare would surely have known. Father went up to her and patted her cheeks. "You're a good mare, Brownie. It's not my fault if you have suffered. May God forgive me——" Before the words were out of his mouth Brownie's skull was split open. "Clean the axe," Father said to me. "Now we have nothing." How I cried that night!—outside, because they would have beaten me if I'd cried in the house. I think everybody in the village hid somewhere and cried . . .' Romachkin gave her an extra fifty copecks. Then she wanted to kiss him on the mouth—'You'll see how, darling'—but he said 'No, thank you,' humbly, and walked away among the dark trees, his shoulders sagging.

All the nights of his life were alike, equally empty. After leaving the office, he wandered from co-operative to co-operative with a crowd of idlers like himself. The shelves in the shops were full of boxes, but, to avoid any misunderstanding, the clerks had put labels on them: *Empty Boxes*. Nevertheless, graphs showed the rising curve of weekly sales. Romachkin bought some pickled mushrooms and reserved a place in a line that was forming for sausage. From a comparatively well-lighted street he turned into another that was dark, and walked up it. Electric signs, themselves invisible, filled the end of it with an orange glory. Suddenly heated voices filled the darkness. Romachkin stopped. A brutal masculine voice was lost in uproar, a woman's voice rose, rapid and vehement, heaping insults on the traitors, saboteurs, beasts in human guise, foreign agents, vermin. The insults spewed into the darkness from a forgotten loud-speaker in an empty office. It was frightful —that voice without a face, in the darkness of the office, in the solitude, under the unmoving orange light at the end of the street. Romachkin felt terribly cold. The woman's voice clamoured: 'In the name of the four thousand women workers . . .' Romachkin's brain passively echoed: *In the name of the four thousand women workers in this factory* . . . And four thousand women of all ages—seductive women, women prematurely old (why?), pretty women, women whom he would never know, women of whom he dared not dream—were present in him for an uncalculable instant, and they all cried: 'We demand the death penalty for these vile dogs! No pity!' ('Can you mean it, women?' Romachkin answered severely. 'No pity? All of us need pity so much, you and I and all of us . . .') 'To the firing squad with them!' Factory meetings continued during the trial of the engineers—or was it the economists, or the food control board, or the Old Bolsheviks, who were being tried this time? Romachkin walked on. Twenty steps farther he stopped again, this time in front of a lighted window. Between the curtains he saw a table set for supper—tea, plates, hands, only hands on the checked linoleum: a fat hand holding a fork, a grey slumbering hand, a child's hand . . . A loud-speaker in the room showered the hands with the cry of the meetings: 'Shoot them, shoot them, shoot them!' Who? It didn't matter. Why?

Because terror and suffering were everywhere mingled with an inexplicable triumph tirelessly proclaimed by the newspapers. 'Good evening, Comrade Romachkin. Have you heard? Marfa and her husband have been refused passports because they were disenfranchised as artisans formerly working on their own account. Have you heard? Old Bukin has been arrested, they say he had hidden dollars sent him by his brother, who is a dentist in Riga . . . And the engineer has lost his job, he's suspected of sabotage. Have you heard? There is going to be a fresh purge of employees, get ready for it, I heard at the house committee meeting that your father was an officer . . .'—'It's not true,' said Romachkin, choking, 'he was only a sergeant during the imperialist war, he was an accountant . . .' (But since that right-thinking accountant had belonged to the Russian People's Union, Romachkin's conscience was not entirely at ease.)—'Try to produce witnesses, they say the commissions are severe . . . They say there is trouble in the Smolensk region—no more wheat . . .'—'I know, I know . . . Come and play checkers, Piotr Petrovich . . .' They went to Romachkin's room, and his neighbour began telling his own troubles in a low voice: his wife's first husband had been a shopkeeper, so it was more than likely that her passport for Moscow would not be renewed. 'They give you three days to get out, Comrade Romachkin, and you have to go somewhere at least two hundred miles away—but will they give you a passport there?' If it turned out that way, their daughter obviously couldn't enter the Forestry School. Gilded by the lamplight, the axe came down on the head of a horse with human eyes, voices lashed through fiery darkness demanding victims, stations were filled with crowds waiting almost hopelessly for trains which crawled over the map towards the last wheat, the last meat, the last combines; a prostitute from the Boulevard Trubnoy lay gaping wide open on a pallet beside a sleeping child pink as a sucking pig, pure as the innocents Herod slaughtered, and a prostitute cost money, five roubles, a day's pay—yes, he must find witnesses to face the new purge with, was the new rent scale going into effect? If in all this there was not some immense wrong, some boundless guilt, some hidden villainy, it must be that a sort of madness filled everyone's brain. The game of checkers was over. Piotr Petrovich went home, thinking of his troubles: 'Most serious, the matter of the interior passport . . .' Romachkin turned down his bed, undressed, rinsed out his mouth, and lay down. The electric light burned on his bed table, the sheet was white, the portraits mute—ten o'clock. Before he went to sleep, he read the paper carefully. The face of the Chief filled a third of the front page, as it did two or three times a week, surrounded by a seven-column speech: *Our economic successes . . .* Prodigious, they were. We are the chosen people, the most fortunate of peoples, envied by a West destined to crises, unemployment, class struggle, war; our welfare increases daily, wages, as the result of Socialist emulation by our shock brigades, show a rise of 12 per cent over the past year; it is time to stabilize them, since production has shown an increase of only 11 per cent. Woe to the sceptics, to those of little faith, to those who nourish the venomous serpent of Opposition in their secret hearts!—It was set forth in angular periods, numbered 1, 2, 3, 4, 5; numbered too were the five conditions (all now fulfilled) for the realization of Socialism; numbered too the six commandments of Labour; numbered too the four grounds for historic certainty . . . Romachkin could not believe his senses, he turned a sharp eye on the 12 per cent increase in wages. This increase in nominal wages was accompanied by a reduction at least three times as great in real wages, as a result of the depreciation of paper money and the rise in prices. . . . But in this connection the Chief, in his peroration, made a mocking allusion to the dishonest specialists of the Commissariat of Finance, who would receive exemplary punishment. 'Continued applause. The audience rise and acclaim the orator for minutes. Salvos of shouts: "Long live our unconquerable Chief! Long live our great Pilot! Long live the Political Bureau! Long live the Party!" The ovation is resumed. Numerous voices: "Long live the Secret Police!" Thunderous applause.'

Feeling unfathomably sad, Romachkin thought: How he lies!—and was terrified at his own audacity. No one, fortunately, could hear him think; his room was empty; somebody came out of the toilet, walked down the hall dragging his slippers—no doubt it was old Schlem, who had stomach trouble; a sewing machine purred softly; before getting into bed, the couple across the hall were quarrelling in little sentences that hissed like lashes. He felt the man pinching the woman, slowly twisting her hair, making her kneel down, then hitting her across the face with the back of his hand; the whole hall knew it, the couple had been reported, but they denied it and were reduced to torturing each other without making any noise, as, afterwards, they cohabited without making any noise, moving like wary animals. And the people listening at the door heard almost nothing, but sensed everything.—Twenty-two people lived in the six rooms and the windowless nook at the back: twenty-two people, all clearly recognizable by the most furtive sounds they made in the stillness of night. Romachkin turned out the light. The feeble glow of a street light came through the curtain, tracing the usual pictures on the ceiling. They varied monotonously from day to day. In the half-light, the Chief's massive profile was superimposed on the figure of the man who was silently beating his wife in the room across the hall. Would she ever escape from her bondage? Shall we ever escape from falsehood? The responsibility was his who lied in the face of an entire people. The terrible thought which, until now, had matured in the dark regions of a consciousness that feared itself, that pretended to ignore itself, that struggled to disguise itself before the mirror within, now stripped off its mask. So, at night, lightning reveals a landscape of twisted trees above a chasm. Romachkin felt an almost visual revelation. He saw the criminal. A translucent flame flooded his soul. It did not occur to him that his new knowledge might avail him nothing. Henceforth it would possess him, would direct his thoughts, his eyes, his steps, his hands. He fell asleep with his eyes wide open, suspended between ecstasy and fear.

Romachkin took to haunting the Great Market—sometimes before the office opened in the morning, sometimes late in the afternoon after his work was done. There, from dawn to dark, several thousand human beings formed a stagnant crowd which might almost have appeared motionless, so patient and wary were their comings and goings. Patches of colour, human faces, objects, were all overwhelmed by the uniform grey of the trodden muddy ground which never dried out; misery marked every creature there with its crushing imprint. It was in the suspicious eyes of market women swathed in shapeless wool or prints, in the earthy faces of soldiers who could no longer really be soldiers, though they still wore vague uniforms that had been in battle only to flee; it was in the frayed cloth of overcoats, in hands that held out unexpected wares: a Samoyed reindeer glove fringed with red and green and lined inside—'Soft as down, citizen, just feel it'—a solitary glove, as it was the solitary merchandise the little Kalmuck thief had to offer to-day. Difficult to tell sellers from buyers, as they stood shifting their feet or prowled slowly around one another. 'A watch, a watch, a good Cyma watch—buy it?' The watch ran only seven minutes—'What a movement, listen, citizen!'—just long enough for the seller to pocket your fifty roubles and vanish. A sweater, worn at the collar and patched in the body, ten roubles—done! A man dead of typhoid had soaked it with his sweat?—Certainly not, citizen, that's only the smell of the trunk it was in. 'Tea, real caravan tea, *t'ai, t'ai*.' The slant-eyed Chinaman chants the magic syllables over and over, looking at you hard, then passes on; if you answer him with a wink he half pulls out of his sleeve a tiny, square painted packet in which Kutzetsov tea used to come in the old days. 'It's the real thing. From the Gepeou co-op.' Is he sneering, the Chinese, or is it the shape of his mouth, with those greenish teeth, that makes him look as if he were sneering? Why does he mention the Gepeou? Can he belong to it? Strange that he's not arrested, that he's there every day—but they are all there every day, the three thousand speculators, male and female, between the ages of ten and eighty—no doubt because it's impossible to arrest them all at once, and because, no matter how many raids the police make, the creatures are legion. Among them too, their caps pulled down to their eyes, stalk the police detectives in search of their prey: murderers, escaped convicts, crooks, renegade counter-revolutionaries. This swarming mass of human beings has an imperceptible structure, like an ancient bog. (Watch your pockets and shake yourself well when you leave, you will certainly have picked up some lice; and beware of those lice, they come from the country, from prisons, from trains, from the huts of Eurasia—they carry typhus; you can pick them up from the ground, you know; people that have them sow them as they walk, and the filthy little insect, who's looking for a living too, climbs up your legs till it gets to the warm place—they know what they're doing, the little beasts! What—you really believe that the day will come when men won't have lice? True Socialism—eh?—with butter and sugar for everybody? Maybe, to increase human happiness, there'll be soft, perfumed lice that caress you?) Romachkin vaguely listened to the tall bearded man who was discussing lice with evident enjoyment. He followed 'Butter Alley,' where of course there was no alley and no butter to be seen, but simply two lines of standing women, some of them holding lumps of butter wrapped in cloths; others, who had not paid the inspector for their places, kept their butter hidden in their bodices, between waist and breasts. (Now and again one of them was arrested: 'Aren't you ashamed of yourself, speculator!') Farther on was the section of illegally slaughtered cattle, meat brought in the bottoms of sacks, under vegetables, under grain, under anything, and which the sellers scarcely showed. 'Good fresh meat—buy it?' From under her cloak the woman produced a shin of beef wrapped in a bloodstained newspaper. How much? Just feel it! A sinister fellow with an epileptic tic held a peculiar piece of black meat in his crooked sorcerer's claws, saying not a word. You can even eat that, it's cheap, all you have to do is cook it well, and the only way to cook it, of course, is in a tin dish over a fire in some empty lot! Do you like stories about women who have been dismembered, citizen? I know some interesting ones. A small boy went by, carrying a kettle and glasses, selling boiled water at ten copecks a glass. Here began the legally constituted market, with its wares duly displayed on the ground. But what wares! An incredible juxtaposition of dark glasses, oil lamps, chipped teapots, old snapshots, books, dolls, scrap iron, dumb-bells, nails (the big ones were sold by the piece, the small ones, which you examined one by one to make sure the points weren't broken, by the dozen), china, bibelots from the old days, shells, spittoons, teething rings, dancing slippers still vaguely gilt, a top hat which had belonged to a circus rider or a dandy under the old régime, things impossible to classify, but which *could* be sold because they *were* sold, because people lived by selling them—flotsam from innumerable wrecks battered by the waves of more than one flood. Not far from the Armenian theatre, Romachkin at last found himself interested in someone, in something. The Armenian theatre was composed of a number of large boxes covered with black cloth and pierced with a dozen oval holes, into which the spectators put their faces—thus their bodies remained outside while their heads were in wonderland. 'Still three places free, comrades, only fifty copecks, the show is about to begin—The Mysteries of Samarkand in ten scenes with thirty actors in real colours.' Having found his three clients, the Armenian disappeared behind the curtain to pull the strings of his mysterious marionettes and make them all talk himself, in thirty different voices—houris with long eyes, wicked old women, servants, children, fat Turkish merchants, a gipsy fortune-teller, a thin devil with a beard and horns—imitating the fire-eating assassin, the amorous tenor, the brave Red soldier . . . Not far away a squatting Tatar watched over his merchandise: felt hats, carpets, a saddle, daggers, a yellow quilt covered with strange stains, a very old fowling piece. 'A good gun,' he said soberly as Romachkin bent over it. 'Three hundred.' Thus they became acquainted. The fowling piece was useless, except to attract the dangerous client. 'I have another one at home that's brand new,' the Tatar—Akhim—finally said at their fourth meeting, after they had drunk tea together. 'Come and see it.'

Akhim lived at the end of a courtyard surrounded by white birches, in the district of quiet, clean little alleys around Kropotkin Street (they had to go through Death Street to reach it). There, in a cavern darkened by the hides and felts that hung from the ceiling, Akhim displayed a magnificent Winchester with two shining blue barrels—'twelve hundred roubles, my friend.' That was Romachkin's salary for six months, and the gun was not at all the weapon for what he had in mind—only two shots, clumsy to transport. Well, by sawing off part of the barrel and two-thirds of the stock, it could be carried under an ordinary suit. Romachkin hesitated, weighing the pros and cons. By going into debt, by selling everything he owned which was saleable, and even stealing a few things from the office besides, he could not get together six hundred . . . A series of dull explosions shook the walls and rattled the window-panes. 'What's that?'—'Nothing, my friend, they're dynamiting St. Saviour's Cathedral.' They dropped the subject. 'No, really,' Romachkin said, 'I can't, it's too expensive. Besides . . .' He had said that he was a hunter, a member of the official hunter's association, and consequently had a permit . . . Akhim's face changed, Akhim's voice changed, he went for the singing tea-kettle, poured tea into their glasses, sat down opposite Romachkin on a low stool, and drank the amber beverage with relish; doubtless he was getting ready to say something important, perhaps his final price, nine hundred? Romachkin could no more get together nine hundred than twelve hundred. It was devastating. After a long silence he heard Akhim's caressing voice mingling with the distant boom of an explosion:

'If it is to kill somebody, I have something better . . .'

'Better?' Romachkin asked, gasping for breath . . .

On the table, between their glasses, lay a Colt revolver with a short barrel and a black cylinder—a forbidden weapon, the mere presence of which was a crime—a fine clean Colt, calling the hand, fortifying the will.

'Four hundred, my friend.'

'Three hundred,' said Romachkin unconsciously, already filled with the Colt's spell.

'Three hundred—take it, my friend,' said Akhim, 'because my heart trusts you.'

It was only as he went out that Romachkin noticed how strangely neglected and disorderly Akhim's quarters looked. It was not a place where anyone lived, it was a place where someone was waiting to vanish, in a confusion like a station platform during the rout of an army. Under the white birches, Akhim smiled at him mildly. Romachkin set out through the peaceful little streets. The heavy Colt lay against his chest, in the inside pocket of his coat. From what robbery, what murder on the distant steppe, did it come? Now it lay against the heart of a pure man whose one thought was justice.

He stopped for a moment at the entrance to a huge construction yard. There was a wide view under the liquid blue of the moon. In the distance, through scaffolding and the rubble of demolished buildings, he could see the waters of the Moskva, as through the crenellations of a ruined fortress. To the right was the scaffolding of an uncompleted skyscraper; to the left rose the citadel of the Kremlin, with the heavy flat façade of the Great Palace, the tall tower of Tsar Ivan, the pointed turrets of the enclosing wall, the bulbous domes of the cathedrals rising against the starry sky. Here searchlights reigned, men ran through a zone of harsh white light, a sentry ordered back a crowd of gapers. The wounded mass of the Cathedral of St. Saviour occupied the foreground; the great gilded cupola that had crowned it was gone like an ancient dream, the building rested heavily on the beginning of its own ruins; a dark crack a hundred feet long split it from top to bottom, like a dead lightning bolt in the masonry. 'There it goes!' someone said. A woman's voice murmured, 'My God!' Thunder burrowed through the ground, shook the ground, made the whole moonlit landscape rock fantastically, set the river sparkling, set people shuddering. Smoke rose slowly, the thunder rolled over the ground and vanished in a silence like the end of the world; a deep sigh rose from the mass of stone, and it began to sink in upon itself with a snapping of bones, a cracking of beams, a desolate look of suffering. 'That's done it!' cried a little bare-headed engineer to several dust-covered workmen who, like himself, had emerged from the cloud. Romachkin, having read it in the papers, thought that life progressed through destruction, that things must perpetually be torn down so that things could be built, that the old stones must be killed so that new buildings, better ventilated and worthier of man, might rise; that on this spot would one day stand the beautiful Palace of the Peoples of the Union—in which perhaps iniquity would no longer reign. A slight unacknowledged grief mingled with these grandiose ideas as he resumed his walk towards the place where he could catch tram-car A.

He put the Colt on the table. Bluish-black, it filled the room with its presence. Eleven o'clock. He bent over it in thought for a moment before he went to bed. On the other side of the partition Kostia moved; he was reading, from time to time he looked up at the radiant miniature. The two men felt each other's nearness. Kostia drummed gently against the partition with his fingertips. Romachkin answered in the same fashion: Yes, come! Should he hide the Colt before Kostia came in? His hesitation lasted only a hundredth part of a second. The first thing Kostia saw as he entered was the magical blue-black steel on the white paper tablecloth. Kostia picked up the Colt and bounced it happily up and down in his hand. 'Magnificent!' He had never held a revolver before, he felt childishly happy. He was rather tall, with a high forehead, unruly hair, and sea-green eyes. 'How well you hold it!' said Romachkin admiringly. And in fact the Colt increased Kostia's stature, giving him the look of a proud young warrior. 'I bought it,' Romachkin explained, 'because I like firearms. I used to hunt, but a shotgun is too expensive . . . A double-barrelled Winchester costs twelve hundred—think of it!' Kostia only half listened to the embarrassed explanation: that his timid neighbour should own a revolver amused him, and he made no attempt to hide his amusement—his whole face lit up with a smile . . . 'You will certainly never use it, Romachkin,' he said. Romachkin answered warily: 'I don't know . . . Of course I have no use for it. What should I use it for? I have no enemies . . . But a firearm is a beautiful thing. It makes you think . . .'

'Of assassins?'

'No. Of just men.'

Kostia suppressed a guffaw. A fine hero *you'd* make, my poor friend! —A good sort, though. The little man was looking at him quite seriously. Kostia feared that he would hurt him if he joked. They

chatted a few minutes just as usual. 'Have you read Issue 12 of *Prison*?'
Romachkin asked before they separated.—'No—is it interesting?'—
'Very. It has the story of the attempt on Admiral Dubassov in 1906 . . .'
Kostia took Issue 12 with him.

But Romachkin himself did not want to re-read any accounts of
those red-letter days of the Revolution. They were too discouraging.
Those historic assassinations had required meticulous preparation, disciplined organization, money, months of work, of watching, of waiting,
courage linked with courage; besides, they had often failed. If he had
really thought about it, his plan would have appeared completely
visionary. But he did not think—thoughts formed and dissolved in him
without control, almost like a reverie. And since he had got through
life in that fashion, he did not know that it is possible to think better,
more accurately, more clearly, but that such thinking is a strange
labour which one performs almost in spite of oneself and which often
results in a bitter pleasure, beyond which there is nothing. Whenever
he could—whether in the morning, afternoon, or evening—Romachkin
explored a certain locality in the centre of the city: Staraia Place, an old
square on which stands a sort of bank building in grey freestone; at
the entrance there is a black glass plate with gold lettering: *Communist
Party (Bolshevik) of the U.S.S.R., Central Committee*. A guard sil-
houetted in the hall. Lifts. Across the narrow square, the old white
crenellated wall of Kitai-Gorod, the 'Chinese City.' Cars drew up.
There was always someone smoking thoughtfully at the corner . . . No,
not here. Impossible here. Romachkin could not have said why.
Because of the white crenellated wall, the severe grey freestone blocks,
the emptiness? The ground was too hard, it bewildered his feet, he felt
that he had neither weight nor substance. In the vicinity of the Kremlin, on the other hand, the breezes that swept through the gardens
carried him across Red Square in all his insignificance, and when he
stopped for a moment before Lenin's tomb, he was as anonymous as
the gaping provincials who stopped with him; the faded, twisted domes
of St. Vasili the Blessed dwarfed him even more. It was not until he
had mounted the three steps of the Place of Execution that he felt
himself again. It had been there for centuries, surrounded by a
small circular stone balcony. How many men had died there? Of
them all, nothing survived in the souls of the passers-by—except in
his. Just as simply would he have laid himself on the wheel that
should break his limbs. The mere thought of the atrocious torture set

his skin shivering. But what else was there to do when one had come thus far? From that day on, he carried the Colt whenever he went out.

Romachkin liked the public gardens that border the outer wall of the Kremlin on the side towards the city. He gave himself the pleasure of walking there almost every day. It was there that the thing hit him between the eyes. He was walking in the gardens eating a sandwich (it was between 1.15 and 1.50), instead of chatting with his colleagues in the Trust restaurant. As usual, the central walk was almost deserted; the tram-cars, making the turn outside the fence, rattled and clanged their bells. Where the walk curves in the direction of the rusty foliage that borders the high wall of the Kremlin, a man in uniform appeared. Two men in civilian clothes followed him, smoking. Tall, almost gaunt, the visor of his military cap pulled down over his eyes, his uniform bare of insignia, his face hard, bristlingly moustached, and inconceivably sensual, the man stepped out of the portraits published in the papers, displayed four stories high on buildings, hung in offices, impressed, day after day, on the minds of the nation. There was no possible doubt: it was *He*. The air of authority, the hands—the right in the pocket, the other swinging . . . As if in final proof of his identity, the Chief drew a short pipe from his pocket, put it between his teeth, and walked on. Now he was only thirty feet from Romachkin. Romachkin's hand flew into his coat pocket, groping for the butt of the Colt. At that moment the Chief, still walking, drew out his tobacco pouch; less than six feet from Romachkin he stopped, daring him; his cat eyes shot a little cruel gleam in Romachkin's direction. His mocking lips muttered something like, 'You abject worm Romachkin,' with devastating scorn. And he passed by. Demolished, Romachkin stumbled over a stone, tottered, almost fell. Two men, sprung from nowhere, caught him in time. 'Do you feel ill, citizen?' They must be members of the Chief's secret-police escort. 'Let me alone!' Romachkin shouted at them, beside himself with rage—but actually he barely breathed the words, or other words, in a despairing whisper. The two men, who were holding him by the elbows, let him go. 'Don't drink when you don't know how, idiot,' muttered one. 'Damned vegetarian!' Romachkin sank onto a bench beside a young couple. A voice of thunder—his own—rang in his head: 'Coward, coward, coward, coward . . .' The couple, paying no attention to him, went on quarrelling.

'If you see her again,' the woman said, 'I . . .' (the next words were inaudible) 'I've had enough. I've suffered too much, I . . .' (more inaudible words). 'I beg you . . .'

An anæmic creature, hardly more than a girl—lifeless blonde hair, a face covered with pink pimples. The fellow answered:

'You make me tired, Maria. Stop it. You make me tired.' And he stared into the distance.

It was all relentlessly logical. Romachkin rose as if pushed up by a spring, looked at the couple implacably, and said:

'We are all cowards—do you hear me?'

It was so obvious, that the tension of his despair snapped; he was able to get up, to walk as he had walked before, to reach the office without being a minute late, go back to his graphs, drink his glass of tea at four o'clock, answer questions, finish his day's work, go home . . . Now, what should he do with the Colt? He could not bear to have the useless weapon in his room any longer.

It was lying on the table, the blue-black steel gleaming with a coldness that was an insult, when Kostia came in and seemed to smile at him. Romachkin was sure he saw him smile. 'Do you like it, Kostia?' he asked. Around them spread the peace of evening. Kostia, with the revolver in his hand and smiling at him quite openly, became a young warrior again. 'It's a beautiful thing,' he said.

'I have no use for it,' said Romachkin, torn with regret. 'You can have it.'

'But it's worth a lot,' the young man objected.

'Not to me. And you know I can't sell it. Take it, Kostia.' Romachkin was afraid to insist, because suddenly he so much wanted Kostia to take it. 'Really?' Kostia spoke again. And Romachkin answered: 'Yes, really. Take it.' Kostia carried away the Colt, put it on his own table, under the miniature, smiled once more at the faithful eyes that looked out of the frame, then at the clean weapon—mortally clean and proud it was! He did a few gymnastics for very joy. Romachkin enviously heard his joints crack.

Almost every evening they talked for a few minutes before they went to bed—the one ponderously insidious, returning to the same ideas over and over, again and again, like a plough ox making one furrow, then beginning again, to plough one beside it, again and yet again; the other mocking, attracted despite himself, sometimes leaping out of the invisible circle that had been drawn around him, only to find himself unwittingly back in it again. 'What do you think, Romachkin?' he asked at last. 'Who is guilty, guilty of it all?'

'Obviously it is whoever has the most power. If there were a God, it would be God,' Romachkin said softly. 'That would be very convenient,' he added, with a little devious laugh.

Kostia felt that he had understood too many things at once. It made his head spin. 'You don't know what you are saying, Romachkin. And it's a good thing for you that you don't! Good night.'

From nine in the morning to six in the evening, Kostia worked in the office of a subway construction yard. The rhythmic and raucous throb of the excavating machine was communicated to the planking of the shanty. Trucks carried away the excavated earth. The first layers appeared to be composed of human debris, as humus is composed of vegetable debris; they had an odour of corpses, of the decaying city, of refuse long fermented under alternate snow and hot pavements. The truck engines, fed on an inconceivable gasolene, filled the yard with staccato explosions so violent that they drowned out the swearing of the drivers. A thin board fence separated Yard No. 22 from the bustling, klaxoning street, with its two surging streams flowing in opposite directions, its hysterically ringing tram-cars, brand new police vans, ramshackle hackney carriages, swarming pedestrians. The shanty, the centre of which was occupied by a stove, housed the timekeeping department, the accounting department, the technicians' office, the desk reserved for the Party and the Young Communists, with its file cases, the corner allocated to the Secretary of the Syndical Cell, the office of the yard chief—but the latter was never there, he ran from one end of Moscow to the other looking for materials, with the Control Commissions running after him. So his space could be used. The Party secretary took it as of right: from morning to night he received the complaints of mud-covered workers, male and female, who descended into the earth, then came up out of the earth—one because he had no lamp, the second because he had no boots, the third no gloves; the fourth had been hurt; the fifth, fired for arriving drunk and late, furious because he was not allowed to go now that he had been fired: 'I demand that the law be obeyed, Comrade Part.-Org. [Party Organizer]. I came late, I was drunk, I made a row. Throw me out— it's the law!' The Part.-Org. burst out, turning crimson: 'In the name of God and all the stinking saints, you rub your dirty nose in the law because you want to quit, eh? Think you'll get yourself some more work clothes somewhere else, eh? Damed dirty . . .'—'The law's the law, Comrade.' Kostia checked the time-cards for absences, went down into the tunnel with messages, helped the organizer of the Young Communists in his various educational, disciplinary, and secret-service duties. A short, dark, bobbed-haired, energetic eighteen-year-old girl with rouged lips and small acid eyes passed. He waved to her. 'So your little pal Maria hasn't shown up for two days? I'll have to take it up with the Y.C. office.'

The girl stopped short and pulled up her skirt with a masculine gesture. A miner's lamp hung from her leather apron. With her hair hidden under a thick kerchief, she looked as if she were wearing a helmet. She spoke passionately, slowly, in a low voice:

'You won't see Maria again. Dead. Threw herself in the Moskva yesterday. She's in the morgue this minute. Go take a look at her if you feel like it. You made her do it—you and the Bureau. And I'm not afraid to tell you so.'

The edge of her shovel gleamed evilly over her shoulder. She pushed her way into the gaping lift. Kostia telephoned to the department, the police, the Y.C. secretary (private wire), the secretary of the yard newspaper, and even others. Everywhere the same news echoed back to him—numbing, and now banally irreparable. At the morgue, on the marble slabs, in a lugubrious grey chill riddled with electric bulbs, lay a nameless boy who had been run over by a tram. He lay sleeping on his back, his skin white as wax, his two hands open as if they had just dropped two marbles. There was an old Asiatic in a long overcoat, hook-nosed, blue-lidded, with his cut throat gaping and black (his face had been crudely painted for a photograph). He looked like an actor made up as a corpse—greenish, the high cheek-bones rose-pink. There was Maria, with her blue and white polka-dot blouse, her thin neck horribly blue, her little snub nose, her red curls plastered to her skull, but with no eyes at all, no eyeballs, only those pitiable folds of torn flesh, strangely sunk into the eye sockets. 'Why did you do it, poor Marussia?' Kostia asked stupidly, while his unhappy hands kneaded his cap. This was death, the end of a universe. But a red-haired girl wasn't the universe? The guardian of the morgue, a morose Jew in a white blouse, came up:

'You know her, citizen? Then there's no use staying here any longer. Come and fill out the questionnaire.'

His office was warm, comfortable, full of papers. *Drownings. Street Accidents. Crimes. Suicides. Doubtful Cases.* 'Under what heading should we put the deceased, in your opinion, citizen?' Kostia shrugged his shoulders. Then he asked angrily:

'Is there a heading, "Collective Crimes"?'

'No,' said the Jew. 'I call your attention to the fact that the deceased has already been examined by the medical expert and shows neither ecchymoses nor signs of strangulation.'

'Suicide,' Kostia interrupted furiously.

He pushed through the drizzle, his right shoulder forward. If he could have fought somebody, broken somebody's nose, or taken a straight right on the jaw—for you, poor Marussia, you sweet little nit-wit—it would have done him good. You big fool, why let yourself get so desperate? Everybody knows that men are bastards. Nobody pays any attention to the Wall Gazette, it's only fit to wipe your arse with! How could you be so dumb, you poor baby, oh for God's sake, oh hell!—The whole thing had been perfectly simple. The horror-stricken Y.C. secretary kept her brief statement to himself. It was written on a page from a school notebook and solemnly signed 'Maria' (and her family name):

'As a proletarian, I will not live with this filthy dishonour. Accuse no one of my death. Farewell.'

And that was that! On orders from the Y.C. Central Committee, the branch committees were making a campaign 'for health, against demoralization.' How should the campaign be conducted? The five young men who made up the Bureau had beaten their brains, until one of them had said: 'Outlaw venereal diseases.' It seemed like a brilliant idea. Of the five, two were probably V.D. cases themselves, but they were clever enough to take their treatments in distant clinics. 'There's Maria, the redhead.'—'Perfect!'—A strange girl—she never said anything at meetings, she was always clean and tidy, she repulsed any advances, frightened to death, yet flared up when she was pinched—where had she ever caught her case? Not in the organization, that was certain. Then it must have been from the demoralized petty-*bourgeois* element? 'She has no class instinct,' said the secretary severely. 'I propose that we publish her expulsion in the yard Wall Gazette. We must make an example.' The Wall Gazette, illustrated with caricatures in water colours which showed a Maria recognizable only by her holiday blouse and her red hair, and grotesquely loaded with a pair of rhinestone ear-rings, tumbling out of a door from which projected the shadow of an enormous broom—the typewritten Wall Gazette was still posted in the vestibule of the shanty. Kostia calmly took it down, tore it into four pieces, and put the pieces in his desk drawer, because they might be used as evidence in court . . .

Autumn and the rains carried away the insignificant episode of Maria's suicide. Submitted to the Branch Committee for a recommendation, the case disappeared under the directives for an urgent and immediate campaign against the Right opposition, which was followed by incomprehensible expulsions; then under another campaign, slower in getting started but actually far more drastic, against corruption among Y.C. and Party officials. Under the whirlwind, the yard Y.C. secretary sunk into an abyss of opprobrium—exclusion, derision, Wall Gazette (the broom reappeared, driving him out with his hair standing on end and his papers swirling over the dump heap), and, finally, dismissal for having granted himself two months' vacation in a rest house whose dazzling white walls rose among the rockslides and bursting flowers of Alupka in the Crimea.

Kostia, accused of 'having demonstratively torn up an issue of the Wall Gazette (a serious breach of discipline) and having attempted to exploit the suicide of an excluded member as part of an intrigue to discredit the Young Communist Bureau,' was 'severely censured.' What did he care? Every night—after the yard, the city, his suppressed rages, his soleless shoes, the sour soup, the icy wind—he returned to the soothing eyes of his miniature. He knocked at Romachkin's door— Romachkin had aged a good deal only recently, and read strange books of a religious tendency. Kostia warned him: 'Watch out, Romachkin, or you'll find yourself a mystic.' 'Impossible,' the shrivelled little man answered. 'I am so profoundly a materialist that . . .'

'That?'

'Nothing. I believe it is always the same unrest in contradictory forms.'

'Perhaps,' said Kostia, struck by the idea. 'Perhaps the mystic and the revolutionary are brothers . . . But one has to extirpate the other . . .'

'Yes,' said Romachkin.

He opened a book—*Isolation*, by Vladimir Rozanov. 'Here—read this. How true it is!' His yellow fingernail pointed to the lines:

'The hearse moves slowly, the road is long. "Well, farewell, Vassili

Vassilievich, it's bad underground, old man, and you lived a bad life; if you had lived better, you would rest easier underground. Whereas, with *iniquity* . . .'

'My God, to die *in iniquity* . . .
And I am in iniquity.'

'Dying in iniquity is no use,' Kostia answered; 'the thing is to fight while we are alive . . .'

He was surprised to have thought so clearly. Romachkin observed him with the keenest attention. The conversation shifted to the issuing of passports, the stricter enforcement of discipline among workers, the Chief's edicts, the Chief himself.

'Eleven o'clock,' said Kostia. 'Good night.'

'Good night. What have you done with the revolver?'

'Nothing.'

One February night, about ten o'clock, the snow stopped falling on Moscow; a mild frost draped everything in sparkling crystals. The lifeless branches of trees and shrubs in the gardens were magically covered with them. Crystals full of a secret light flowered on stones, covered the house fronts, clothed monuments. You walked on powdered stars through a stellar city: myriads of crystals floated in the globes of light around the street lamps. Towards midnight the sky became incredibly clear. The smallest light shot skyward like a sword. It was a festival of frost. The silence seemed to scintillate. Kostia became aware of the enchantment only after he had been walking through it for several minutes, after a Y.C. meeting devoted, like so many before it, to discussing the relaxation of discipline at work. The month was drawing to its close; Kostia, like many others, was going without food. At the meeting he had said nothing, knowing that his formula would be inacceptable: 'For more discipline, more food. Soup first! Good soup will put a stop to drinking.' What was the use of saying it? The magic of the night laid hold of him, lightened his stride, cleared his mind, made him forget his hunger, even made him forget the execution of six men the night before, though it had made an unusual impression on him. 'Food supply saboteurs,' said the curt official announcement. No doubt they stole, like everybody else—but could they help stealing? Could I—in the long run? The pillars of light above the street lamps tapered upward, very high into a darkness filled with minute frost crystals.

Kostia was going down a narrow street, on one side of which was a row of small private houses from the previous century, on the other a row of six-story apartment buildings. Here and there a discreet light showed through a window. Odd how everybody leads his own individual life! The snow crackled softly under his feet, like rustling silk. A powerful black car, slipping silently over the snow, stopped a few paces ahead of him. A stout man in a short fur-lined coat and an astrakhan cap got out, with a brief case under his arm. As Kostia came almost abreast of him, he saw that the man had thick down-turning moustaches, full cheeks, and a broad flat nose. He thought he vaguely recognized the face. The man said something to his chauffeur, who answered deferentially:

'Very good, Comrade Tulayev.'

Tulayev? Of the Central Committee? Tulayev, of the mass deportations in the Vorogen district? Tulayev of the university purges? Curious, Kostia turned to get a better view of him. The car disappeared down the street. Walking quickly and heavily, Tulayev overtook Kostia, passed him, stopped, looked up at a lighted window. Fine frost crystals fell on his raised face, powdering his eyebrows and moustache. Kostia came up behind him, Kostia's hand remembered the Colt, Kostia's hand drew it out of his pocket, and——

The explosion was deafening and brief. Deafening in Kostia's soul, like a sudden clap of thunder in a dead silence. Incredible in that boreal night. Kostia saw the thunder burst within him: it was a cloud which swelled, became an enormous black flower fringed with flames, and vanished. A piercing whistle signal whipped the night, very near. Another answered from farther away. The night filled with an invisible panic. Whistles cut across one another, wildly, precipitately, sought one another, collided, cut through the aerial pillars of light. Kostia fled over the snow through small quiet streets, running with his elbows close to his sides, as he ran at the Youth Stadium. Round a corner, now another—he told himself that it was time to walk without any show of hurry. His heart was beating very hard. 'What have I done? Why? It was madness . . . I acted without thinking . . . Without thinking, like a man of action . . .' Like snow squalls, fragments of ideas chased one another through his mind. 'Tulayev certainly deserved to be shot . . . Was it my business to know it? Am I sure of it? Am I sure of justice?

Am I mad?' A sleigh appeared—could anything be more fantastic?—
the driver thrust his crafty eyes and snow-covered beard towards
Kostia as he passed.

'What's going on back there, young fellow?'

'I don't know. Drunks fighting again, I suppose. Devil take them!'

The sleigh turned slowly around in the street, to avoid trouble. The
exchange of ordinary words had completely sobered Kostia and made
him feel extraordinarily calm. Crossing a well-lighted square, he passed
a sentry at his post. Had he not been dreaming? In his pocket the
barrel of the Colt was still devastatingly hot. In his heart, joy grew
inexplicably. Pure joy. Luminous, cold, inhuman, like a starry winter
sky.

There was a thread of light under Romachkin's door. Kostia went
in. Romachkin was reading—in bed, because of the cold. Grey heather
covered the windowpanes. 'What are you reading, Romachkin? It's
cold in here. It's wonderful outdoors, you have no idea!'

'I wanted to read something about the happy life. But there are no
books on the subject. Why have none been written? Don't writers
know any more about it than I do? Don't they want to know what it is,
as I do?'

Kostia was amused. What a man!

'All I could find was this—in a second-hand bookshop. It's a very
old book and very beautiful . . . *Paul and Virginia*. It happens on an
island full of happy birds and plants; they are young and pure and love
each other . . . It's unbelievable.' He noticed Kostia's exalted face.
'But, Kostia, what has happened to you?'

'I'm in love, Romachkin, my friend—it's terrible.'

THE SWORD IS BLIND

THE PAPERS briefly announced 'the premature death of Comrade Tulayev.' The first secret investigation produced sixty-seven arrests in three days. Suspicion at first fell on Tulayev's secretary, who was also the mistress of a student who was not a Party member. Then it shifted to the chauffeur who had brought Tulayev to his door—a Security man with a good record, not a drinker, no questionable relations, a former soldier in the special troops, and a member of the Bureau of his garage cell. Why had he not waited until Tulayev had entered the house, before driving off? Why, instead of going in immediately, had Tulayev walked a few paces down the pavement? Why? The entire mystery of the crime seemed to centre in these two unknowns. No one was aware that Tulayev had hoped to spend a few minutes with the wife of an absent friend; that a bottle of vodka and two dimpled arms, a milky body, warm under a house dress, were waiting for him . . . But the fatal bullet had not been shot from the chauffeur's pistol; and the fatal weapon remained undiscoverable. Interrogated for sixty consecutive hours by inquisitors who themselves became exhausted and relayed each other every four hours, the chauffeur sank to the verge of insanity without changing his declarations, except insofar as he finally lost the power of speech, the faculty of reason, and even the use of the facial muscles which the nerves must activate in order to produce speech and expression. After thirty-four hours of questioning, he was no longer a man but a lay figure of suffering flesh and shapeless clothes. They dosed him with strong coffee, brandy, as many cigarettes as he wanted. They gave him an injection. His fingers dropped the cigarettes, his lips forgot to drink when a glass was held to them; every hour two men from the special detachment dragged him to the washroom, held his head under the tap, doused him with ice-cold water. He scarcely moved, limp in their hands even under the icy water, and the men thought that he took advantage of these moments of respite to sleep while they held him up; handling that human rag demoralized them after a few hours, and they had to be replaced. They held him in his chair to keep him from falling onto the floor. Suddenly the examining judge hammered the butt of his revolver on the table and roared:

'Open your eyes, prisoner. I forbade you to sleep! Answer! After you fired, what did you do?'

At this three hundredth repetition of the same question, the man from whom all intelligence, all resistance had been drained, the man who had no self left, his eyes bloodshot, his sagging face horribly scarred, began to answer:

'I . . .'

Then he collapsed onto the table with a sound like a snore. Foamy saliva ran from his mouth. They sat him up. They poured a drink of Armenian brandy between his teeth.

'. . . didn't fire . . .'

'Liar!'

The judge was so exasperated that he slapped him with all his strength; and the judge felt as if he had hit a swinging manikin. The judge swallowed half a glass of tea at one gulp—but the tea was really warm brandy. A sudden chill seized him. Low voices crept behind him. The partition was merely a curtain drawn across a darkened room, six feet away. From behind it, everything that went on in the lighted room was clearly visible. Several persons had silently entered the darkened room, all respectfully following the first. Tired of picking up the telephone and asking 'What about the plot?' only to hear the High Commissar's unstrung voice repeat the idiotic formula, 'The investigation is being pursued without yielding any substantial results'—the Chief had come himself. Boots, short coarse tunic, bare head, low brow, tense face, bushy moustache—from the invisible hide-out he had avidly fixed his eyes on the eyes of the chauffeur—who did not see him, who could no longer see anything. He had listened. Behind him stood the exhausted High Commissar, straight as a sentry; behind them again, nearer to the door, in complete darkness, other gold-braided personages, mute and petrified. The Chief turned to the High Commissar and, in a very low voice, said:

2*

'Have this useless torture stopped instantly. You can see for yourself that the man knows nothing.'

The uniforms drew to either side before him. He strode towards the lift—alone, jaws clenched, frowning—followed by a single absolutely trustworthy guard, of whom he was fond. 'Don't come with me,' he had said to the High Commissar severely. 'Attend to the plot.'

Terror and feverish activity reigned in the building, concentrated in the story where, at twenty tables, interrogations were being carried on without a break. In the private office which he had reserved for himself on the spot, the High Commissar stupidly opened a pointless dossier, then another even more pointless. Nothing! He felt sick. He could have vomited like the chauffeur, who, his mouth ringed with foam, was at last being carried away on a stretcher—to sleep. For a time the High Commissar wandered from office to office. In No. 266, the chauffeur's wife was weeping as she admitted that she often consulted fortune-tellers, that she had secretly attended religious services, that she was jealous, that . . . In No. 268, the sentry who had been on duty at the time and place of the assassination repeated again that he had gone into the court to warm himself at the brazier, because Comrade Tulayev never came home before midnight; that, hearing the shot, he had rushed out into the street; that at first he had seen no one because Comrade Tulayev had fallen against the wall; that he had only been intensely surprised by the peculiar light . . .

The High Commissar entered. The sentry was testifying standing at attention, calmly, in a voice that showed emotion. The High Commissar asked:

'What light are you referring to?'

'An extraordinary light, a supernatural light—I can't describe it—there were pillars of light up to the sky, glittering, dazzling . . .'

'Are you a Believer?'

'No, Comrade Chief, member of the Society of the Godless for four years, dues paid up.'

The High Commissar turned on his heel, shrugging his shoulders. In No. 270 a thick market woman's voice was relating, with many interpolated sighs and exclamations of 'Oh Jesus, my God,' that at the Smolensk market everyone said that poor Comrade Tulayev, beloved of the great Comrade Chief, had been found at the gate of the Kremlin with his throat cut and his heart pierced by a dagger with a triangular blade, like poor little Tsarevich Dimitri long ago, and the monsters had gouged out his eyes, and she had cried over it with Marfa who sells grain, with Frossia who resells cigarettes, with Niucha who . . . Her intolerable and endless chatter was being patiently recorded by a young officer in a tight uniform and eyeglasses, with a medal bearing the Chief's profile on his chest—he wrote it all down rapidly on long sheets of paper. He was so occupied that he did not look up at the High Commissar, who stood framed in the door and who left without uttering a word.

On his own desk the High Commissar found a red envelope from the Central Committee, General Secretariat, *Urgent Strictly Confidential* . . . Three lines, ordering him to 'follow the Titov matter with the greatest attention and report to us personally on it.' Very significant, that! Bad. So the new Deputy High Commissar was spying without even trying to save appearances. Only *he* could have informed the General Secretariat (and without the knowledge of his superior) of the Titov matter—the mere mention of which made you want to spit with disgust! An anonymous denunciation, in big schoolboy handwriting, which had arrived that morning: 'Matvei Titov said that it's Security that had Comrade Tulayev killed because there's a long reckoning between them. He said: Me, I feel it in my bones that it's the Gepeous, I tell you. He said that in front of his servant Sidorovna, and Palkin the coachman, and a clothes seller who lives at the corner of Ragman Alley and Holy Field Street, at the end of the court, one flight up, on the right. Matvei Titov is an enemy of the Soviet government and our beloved Comrade Chief and an exploiter of the people who makes his servant sleep in the hall with no fire and has got the poor daughter of a collectivized peasant pregnant and refuses to pay the food allowance for her child who will come into this world in pain and misery . . .' And twenty more lines of the same. Deputy High Commissar Gordeyev was having this document photographed and typewritten for immediate transmission to the Political Bureau!

At that moment, Gordeyev came in: stout, blond, his hair pomaded, round face, a suspicion of downy moustache, big tortoise-shell spectacles. There was something porcine about him, and with it the servile insolence of a domestic animal too well fed by its human masters.

'I fail to understand you, Comrade Gordeyev,' the High Commissar said carelessly. 'You have communicated this absurd statement to the Political Bureau? To what end?'

Gordeyev looked offended. 'But, Maxim Andreyevich,' he protested, 'there is a C.C. circular which prescribes that all complaints, denunciations, and even allusions to which we are subjected shall be submitted to the P.B. Circular dated March 16 . . . And the Titov matter is hardly to be called absurd—it reveals a state of mind among the masses of which we should be more fully informed . . . I have had Titov arrested, together with a number of his acquaintances . . .'

'Perhaps you have even interrogated him yourself by now?'

The High Commissar's mocking tone appeared to escape Gordeyev, who thought it his best tactics to appear stupid:

'Not personally. My secretary was present at the interrogation. It is extremely interesting to trace the origins of the myths which get into circulation about us. Don't you think so?'

'And have you found the origin of this one?'

'Not yet.'

On the sixth day of the investigation, High Commissar Erchov, summoned by telephone to present himself at the General Secretariat immediately, waited in an ante-room there for thirty-five minutes. Everyone in the Secretariat knew that he was counting the minutes. At last the tall doors opened to him, he saw the Chief at his desk, before his telephones—solitary, greying, his head bowed. It was a massive head; and seen, as Erchov saw it, against the light, it looked sombre. The room was large, high-ceilinged and comfortable, but almost bare . . . The Chief did not raise his head, did not hold out his hand to Erchov, did not ask him to sit down. To maintain his dignity, the High Commissar advanced to the edge of the table and opened his brief case.

'The plot?' the Chief asked, and Erchov saw that his face had the concentrated look, the hard lines, of his cold rages.

'I am inclined to accept the view that the assassination of Comrade Tulayev was the act of an isolated individual . . .'

'Very efficient, your isolated individual! Remarkably well organized!'

Erchov felt the sarcasm in the back of his neck, the place where the executioner's bullet lodges. Could Gordeyev have sunk so low as to carry on a secret investigation of his own and then conceal the results? It would have been almost impossible. In any case, there was nothing to answer . . .

The silence which followed annoyed the Chief.

'Let us accept your view provisionally. By the decision of the

Political Bureau, the case will not be closed until the criminals have been punished . . .'

'Exactly what I was about to propose,' said the High Commissar, playing up.

'Do you propose any sanctions?'

'I have them here.'

The sanctions filled several typewritten sheets. Twenty-five names. The Chief glanced over them.

'You are losing your mind, Erchov,' he said angrily. 'This doesn't sound like you! Ten years for the chauffeur! When it was his duty not to leave the person entrusted to him until he had seen him safely home?'

To the other proposals he said nothing. On the other hand, his outburst caused the High Commissar to increase all the suggested sentences. The sentry who had been warming himself at the brazier during the assassination would be sent to the Pechora labour camp for ten years instead of eight. Tulayev's secretary and her lover, the student, would be deported—the woman to Vologda, which was mild, the student to Turgai, in the Kazakstan desert—for five years each (instead of three). As he handed the revised sheet to Gordeyev, the High Commissar allowed himself the pleasure of saying:

'Your proposals were considered too mild, Comrade Gordeyev. I have corrected them.'

'Thank you,' said Gordeyev, with a polite bow of his pomaded head. 'For my part, I have permitted myself to take a step which you will certainly approve. I have had a list made of all persons whose antecedents might make them suspect of terrorism. So far we have found seventeen hundred names of persons still at liberty.'

'Very interesting . . .'

(He hadn't thought that up himself, the greasy-headed stool pigeon! Perhaps the idea had come from high up, from very high up . . .)

'Of these seventeen hundred persons, twelve hundred are Party members; about a hundred still hold important offices; several have repeatedly occupied positions in the immediate circle of the Chief of the Party; three are actually in Security . . .'

He had spoken with assurance but without emotion, and every sentence had told. What are you doing, who are you after, you climber? You have your sights on the very heart of the Party! The High Commissar remembered that, during the trouble in Tashkent in 1914, he had fired on the mounted militia, and as a result had been imprisoned in a fortress for eighteen months . . . Then am I suspect? Am I one of the three 'ex-terrorists,' 'members of the Party,' with jobs in Security?

'Have you informed anyone whomsoever of your researches in this direction?'

'No, naturally not,' the pomaded head replied suavely, 'certainly not. Only the General Secretary, who made the necessary arrangements for me to obtain certain dossiers from the Central Control Commission.'

This time, the High Commissar felt definitely caught in the meshes of a net that was closing about him for no reason at all. To-morrow or next week, on one pretext or another, they would finish the process of removing the last colleagues in whom he could trust: Gordeyev would replace them by men of his own . . . For years this same office had been occupied by someone else—a man whose figure and voice, whose peculiarities of speech, whose trick of clasping his hands, of frowning and holding his pen suspended over a document he was to sign, Erchov knew intimately; a man who had worked zealously and conscientiously ten or twelve hours a day . . . Around that obedient, skilful, and implacable man, too, the net had closed; he had struggled in its inextricable meshes, refusing to understand, to see, yet feeling more defeated day by day, growing visibly older; in a few weeks he had acquired the look of a little clerk who had taken orders all his life; he had let his subordinates make his decisions for him; he had spent his nights drinking with a little actress from the Opera, his days thinking of blowing out his brains—until the evening when they had come and arrested him . . . But perhaps he was actually guilty, whereas I . . .

Gordeyev said:

'I have made a selection from the list of seventeen hundred—some forty names for the present. Some of them are very highly placed. Do you care to go over it?'

'Have it brought to me immediately,' said the High Commissar in a tone of authority, while an uncomfortable chill crept through his limbs.

Alone in his huge office, communing with the dossiers, with suspicion, fear, power, powerlessness, the High Commissar became his simple self—Maxim Andreyevich Erchov, a man forty years old, in vigorous health, prematurely wrinkled, with puffy eyelids, a thin-lipped mouth, and uneasy eyes . . . His predecessors here had been Henri Grigoryevich, who had breathed the air of these offices for ten years and was executed after the trial of the Twenty-one; then Piotr Eduardovich, who had disappeared—that is to say, who was confined on the second floor of the subterranean prison under the particular supervision of an official appointed by the Political Bureau. What admission did they want from him? Piotr Eduardovich had been fighting for five months—if 'fighting' was the proper term for turning grey at thirty-five and repeating 'No, no, no, it is not true,' with no hope except to die in silence—unless solitary confinement had driven him mad enough to hope for anything else.

Erchov, recalled from the Far East, where he had thought himself happily forgotten by the Personnel Service, had been offered an unparalleled promotion: High Commissar for Security in conjunction with Commissar of the People for Internal Affairs, which practically carried with it the rank of marshal—the sixth marshal—or was it the third, since three of the five had disappeared? 'Comrade Erchov, the Party puts its confidence in you! I congratulate you!' The words were spoken, his hand shaken, the office (it was one of the Central Committee offices, on the same floor as the General Secretariat) was full of smiles. Unannounced, the Chief entered quickly, looked him up and down for a split second—a superior studying an inferior; then, so simply, so cordially, smiling like the others and perfectly at ease, the Chief shook Maxim Andreyevich Erchov's hand and looked into his eyes with perfect friendliness. 'A heavy responsibility, Comrade Erchov. Bear it well.' The press photographer flashed his magnesium lightning over all the smiles . . . Erchov had reached the pinnacle of his life, and he was afraid. Three thousand dossiers, of capital importance because they called for capital punishment, three thousands nests of hissing vipers, suddenly descended like an avalanche upon his life, to remain with him every instant. For a moment the greatness of the Chief reassured him. The Chief, addressing him as 'Maxim Andreyevich' in a cordial tone, paternally advised him 'to go easy with personnel, keeping the past in mind yet never failing in vigilance, to put a stop to abuses.'—'Men have been executed whom I loved, whom I trusted, men precious to the Party and the State!' he exclaimed bitterly. 'Yet the Political Bureau cannot possibly review every sentence! It is up to you,' he concluded. 'You have my entire confidence.' The power that emanated from him was spontaneous, human, and perfectly simple; the kindly smile, in which the russet eyes and the bushy moustache joined, attested it; it made you love him, believe in him, praise him as he was praised in the press and in official speeches, but sincerely, warmly. When the General Secretary filled his pipe, Maxim Andreyevich Erchov, High Commissar for Interior Defence, 'sword of the dictatorship,' 'keen and ever-wakeful eye of the Party,' 'the most implacable and the most human of the faithful collaborators of the greatest Chief of all times' (these phrases had appeared in the *Political Service Schools Gazette* that very morning)—Maxim And-reyevich Erchov felt that he loved the man and that he feared him as one fears mystery. 'No bureaucratic delays, now!' the Chief added. 'Not too much paper work! Clear, up-to-date dossiers, with no official rigmarole and no missing documents—and action! Otherwise you will find yourself drowned in work.'—'An inspired directive' was the sober comment of one of the members of the Special Commission (composed of the heads of bureaus) when Erchov repeated it to them word for word.

Nevertheless, the swarming, proliferating, overflowing, all-conquer-ing dossiers refused to relinquish the most minor memorandums; on the contrary, they continued to swell. Thousands of cases had been opened during the first great trial of traitors, a trial 'of world-wide importance'; thousands more had been opened, before the original thousands had been disposed of, during the second trial; thousands during the third trial; thousands during the preliminary investigations for the fourth, fifth, and sixth trials, which never came into court because they were suppressed. Dossiers arrived from the Ussuri (Japanese agents), from Yakutia (sabotage, espionage, and traitors in the gold placers), from Buriat-Mongolia (the case of the Buddhist monasteries), from Vladivostok (the case of the submarine fleet com-mand), from the construction yards of Komsomolsk, City of the Young Communists (terrorist propaganda, demoralization, abuse of power, Trotskyism-Bukharinism), from Tsing-kiang (smuggling, con-tacts with Japanese and British agents, Moslem intrigues), from all the Turkestan republics (separatism, Pan-Turkism, banditry, foreign intelligence services; Mahmudism—but who on earth was Mahmud? —in Uzbekistan, Turkmenistan, Tadjikistan, Kazakstan, Old Bok-hara, Syr Darya); the Samarkand assassination was connected with the Alm Ata scandal, the Alm Ata scandal with the case of espionage (aggravated by the kidnapping of an Iranian national) at the Ispahan

Consulate; forgotten cases came to life again in concentration camps in the Arctic, new cases were born in prisons; memorandums in code, dated from Paris, Oslo, Washington, Panama, Hankow, Canton in flames, Guernica in ruins, bombed Barcelona, Madrid desperately surviving under a succession of terrors (and so on—consult a map of the two hemispheres) demanded investigations; Kaluga announced suspicious epidemics among livestock, Tambov agrarian discontent, Leningrad presented twenty dossiers simultaneously—the Sailors' Club case, the Red Triangle Factory case, the Academy of Sciences case, the Former Revolutionary Prisoners case, the Leninist Youth case, the Geologic Committee case, the Free Masons case, the matter of homosexuality in the Fleet . . . Now here, now there, a succession of shots traversed this mass of names, documents, figures, mysterious lives whose mystery was never entirely laid bare, supplementary investigations, denunciations, reports, insane ideas. Several hundred uniformed men, ranked in a strict hierarchy, dealt with these papers day and night, were dealt with by them in their turn, suddenly vanished into them, passing the perpetual labour on to other hands. On the summit of the pyramid stood Maxim Andreyevich Erchov. What could he do?

From the P.B. meeting which he had attended he brought back an oral directive which the Chief had repeated several times: 'You must make good your predecessor's errors!' Predecessors were never mentioned by name; Erchov felt grateful to the Chief (but why, after all?) for not having said, 'the traitor's errors.' From every branch of the Central Committee arrived complaints concerning the disorganization of personnel, which had been so affected by purges and repressive measures in the last two years that instead of being rejuvenated it was melting away; the result had been fresh cases of sabotage, clearly due to the muddle-headedness, incompetence, insecurity, and pusillanimity of industrial personnel. Without arousing the Chief's disapproval, a member of the Organization Bureau had emphasized the urgent necessity of restoring to productive employment those who had been wrongfully sentenced, upon calumnious denunciations, as a result of mass campaigns, and so forth, and even of guilty persons towards whom indulgence seemed feasible. 'Are we not,' he had cried, 'the country which remakes men? We transform even our worst enemies . . .' This oratorical sally had fallen into a sort of void. For a second the High Commissar's mind dwelt on an annoying counter-revolutionary joke: 'Remaking men consists in reducing them, by persuasion, to the condition of corpses . . .' Precisely at that moment the Chief's kindly eyes looked meaningfully at Erchov. Erchov put his entire staff on their mettle: within ten days, ten thousand dossiers, preferably those of industrial administrators (Communists), technicians (non-Party members), and officers (Communists and non-Party members), were carefully reviewed, which made possible 6,727 releases, of which 47.5 per cent resulted in rehabilitations. The more thoroughly to overwhelm his 'predecessor'—whose chief assistants had just been executed—the papers announced that, during the late purges, the percentage of innocent persons sentenced had risen to over 50; this seemingly produced a good effect; but the C.C. statisticians responsible for the figures, and the assistant press director who had authorized their publication, were immediately dismissed when it was learned that an *émigré* newspaper published in Paris had perfidiously commented upon the facts thus revealed. Erchov and his staff fell upon yet more mountains of dossiers, working day and night. At this point two pieces of news threw them into confusion. An ex-Communist, expelled from the Party on the basis of an undeniably calumnious denunciation which accused him of being a Trotskyist and the son of a priest (the documents proved that he had been conspicuous in the campaigns against Trotskyism from 1925 to 1937, and that he was the son of a mechanic in the factory at Bryansk), having been released from the 'special cases' concentration camp at Kem, on the White Sea, returned to Smolensk and there killed a member of the Party Committee. A woman doctor, released from a work camp in the Urals, was arrested as she attempted to cross the border into Estonia. Seven hundred and fifty new denunciations against recently released persons appeared; in thirty instances the supposedly innocent turned out to be undeniably guilty—or at least so divers committees affirmed. A rumour gained headway: Erchov was not doing the job. Too liberal, too hasty, not sufficiently versed in the technique of repression.

Then came the Tulayev case.

Gordeyev was still following it, in accordance with special instructions from the Political Bureau. When Erchov questioned him about the chauffeur's execution, he answered, with offensive reserve:

'. . . Night before last, with the four Fur Trust saboteurs and the little music-hall actress condemned for espionage . . .'

Erchov flinched—but imperceptibly, for he made every effort to keep his feelings concealed. Was it chance, coincidence, or a slap? He had admired the little actress—her lithe body leaping onto the stage, more attractive in the yellow-and-black tights than if it had been naked!—had admired her enough to send her flowers. Gordeyev went on (was it a second slap?):

'The report was submitted to you . . .'

So he didn't read all the reports that came to his desk? . . .

'It is most unfortunate,' Gordeyev resumed innocuously, 'because, only yesterday, we found material which throws quite a new light on the chauffeur's personality . . .'

Erchov raised his head, obviously interested.

'Yes. Imagine! During 1924–25 he was Bukharin's chauffeur for seven months; four letters of recommendation from Bukharin were found in his Moscow dossier. The latest was dated only last year! There is more besides: While serving as a battalion commissar on the Volhynia front in 1921 he was accused of insubordination. The man who got him out of it was Kiril Rublev!'

Another slap! By what inconceivable negligence could such facts have escaped the commissions whose duty it was to investigate the past careers of agents attached to the persons of C.C. members? The responsibility was the High Commissar's. What were the commissions under his orders doing? Who were their members? Bukharin, one-time ideologist of the Party, 'Lenin's favourite disciple,' whom Lenin called 'son,' was now the incarnation of treachery, espionage, terrorism, the dismemberment of the Union. And Kiril Kirillovich Rublev, his old friend—was he still alive after so many proscriptions? 'Yes indeed,' Gordeyev bore witness. 'He is at the Academy of Sciences, buried under tons of sixteenth-century archives. I have someone watching him . . .'

A few days later, one of Erchov's recent appointees went insane. The First Examining Magistrate of the Forty-first Bureau was a conscientious ex-soldier, taciturn-looking, with a high, deeply lined forehead. Erchov had just approved his promotion, despite the cautious hostility of the Cell secretary, a Party member. Erchov's appointee suddenly turned on a high Party official and drove him out of his office. He was heard shouting:

'Get out, stool pigeon, informer! I order you to keep your mouth shut!' He locked himself in his office. Several revolver shots rang out. The magistrate appeared in the doorway, standing on tiptoe, his hair rumpled, the smoking revolver in his hand. He shouted: 'I am a traitor! I have betrayed everything! Gang of beasts!'—and, to the general consternation, it was seen that he had riddled the Chief's portrait with bullets, shooting out the eyes, making a gaping hole in the forehead . . . 'Punish me!' he went on shouting. 'Eunuchs!' It took six men to subdue him. When they had tied him up with their belts, he shook with laughter, inextinguishable, grating, convulsive bursts of laughter. 'Eunuchs! Eunuchs!' Erchov, preyed on by an unspoken fear, went to see him. He was tied to a chair, which had fallen over backwards, so he lay with his boots in the air and his head on the carpet. At sight of the High Commissar he foamed: 'Traitor, traitor, traitor, traitor! I see the depths of your soul, hypocrite! So you've been gelded too, eh?'

'Shall we gag him, Comrade Chief?' an officer asked respectfully.

'No. Why isn't the ambulance here yet? Have you called the hospital? What are you thinking of? If an ambulance is not here in fifteen minutes, you will consider yourself under arrest!'

A short, extremely blond clerk, with irritating side curls, who had entered out of curiosity, papers in hand, looked at them both—Erchov and the lunatic—with the same horror, and did not recognize the High Commissar. Erchov drew himself up, squared his shoulders. He felt the slight giddiness and nausea he used to feel when he was obliged to be present at executions. He left the room without a word, got into the lift . . . The departmental heads were obviously avoiding him. Only one of them came to meet him—an old friend who had shared his sudden rise and who was now in charge of the foreign department.

'Well, Ricciotti, what is it?'

Ricciotti's Italian name was a legacy from a childhood spent on the shores of a picture-postcard bay, as was the useless, Neapolitan-fisherboy beauty which he still possessed, the touch of gold in the eyes, the warm guitar player's voice, an imagination and a loyalty so unusual that—on due consideration—they seemed feigned. The general opinion was that he 'aimed to be original.'

'Oh, the daily ration of troubles, my dear Maximka.'

Ricciotti took Erchov familiarly by the arm and accompanied him into his office, talking fluently all the while: about the secret service at Nanking which had been abominably taken in by the Japanese; the work of the Trotskyists in Mao Tse-tung's army; an intrigue in the White military organization at Paris, 'where we now hold all the cards'; things in Barcelona, which were going as badly as possible—Trotskyists, Anarchists, Socialists, Catholics, Catalans, Basques, being all equally ungovernable—a military defeat there was inevitable, no use blinking the fact; the complications which had arisen in connection with the gold reserve; five or six different sets of spies all operating at once . . . A ten-minute talk with him, as he strode up and down the office, was worth many long reports. Erchov admired and slightly envied the supple intelligence which embraced all things at once and yet remained singularly unencumbered. Lowering his voice, Ricciotti led him to the window. It offered a view of Moscow—a vast white open space, over which human ants hurried in all directions, following dirty paths in the snow; a mass of houses, and, still towering over all, the bulbous domes of an old church, painted an intense blue fretted with golden stars. Erchov would have thought it beautiful if he had been able to think.

'Listen, Maximka, watch out . . .'

'For what?'

'I have been told that the agents sent to Spain were an unfortunate choice. Of course, so far as appearances go, the remark was aimed at me. But it is you they are after.'

'Right, Sacha. Don't worry. He has confidence in me, you know.'

The hands of the clock were circling inexorably. Erchov and Ricciotti parted. Four minutes to run through *Pravda*. What's this?—The front-page picture: Erchov should be in it—second to the left from the Chief, among the members of the Government; the photograph had been taken two afternoons ago in the Kremlin, at the reception for Elite women textile workers . . . He unfolded the paper: instead of one picture there were two, and they had been trimmed in such a way that the High Commissar for Security appeared in neither. Amazement. Telephone. The editorial office? The High Commissar's office calling . . . Who made up the first page? Who? Why? You say the pictures were supplied by the General Secretariat at the last moment? Yes—very well—that is what I wanted to know . . . But the truth was that he had learned too much.

Gordeyev came in and amiably informed him that two of the three men who made up his personal escort had had to be replaced—one was ill, the other had been sent to White Russia to present a flag to the workers of a frontier military-agricultural group. Erchov refrained from remarking that he might have been consulted. In the courtyard three men came to attention beside his car and received him with a single 'Greetings, Comrade High Commissar,' irreproachably released from three arching chests. Erchov answered them pleasantly and, pointing to the steering wheel, nodded to the only one of the three whom he knew—the one who would doubtless soon be relieved of his job, leaving the High Commissar thenceforth to travel surrounded by strangers, who would perhaps be under secret orders, obeying a will that was not his own.

The car emerged from under a low archway, passed between iron gates guarded by helmeted sentries, who presented arms; the car leaped into a square at the grey hour of twilight. Blocked for a moment between a bus and the stream of pedestrians, it slowed down. Erchov saw the unknown faces of people who did not signify: clerks, technicians still wearing their school caps, a melancholy old Jew, graceless women, hard-faced workmen. Preoccupied, silent, insubstantial against the snow, they saw him without dreaming of recognizing him. How do they live, what do they live on? Not one of them, not even those who read my name in the papers, imagines or can imagine what I am. And I—what do I know of them, except that I do not know them, that though their million names are filed somewhere, can be catalogued and classified, each of their identities is a different unknown, each a mystery that will never wholly be solved . . . The lights were going on in Theatre Square, up and down the steep slope of Tverskaya Street surged the evening crowds. Stifling, swarming city—raw lights slashing across patches of snow, fragments of crowd, rivers of pavement, rivers of mud. The four uniformed men in the high-powered government car were silent. When at last, after circling a ponderous triumphal arch which resembled the door of a huge prison, the car picked up speed down the long perspective of Leningrad Boulevard, Erchov bitterly remembered that he loved driving—the road, the speed, his own quick perception governing speed and motor. They objected to his driving these days. In any case he was too nervous, too preoccupied with work, to drive. A fine stretch of road— we know how to build. A road like this paralleling the Trans-Siberian —that's what we need to make the Far East secure. It could be done in a few years if we put five hundred thousand men to work on it, and four hundred thousand might well be drafted from prisons. Nothing impractical in the idea—I must give it further consideration. The image of the lunatic, bound to an overturned chair in a wrecked office, suddenly hung floating over the magnificent road whose precise black length was bordered on either side by immaculate white. 'Well, it's enough to drive anyone mad . . .' The lunatic laughed derisively, the lunatic began: 'You're the one who's mad, not me, it's you, not me, you'll see . . .' Erchov lit a cigarette, he wanted to see the flame of the lighter flickering between his gloved hands. And the touch of nightmare yielded and was gone. His nerves were ragged . . . he must take a whole day off, rest, get out in the fresh air . . . The street lights became fewer, a sky of stars flooded the woods with pale light. Erchov stared at it. Deep within him there was a reverent joy—but he was not conscious of it, his mind pondered figures, intrigues, plans, aspects of cases. The car passed into the shadow of tall spruces covered with snow like shaggy fur. It was very cold. The car turned on smooth snow. The pointed Norwegian gables of a large house stood densely black against the sky—Villa No. 1 of the People's Commissariat for Internal Affairs.

Here, over objects plain or flamboyantly coloured, but all contributing harmoniously to the decorative scheme, a soundproofed silence reigned. No visible telephone, no newspapers, no official portraits (it was a daring thing to exclude them), no weapons, no administrative memo pads. Erchov would have nothing that reminded him of work: when the human animal puts forth its maximum effort, it requires complete rest: the highly responsible official has a greater right to it than anyone else. Here there should be nothing but his private life—our private life, Valia, you and I. A portrait of Valia as a proper little schoolgirl hung in a cream-white oval wooden frame with a sculptured knot of ribbon at the top. Valia . . . Valentina. The tall mirror reflected warm Central Asiatic colours. Nothing suggested winter—not even the miraculous snow-laden branches which were visible through the windows. They were only a magnificent stage-set, a piece of white magic. Erchov went to the phonograph. There was a Hawaiian blues record on the turntable. No—not that! Not to-day! The poor wretched lunatic had cried: 'Traitors, we are all of us traitors!' But did he really say 'all of us'?—or did I add that? Why should I add it? The professional investigator found himself considering an odd problem. Would the most humane thing be to do away with the insane?

Valentina came out of the bathroom in a *peignoir*. 'Hello, darling.'

Hours devoted to caring for her body, and an intense well-being, had transformed the Valia he had first known as a typical young provincial woman from the Yeniseisk; her whole supple, radiant being proclaimed that it was good to live. Yes, when Communist society was at last firmly built up, after many difficult but enriching transition periods, all women would develop as fully . . . 'You are a living anticipation, Valia'—'Thanks to you, Maximka, who work and fight, thanks to men like you . . .' They sometimes said such things to each other—doubtless to justify their privileges in their own eyes; thus privilege conferred a mission. Their union was clean and uncomplicated—like the union of two healthy bodies which are attracted to each other. Eight years previously, during a tour of inspection in the vicinity of Krasnoyarsk, where he commanded a division of special Security troops, Erchov stopped at the house of a battalion commander in a military city deep in the forest. When his subordinate's young wife entered the room, Erchov found himself dazzled by her innocent and self-assured animality. It was the first time a woman had ever affected him so powerfully. Her presence evoked forests, the chill waters of untamed brooks, the pelts of suspicious beasts, the taste of new milk. She had prominent nostrils which seemed to be perpetually scenting something, and big, feline eyes. He desired her instantly—not for a chance hour, not for a night—he wanted to possess her wholly, forever, proudly. 'Why should she belong to someone else, when I want her?' The 'someone else,' an officer of low rank, with no future, absurdly deferential to his chief, had a ridiculous way of using shopkeepers' expressions in his speech. Erchov loathed him. To get him out of the way, he sent him off to inspect posts in the forest. When Erchov was alone with the woman he wanted, he first smoked a cigarette in silence; he had given himself that much time to summon up his courage. Then: 'Valentina Anisimovna, I have something to say to you . . . listen carefully. I never go back on my word. I am as straightforward and trustworthy as a good cavalry sabre. I want you to be my wife . . .' Ten feet away, firmly planted in his chair, he looked rather as if he had given a command, as if she must inevitably obey—and the young woman was attracted. 'But I don't know you,' she said, desperately frightened—and it was as if she had fallen into his arms. 'That doesn't matter. I knew you through and through the first minute I saw you. I am trustworthy and plain, I give you my word that . . .'—'I don't doubt it,' Valentina murmured, not aware that she was already con-

senting, "but . . .'—'There are no buts. A woman is free to choose.'
He refrained from adding: 'I am chief of the division, your husband
will never get anywhere.' She must have thought the same thing, for
they looked at each other in embarrassment, with such a feeling of
complicity that they both blushed for shame. Erchov turned her husband's portrait to the wall, took her in his arms, and kissed her eyelids
with a sudden strange tenderness. 'Your eyes, your eyes, you are all
sunlight, my . . .' She made no resistance, wondering dully whether
this important official—quite handsome, too—was going to take her
then and there, on the uncomfortable little sofa—luckily she had no
underwear on, luckily . . . He did nothing of the sort. He merely said,
in the clipped tones of a man making a report: 'You will leave with me
the day after to-morrow. As soon as Battalion Commander Nikudychin
returns, I shall explain matters to him as man to man. You will get
your divorce to-day—have the papers by five o'clock.' What could the
battalion commander say to the division commander? Woman is free,
and Party ethics prescribe respect for freedom. Battalion Commander
Nikudychin (whose name means, approximately, 'Good-for-nothing')
stayed drunk for a week before he visited the Chinese prostitutes of
the city for another sort of forgetfulness. Informed of his misconduct,
Erchov treated his subordinate indulgently, for he understood his
grief. Nevertheless, he had the Party secretary read him a lecture . . .
A Communist must not lose his moral equilibrium because his wife
leaves him—obviously . . .

In these rooms, Valentina liked to pass the days almost naked, wearing only the gauziest of materials. Always her body was as completely
present as her eyes, her voice. Her big eyes looked as golden as the
curls that tumbled over her forehead. She had full lips, prominent
cheek-bones, a clear pink complexion, a figure as supple and fresh as a
good swimmer's. 'You always look as if you had just come bounding
out of cold water into the sun,' her husband said to her one day. She
glanced into the mirror and answered with a proud little laugh:
'That's what I am—cold and full of sunlight. Your little golden fish.'
To-night she held out her beautiful bare arms to him:
'Why so late, darling? What is it?'
'Nothing,' Erchov said with a forced smile.
At that moment he became clearly aware that, on the contrary, there
was something, something enormous; it was here, and it would be

wherever he went—an infinite threat to himself and to this woman. Perhaps she was too beautiful, perhaps too privileged, perhaps . . . Footsteps measured the hall—the night guard going to check on the service entrance.

'Nothing. Two of my personal guards have been changed. It annoys me.'

'But you're the master, darling.' She stood there before him very straight, her *peignoir* half open over her breasts.

She finished filing a lacquered fingernail. Erchov knit his brow and stared dully at a fine firm breast, tipped with a lavender nipple. Still frowning, he met her untroubled eyes, beautiful as a field of flowers. She went on:

'. . . Don't you do as you please?'

Really, he must be very tired, or such a trifling phrase could never have produced such a strange effect on him . . . When he heard her casual words, Erchov became aware that actually he was master of nothing, that his will determined nothing, that any attempt he made to fight would fail. 'Only lunatics do as they please,' he thought. Aloud he answered with a bitter smile:

'Only lunatics imagine that they do as they please.'

It came to her: 'Something is up . . .' And she was so certain of it, and it made her so afraid, that her impulse to throw her arms around him died. She forced herself to be vivacious. 'Isn't it time we kissed each other, Sima?' He picked her up, putting his hands under her elbows as he always did, and kissed her—not on the mouth, but between her mouth and her nose and on the corners of her lips, sniffing to catch the odour of her skin. 'Nobody else kisses like that,' he had said to her when he was courting her—'just us.'

'Go and take a bath,' she said.

If he did not believe in cleansing the soul—what old-fashioned jargon!—he believed in the blessing of a clean body—soaped, rinsed, doused with cold water after a warm bath, massaged with eau-de-Cologne, admired in the mirror. 'Damned if the human animal isn't a beautiful thing!' he would sometimes exclaim in the bathroom. 'Valia, I'm beautiful too.' She would come running, and they would kiss in front of the mirror—he naked and solidly built, she half-naked, supple in some vividly striped *peignoir* . . . Those were dim memories now, dating from a distant past. In those days, as chief of secret operations in a district on the Far Eastern frontier, Erchov himself tracked down spies in the forest, directed silent man hunts, dealt with double-crossing agents, shuddered in sudden anticipation of the bullet that strikes you down from the brush, and no one ever finds out who fired it . . . He loved the life, not knowing that he was destined for the heights . . . The warm water showered over his shoulders. All he could see of himself in the mirror was a drawn face, with anxious eyes between puffy lids. 'I look like a man who's just been arrested, damn it!' The bathroom door was open; in the next room Valia put on a Hawaiian record—steel guitar and a Negro or Polynesian voice: 'I am fond of you . . .'

Erchov exploded.

'Valia, do me the favour of breaking that record this minute!'

The record cracked in two, the cold water came down on his neck like a solace.

'I broke it, Sima darling. And I'm tearing up the yellow cushion.'

'Thank you,' he said, straightening up. 'You're as good as cold water.'

The cold water came from under the snow. Somewhere wolves quenched their thirst in it.

They had sandwiches and sparkling wine brought to the bedroom. His apprehension had faded . . . better not to think about it or it would come back. There was not much of tenderness between them; theirs was an intimacy of two very clean and intelligent bodies profoundly delighted by each other. 'Want to go ski-ing to-morrow?' Valia asked, and her eyes opened wide, her nostrils opened wide. He almost knocked over the low table in front of them, so instantaneous was the reflex that carried him to the door. He flung it open—and a woman's voice in the hall cried: 'What a fright you gave me, Comrade Chief!' He saw the chambermaid, bent over the carpet, picking up towels. 'What are you doing here?' Erchov could hardly articulate for anger. 'I was just going by, Comrade Chief. You frightened me . . .' He closed the door and came back to Valia, his face sullenly angry, his moustache bristling. 'That bitch was listening at the keyhole!' This time Valia felt definitely frightened. 'Impossible, darling, you're overtired, you don't know what you're saying.' He crouched on the floor at her feet. She took his head in both hands and rocked it on her lap. 'Stop saying such foolish things, darling. Let's get some sleep.' He thought: 'Do you think it's so easy to sleep?' and his hands moved up her thighs to her warm belly.

'Put on a record, Valia. Not Hawaiian, or Negro, or French . . . Something of our own . . .'

'How about "The Partisans"?'

He walked up and down the room while, from the phonograph, came the masculine chorus of Red Partisans riding across the taiga: 'They conquered the Atamans—they conquered the Generals—they won their last victories—on the shores of the sea . . .' Columns of grey-cloaked, singing men marched through the streets of a small Asiatic city. It was late in the afternoon. Erchov stopped to watch them. A strapping fellow sang the first lines of each stanza alone, then they were repeated in well-disciplined chorus. The rhythmic tread of boots on the snow made a muffled accompaniment. Those conscious voices, those mingled and powerful voices, those voices with the strength of the earth in them—that is what we are . . . The song ended. Erchov said to himself: 'I'll take a little gardenal . . .' and there was a knock at the door.

'Comrade Chief, Comrade Gordeyev wishes to speak to you on the telephone.'

And Gordeyev's calm voice came over the wire, announcing new leads on the assassination, discoveries only just made—'so I had to disturb you, please excuse me, Maxim Andreyevich. There is an important decision to be made . . . Very strong evidence pointing to the indirect complicity of K. K. Rublev.' Which would establish a curious connection between this case and the two previous trials . . . 'As K. K. Rublev is on the special list of former members of the Central Committee, I did not wish to assume the responsibility . . .'

So you want me to take the responsibility of ordering his arrest or leaving him at liberty, you vermin . . . Erchov curtly asked:

'Biography?'

'I have it before me. In 1905, medical student at the University of Warsaw; Maximalist in 1906, fired two bullets from a revolver at Colonel Golubev, wounding him—escaped from military prison in 1907 . . . member of the Party, 1908. Intimate with Innokentii [Dubrovinsky], Rykov, Preobrazhensky, Bukharin' (and the names of these men, who had been shot as traitors after having been leaders of the Party, seemed enough to condemn Rublev). 'Political Commissar with the Nth Army, special mission in the Baikal district, secret mission in Afghanistan, president of the Chemical Fertilizers Trust, instructor at Sverdlov University, member of the C.C. until . . . member of the

Central Control Commission until . . . Censured and warned by the Moscow Control Commission for factional activity. Request for his expulsion on the grounds of Right Opportunism . . . Suspected of having read the criminal document drawn up by Riutin . . . Suspected of having attended the clandestine meeting in Zyelony Bor forest . . . Suspected of having helped Eysmont's family when Eysmont was imprisoned . . . Suspected of having translated a German article by Trotsky, which was found when the premises of his former pupil B. were searched.' (From all directions, suspicion pointed at the man who now supervised the general history section of a library.)

Erchov listened with increasing irritation. We knew all this before, you rat. Suspicions, denunciations, presumptions—we've had our fill of them! There is not a shadow of a connection between all this and the Tulayev case, and you're only trying to set a trap for me, you want me to arrest an old member of the C.C. If he has been let alone up to now, it must be because the Political Bureau wants him let alone. Erchov said:

'Very well. Wait till you hear from me. Good night.'

When Comrade Popov, of the Central Control Commission—a figure unknown to the general public but whose moral authority was of the highest (especially since the execution for treason of two or three men even more respected than himself)—when Comrade Popov sent in his name to the High Commissar, the latter had him ushered in immediately, and not without a decided feeling of curiosity. It was the first time Erchov had ever seen Popov. On very cold days Popov wore a cap over his thick dirty-grey head of hair—a workman's cap, for which he had paid six roubles at Moscow Ready-to-Wear. His faded leather overcoat had been new ten years ago. Popov had an ageing, deeply-lined face, pimply from bad health, a thin faded beard, steel-rimmed spectacles. So he entered—the cap on his grey head, a bulging brief case under his arm, a strange little half-smile in his eyes. 'Everything going well, I hope, my dear comrade?' he asked, as if he were an old friend; and, for a fraction of a second, Erchov was taken in by the old fox's guileless manner. 'Very happy to meet you at last, Comrade Popov,' the High Commissar answered.

Popov unbuttoned his overcoat, dropped heavily into a chair, murmured: 'I'm tired out, damn it! Nice place you have here—well designed, these new buildings,' and began filling his pipe. 'It wasn't like this in my day. I was in the Cheka at the very beginning, you know with Felix Edmundovich Djerzhinski. No, there was nothing like the comfort, the system you have to-day . . . The land of the Soviets is progressing by leaps and bounds, Comrade Erchov. You're lucky to be young . . .'

Erchov politely let him take his time. Popov raised a flabby, earth-coloured hand with cracked and dirty nails.

'But to come to the point, my dear comrade. The Party has you in mind. It has us all in mind, the Party. You work long hours, you work hard, the Central Committee knows your worth. Of course you have had almost too much on your hands, what with straightening out the situation you inherited' (the allusion to his predecessors was discreet), 'the period of plots through which we are passing——'

What was he getting at?

'History proceeds by stages—during one period there are polemics, during another there are plots . . . To come to the point—you are obviously tired. This matter of the terrorist attack on Comrade Tulayev seems to have been a little beyond you . . . You will excuse me for saying this to you with my usual frankness, absolutely between ourselves, my dear comrade, and as man to man—just as once in 'eighteen Vladimir Ilich himself said to me . . . Well, because we know your worth . . .'

What Lenin may have said to him twenty years earlier, he had not the least intention of relating. It was his way of talking—a counterfeit vagueness, with a liberal sprinkling of 'well nows,' a quavering voice—how old I'm getting, one of the oldest members of the Party, always in the breach . . .

'Well now, you must take a rest—just a couple of months in the country, under the Caucasian sun . . . Taking the waters, comrade—how I envy you! Ah—Matsesta, Kislovodsk, Sochi, Tikhes-Dziri, what wonderful country . . . You know Goethe's poem:

'*Kennst du das Land wo die Zitronen blühn?*

'. . . don't you know German, Comrade Erchov?'

A chill ran through the High Commissar. At last he was beginning to grasp the meaning of Popov's chatter.

'Excuse me, Comrade Popov, I am not sure that I quite understand you. Is this an order?'

'No, my dear comrade. We are simply giving you a word of advice. You are overtired—just as I am. Anyone can see it. We all belong to the Party, and we are responsible to the Party for our health. And the Party looks out for us. The old stalwarts have thought of you, your name has been mentioned in the Organization Bureau.' (He used the term to avoid naming the Political Bureau.) 'It has been decided that Gordeyev shall replace you during your absence ... We know how well you and he get on together ... so it will be a colleague in whom you have complete confidence who ... yes, two months ... not a day more ... the Party cannot give you longer, my dear comrade ...'

Moving with exaggerated slowness, Popov uncrossed his legs and stood up: rancid smile, muddy complexion. Benevolently he held out his hand. 'Ah—you aren't old enough yet to know what rheumatism is ... Well, when will you be off?'

'To-morrow evening—for Sukhum. I shall begin my leave of absence this afternoon.'

Popov seemed delighted.

'Good! That's what I like—military promptness in making decisions ... Even I, old as I am ... Yes, yes ... Get a good rest, Comrade Erchov ... A magnificent country the Caucasus—the jewel of the Union ... *Kennst du das Land* ...'

Erchov firmly shook a slimy hand, saw Popov to the door, shut the door, and stood helplessly in the centre of his office. Nothing here was his any longer. A few minutes of hypocritical conversation had been enough to remove him from the controls. What did it mean? The telephone buzzed. Gordeyev asked at what time he should summon the department heads for the projected conference?

'Report to me for orders,' said Erchov, controlling himself with difficulty. 'No—cancel that. No conference to-day.'

He drank down a glass of ice water.

He did not tell his wife that he was taking this sudden vacation by order. At Sukhum (palms beside an unimaginably blue sea, hot summer weather), the 'strictly secret' envelopes reached him for a week—then stopped. He did not dare to ask for more. Instead he spent his time in the bar, with several taciturn generals on their way back from Mongolia. Whisky gave them a common mentality—fiery and ponderous. The news that a member of the Political Bureau had come to stay in a nearby villa sent Erchov into a panic. Suppose he should ignore the High Commissar's presence? 'We'll take a trip to the mountains, Valia.' Under a blazing sun the car climbed a zigzag road: dazzling rocks, ravines, the immense enamel beaker that was the sea. Blindingly blue, the sea's horizon rose higher and higher. Valia began to be afraid. She sensed flight, but a flight that was ridiculous, impossible. 'Don't you love me any more?' she asked him at last. They had reached four thousand feet and still there was nothing but rocks, sea, and sky. He kissed her fingertips, not knowing if his sickening fear left him capable of desiring her. 'I am too afraid to think about love now . . . I am afraid—what nonsense! . . . No, it's not nonsense—I am afraid because it is my turn to die . . .' The landscape of sun-drenched rocks was deliciously fatiguing—and the sea, the sea, the sea! 'If I must die, let me at least enjoy this woman and these colours!' It was a brave thought. Avidly he kissed Valia on the mouth. The purity of the landscape filled them with an ecstasy that was like light. They spent three weeks in a chalet high in the mountains. An Abkhasian couple dressed in white (husband and wife were equally beautiful) served them in silence. They slept on a terrace in the open air, their bodies clothed in silk; and, after making love, they were together again as they gazed up at the stars. Once Valia said: 'Look, darling, we're going to fall into the stars . . .' So, occasionally, he tasted peace. But all the rest of the time he was obsessed by two thoughts—one rational and reassuring, the other disguised and perfidious, following its own obscure course, tenacious as decay in a tooth. The first was clearly formulated: 'Why shouldn't they retire me for just long enough to get this accursed case settled, since I seem to have made a mess of it? The Chief has shown that he is favourably disposed towards me. After all, all they have to do is send me back to the army. I can't have offended anyone, because I have no past. Suppose I ask to be sent back to the Far East?' The second, the insidious one, murmured: 'You know too much—they're never going to believe you'll keep your mouth shut. You will be made to disappear as your predecessors disappeared. Your predecessors went through all this—work, clues, anxiety, doubt, leaves of absence, irrational flight, resignation, and return—and they were shot.'—'Valia,' he suddenly called, 'come hunting with me!' He took her on long climbs to inaccessible spots, from which, suddenly, the sea would be visible, fringing an immense map; capes and rocks jutted out into a whirlpool of light. 'Look, Valia!' On a rock peak rising from the sunny scree an ibex stood against the blue, horns lifted. Erchov handed Valia the rifle; she put it cautiously to her shoulder; her arms were bare, beads of sweat gleamed on the back of her neck. The sea filled the cup of the world, silence reigned over the universe, the creature stood tense and alive, a golden silhouette. 'Aim carefully,' Erchov whispered into her ear. 'And above all, darling, miss him. . . .' Slowly the rifle rose, rose; Valia's head dropped back; when the barrel pointed straight up into the sky, she fired. Valia was laughing, her eyes were full of the sky. The report faded to a faint rasp like tearing cloth. Calmly the ibex turned its slim head towards the two distant white figures, stared at them for a moment, bent its hocks, bounded gracefully towards the sea, and disappeared. . . . It was that evening, when they got back, that Erchov found a telegram summoning him to Moscow immediately.

They travelled in a private railway car. On the second day the train stopped at a forgotten station in the middle of snow-covered cornfields. An impenetrable grey mist darkened the horizon. Valia was sulking a little, with a cigarette between her lips and a book of Zoschenko's in her hands. . . . 'What do you find to interest you,' he had asked, 'in that sort of sour humour which is a libel on us?' She had just answered, angrily, 'Nowadays you never say anything that isn't official. . . .' Going back to everyday life had set them both on edge. Erchov began looking through a newspaper. The orderly officer entered, announcing that Erchov was wanted on the telephone in the station—a defect in the equipment made it impossible to connect the through wire with the private car. Erchov's face darkened: 'When we reach Moscow, you will have the rolling-stock supervisor put under arrest for a week. Telephones in private cars must function ir-re-proach-ab-ly. Make a note of it.'

'Yes, Comrade High Commissar.'

Erchov put on his overcoat, which bore the emblems of the highest power, stepped down onto the wooden platform of the deserted little station, noticed that the train was only three cars long, and strode rapidly towards the only visible building. The orderly officer followed him respectfully, three paces behind. *Security, Railway Supervision.* Erchov entered; several soldiers came to attention, and saluted. 'This way, Comrade Chief,' said the orderly officer, blushing oddly. In the little back room, overheated by an iron stove, two officers rose as he entered, puppets jerked by the strings of discipline, one tall and thin, the other short and fat, both smooth-faced and of high rank. A little surprised, Erchov returned their salute. Then curtly:

3

'The telephone?'

'We have a message for you,' the tall, thin one answered evasively. He had a long wrinkled face and grey eyes that were absolutely cold.

'A message? Let me have it.'

The tall, thin one reached into his brief case and drew out a sheet of paper on which were a few typewritten lines. 'Have the goodness . . .'

'By decision of the Special Conference of the People's Commissariat for Internal Affairs . . . dated . . . concerning Item No. 4628g . . . order for the preventive arrest . . . ERCHOV, Maxim Andreyevich, forty-one years of age . . .'

A sort of cramp settled on Erchov's throat, yet he found the strength to read it all through, word by word, to examine the seal, the signatures —'Gordeyev,' countersigned Illegible—the serial numbers . . . 'No one has a right,' he said absurdly after a few seconds, 'I am . . .' The short, fat one did not let him finish:

'You are so no longer, Maxim Andreyevich. You have been relieved of your high office by a decision of the Organization Bureau.'

He spoke with unctuous deference.

'I have a copy of it here . . . Be so good as to surrender your weapons . . .'

The table was covered with black oilcloth; Erchov laid his regulation revolver down on it. As he reached into his back pocket for the little spare Browning he always carried, he felt an urge to send a bullet into his heart; imperceptibly, he forced his hand to move more slowly, and he thought that he let no expression appear in his face. The gilded ibex on the pyramid of rock, between sea and sky. The gilded ibex threatened by the hunter's gun; Valia's teeth, her straining neck, the blueness . . . it is all over. The tall thin one's transparent eyes never left his, the short fat one's hands gently grasped the High Commissar's hand and secured the Browning. An engine gave a long whistle. Erchov said:

'My wife . . .'

The short, fat one broke in cordially:

'Set your mind at ease, Maxim Andreyevich, I shall look out for her myself . . .'

'Thank you very much,' said Erchov stupidly.

'Be so good as to change your clothes,' said the tall, thin one, 'because of the insignia . . .'

Ah yes, his insignia . . . A military tunic without insignia, a military overcoat much like his own, but without insignia, lay over the back of a chair. It had all been carefully thought out. He dressed like a somnambulist. Everything was becoming clear—first of all, certain things that he had done himself . . . His own portrait, yellowed by the sun and dirtied with flyspecks, looked at him. 'Have that portrait taken down,' he said severely. The sarcasm did him good, but it was received in silence.

When Erchov came out of the little back room, walking between the tall, thin officer and the short, fat one, the outer room was empty. The men who had seen him come in wearing the stars of power on collar and sleeves did not see him walk out disgraced. 'Whoever organized this deserves to be complimented,' thought the ex-High Commissar. He did not know whether the idea had come to him from force of habit, or whether he was thinking ironically. The station was deserted. Black rails against the snow, empty space. The special train was gone—carrying away Valia, carrying away the past. A hundred yards away another car waited—an even more special car. Towards it Erchov strode, between the two silent officers.

MEN AT BAY

BORN IN the Arctic, sweeping across the sleeping forests along the Kama, slow-falling, eddying snowstorms, before which packs of wolves fled here and there, bore down on Moscow. They seemed to be torn to shreds over the city, worn out by their long journeyings through the air, suddenly blotting out the blue sky. A dull milky light spread over the squares, the streets, the little forgotten private houses in ancient alleys, the trams with their frost-traced windows . . . Life went on in a soft swirling and eddying that was like a burial. Feet trod on millions of pure stars, fresh every instant. And suddenly, high up, behind church domes, behind delicate crosses springing from inverted crescents and still showing traces of gilt, the blue reappeared. The sun lay on the snow, caressed dilapidated old façades, shone in through double windows . . . Rublev never tired of watching these changes. Delicate, be-diamonded branches appeared in the window of his office. Seen from there, the universe was reduced to a bit of forsaken garden, a wall, and, behind the wall, an abandoned chapel with a greenish-gold dome growing pink under the patina of time.

Rublev looked up from the four books which he was simultaneously consulting: the same series of facts appeared in them under four undeniable but unsubstantiated aspects—whence the errors of historians, some purposeful, others unconscious. You made your way through error as you did through snowstorms. Centuries later, the truth became apparent to someone—to-day it is to me—out of the tangle of contradictions. Economic history, Rublev made a note, often has the deceitful clarity of a coroner's report. Something, fortunately, escapes them both—the difference between corpse and living man.

'My handwriting looks neurotic.'

Assistant Librarian Andronnikova came in. ('She thinks that *I* look neurotic . . .') 'Be so good, Kiril Kirillovich, as to look over the list of banned books for which special permissions have been requested . . .' Usually Rublev carelessly O.K.'d all such requests—whether they came from idealistic historians, liberal economists, social-democrats with a tinge of *bourgeois* eclecticism, cloudy intuitionists . . . This time he gave a start: a student at the Institute of Applied Sociology had asked for *The Year* 1905 by L. D. Trotsky. Assistant Librarian Andronnikova, with her small face framed in a foam of white hair, had expected that Rublev would be surprised.

'Refused,' he said. 'Tell him to apply to the Library of the Party History Commission . . .'

'I did,' Andronnikova answered gently. 'But he was very insistent.'

Rublev thought he read a childish sympathy in her eyes, the sympathy of a weak, clean, and good creature.

'How are you, Comrade Andronnikova? Did you find any cloth at the Kuznetsky-most Co-op?'

'Yes, thank you, Kiril Kirillovich,' she said, a restrained warmth colouring her voice.

He took his overcoat down from the coat stand, and, as he put it on, joked about the art of life:

'We lie in wait for luck, Comrade Andronnikova, for our friends and for ourselves . . . We are living in the jungle of the transition period, eh?'

'Living in it is a dangerous art,' thought the white-haired woman, but she merely smiled, more with her eyes than with her lips. Did this singular man—scholarly, keen-minded, passionately fond of music— really believe in the 'twofold period of transition, from Capitalism to Socialism and from Socialism to Communism,' about which he had published a book in the days when the Party still allowed him to write? Citizeness Andronnikova, sixty, ex-princess, daughter of a great liberal (and monarchist) politician, sister of a general massacred by his soldiers in 1916, widow of a collector of pictures the only loves of whose life had been Matisse and Picasso, deprived of the ballot because of her social origins, lived by a private cult whose saint was Wladimir Soloviev. The philosophy of mystical wisdom, if it did not help her to understand the species of men called 'Bolsheviks'—men strangely stubborn, hard, limited, dangerous, yet some of whom had souls of unequalled richness—helped her to regard them with an indulgence in which, of late, there was an admixture of secret compassion. If the worst were not also to be loved, what place would there be for Christian charity here below? If the worst were not sometimes very near to the best, would they really be the worst? Andronnikova thought: 'They certainly believe what they write . . . And perhaps Kiril Kirillovich is right. Perhaps it really is a period of transition . . .' She knew the names, faces, histories, smiles, characteristic gestures, of several prominent Party members who had recently disappeared or been executed in the course of incomprehensible trials. They were true brothers of the man before her; they all called each other by nicknames; they all talked of a 'period of transition,' and no doubt it was because they believed in it that they had died . . . Andronnikova watched over Rublev with an almost painful anxiety, though he did not suspect it. She repeated the name of Kiril Kirillovich in her mental prayers at night, before she went to sleep with the covers pulled up to her chin, as she had at sixteen. Her room was tiny and full of faded things—old letters in elaborate boxes, portraits of handsome young men, cousins and nephews, most of them buried no one knew where, in the Carpathians, at Gallipoli, before Trebizond, at Yaroslavl, in Tunisia. Two of these aristocrats were presumably still alive—one a waiter in Constantinople, the other, under a false name, a tram-car motorman in Rostov. But when Andronnikova managed to get hold of some half-decent tea and a little sugar, she still found a certain pleasure in life . . . As a means of getting a few minutes' conversation with Rublev every day she had hit on the idea of searching the shops for dress goods, letter paper, choice foods, and telling him the difficulties she encountered. Rublev, who liked to walk the streets of Moscow, went into shops to get information for her.

Since he enjoyed breathing the cold air, Rublev went home on foot through the white boulevards. Tall, thin, and broad-shouldered, he had begun to stoop during the last two years, not under the burden of years but under that heavier burden, anxiety. The little boys chasing each other on skates over the snowy boulevard knew his old fur-lined coat, much faded about the shoulders, the astrakhan cap which he wore pulled down to his eyes, his scanty beard, his big bony nose, his bushy eyebrows, the bulging brief case he carried under his arm. As he passed he heard them call: 'Hi, Vanka, here's Professor Checkmate,' or 'Watch out, Tiomka, here comes Tsar Ivan the Terrible.'

The fact is that he both looked like a schoolmaster who was a champion chess player and resembled the portraits of the Bloody Tsar. Once a schoolboy who had come whizzing along at top speed on a single skate and had crashed into him muttered this odd apology: 'Excuse me, Citizen Professor Ivan the Terrible'—and could not understand the strange fit of laughter with which the stern old codger answered him.

He passed the ironwork gateway of No. 25 Tverskoy Boulevard, 'Writers' House.' On the façade of the little building a medallion displayed the noble profile of Alexander Herzen. Out of the basement windows wafted the odours of the 'Writers' Restaurant'—or rather of the scribblers' trough. 'I sowed dragons,' said Marx, 'and reaped fleas.' This country is forever sowing dragons, and in times of stress it produces them, strong with wings and claws, furnished with magnificent brains, but their posterity dies out in fleas, trained fleas, stinking fleas, fleas, fleas! *In this house was born Alexander Herzen*, the most generous man in the Russia of his time, and therefore driven to live in exile; and because he had perhaps exchanged messages with him, a man of the high intelligence of Chernyshevski was manhandled by the police for twenty years. Now in this house the scribblers filled their bellies by writing, in verse or prose, and in the name of the Revolution, the stupidities and infamies which despotism ordered them to write. Fleas, fleas. Rublev still belonged to the Writers' Syndicate, whose members, who not long ago sought his advice, now pretended not to see him in the street for fear of compromising themselves ... A sort of hate came into his eyes when he saw the 'poet of the Young Communists' (forty years old) who had written, for the executed Piatakov and certain others:

> *Shooting them is little,*
> *Is too little, is nothing!*
> *Poison carrion, profligates,*
> *Imperialist vermin,*
> *Who soil our proud Socialist bullets!*

All in double rhymes. There were a hundred lines of it. At four roubles a line, it came to a skilled workman's wages for a month, a ditch-digger's for three months. The author of it, dressed in a sport suit made of good brown German cloth, displayed a rubicund face in editorial offices.

Strastnaya Square—Square of the Monastery of the Passion. Push-kin meditated on his pedestal. May you be forever blessed, Poet of Russia, because you were not a rat, because you were only a little of a coward, just enough, probably, to save your neck under an enlightened tyranny, when they hanged your friends the Decembrists! The little monastery tower across the square was being gradually demolished. The reinforced concrete *Izvestia* building, distinguished by a clock, rose above the gardens of the old monastery. At the four corners of the square: a little white church, cinema theatres, a book shop. People in single file waited patiently for a bus. Rublev turned right, into Gorki Street, looked idly into the windows of a big grocer's shop displaying fat fish from the Volga, magnificent fruits from Central Asia, de-luxe viands for handsomely paid specialists. He lived in an eleven-story block of flats in the next little side street. The spacious halls were scantily lighted. Slowly the lift rose to the eighth floor. Rublev went down a dark gloomy corridor, knocked softly at a door. It opened, he entered and kissed his wife on the forehead:

'Any heat to-day, Dora?'

'Not much. The radiators are barely warm. Put on your old field jacket.'

Neither meetings of the tenants of Soviet House nor the annual arrest and trial of the technicians of the Regional Bureau of Com-bustibles did anything to improve the situation. The cold brought a sort of desolation into the big room. Touched by the twilight, the whiteness of roofs filtered through the window. The green leaves of the plants seemed to be made of metal, the typewriter displayed a dusty keyboard that looked like a fantastic set of false teeth. The strong radiant human bodies which Michael Angelo had painted for the Sistine Chapel, reduced to black and grey by photography, had be-come uninteresting blotches on the wall. Dora lit the lamp on the table, sat down, crossed her arms under her brown woollen shawl, and looked up at Kiril out of her calm grey eyes. 'Did you have a good day?' She kept down her joy at having him back, as a moment earlier she had kept down her fear that he would not come back. It would always be like that. 'Have you read the papers? . . . I ran through them . . . A new People's Commissar for Agriculture has been ap-pointed in the R.S.F.S.R.; the one before has disappeared. And this one will disappear before six months are out, Dora, I assure you. And the one who follows him too! Which of them will make things any better?' They talked in low voices. If there had been any occasion to draw up a list of tenants of this very building, all influential people, who had disappeared in the last twenty months, they would have discovered surprising percentages, would have concluded that certain floors were unlucky, would have seen twenty-five years of history under more than one murderous aspect. But the list was there—it was in them, obscurely. That was what was ageing Rublev. It was the only way in which he yielded.

In that same room, between the plants with their metallic leaves and the dim reproductions of the Sistine frescoes, they had listened all day and late into the night to the senseless, demonic, inexorable, incredible voices that poured from the loud-speaker. Those voices filled hours, nights, months, years, they filled the soul with delirium, and it was astonishing that one could go on living after having heard them. Once, Dora had stood up, pale and shattered, her hands hanging limp, and said:

'It is like a snowstorm covering a continent. No roads, no light, no possible way of travelling, everything will be buried . . . It is an avalanche coming down on us, carrying us away . . . It is a horrible revolution . . .'

Kiril was pale too, the room flickered with white light. From the varnished case of the radio came a slightly hoarse, shaky, hesitating voice, with a heavy Turkish accent—the voice of an ex-member of the Turkmanistan Central Committee, who, like everyone else, was confessing to unending treason. 'I organized the assassination of . . . I took part in the attempt on . . . which failed . . . I prevented the irrigation plans from succeeding . . . I incited the revolt of the Basmachi . . . I dealt with the British Intelligence . . . The Gestapo sent me . . . I was paid thirty thousand . . .' Kiril turned a knob and stopped the flood of insanity. 'Abrahimov on the stand,' he murmured. 'Poor devil!' He knew him—an ambitious young fellow from Tashkent who liked to drink good wine, hard-working, not stupid . . . Kiril rose to his feet and said solemnly:

'It is the counter-revolution, Dora.'

The voice of the Supreme Prosecutor went dismally on and on, rehashing conspiracies, assassinations, crimes, destruction, felonies, treason; it became a sort of weary barking, heaping insults upon men who listened, their heads bowed, desperate, done for, under the eyes of a mob, between two guards: among those men there were several

3*

who were spotless, the purest, the best, the most intelligent men of the Revolution—and precisely for that reason they were undergoing martyrdom, they accepted martyrdom. Hearing them over the radio, he sometimes thought: 'How he must be suffering! . . . But no—that is his normal voice—what is it? Is he mad? Why is he lying like that?' Dora walked back and forth across the room, bumping against the walls, Dora collapsed onto the bed, shaken by dry sobs, choking. 'Wouldn't it be better if they let themselves be torn to pieces alive? Don't they realize that they are poisoning the soul of the proletariat? That they are poisoning the springs of the future?'

'They do not realize it,' Kiril Rublev said. 'They believe that they are still serving Socialism. Some of them hope that they will be allowed to live. They have been tortured . . .'

He wrung his hands. 'No, they are not cowards; no, they have not been tortured. I do not believe it. They are true, that is it, still true to the Party, and there is no more Party, there are only inquisitors, executioners, criminals . . . No, I'm talking nonsense, it is not so simple. Perhaps I would do as they are doing if I were in their place . . .'

At that instant he thought, perfectly clearly: 'Their place is mine, and some day I shall be there, infallibly . . .' and his wife knew, perfectly clearly, that he was thinking it.

'They assure themselves that it is better to die dishonoured, murdered by the Chief, than to denounce him to the international *bourgeoisie* . . .'

He almost screamed, like a man crushed in an accident:

'And in that, they are right.'

For a long time they returned to this obsessing thought again and again, discussed it again and again. Their minds worked on nothing else, they scrutinized this single theme from every standpoint, because in that part of the world—the Great Sixth—history had nothing to work on but this darkness, these lies, this perverse devotion, this blood that was shed day in and day out. Old Party members avoided one another—so that they should not have to meet each other's eyes, or lie ignobly to each other's faces out of a reasonable cowardice, so that they might not stumble over the name of a comrade who had disappeared, not have to compromise themselves by a handshake, or disgust themselves by not giving it. Nevertheless, they came to know of the arrests, the disappearances, the fantastic sick leaves, the ill-omened transfers, bits of secret interrogations, sinister rumours. Long before a member of the General Staff—ex-coal miner, a Bolshevik in 1908, once famous for a campaign in the Ukraine, a campaign in the Altai, a campaign in Yakutsk, thrice decorated with the Order of the Red Flag—long before this general disappeared, a perfidious rumour followed him everywhere, making the women whom he met look at him with eyes that were strangely wide, emptying the ante-chambers of the Defence Commissariat when he passed through them. Rublev saw him one evening at Red Army House: 'Imagine it, Dora. The reception line was not ten feet from him . . . Those who found themselves face to face with him smiled sweetly and too politely, and disappeared . . . I watched him for twenty minutes. He sat all alone, between two empty chairs—brand-new uniform, all his decorations, looking like a wax doll as he watched the dancing. Fortunately some young lieutenants, who knew nothing, danced with his wife . . . Arkhinov came up, recognized him, hesitated, pretended to look for something in his pockets—and slowly turned his back on him . . .' A month later, when he was arrested as he left a committee meeting at which he had not opened his mouth, the general felt relieved; in fact, everyone felt the relief that comes at the end of a long wait. When the same icy atmosphere began to surround another Red general, summoned to Moscow from the Far East to receive mythical orders, he blew out his brains in the bathtub. Contrary to all expectations, the Artillery Command gave him a handsome funeral; three months later, in accordance with the decree providing that the families of traitors must be deported to 'the most remote districts of the Union,' his mother, his wife, and his two children were ordered to set forth into the unknown. News of such cases—and they were many—came to people by chance, confidentially, in whispered conversations, and the details were never fully known. You knocked at a friend's door, and the maid looked at you in terror when she opened it. 'I don't know anything about it, he is not here, he will not be back, I have been told to go to the country . . . No, I don't know anything, no . . .' She was afraid to say another word, afraid of you as if danger were at your heels. You telephoned to a friend—from a public booth, by way of precaution—and the voice of an unknown man asked, 'Who is calling?' very clearly, and you understood that a spy had been posted there and you answered mockingly, though you felt disturbed, 'The State Bank, on business,' and then you got away as fast as you could because you knew that the booth would be searched within ten minutes. New faces appeared in offices instead of the faces you had known; you felt ashamed when you mentioned the former incumbent's name, and ashamed when you did not mention it. The papers published the names of new members of the federated governments without saying what had become of their predecessors—which was obvious enough. In communal apartments, occupied by several families, if the bell rang at night, people thought: 'They've come for the Communist'—as in earlier days they would immediately have thought it was the technician or the ex-officer who was being arrested. Rublev checked over the list of his earlier comrades and found only two still alive with whom he was more or less intimate: Philippov, of the Plan Commission, and Wladek, a Polish *émigré*. The latter had once known Rosa Luxembourg, had belonged, with Warsky and Waletsky, to the first Central Committees of the Polish C.P., had done secret-service work under Unschlicht . . . Warsky and Waletsky, if perhaps they were still alive, were alive in prison, in some secret isolator reserved for those who had once been influential leaders of the Third International; the corpulent Unschlicht, with his big face and spectacles, was generally supposed to have been executed—it was almost a certainty. Wladek, holding an obscure post in an Institute of Agronomy, did his utmost to remain forgotten there. He lived some twenty-five miles from Moscow in a dilapidated villa in the heart of the forest; he came to the city only for his work, saw no one, wrote to no one, received no letters, and made no telephone calls.

'Perhaps in that way they will forget me? Do you understand?' he said to Rublev. 'There were some thirty of us Poles who belonged to the old Party cadres; if four are still alive, it is surprising.'

Short, almost bald, bulb-nosed, extremely shortsighted, he surveyed Rublev through extraordinarily thick glasses; yet his expression remained cheerful and young, his thick lips were playful.

'Kiril Kirillovich, all this nightmare is basically very interesting and very old. History doesn't give a damn for us, my friend. "Ah-ha, my little Marxists," she says, like one of Macbeth's witches, "you make plans, you worry over questions of social conscience!" And she turns Little Father Tsar Iohan the Terrible loose on us, with his hysterical fears and his big ironshod stick . . .'

They were whispering together in a dim antechamber lined with showcases containing an exhibition of grains. Rublev answered with a faint laugh:

'You know the schoolboys think that *I* look like Tsar Iohan . . .'

'We are all like him in one way or another,' said Wladek, half serious, half joking. 'We are all of us professors descended from the Terrible Tsar . . . Even I, despite my baldness and my Semitic ancestry —even I feel a little frightened when I look inside myself, I assure you.'

'I cannot in the least agree with your bad literary psychology, Wladek. We must talk seriously. I will bring Philippov.'

They arranged to meet in the woods, on the bank of the Istra, because it would not have been prudent to meet either in the city or at Philippov's, whose neighbours were railwaymen. 'I never let anyone come to my place,' said Philippov. 'That is the safest way. Besides, what is one to talk about?'

Without in the least knowing why, Philippov had survived several sets of economists on the Central Plan Commission. 'The only plan which will be completely carried out,' he said lightly, 'is the plan of arrests.' Member of the Party since 1910, president of a Siberian Soviet when the spring floods of March, 1917, carried away the double-headed eagles (thoroughly worm-eaten), later commissar with little troops of Red partisans who held the taiga against Admiral Koltchak, he had for almost two years been collaborating on plans for the production of goods of prime necessity—an incredible task, enough to get a man thrown into prison instantly, in a country where there was a simultaneous lack of nails, shoes, matches, cloth, et cetera. However, since he was a man to fear because of his long connection with the Party, directors who wanted primarily to keep out of trouble had set him to work on the plan for the distribution of popular musical instruments—accordions, harmoniums, flutes, guitars, and zithers and tambourines for the East (the equipment of orchestras being undertaken by a special bureau, orchestral instruments did not fall within his province). This appointment provided an oasis of safety, since the supply always exceeded the demand in almost all markets, except those of Buriat-Mongolia, Birobidjan, the Autonomous Region of Nakhichevan, and the Autonomous Republic of the Karabakh Mountains, which were regarded as of secondary importance. 'On the other hand,' Philippov commented, 'we have introduced the accordion into Dzungeria . . . The shamans of Inner Mongolia demand our tambourines . . .' He scored unexpected successes. As a matter of fact everyone knew that the thriving trade in musical instruments was due to the lack

of more useful goods, and that their production in sufficient quantities
was partly due to the labour of artisans refractory to co-operative
organization, partly to the uselessness of the instruments themselves
. . . But that was the responsibility of the higher echelons of the
Central Plan Commission . . . Philippov, with his round head, his
freckled face, his straight black moustache, trimmed very short, his big
sagacious eyes which shone from between puffy lids, arrived at the
meeting place on skis, as did Rublev. Wladek came from his villa in
felt boots and a sheepskin coat, like a fantastic and extremely shortsighted woodcutter. They met under pines whose straight black trunks
rose forty feet above the bluish snow before branching. Under the
wooded hills, the river traced slow curves of grey-pink and pale azure
such as are to be found in Japanese prints. The three men had known
each other for many years. Philippov and Rublev had slept in the same
room in a wretched hotel on the Place de la Contrescarpe, in Paris,
shortly before the Great War; in those days they lived on brie and
blood pudding; at the Bibliothèque Ste.-Geneviève they commented
scathingly on the insipid sociology of Dr. Gustave Le Bon; together
they read the accounts of Madame Caillaux's trial in Juarès's newspaper; they shopped at the stalls in the Rue Mouffetard, looking with
delight at the old houses which had seen the revolutions, amusing
themselves by recognizing Daumier's types in the figures they saw
emerging from corridors and halls that were like vaults . . . Philippov
sometimes slept with little Marcella, chestnut-haired, smiling, and
serious, who was generally to be found at the Taverne du Panthéon.
There, late at night, she and her girl friends danced lusty waltzes in
the small rooms downstairs, to the music of violins. They went to the
Closerie des Lilas to see Paul Fort, surrounded by admirers. The poet
always got himself up to look like a musketeer. In front of the café,
Marshal Ney, on his pedestal, marched to his death, brandishing his
sabre—and Rublev insisted that he must be cursing: 'Swine, swine!'
Together they recited poems by Constantin Belmont:

Be we like the sun! . . .

They quarrelled over the problem of matter and energy, which was
being restated by Avenarius, Mach, and Maxwell. 'Energy is the only
cognizable reality,' Philippov asserted one evening. 'Matter is only an
aspect of it . . .'—'You are nothing but an unconscious idealist,' Rublev

retorted, 'and you are turning your back on Marxism . . . In any case,' he added, 'the petty-*bourgeois* frivolity of your private life had given me due warning . . .' They shook hands coldly at the corner of the Rue Soufflot. The ponderous black silhouette of the Panthéon rose from the wide deserted street with its lines of funereal street lamps. The paving stones gleamed, a solitary woman, a prostitute who kept her veil down, waited in the darkness for an unknown man. The war aggravated their long disagreement, although they both remained internationalists; but one of them had enlisted in the Foreign Legion, the other was interned. They met again at Perm in 'eighteen, and were too busy to be surprised or to celebrate the occasion for more than five minutes. Rublev was bringing a detachment of workers into the city to suppress a mutiny of drunken sailors. Philippov, a muffler around his neck, his voice a whisper, one arm wounded and in a sling, had just escaped by the merest chance from the clubs of peasants in revolt against requisitionings. Both of them were dressed in black leather, armed with Mausers sheathed in wood, carrying urgent orders, living on boiled groats and pickled cucumbers, exhausted, enthusiastic, radiating a sombre energy. They held a council of war by candlelight, guarded by proletarians from Petrograd with cartridge belts over their overcoats. Inexplicable shots sounded in the dark city; its gardens were full of excitement under the stars.

Philippov spoke first: 'We have to shoot people or we'll get nothing done.'

One of the men on guard at the door said soberly: 'By God, you're right!'—'Shoot who?' Rublev asked, overcoming his fatigue, his desire to sleep, his desire to vomit.

'Some hostages—there are officers, a priest, manufacturers . . .'

'Is it really necessary?'

'I'll say it is,' growled the man at the door, 'or we're done for.' And he came towards them, holding out his black hands.

And Rublev rose, seized by wild anger. 'Silence! There will be no interrupting the deliberations of the Army Council! Discipline!' Philippov put his hand on his shoulder and pushed him back into his chair. Then, to end the quarrel, he whispered ironically: 'Do you remember the Boul' Miche'?'

'What?' said Rublev in amazement. 'Not another word, you Tatar, I beg of you. I am absolutely against the execution of hostages. Let us not become barbarians.'

Philippov answered: 'You have to consent to it. First, our retreat is cut off on three sides out of four. Second, I absolutely must have several carloads of potatotes and I can't pay for them. Third, the sailors have behaved like gangsters, and it's they who ought to be shot; but we can't shoot them, they're splendid physical specimens. Fourth, as soon as our backs are turned, the whole countryside will rise . . . So sign.'

The order for execution, written in pencil on the back of a receipt, was ready. Rublev signed it, muttering: 'I hope we have to pay for this, you and I; I tell you we are besmirching the Revolution; the devil knows what all this is about . . .' They were still young then. Now, twenty years later, growing fat and grey, they glided on their skis through the admirable Hokusai landscape, and wordlessly the past re-awoke within them.

Philippov lengthened his stride and shot ahead. Wladek came to meet them. They set their skis up in the snow and followed the edge of the wood, above a river of ice fringed with astonishing white shrubbery.

'It's good to meet again,' said Rublev.

'It's wonderful that we are alive,' said Wladek.

'What are we going to do?' asked Philippov. ' "That is the question." '

Space, the woods, the snow, the ice, the blue, the silence, the clarity of the cold air surrounded them. Wladek spoke of the Poles, all vanished into prisons—the Left, led by Lensky, after the Right, led by Koschewa. 'The Jugoslavs, too,' he added, 'and the Finns . . . It happens to the whole Comintern . . .' He studded his narrative with names and faces.

'Why, it's even worse than at the Plan Commission!' Philippov exclaimed cheerfully.

'As for me,' Philippov said, 'I'm quite sure that I owe my life to Bruno. You knew him, Kiril, when he was legation secretary at Berlin —can you see his Assyrian profile? After Krestinsky's arrest, he expected to be liquidated too and, incredible as it may seem, he had been appointed assistant director of a central bureau in Internal Affairs— which gave him access to the master files. He told me that he hoped he had managed to save a dozen comrades by destroying their cards. "But I am done for," he said. "There are still the dossiers, of course, and there is the Central Committee file, but one doesn't show up so much there, sometimes names are hard to find . . ." '

'And then?'

'*Finis*—I don't know how or where—last year.'

Philippov repeated: 'What is to be done?'

'For my part,' said Wladek, searching his pockets for a cigarette, and looking more than ever like a mocking, prematurely old child, 'if they come to arrest me, I will not let them take me alive. No, thanks.'

'But there are people,' said Philippov, 'who are released or deported. I know of cases. Your solution is not reasonable. Besides, there is something about it I don't like. It smacks of suicide.'

'Have it your own way.'

Philippov went on:

'If I am arrested I shall politely tell them that under no circumstances will I enter into any scheme, either with a trial or without. Do as you please with me . . . Once that is absolutely clear, I think one has a chance of getting out of it. You go to Kamchatka or you draw up plans for timber cutting. I'm willing. How about you, Kiril?'

Kiril Rublev took off his fur cap. His high forehead, under curls that were still dark, stood bare to the cold.

'Ever since they shot Nicolai Ivanovich, I have sensed that they were prowling around me, imperceptibly. And I am waiting for them. I haven't told Dora, but she knows. So, in my case it is a very practical question, which I may have to answer any day . . . And . . . I don't know . . .'

They began to walk, sinking in the snow to their calves. Above them, crows flew from branch to branch. The light was charged with wintry whiteness. Kiril was a head taller than either of his companions. He differed from them in spirit as well. He spoke in a calm voice:

'Suicide is only an individual solution—therefore not Socialist. In my case it would set a bad example. I don't say this to shake your resolution, Wladek: you have your reasons, and I believe that they are valid for you. To say that one will confess nothing is courageous, perhaps overly courageous: no one knows precisely how strong he is. And then, it is all more complex than it appears.'

'Yes,' said the other two, stumbling through the snow.

'One has to become conscious of what is going on . . . become conscious . . .'

Rublev, repeating his words in a doubtful voice, wore an expression which was often seen on his face—the look of a preoccupied pedant. Wladek flew into a rage, turned purple, waved his short arms:

'Damned theoretician! There's no curing you! I can still see the articles in which you cut up the Trotskyists in 'twenty-seven by maintaining that the proletarian party cannot degenerate ... Because if it degenerates, obviously it is not the proletarian party ... You casuist! What is going on is as clear as daylight. Thermidor, Brumaire, and all the rest of it, on an unheard-of social scale and in the country where Genghis Khan has the use of the telephone, as old Tolstoy put it.'

'Genghis Khan,' said Philippov, 'is a great man not properly appreciated. He was not cruel. If he had his servants build pyramids of severed heads, it was not out of cruelty nor to satisfy a primitive taste for statistics, but to depopulate the countries which he could not otherwise dominate and which he intended to bring back to a pastoral economy, the only economy which he could understand. Already, it was differences in economies which made heads fall ... Note that the only way he could assure himself that the massacres had been properly carried out, was to collect the heads. The Khan distrusted his manpower ...'

They walked a little while longer in deeper snow. 'A marvellous Siberia,' murmured Rublev, whom the landscape had calmed. And Wladek turned abruptly towards his two companions, planted himself in front of them in comic exasperation:

'What eloquence! One of you lectures on Genghis Khan, the other advocates becoming fully conscious! You are making a mock of your own selves, my dear comrades. Permit *me* to reveal something to you! It's *my* turn, my turn ...'

They saw that his thick lips were trembling, that there was mist on the lenses of his glasses, that straight lines cut horizontally across his cheeks. For several seconds he kept muttering 'my turn, my turn' almost unintelligibly.

'But doubtless I am of a grosser constitution, my dear comrades. As for *me*—the fact is—I am afraid. I am deathly afraid—do you hear me? —whether it is worthy of a revolutionary or not. I live alone like an animal among all these woods and all this snow, which I loathe— because I am afraid. I live without a wife, because I don't want two of us waking up at night to ask ourselves if it is the last night. I wait for them every night, all by myself, I take a bromide, I go to sleep in a stupor, I wake with a start, thinking they've come, crying out "Who's there?" and the woman next door answers, "It's the blind banging, Vladimir Ernestovich, sleep well," and I can't get back to sleep. I am afraid and I am ashamed, not of myself, but of all of us. I think of those who have been shot, I see their faces, I hear their jokes, and I have migraines that medicine has not yet named—a little pain the colour of fire fixes itself in the back of my neck. I am afraid, afraid, not so much afraid of dying as of nothing and everything—afraid to see you, afraid to talk to people, afraid to think, afraid to understand . . .'

And indeed it could be read in his puffy face, in his red-rimmed eyes, in his precipitate speech. Philippov said:

'I am afraid too, of course—but it doesn't do any good. I have grown used to it. One lives with fear as one lives with a hernia.'

Kiril Rublev slowly pulled off his gloves and looked at his hands, which were long and strong, a little hairy between the joints—'hands still full of vitality,' he thought. And, picking up some snow, he began kneading it violently.

'Everyone is an ignoble coward,' he said, 'it's an old, old story. Courage consists in knowing that fact and, when necessary, acting as if fear did not exist. You are wrong, Wladek, in thinking that you are different from anyone else. However, it is hardly worth our meeting in this magnificent landscape if we are only going to make useless confessions to one another . . .'

Wladek did not answer. His eyes searched the deserted, barren, luminous landscape. Ideas as slow-moving as the flight of the crows in the sky passed through his mind: Whatever we say is useless now . . . I wish I had a glass of hot tea . . . Kiril, suddenly dropping the burden of his years, jumped back, raised his arm—and the hard snowball he had just finished making struck an astonished Philippov square on the chest. 'Defend yourself, I attack,' Kiril cried gaily and, his eyes laughing, his beard askew, he grabbed up handfuls of snow. 'Son of a sea-cook,' Philippov shouted, transfigured. And they began to fight like two schoolboys. They leaped, laughed, sank into snow up to their waists, hid behind trees to make their ammunition and take aim before they let fly. Something of the nimbleness of their boyhood came back to them, they shouted joyous 'ughs,' shielded their faces with their elbows, gasped for breath. Wladek stood where he was, firmly planted, methodically making snowballs to catch Rublev from the flank, laughing until the tears came to his eyes, showering him with abuse: 'Take that, you theoretician, you moralist, to hell with you,' and never once hitting him . . .

They got very hot, their hearts pounded, their faces relaxed. From a sky which had imperceptibly grown grey, night suddenly fell on lustreless snow, on misty and petrified trees. Breathing hard, the three started back in the direction of the railroad. 'How about that one I landed on your ear, Kiril,' said Philippov, chortling. 'How about the one I landed on the back of your neck?' Rublev retorted. It was Wladek who returned to serious matters:

'You know, my nerves are all to pieces, I admit—but I am not as afraid as I might be. Come what may, my death will fertilize Socialist soil, if it is Socialist soil . . .'

'State Capitalism,' said Philippov.

Rublev:

'. . . We must cultivate consciousness. There is sure progress under this barbarism, progress under this retrogression. Look at our masses, our youth, all the new factories, the Dnieprostroi, Magnitogorsk, Kirovsk . . . We are all dead men under a reprieve, but the face of the earth has been changed, the migrating birds must wonder where they are when they see what were deserts covered with factories. And what a new proletariat! Ten million men at work, with machines, instead of three and a half million in 1927. What will that effort not accomplish for the world in half a century!'

'. . . When nothing of us will remain, not even our smallest bones,' Wladek chanted, perhaps without irony.

By way of precaution, they parted before they reached the first houses. 'We must meet again,' Wladek proposed. And the other two said, 'Yes, yes, absolutely,' but none of them believed that it would really be possible or of any use. When they parted they all shook hands warmly. Kiril Rublev skied rhythmically to the nearest station, following the silent forest where darkness seemed to grow out of the ground like an imperceptible mist. A thin, blue, terribly sharp crescent moon, curved like an ideal breast, rose into the sky. Rublev thought: 'Ill-omened moon. Fear comes exactly like night.'

One evening as the Rublevs were finishing dinner, Xenia Popova came to tell them a great piece of news. On the table there were a dish of rice, a sausage, a bottle of Narzan mineral water, grey bread. The primus stove hissed under the kettle. Kiril Rublev was sitting in the old arm-chair, Dora in the corner of the sofa. 'How pretty you are,' Kiril said to Xenia affectionately. 'Let me see your big eyes.' She turned them towards him frankly—wide, well-shaped eyes, fringed with long lashes. 'Neither stones, nor flowers, nor the sky have that colour,' said Rublev to his wife. 'It is the eye's own miracle. You can be proud, child.'

'You'll have me embarrassed soon,' she said.

The clear features, the high forehead, the little rolls of blonde hair above the ears, the eyes that always seemed to be smiling at life— Rublev scanned them almost maliciously. So purity was born of dirt, youth of attrition. He had known Popov for more than twenty years— an old fool who, because he could not understand the a-b-c of political economy, had specialized in matters of Socialist ethics. In pursuit of his speciality, he had buried himself in the dossiers of the Central Control Commission of the Party, and now his entire life was devoted to the adulteries, lies, drinking bouts, and abuses of power perpetrated by old revolutionaries. It was he who found grounds for reprimands, distributed warnings, prepared indictments, planned executions, and proposed rewards for the executioners. 'Many vile tasks must needs be performed, so there must needs be many vile beings,' as Nietzsche said. But how, by what miracle, did the rancid flesh and the rancid spirit of a Popov produce this creature, Xenia? So life triumphs over our base clay. Kiril Rublev looked at Xenia with a delight in which there was both hunger and malice.

Sitting with her knees crossed, the girl lit a cigarette. She was so happy that she had to do something—anything—to keep it from showing. Making a very unsuccessful attempt to look detached, she said:

'Papa is having me sent abroad—a mission to Paris—six months— for the Central Textile Bureau. I'm to study the new technique for printing cloth . . . Papa knew that I had been wanting to go abroad for years . . . I jumped for joy!'

'Why shouldn't you?' said Dora. 'I'm terribly glad. What are you going to do in Paris?'

'It makes me dizzy to think of it. I'll see Notre-Dame, Belleville. I'm reading a biography of Blanqui and the history of the Commune. I'll go to see the Faubourg-St.-Antoine, the Rue St.-Merri, the Rue Haxo, the Wall of the Confederates . . . Bakunin lived in the Rue de Bourgogne, but I haven't been able to find out the number. Anyway, the number may have been changed. Do you know where Lenin lived?'

'I went to see him in Paris,' said Rublev slowly, 'but I have no idea where it was . . .'

'Oh!' said Xenia reproachfully. How could anyone forget such things?' Her big eyes opened wide. 'Really? You knew Vladimir Ilich? What luck!'

'What a child you are!' Rublev thought. 'But you are right.'

'And then,' she said, overcoming a slight hesitation, 'I mean to get some clothes. Pretty French things—is that wrong, do you think?'

'Not a bit,' said Dora. 'It's a fine idea. I wish all our young people could have lovely things.'

'That's what I thought—just that! But my father is always saying that clothes ought to be practical, that elaborate clothes are a survival from barbaric cultures, that fashion is a characteristic of the capitalist mentality . . .' The incomparably blue eyes smiled.

'Your father is a damned old puritan . . . What is he doing these days?'

Xenia chattered on. Sometimes, at the bottom of a clear stream flowing over pebbles, a shadow appears, troubles the eye for a moment, and vanishes, leaving one wondering what it was, what mysterious life was following its destiny in those depths. Suddenly the Rublevs found themselves listening intently. Xenia was saying:

'. . . Father has been very busy with the Tulayev case, he says it is another plot . . .'

'I had some contact with Tulayev in the past,' said Rublev in a subdued voice. 'I spoke against him in the Moscow Committee four years ago. Winter was coming on, and of course there was a fuel shortage. Tulayev proposed that the directors of the Combustibles Trust be brought to trial. I got his idiotic proposal turned down.'

'. . . Father says that a great many people are compromised . . . I think—don't repeat this, it's very serious—I think Erchov has been arrested . . . He was recalled from the Caucasus, but he has never shown up anywhere . . . I happened to overhear a telephone conversation about his wife . . . She has apparently been arrested too . . .'

Rublev picked up his empty glass from the table, held it to his lips as if he were drinking, and set it down. Xenia watched him in amazement. 'Kiril,' Dora asked, 'what have you been drinking?' 'Why, nothing,' he said with a bewildered smile.

An uncomfortable silence followed. Xenia bowed her head. The useless cigarette burned out between her fingers.

'And our Spain, Kiril Kirillovich,' she asked at last, with an effort

. . . 'do you think it can hold out? . . . I should like . . .' She did not say what she would like.

Rublev picked up the empty glass again.

'Defeated. And it will be partly our doing.'

The end of their conversation was laboured. Dora tried to start other subjects. 'Have you been to the theatre lately, Xenia? What are you reading?' Her questions found no answers. A damp, chill mist irresistibly invaded the room. It dimmed the lamp. Xenia felt a stab of cold between her shoulder blades. Rublev and Dora rose as she did. Standing there, they overcame the mist for a moment.

'Xenia,' said Dora gently, 'I wish you every happiness.'

And Xenia felt a little sad—it was like a good-bye. How was she to return their good wishes? Rublev affectionately put his arm around her waist.

'You have shoulders like an Egyptian statuette, wider than your hips. With those shoulders and those bright eyes of yours, you must take very good care of yourself, Xeniuchka!'

'What do you mean?'

'Only too much. Some day you'll understand. *Bon voyage!*'

At the last moment, in the narrow vestibule cluttered with heaps of newspapers, Xenia remembered something important that she could not leave unsaid. Her eyes clouded; she spoke in a low voice.

'I heard my father say that Ryzhik has been brought back to a prison in Moscow, that he is on a hunger strike and very ill . . . Is he a Trotskyist?'

'Yes.'

'A foreign agent?'

'No. A man as strong and pure as crystal.'

There was terror in the helpless look Xenia gave him.

'Then why . . . ?'

'Nothing happens in history that is not, in some sense, rational. The best sometimes have to be broken, because they do harm precisely by being the best. You cannot understand that yet.'

Something in her carried her towards him; she almost fell on his chest.

'Kiril Kirillovich, are you an Oppositionist?'

'No.'

On that word, after a few caressing gestures, a few swift kisses on Dora's unhappy lips, they parted. Xenia's youthful footfalls grew fainter down the hall. To Kiril and Dora, the room looked larger, more inhospitable. 'So it goes,' said Kiril. 'So it goes,' said Dora with a sigh.

Rublev poured himself a big drink of vodka and swallowed it down. 'And you, Dora, you who have lived with me for sixteen years—do you think I am an Oppositionist? Yes or no?'

Dora preferred not to answer. He sometimes talked to himself like that, asking her questions with a sort of fierceness.

'Dora, I'd like to get drunk to-morrow, I think I should see more clearly afterwards . . . Our Party can have no Opposition, it is mono-lithic because we reconcile thought and action for the sake of a higher efficiency. Rather than settle which of us is right and which wrong, we prefer to be wrong together because in that way we are stronger for the proletariat. And it was an old mistake of *bourgeois* individualism to seek truth for the sake of conscience, one conscience, *my* conscience. We say: To hell with my and me, to hell with self, to hell with truth, if the Party can be strong!'

'What Party?'

Dora's two words, spoken in a low, cold voice, reached him at the instant when the pendulum within him began its swing in the opposite direction.

'. . . Obviously, if the Party is betrayed, if it is no longer the Party of the Revolution, that position of ours is ridiculous and meaningless. We ought to do exactly the opposite—in that case, each of us should recover his conscience . . . We need unfailing unity to hold back the thrust of hostile forces . . . But if those forces exercise themselves pre-cisely through our unity . . . What did you say?'

He could not sit still in the huge room. His angular frame moved across it obliquely. He looked like a great emaciated bird of prey shut up in a cage that was quite large but still too small. So Dora saw him. She answered:

'I don't know.'

'The conclusions reached concerning the Opposition from seven to ten years ago and formulated between 1923 and 1930 would have to be revised. We were wrong then, perhaps the Opposition was right— *perhaps*, because no one knows if the course of history could be different from what it is . . . Revise our conclusions concerning a time now dead, struggles that are ended, outworn formulas, men sacrificed in one way or another?'

Several days passed—Moscow days, crowding on each other, crowded with events, cluttered with things to do, then suddenly interrupted by limpid moments when you forget yourself in the street to stare at the colours and the snow under a cold bright sky. Healthy young faces pass, and you wish you could know the souls behind them, and you think that we are a people numerous as grass, a mixture of a hundred peoples, Slavs, Finns, Mongols, Turks, Jews, all on the march and led by girls and youths whose blood runs golden. You think of the machines waking to strength in the new factories; they are agile and shining, they contain the power of millions of insentient slaves. In them the old suffering of toil is extinguished forever. This new world is arising little by little out of evil—and its people lack soap, underwear, clothes, clear knowledge, true, simple, meaningful words, generosity; we hardly know enough to animate our machines; there are sordid hovels around our giant factories, which are better equipped than the factories of Detroit or the Ruhr; in those hovels men bowed under the relentless law of toil still sleep the sleep of animals; but the factory will conquer the hovel, the machines will give these men—or the men who will follow them, it matters little—an astounding awakening. This unfolding of a world—machines and masses progressing together, inevitably—makes up for many things. Why should it not make up for the end of our generation? Overhead expenses, an absurd ransom paid to the past. Absurd—that was the worst part of it. And that the masses and the machines should still need us; that, without us, they might lose their way—that was dismaying, it was horrible. But what are we to do? To accomplish things consciously, we have only the Party, the 'cohort of iron.' Of iron and flesh and spirit. None of us any longer thought alone or acted alone: we acted, we thought, together, and always in the direction of the aspirations of innumerable masses, behind whom we felt the presence, the burning aspiration, of other yet greater masses—Proletarians of all countries, unite! The spirit became confused, the flesh decayed, the iron rusted, because the cohort—chosen by successive trials of doctrine, exile, imprisonment, insurrection, power, war, work, fraternity, at a moment perhaps unique in history—wore away, gradually invaded by intruders who spoke our language, imitated our gestures, marched under our banners, but who were utterly different from ourselves—moved by old appetites, neither proletarians nor revolutionaries—profiteers . . . Enfeebled cohort, artfully invaded by your enemies, we still belong to you! If you could be cured, were it by red-hot iron, or replaced, it would be worth our lives. Incurable,- and, at present, irreplaceable. Nothing remains for us, then, but to go on serving nevertheless, and, if we are murdered, to submit. Would our resistance do anything but make bad worse? If—as they could have done at any instant—a Bukharin, a Piatakov had suddenly risen in the dock to unmask their poor comrades lying through their last hours by command, the fraudulent prosecutor, the abetting judges, the double-dealing inquisition, the gagged Party, the stupid and terrorized Central Committee, the devastated Political Bureau, the Chief ridden by his nightmare—what demoralization there would have been in the country, what jubilation in the capitalist world, what headlines in the fascist press! 'Read all about it—The Moscow Scandal, The Bolshevik Sink, The Chief Denounced by his Victims.' No, no— better the end, any end. The account must be settled between ourselves, in the heart of the new society preyed on by old ills . . .

In that iron circle Rublev's thoughts never ceased to travel.

One evening after dinner he put on his short overcoat and his astrakhan cap, said to Dora, 'I'm going up for a breath of air,' took the lift, and got out on the terrace roof above the eleventh floor. An expensive restaurant occupied it in summer; and the diners, as they listened vaguely to the violins, looked at the innumerable lights of Moscow, spellbound despite themselves by those terrestrial constellations, whose tiniest lights guided lives at work. The place was even more beautiful in winter, when there were neither diners, nor flowers, nor coloured lamp shades on the little tables, nor violins, nor odours of broiled mutton, champagne, and cosmetics—only the vast calm night over the vast city, the red halo of Passion Square, with its electric signs, its snow stained by black ruts and footpaths, its swarm of people and vehicles under the arc lights, the discreet, secret glow of its windows . . . At that height, the electric lights did not interfere with vision, the stars were clear and distinct. Fountains of reddish light in the midst of the dense black of buildings indicated the squares; the white boulevards disappeared into darkness. His hands in his pockets, Rublev made the circuit of the terrace, thinking nothing. A faint smile came to his lips. 'I should have made Dora come up to see this—it is magnificent, magnificent . . .' And he stopped short, surprised—for a couple with their arms around each other's waists were swiftly bearing down on him, leaning forward in a graceful attitude of flight. Skating alone on the terrace, the two lovers swept up to Kiril Rublev, their ravished faces shone on him, they smiled at him, leaned into a long airy curve, and were off towards the horizon—that is, towards the other end of the terrace, from which there was a view of the Kremlin. Rublev watched them stop there and lean on the railing; he joined them and leaned on the railing too. They could clearly see the high crenellated wall, the heavy watch-towers, the red flame of the flag, lit by a searchlight, on the cupola of the Executive offices, the domes of the cathedrals, the vast halo of Red Square.

The girl looked towards Rublev, in whom she recognized the old and influential Bolshevik for whom a Central Committee car came every morning—last year. She half turned to him. Her companion stroked the back of her neck with his fingers.

'Is that where the Chief of our Party lives?' she asked, looking off towards the towers and crenellations bright against the night.

'He has an apartment in the Kremlin, but he doesn't often stay there,' Rublev answered.

'Is that where he works? Somewhere under the red flag?'

'Yes, sometimes.'

The young face was thoughtful for a moment, then turned to Rublev:

'It is terrible to think that a man like him has lived for years surrounded by traitors and criminals! It makes you tremble for his life ... Isn't it terrible?'

Rublev echoed her hollowly: '. . . terrible.'

'Come on, Dina,' the young man murmured.

They put their arms around each other's waists, became aerial again, leaned forward, and, borne by a magic power, set off on their skates towards another horizon ... A little tense, Rublev made his way to the lift.

In the apartment he found Dora sitting opposite a young well-dressed man whom he did not know. Her face was pale. 'Comrade Rublev, I have brought you a message from the Moscow Committee...' A big yellow envelope. Merely a summons to discuss urgent business. 'If you could come at once, there is a car waiting ...'

'But it is eleven o'clock,' Dora objected.

'Comrade Rublev will be back in twenty minutes, by car. I was told to assure you of that.'

Rublev dismissed the messenger. 'I'll be down in three minutes.' His eyes upon hers, he looked at his wife: her lips were colourless, her cheeks yellowish, it was as if her face were disintegrating. She murmured:

'What is it?'

'I don't know. It happened once before, you remember. A little peculiar, even so.'

No light anywhere. No possible help. They kissed hurriedly, blindly, their lips were cold. 'See you later.'—'See you later.'

The Committee offices were deserted. In the secretary's office a stout, bemedalled Tatar, with cropped skull and a thin fringe of black hairs on his upper lip, was reading the papers and drinking tea. He took the summons. 'Rublev? Right away . . .' He opened a dossier in which there was only a single typewritten sheet, read it, frowning, raised his face—the puffy, opaque, heavy face of a big eater.

'Have you your Party card with you? Please let me see it.'

From his pocketbook Rublev took the red folder in which was written: 'Member since 1907.' Over twenty years. What years!

'Right.'

The red folder disappeared into a drawer, the key turned.

'You are charged with a crime. Your card will be returned to you, if necessary, after the investigation. That is all.'

Rublev had been waiting for the blow too long. A sort of fury bristled his eyebrows, clenched his jaws, squared his shoulders. The secretary slid back a little in his revolving chair:

'I know nothing about it, those are my orders. That is all, citizen.'

Rublev walked away, strangely light, borne by thoughts like flights of birds. So that's the trap—the beast in the trap is you, the trapped beast, you old revolutionist, it's you . . . And we're all in it, all in the trap . . . Didn't we all go absolutely wrong somewhere? Scoundrels, scoundrels! An empty hall, rawly lighted, the great marble stairway, the double revolving door, the street, the dry cold, the messenger's black car. Beside the messenger, who was smoking while he waited, someone else, a low voice saying thickly: 'Comrade Rublev, be so good as to come with us for a short conversation . . .'—'I know, I know,' said Rublev furiously, and he opened the door, flung himself into the icy Lincoln, folded his arms, and summoned all his will power to hold down an explosion of despairing fury . . .

The snow-white and night-blue of the narrow streets passed over the windows in parallel bands. 'Slower,' Rublev ordered, and the driver obeyed. Rublev let down the window—he wanted a good look at a bit of street, it did not matter what street. The pavement glittered with untrodden snow. A nobleman's residence of the past century, with its pillared portico, seemed to have been sleeping for the last hundred years behind its ornamental iron fence. The silvery trunks of birches shone faintly in the garden. That was all—forever, in a perfect silence, in the purity of a dream. City under the sea, farewell. The driver pushed down the accelerator.—It is we who are under the sea. It doesn't matter—we were strong men once.

TO BUILD IS TO PERISH

MAKEYEV WAS exceptionally gifted in the art of forgetting in order to grow greater. Of the little peasant from Akimovka near Kliuchevo-the-Spring, Tula Government—a country of green and brown valleys, dotted with thatched roofs—he preserved only a rudimentary memory, just enough to make him proud of his transformation. A little reddish-haired lad like a million others, like them destined to the soil, the village girls would have none of him—they called him 'Artyomka the Pockmarked' with a shade of mockery. Rickets in childhood had left him with awkward bowlegs. Nevertheless, at seventeen, in the Sunday evening fights between the lads of Green Street and the lads of Stink Street, he brought down his enemy with a blow of his own invention which landed between neck and ear and caused instantaneous dizziness . . . After these rough-and-tumble fights, since even now no girl would have him, he sat on the dilapidated steps of his house, chewing his nails and watching his big strong toes wriggling in the dust. If he had known that there are words to express the vicious torpor of such moments, he would have muttered, as Maxim Gorki muttered at his age: 'What boredom, what loneliness, what a desire to smash someone in the face!'—not for the pleasure of victory this time, but to escape from himself and an even worse world. In 1917 the Empire made Artyem Makeyev a soldier under its double eagles—a passive soldier, as dirty and with as little to do as all his fellows in Volhynia trenches. He spent his time marauding through a countryside which had already been visited by a hundred thousand marauders just like himself; laboriously delousing himself at twilight; dreaming of raping the peasant girls—they were few and far between—whom night caught on the roads, and who, incidentally, had been frequently raped before by many another . . . As for him, he did not dare. He followed them through a chalk countryside of shattered trees and fields full of shell holes; suddenly the ground would hold up a clutching hand, a knee, a helmet, a jagged tin can. He followed them, his throat dry, his muscles painfully thirsting for violence; but he never dared.

A curious strength, which at first made him uneasy, awoke in him when he learned that the peasants were taking possession of the land. Before his eyes hung the manor of Akimovka, the manor house with its low portico on four white columns, the statue of a nymph beside the pool, the fallow fields, the woods, the marsh, the meadows . . . He felt an inexpressible hatred for the owners of that unknown universe, which was really his, his from all eternity, his in all justice, but which had been taken from him by a nameless crime perpetrated long before his birth, an immense crime against all the peasants on earth. It had always been thus, though he had not known it; and that hatred had lain asleep in him always. The gusts of wind that blew at evening over fields which the war had disinherited brought him intelligible sentences, revealing words. The people of the manor—'Sir' and 'Madam' —were 'blood-drinkers.' Private Artyem Makeyev never having seen them, no human image disturbed the image which the words called up in him. But blood he had seen often enough—the blood of his comrades after a burst of shrapnel, when the earth and the yellowed grass drank it—very red at first, so red it turned your stomach, then black, and, very soon, the flies settled on it.

About this period Makeyev thought of his life for the first time. It was as if he had started talking with himself—and he almost laughed, it was funny—he was making a fool of himself! But the words that arranged themselves in his mind were so serious that they killed his laughter and made him screw up his face like a man who tries to raise a weight too heavy for his muscles. He told himself that he must *get away, carry grenades under his greatcoat, get back to his village, set fire to the manor house, take the land.* Where did he hit on the idea of fire? The forest sometimes catches fire in summer, no one knows how. Villages burn and no one knows where the fire started. The idea of a fire made him think further. A shame, of course, to burn down the beautiful manor house, it could be used for—what? What could it be made into for the peasants? To have the clodhoppers in it themselves —no, that would never do . . . Burn the nest and you drive away the birds. Burn the manorial nest, and a trench full of terror and fire would separate past from present, he would be an incendiary, and incendiaries go to jail or the gallows, so we must be the stronger—but this was beyond Makeyev's reasoning ability, he felt these things rather than thought them. He set out alone, leaving the louse-infested trench by way of the latrines. In the train he found himself with men like himself, who had set off like himself; when he saw them his heart filled with strength. But he told them nothing, because silence made him strong. The manor house went up in flames. A troop of Cossacks rode through the green roads towards the peasant uprising: wasps buzzed around their horses' sweating flanks; mottled butterflies fled before the mingled stench of human sweat and horse sweat. Before they reached the offending village, Akimovka near Kliuchevo-the-Spring, telegrams mysteriously reached the district, spreading good news: 'Decree concerning the seizure of lands,' signed, 'The People's Commissars.' The Cossacks had the news from a white-haired old man who popped out from among the roadside shrubbery, under the silver-scaled birches. 'It's the law, my lads, the law, you can't do anything about it. It's the law.' The land, the land, the law!—there was an astonished murmuring among the Cossacks, and they began to deliberate. The stupefied butterflies settled in the grass, while the troop, restrained by the invisible decree, halted, not knowing whether to go forward or back. What land? Whose was the land? The land-lords'? Ours? Whose? Whose? The amazed officer suddenly felt afraid of his men; but no one thought of stopping him from escaping. In Akimovka's single street, where the mud-daubed log houses leaned each its own way in the centre of a little green enclosure, heavy-breasted women crossed themselves. This time there could be no mistake—the days of Anti-christ were really come! Makeyev, who still clung to his beltload of grenades, came out onto the stairs of his house, a ruinous isba with a leaky roof, and shouted to the old witches to shut up, God damn it, or they would soon see, God damn it—his face growing more and more crimson . . . The first assembly of the poor peasants of the district elected him president of its Executive Committee. The first DECREED which he dictated to his scribe (who had been clerk to the district justice of peace) ordered that any woman who spoke of Antichrist in public should be whipped; and the text of it, written in a round hand, was posted in the main street.

Makeyev began a rather dizzying career. He became Artyem Artyemich, president of the Executive, without exactly knowing what the Executive was, but with eyes that were deeply set under arching brows, shaven head, shirt freed of vermin, and, in his soul, a will as tough as knotted roots in a rock crevice. He had people who regretted the former police turned out of their houses; other police, who were sent into the district, he had arrested, and that was the last that was seen of them. People said that he was just. He repeated the word from the depths of his being, with a subdued fire in his eyes: Just. If he had had time to watch himself live, he would have been astonished by a new discovery. Just as the faculty of reason had suddenly revealed itself to him so that he could seize the land, another more obscure faculty, which sprung inexplicably to life in his muscles, his neck, his viscera, led him, roused him, strengthened him. He did not know its name. Intellectuals would have called it will. Before he learned to say *It is my will*, which was not until several years later when he had grown accustomed to addressing assemblies, he instinctively knew what he had to do in order to obtain, dominate, order, succeed, then feel a calm content almost as good as that which comes after possessing a woman. He rarely spoke in the first person, preferring to say *We*. It is not my will, it is our will, brothers. His first speeches were to Red soldiers in a freight car; his voice had to rise above the rattle and clank of the moving train. His faculty of comprehension grew from event to event, by successive illuminations. He saw causes, probable effects, people's motives, he sensed how to act and react; he had a hard time reducing it all to words in his mind, and then reducing the words to ideas and memories, and he never wholly succeeded.

The Whites invaded the district. The Makeyevs met with short shrift from these gentry, who hanged them as soon as they captured them, pinning insulting inscriptions on their chests: *Brigand* or *Bolshevik* or both together. Makeyev managed to join comrades in the woods, seized a train with them, left it at a steppe city which greatly delighted him, for it was the first large city he had ever seen and it lived pleasantly under a torrid sun. In the market big juicy melons were sold for a few copecks. Camels paced slowly through the sandy streets. A few miles from the city, Makeyev shot down so many white-turbaned horsemen that he was made a deputy chief. A little later, in 'nineteen, he joined the Party. The meeting was held around a fire in the open fields, under glittering stars. The fifteen Party members were grouped around the Bureau of Three, and the Three crouched in the

4

firelight, with notebooks on their knees. After the report on the international situation, given in a harsh voice which imparted an Asiatic
flavour to strange European names—Cle-mansso, Loy-Djorje, Guer-
mania, Liebkneckt—Commissar Kasparov asked if anyone raised any
objection to the admission of candidate Makeyev, Artyem Artyemi-
yevich, into the Party of the Proletarian Revolution? 'Stand up,
Makeyev,' he said imperiously. Makeyev was already on his feet,
straight as a ramrod in the red firelight, blinded by it and by all the
eyes that were fixed on him at this moment of consecration, blinded
too by a rain of stars, though the stars were motionless . . . 'Peasant,
son of working peasants . . .' 'Son of landless peasants!' Makeyev
proudly corrected. Several voices approved his membership. 'Adopted,'
said the Commissar.

At Perekop, when, to win the final battle in the accursed war, they
had to enter the treacherous lagoon of Sivash and march through it in
water up to their waists, up to their shoulders in the worst places—and
what awaited them ten paces ahead, if not the end?—Makeyev,
Deputy Commissar with the Fourth Battalion, had more than one
fierce struggle to save his life from his own fear or his own fury. What
deadly holes might lie under that water which spread so dazzlingly
under the white dawn? Had they not been betrayed by some staff
technician? Jaws clenched, trembling all over, but resolute and cool to
the point of insanity, he held his rifle above his head at arm's length,
setting the example. He was the first out of the lagoon; the first to
climb a sand dune, to lie down, feeling the sand warm against his
belly, to aim and begin firing from ambush on a group of men, taken
by surprise from the rear, whom he distinctly saw scurrying around a
small fieldpiece. . . . On the evening of the exhausting victory, an
officer dressed in new khaki stood on the same fieldpiece to read the
troop a message from the Komandarm (Army Commander), to which
Makeyev did not listen because his back was broken with stooping
and his eyes gummy with sleep. Towards the end of it, however, the
harsh rhythm of certain words penetrated his brain: 'Who is the brave
combatant of the glorious Steppes Division who . . .' Mechanically,
Makeyev too asked himself who the brave combtaant might be and
what he might have done, but to hell with him and with all these
ceremonies because I'll die if I don't get some sleep, I'm done in. At
that moment Commissar Kasparov looked at Makeyev so intently that
Makeyev thought: 'I must be doing something wrong. I must look as

if I were drunk,' and he made an immense effort to keep his eyes from closing. Kasparov called:

'Makeyev!'

And Makeyev staggered from the ranks, amid a murmur: 'It's him, him, him, Artyemich!' The Artyomka whom the village girls once despised entered into glory covered to the neck with dried mud, drunk with weariness, wanting nothing in the world but a bit of grass or straw to lie down on. The officer kissed him on the mouth. The officer's chin was stubbly, he smelled of raw onion and dried sweat and horse. Then, for a brief instant, they looked at each other through a fog, as two exhausted horses reconnoitre each other. Their eyes were wet. And Makeyev came to, as he recognized the partisan of the Urals, the victor of Krasni-yar, the victor of Ufa, the man who turned the most desperate of retreats, Blücher. 'Comrade Blücher,' he said thickly, 'I'm . . . I'm glad to see you . . . You . . . You're a man, you are . . .' It seemed to him that Blücher was reeling with sleep, like himself. 'You too,' Blücher answered with a smile, 'you're a man, all right . . . Come and drink some tea with me to-morrow morning, at Division Headquarters.' Blücher had a tanned face, with deep perpendicular lines and heavy pockets under the eyes. That day was the beginning of their friendship, a friendship between men of the same stuff who saw each other for a brief hour twice a year, in camps, at ceremonies, at the great Party conferences.

In 1922, Makeyev returned to Akimovka in a jolting Ford marked with the initials of the C.C. of the C.P. (b.) of the R.S.F.S.R. The village children surrounded the car. For some seconds Makeyev stared at them with a terrible intensity of emotion: really, he was looking for himself among them, but too awkwardly to recognize how much several of them resembled him. He threw them his whole stock of sugar and change, patted the cheeks of the little girls who were timid and hung back, joked with the women, went to bed with the merriest one—she had full breasts, big eyes, and big teeth—and installed himself, as Party organizing secretary for the district, in the best house. 'What a backward place!' he said. 'We have to begin at the very beginning. Not a ray of light!' Sent from Akimovka to eastern Siberia to preside over a regional Executive. Elected an alternate member of the C.C. the year after the death of Vladimir Ilich . . . Each year new distinctions were added to the service record in his personal dossier as a member of the Party in the most responsible category. Honestly, patiently, with sure tread, he climbed the rungs of power. Meanwhile, as he lost all distinct memories of his wretched childhood and adolescence, of his life of humiliations during the war, of a past without pride and without power, he began to feel himself superior to everyone with whom he came into contact—always excepting men whom the C.C. had appointed to positions of greater power. These he venerated, with no jealousy, as creatures of a nature that was not yet his but which was bound to be his some day. He felt himself, like them, possessed of a legitimate authority, integrated into the dictatorship of the proletariat like a good steel screw set in its proper place in some admirable, supple, and complex machine.

As Secretary of the regional Committee, Makeyev had governed Kurgansk (both the city and the district) for a number of years, with the proud but unspoken thought of giving it his name: Makeyevgorod or Makeyevgrad—why not? The simplest form—Makeyevo—reminded him too much of peasant speech. The proposal, broached in the lobbies of a regional Party conference, was about to pass—by unanimous vote, according to custom—when, suddenly doubtful, Makeyev himself changed his mind at the last moment. 'All the credit for my work,' he cried from the platform, under the huge picture of Lenin, 'belongs to the Party. The Party has made me, the Party has done all.' Applause. But already Makeyev was terrified by the thought that his words might be construed as containing unfortunate allusions to the members of the Political Bureau. An hour later, he mounted the platform again, having meanwhile run through the last two issues of *The Bolshevik*, the magazine devoted to theory, where he found several phrases which he distributed to his audience, pounding them home with short jabs of his fists. 'The highest personification of the Party is our great, our inspired Chief. I propose that we give his glorious name to the new school we are about to build!' His audience applauded confidently, as they would confidently have voted for Makeyevgrad, Makeyevo, or Makeyev City. He came down from the platform wiping his forehead, glad that he had been wise enough to refuse fame for the moment. It would come. His name would be on maps, among the blue curves of rivers, the green blotches of forest, the crosshatched hills, the sinuous black railroad lines. For he had faith in himself as he had faith in the triumph of Socialism—and doubtless it was the same faith.

In this present, which was the only reality, he no longer distin-

guished between himself and the country which—as big as centuries-
old England—lies three-quarters in Europe and one-quarter in an
Asia of plains and deserts still furrowed by caravan routes. A country
without a history: the Khazars had passed that way in the fifth century
on their little long-haired horses, as the Scythians had passed that way
centuries before them, to found an empire on the Volga. Where did
they come from? Who were they? Came too the Pechenegs, Genghis
Khan's horsemen, Kulagu Khan's archers, the Golden Horde's slant-
eyed administrators and methodical headsmen, the Nogai Tatars.
Plain upon plain—migrations vanished in them as water vanishes in
sand. Of that immemorial legend, Makeyev knew only a few names, a
few scenes; but he knew and loved horses as the Pechenegs and the
Nogai did, like them he understood the flight of birds, like them he
could find his way through blizzards by signs which men of other races
could not discern. If by some miracle the weapon of past centuries, a
bow, had been placed in his hands, he could have used it as skilfully
as the divers unknown tribes whom that soil had nourished, who had
died upon it and been absorbed into it . . . 'All is ours!' he said,
sincerely, at public meetings of the Railwaymen's Club, and he could
easily have substituted 'All is mine,' since he was only vaguely aware
where 'I' ended and 'we' began. (The 'I' belongs to the Party, the 'I'
is of value only inasmuch as, through the Party, it incarnates the new
collectivity; yet, since it incarnates it powerfully and consciously, the
'I,' in the name of the 'we,' possesses the world.) Makeyev could not
have worked it out theoretically. In practice, he never felt the slightest
doubt. 'I have forty thousand head of sheep in the Tatarovka district
this year!' he cried happily at the regional Production conference.
'Next year I shall have three brickworks operating. I told the Plan
Commission: "Comrade, you must give me three hundred horses
before autumn—or you'll hold up the plan for the year! You want to
put my only electric power station under the Centre? Not if I can
stop you, it's mine, I'll use every measure, the C.C. will decide." '
(Instead of 'measure' he said 'resource,' or rather he thought he was
saying 'resource' but he actually said 'recourse.')

Two Narychkins successively exiled to Kurgansk—one, at the end of
the eighteenth century, for misappropriations considered excessive
when he fell into disfavour with an ageing and obese empress; the
other, early in the nineteenth, for some witty remarks on the Jacobin-
ism of Monsieur Bonaparte—built a little square palace there in the

Neo-Greek style of the Empire, with a peristyle and columns. On either side of this palace extended the wooden houses of the merchants, the low-walled caravansary, the gardens of the more luxurious dwellings. Makeyev set up his office in one of the drawing-rooms of the old régime governors-general, the very drawing-room to which the liberal Narychkin, waited on by indolent servitors, had been wont to retire to re-read Voltaire. A local antiquarian told Comrade Artyem Artyemi-yevich about it. 'He was a Freemason too—belonged to the same lodge as the Decembrists.'—'Do you really believe any of those feudal dogs could be sincerely liberal?' Makeyev asked. 'Anyway, what does liberal mean?' A copybook containing a part of the family journal, odd volumes of Voltaire, a copy of Montesquieu's *Spirit of the Laws* annotated in the nobleman's own hand, were still in the attic, together with odd pieces of old furniture and some family portraits, one of which, signed by Madame Vigée-Lebrun, a French Revolutionary *émigrée*, represented a stout dignitary of fifty, with penetrating brown eyes and an ironic and sensual mouth . . . Makeyev had it brought down, contemplated Narychkin for a moment, looked sourly at the glittering cross on his chest, touched the frame with the toe of his boot, and pronounced judgment: 'Not bad. A real feudal mug. Send it to the regional museum.' The title of Montesquieu's book was translated for him. He sneered: 'Spirit of exploitation! . . . Send it to the library.' 'I should suggest the museum,' the antiquarian objected. Makeyev turned on him and, in a crushing voice (because he did not understand), said: 'Why?' The frightened antiquarian made no answer. On the double mahogany door a sign was tacked: *Office of the Regional Secretary*. Inside: a large desk; four telephones, one of them a direct wire to Moscow, the C.C., and the Central Executive; dwarf palms between the tall windows; four big leather arm-chairs (the only ones in the district); on the right-hand wall, a map of the district especially drawn by a deported ex-officer; on the left-hand wall, a map from the Economic Plan Commission indicating the sites of future factories, of a projected railway and a projected canal, of three workers' housing developments to be built, of baths, schools, and stadiums to be brought into existence in the city . . . Behind the Regional Secretary's comfortable arm-chair hung a large portrait in oils of the General Secretary, supplied for eight hundred roubles by the Universal Stores in the capital—a slick and shining portrait, in which the Chief's green tunic seemed to be cut out of heavy painted cardboard and his half-smile miscarried into absolute nullity. When the office was completely furnished, Makeyev entered it with suppressed delight. 'Wonderful, that portrait of the Chief. That's real proletarian art!' he said expansively. But what was lacking in the room? What was this strange, irritating, improper, inconceivable blank? He turned on his heel, vaguely displeased, and the people around him—the architect, the secretary of the city Committee, the commandant of the building, the chief clerk, his private stenographer—all felt the same discomfort. 'And Lenin?' he said at last; then added, with almost thunderous reproach: 'You have forgotten Lenin, comrades! Ha, ha, ha!' His laughter rang out insolently amid the general confusion. The secretary of the city Committee was the first to regain his self-possession:

'Not at all, Comrade Makeyev, not at all. We hurried to get things finished this morning and there wasn't time to put in the bookcase— there's where it will stand—with Ilich's *Complete Works*, in the Institute edition, and the little bust that goes on top of it, just like in my place.'

'That's better,' said Makeyev, his eyes still gleaming with mockery. And, before dismissing them, he announced sententiously:

'Never forget Lenin, comrades—that is the Communist's law.'

Left alone, Makeyev sat squarely down in his revolving chair, turned it happily back and forth, dipped the new pen into the red ink, and wrote a large signature, complete with flourishes—A. A. MAKEYEV—on the memorandum pad with its printed heading: *C.P. of the U.S.S.R. Kurgansk Regional Committee. The Regional Secretary.* After admiring it for a while, he looked at the telephones, and his full cheeks creased in a smile. 'Hello, operator. Seven-six.' His voice became soft: 'Is that you, Alia?' Half mockingly, half caressingly: 'Nothing, nothing. Everything going all right? Yes, of course, pretty soon.' He turned to the second telephone: 'Hello, Security? The Chief's office. Hello, Tikhon Alexeyich—come about four o'clock. Is your wife feeling better? Yes—yes—all right.' Great stuff! He looked long and eagerly at the direct Moscow connection, but could think of nothing urgent to tell the Kremlin; yet he put his hand on the receiver (suppose I call the Central Plan Commission about trucks?), but then did not dare. In times past the telephone had been a wonder to him, a magical instrument; awkward about using it, he had long feared it, losing far too much of his self-assurance in the presence of the little black cylinder of the receiver. Now that all its terrifying magic was placed at his service, he saw it as a symbol of power. The little local committees came to fear his calls. His imperious voice burst from the receiver: 'Makeyev speaking.' It was an almost unintelligible roar. 'That you, Ivanov? More lapses, eh? I won't have it . . . immediate sanctions . . . Give you twenty-four hours! . . .' He preferred to act these scenes before a few deferential colleagues. The blood rose to his heavy face, his broad, conical, shaven skull. The reprimand delivered, he slammed down the receiver, stared into space like an angry beast of prey, pretending to see no one, opened a dossier, ostensibly to calm himself. (But it was all only an inner rite.) Woe to the Party member under investigation whose personal dossier fell into Makeyev's hands at such a moment! In less than a minute he infallibly discovered the weak point in the case: 'Claims to be the son of poor peasants, was actually the son of a deacon.' The genuine son of landless peasants laughed harshly, and wrote in the column reserved for suggested action: '*exp.*' (expulsion) followed by an implacable *M.*, all in heavy blue pencil. He had a disconcerting faculty of remembering such dossiers, fishing them out from among a hundred others to confirm his decision a year and a half later, when the file, swelled by a dozen reports, came back from Moscow. If the Central Control Commission happened to favour keeping the poor wretch in the Party 'with a solemn warning,' Makeyev was even capable of renewing his opposition with Machiavellian ingenuity. The C.C.C. was well aware of these cases, and indulgently supposed that Makeyev was settling personal accounts—no one had the least idea of the absolute impartiality of the rages which he put on for the sake of his prestige. Only one of the C.C.C. secretaries occasionally permitted himself to over-ride these decisions of Makeyev's—Tulayev. 'One down for Makeyev,' he muttered into his thick moustache as he ordered the reinstatement of the expelled member whom neither he nor Makeyev had ever seen or would ever see. On the rare occasions when they met in Moscow, Tulayev, who was a bigger man than Makeyev, addressed him genially in the familiar form, though at the same time calling him 'comrade,' to indicate that not all Bolsheviks were equal. Tulayev discerned Makeyev's value. Basically the two men were much alike, though Tulayev was better educated, more adaptable, and more blasé about exercising power (as chief clerk to a substantial Volga merchant, he had taken courses at a commercial school). Tulayev was embarked on a bigger career. He once plunged Makeyev into unbearable embarrassment by reporting to a meeting that the last May Day procession at Kurgansk had included no less than 137 large or small portraits of Comrade Makeyev, Regional Secretary, and then going on to mention the official opening of a Makeyev Day Nursery in a Kazak village which had soon after emigrated in a body to newer pastures ... Crushed by the laughter, Makeyev rose and stood looking into the sea of hilarious faces, his eyes full of tears, his voice half choked, demanding the floor ... He did not get it, for a member of the Political Bureau came in, wearing an elegantly tailored workman's blouse, and the whole assembly rose for the ritual seven-to-eight-minute ovation. After the meeting Tulayev sought out Makeyev: 'That was a pretty good trouncing I gave you, eh, brother? But don't let a little thing like that make you angry. If you get the chance, come back at me as hard as you like. Have a drink?' Those were the good old times of rough-and-ready brotherhood.

In those days the Party was turning over a new leaf. No more heroes —what was needed was good administrators, practical unromantic men. No more venturesome spurts of international or planetary or name-your-own-adjective revolution—we must think of ourselves, build Socialism for ourselves, in our own country. A renovation of cadres, opening the way to second-rank men, rejuvenated the Republic. Makeyev took part in the purges, acquired a reputation as a practical man devoted to the 'general line,' learned the official phrases which bring peace to the soul, and was able to recite them for an hour by the clock. It was with strange emotion that he one day received a visit from Kasparov. The former Commissar of the Steppes Division, the leader of the fiery Civil War days, quietly entered the Regional Secretary's office, without knocking or sending in his name, about three o'clock one torrid summer afternoon. A Kasparov who had aged and grown thinner, in a white blouse and cap. 'You!' Makeyev exclaimed, and flew to embrace his visitor, kissed him, clasped him to his chest. Kasparov gave the impression of being light. They sat down facing each other in the deep arm-chairs, and now a feeling of uneasiness extinguished their joy. 'Well,' said Makeyev, who did not know what to say, 'where are you bound in that outfit?' Kasparov's face looked tense and severe, as it used to look when they camped on the Orenburg steppes, or during the Crimean campaign, or at Perekop ... He looked at Makeyev impenetrably; perhaps he was judging him.

4*

Makeyev felt uncomfortable. 'Appointed by the C.C.,' said Kasparov, 'to be director of river transport in the Far East . . .' Makeyev instantly computed the extent of this disgrace: distant exile, a purely economic position, whereas a Kasparov could have governed Vladivostok or Irkutsk, at the very least.

'And you?' said Kasparov, with something of melancholy in his tone.

To shake off his uneasiness, Makeyev stood up—herculean, massive, shaven-skulled. Sweat stains showed on his blouse.

'I'm building,' he said cheerfully. 'Come and see.' He took Kasparov to the Plan Commission's map—irrigation canals, brickworks, railway yard, schools, baths, stud farms. 'Just look at that—you can see the country growing under your eyes, in twenty years we'll be up with the U.S.A. I believe it because I am in the thick of it.' His voice rang a little false and he noticed it. It was the voice in which he made official speeches . . . With a barely sketched gesture, Kasparov waved aside the vain words, the economic plans, his old comrade's simulated joy—and that was just what Makeyev obscurely feared. Kasparov said:

'All that is fine. But the Party is at the crossroads. The fate of the Revolution is being decided, brother.'

By the greatest of luck, the telephone began buzzing shrilly at that moment. Makeyev gave some orders relative to nationalized trade. Then, taking his turn at dismissing what he preferred to overlook, he spread his broad, plump hands in a conclusive gesture, and, with a guileless look:

'In this country, old man, everything has been decided once and for all. The general line—I don't see any other way. I'm going ahead. Come back here in two or three years, and you won't recognize the town or the district. A new world, old man, a new America! A young Party that doesn't know what fear is, full of confidence. Will you come and review the Young Communist sports parade with me this evening? You'll see!'

Kasparov shook his head evasively. Another played-out Thermidorian, a fine administrative animal who could glibly recite the four hundred current ideological phrases that obviated thinking, seeing, feeling, and even remembering, even suffering the least remorse when you did the vilest things! There were both irony and despair in the little smile that lighted Kasparov's lined face. Makeyev bristled in the presence of feelings utterly foreign to his nature but which he nevertheless divined.

'Yes, yes, of course,' said Kasparov in a peculiar tone. He appeared to make himself at ease, unbuttoned the neck of his shirt, threw his cap into one of the arm-chairs, sat down comfortably in another with his legs crossed:

'A nice office you have here—for whatever that's worth—very nice. But beware of bureaucratic comfort, Artyemich. It's a slough—a man can drown in it.'

Was he trying to be deliberately disagreeable? Makeyev lost a little of his assurance. Kasparov looked at him judicially out of his strange grey eyes, which were calm in danger, calm in excitement.

'Artyemich, I have been thinking things over. Our plans are fifty to sixty per cent impossible to carry out. To carry them out to the extent of the remaining forty per cent, the real wages of the working class will have to be reduced below the level they reached under the Imperial Government—far below the present level even in backward capitalist countries . . . Have you thought about that? I fear not. In six months at most, we shall have to declare war on the peasants and begin shooting them down—as sure as two and two make four. Shortage of industrial goods, plus depreciation of the rouble—or, to put it frankly, hidden inflation; low grain prices imposed by the state, natural resistance on the part of grain owners—you know how it goes. Have you considered the consequences?'

Makeyev had too much sense of reality to demur, but he was afraid someone in the hall might hear such words spoken in his office—words of sacrilege, challenging the Chief's doctrine, challenging everything! They cut him, they troubled him: he became aware that it required his most conscious effort to keep himself from speaking the same terrible language. Kasparov went on:

'I am neither a coward nor a bureaucrat, I know what duty to the Party is. What I am saying to you, I have written to the Political Bureau, with figures to support it. Thirty of us signed it—all survivors of Tsarist prisons, of Taman, Perekop, Kronstadt . . . Can you guess how they answered us? As for me, I was first sent to inspect the schools in Kazakistan, which have neither teachers nor buildings nor books nor pencils . . . Now I am being sent to count barges at Krasnoyarsk— which is all the same to me. But that this criminal stupidity should be continued for the pleasure of a hundred thousand bureaucrats too lazy to realize that they are headed for their own destruction and are dragging the Revolution with them—that is *not* all the same to me. And you, old man, hold an honourable rank in the hierarchy of those hundred thousand. I rather suspected it. I sometimes asked myself: What is going to become of old Makeyich, if he isn't a down-and-out drunk by now?'

Makeyev walked nervously back and forth from map to map. Kasparov's words, his ideas, his very presence, were becoming intolerably distressing—it was as if he suddenly felt dirty from head to foot because of those words, of those ideas, of Kasparov. The four telephones, the smallest details of the office, began to look odious. And anger was no way out—why? In a tired voice he answered:

'Let's talk about something else. You know I am not an economist. I carry out the Party's directives, that's all—to-day, just as I used to in the army with you. And you taught me to obey for the Revolution. What more can I do? Come and have dinner at my house later. I have a new wife, you know—Alia Sayidovna, a Tatar. You'll come?'

Under the indifferent tone, Kasparov read an entreaty: Show me that you still think enough of me to sit down at my table with my new wife—that's all I ask of you. Kasparov put on his cap, stood at the window for a moment humming to himself and looking out into the public garden (a gravel disk flooded with sunshine; a little dark bronze bust exactly in the centre of it). 'Right—see you this evening, Artyemich. A fine town you have here . . .'—'Isn't it?' Makeyev answered quickly, feeling intensely relieved. Below them Lenin's bronze cranium gleamed like polished stone. It was a good dinner, nicely served by Alia. She was short and plump, with a sleek animal grace: clean, well-fed; bluish-black hair twined over her temples, doe eyes, a profile of soft curves, all the lines of her face and body melting into each other. Ancient Iranian gold coins hung at her ears, her fingernails were painted pomegranate red. She served Kasparov to *pilau*, juicy watermelon, real tea—'you can't find it anywhere any more,' she said pleasantly. Kasparov refrained from confessing that he had not eaten such a good meal for six months. He exhibited himself in his most amiable light, told the only three stories he knew (which he privately referred to as his 'three little stories for inane evenings') and showed none of the exasperation aroused in him by her little laugh, which displayed her white teeth and arched her round breasts, and by Makeyev's self-satisfied guffaws; he even went so far as to congratulate them on their happiness. 'You ought to have a canary, in a big, pretty cage—it's just the thing for a nice, homelike place . . .' Makeyev was very nearly aware of the sarcasm, but Alia exploded: 'Just what I've been saying, comrade. Ask Artyem if I haven't!' When they parted, the two men sensed that they would not meet again—unless as enemies.

An ill-omened visit: for soon after it, troubles began. The Party and administrative purges were just completed, under Makeyev's energetic leadership. In the offices of Kurgansk there remained but a small percentage of old-timers—that is, of men formed in the storms of the past ten years. Tendencies—whether Left (Trotskyist), Right (Rykov-Tomsky-Bukharin), or Pseudo-Loyalist (Zinoviev-Kamenev)—appeared to be thoroughly wiped out, though actually they were not entirely so, for wisdom advised laying something aside for the future. But grain was not coming in satisfactorily. In accordance with messages from the C.C., Makeyev visited the villages, broadcast promises and threats, had himself photographed surrounded by *mujiks*, women, and children, got up several parades of enthusiastic farmers who were turning over all their wheat to the state. The carts entered the city in procession, laden with sacks and accompanied by red flags, transparencies proclaiming a single-hearted devotion to the Party, portraits of the Chief and portraits of Comrade Makeyev, carried like banners by the village lads and girls. There was a fine holiday feeling about these manifestations. The Executive of the regional Soviet sent the orchestra of the Railwaymen's Club to meet the parades; film photographers, summoned from Moscow by telephone, arrived by plane to film one of the Red convoys, and the entire U.S.S.R. later saw it on the screen. Makeyev received it, standing on a truck, shouting sonorously: 'Honour to the farmers of a happy land!' The evening of the same day he stayed in his office late into the night, conferring with the President of the Executive of the Soviet and an envoy extraordinary from the C.C. The situation was becoming serious: insufficient reserves, insufficient receipts, the certainty of a reduction in cropping, an illicit rise in market prices, a wave of speculation. The envoy extraordinary announced draconian measures to be applied 'with an iron hand.' 'Certainly,' said Makeyev, afraid to understand.

So began the black years. First expropriated, then deported, some seven per cent of the farmers left the region in cattle cars amid the cries, tears, and curses of urchins and dishevelled women and old men mad with rage. Fields lay fallow, cattle disappeared, people ate the oil cake intended for the stock, there was no more sugar or gasolene, leather or shoes, cloth or clothes, everywhere there was hunger on impenetrable white faces, everywhere pilfering, collusion, sickness; in vain did Security decimate the bureaus of animal husbandry, agriculture, transport, food control, sugar production, distribution . . . The C.C. recommended raising rabbits. Makeyev had placards posted: 'The rabbit shall be the cornerstone of proletarian diet.' And the local government rabbits—his own—were the only ones in the district which did not die at the outset, because they were the only ones which were fed. 'Even rabbits have to eat before they are eaten,' Makeyev observed ironically. The collectivization of agriculture extended over eighty-two per cent of family units, 'so great is the Socialist enthusiasm among the peasants of the region,' wrote *Pravda* and at the same time published a picture of Comrade Makeyev, 'the fighting organizer of this rising tide.' No one stayed out of the kolkhozes except isolated peasants whose houses slumbered far from roads, a few villages populated by Mennonites, a village where there was resistance from an old partisan from the Irtysh, who had twice been decorated with the Order of the Red Flag, had known Lenin, and for that reason was not arrested . . . Meanwhile a meat-canning factory was built, equipped with the latest-model American machinery and supplemented by a tannery, a shoe factory, and a factory to make special leathers for the army: it was finished the year meat and hides disappeared. Further building included comfortable houses for the Party leaders and technicians and a workers' garden city not far from the lifeless factory . . . Makeyev faced everything, actually fought 'on three fronts' to carry out the C.C.'s orders, fulfil the industrialization plan, keep the earth from dying. Where to find seasoned wood for building, nails, leather, work clothes, bricks, cement? There was a perpetual lack of materials, the starving workmen were perpetually stealing or running away—the great builder found himself with nothing on hand but papers, circulars, reports, orders, theses, official predictions, texts of denunciatory speeches, motions voted by the shock brigades. Makeyev telephoned, jumped into his Ford (now as battered as a General Staff car in the old days), arrived unheralded at a building site; counted the barrels of cement and sacks of lime himself, frowning fiercely; questioned the engineers: some of whom defied truth by swearing to build even without wood and bricks, others by demonstrating that it was impossible to build with such cement. Makeyev wondered whether they were not all in a conspiracy to destroy himself and the Union. But basically he knew, he felt, that all they said was true. His brief case under his arm, his cap on the back of his head, Makeyev had himself driven at full speed through woods and plains to the 'Hail Industrialization' kolk-hoze, which had not a horse left, where the last cows were dying for lack of fodder, where thirty bales of hay had recently been stolen at night, perhaps to feed horses which had been reported dead but were really hidden in the dreaming forest of Chertov-Rog, 'The Devil's Horn.' The kolkhoze looked deserted, two Young Communists from the city lived there amid general hostility and hypocrisy; the president, so helpless that he blurted unintelligibly, explained to 'Comrade Secretary of the Regional Committee' that the children were all sick from undernourishment, that he must have at least a truckload of potatoes immediately so that field work could be resumed, since the rations allocated by the State at the end of the previous year (a year of scarcity) had been two months short—'just as we said, don't you remember?' Makeyev grew angry, promised, threatened, both uselessly, overwhelmed by a dull despair . . . The same old story, over and over, over and over—it kept him awake at night. The land was going to ruin, the livestock was dying, the people were dying, the Party was suffering from a sort of scurvy, Makeyev saw even the roads dying— the roads over which no wagons any longer passed, the roads over which grass was spreading . . .

So hated by the inhabitants that he never went out on foot in the city except when he was forced to, and then accompanied by a guard who walked three feet behind him with his hand on his holster, he carried a cane himself to ward off aggressors. He had a fence built around his house, had it guarded by soldiers. Things suddenly came to a head in the third year of scarcity, the day when Moscow telephoned him a confidential order to begin a new purge of the kolkhozes before the autumn sowing, in order to cut down secret resistance. 'Who signed this decision?'—'Comrade Tulayev, third secretary of the C.C.' Makeyev dryly said: 'Thank you,' hung up, and struck the desk with his fist. Into his brain rose a wave of hate against Tulayev, Tulayev's long moustaches, Tulayev's broad face, Tulayev the heartless bureaucrat, Tulayev the starver of the people . . . That evening Alia Sayidovna opened the door to a surly Makeyev, a Makeyev who looked like a bulldog. He very seldom talked to her about business; but he often talked aloud to himself, because under emotional pressure silent thinking was difficult for him. Alia, with her soft sleek profile, with the gold coins dangling from the lobes of her pretty ears, heard him muttering: 'I won't stand for another famine—not me. We've paid our share, old man, and that's enough. I won't play up any longer. The district can't stand any more. The roads are dying! No, no, no, no! I'll write to the C.C.'

He did write, after a sleepless night, a night of agony. For the first time in his life, Makeyev refused to carry out an order from the C.C., denounced it as error, madness, crime. He felt he was saying too much, then again that he was saying too little. When he re-read what he had written, terrified at his own audacity, he told himself that he would have demanded the expulsion and arrest of anyone who dared to criticize a Party directive in such terms. But the fields overrun with weeds, the road overrun with grass, the children with their bellies swollen from starvation, the empty shops of nationalized retail commerce, the black looks of the peasants, were there, really there. One after the other he tore up several drafts. Hot and uneasy, Alia tossed feverishly in the big bed; she attracted him only rarely now, a little female who would never understand. His memorandum on the necessity for postponing or annulling the Tulayev circular regarding the new purge of kolkhozes was dispatched the next morning. Makeyev had a violent headache, drifted from room to room, in his slippers and half-dressed, behind the wooden blinds which were closed against the torrid heat. Alia brought him small glasses of vodka, pickled cucumbers, tall glasses of water so cold that vapour condensed on them in drops. He was red-eyed from lack of sleep, his face was unshaven, he smelled of sweat . . . 'You ought to take a trip somewhere, Artyem,' Alia suggested. 'It would do you good.' He became aware of her; the hallucinating mid-afternoon heat made a furnace of the city, the plains, the surrounding steppes, poured through the walls of the house, flamed in his numb veins. Hardly three steps separated him from Alia, who fell back, tottered beside the divan, was thrown down, felt Artyem's dry hands knead her fiercely from neck to knees, felt his suffocating mouth press down on her mouth, felt him rip her silk kaftan, which would not unfasten quickly enough, felt him bruise her legs, which had not opened quickly enough . . . 'Alia, you are as downy as a peach,' said Makeyev as he rose refreshed. 'Now the C.C. will see who's right, that numskull Tulayev or me!' For a moment, possessing his wife gave him the feeling of conquering the universe.

Makeyev fought a losing battle with Tulayev for two weeks. Accused by his powerful antagonist of tending towards the 'Right opportunist deviation,' he saw himself on the brink of the abyss. Figures and several sentences from his memorandum, quoted to denounce 'the incoherencies of the Political Bureau's agrarian policy' and the 'fatal blindness of certain functionaries,' appeared in a document probably drawn up by Bukharin and delivered to the Control Commission by an informer. Makeyev, seeing that he was lost, abjured instantly and passionately. The Politburo and the Orgburo (Organization Bureau) decided to maintain him in his position since he had renounced his errors and was devoting himself to the new purge of kolkhozes with exemplary energy. Far from sparing his own henchmen, he regarded them with such suspicion that several of them found themselves on their way to concentration camps. Putting the burden of his own responsibility upon them, he harshly refused to see them or intercede for them. From the depths of prisons, some of them wrote that they had merely carried out his orders. 'The counter-revolutionary irresponsibility of these demoralized elements,' Makeyev commented, 'deserves no indulgence. Their only aim is to discredit the Party.' In the end he believed it himself.

Would not his disagreement with Tulayev be remembered during the election for the Supreme Council? A certain vacillation in the Party committees made Makeyev uneasy. Many voices were raised in favour of candidates who were high Security officials or generals, rather than Communist leaders. Happy day! Official rumour repeated a remark by a member of the Political Bureau: 'Makeyev's is the only possible candidacy in the Kurgansk region . . . Makeyev is a builder.' Immediately transparencies appeared across the streets, urging: *Vote for the Builder Makeyev*—who, in any case, was the only candidate. At the first session of the Supreme Council, held in Moscow, Makeyev, at the peak of his destiny, ran into Blücher in the ante-rooms. 'Greetings, Artyem,' said the commander-in-chief of the valorous Special Army of the Red Flag in the Far East. Intoxicated, Makeyev answered: 'Greetings, Marshal! How are you?' They went to the buffet together, arm in arm like the old comrades they were. Both of them were heavier, their faces full and well-massaged, with fatigue pouches under the eyes, both wore well-cut clothes of fine material, both were decorated— Blücher wore four brilliant medals on his right breast, three Orders of the Red Flag and one Order of Lenin; Makeyev, less heroic, had only

one Red Flag and the Medal of Labour . . . The strange thing was that
they had nothing to say to each other. With sincere delight they
exchanged phrases from the newspapers: 'So you're building, old
man? Things going well? Happy? Healthy?'—'So, Marshal, you're
keeping the little Japs in order, eh?'—'Right—they can come whenever
they're ready!' Deputies from the Siberian North, from Central Asia,
from the Caucasus, in their national costumes, flocked to stare at them.
In the soldier's reflected glory, Makeyev admired himself. He thought:
'We'd make a fine snapshot.' The memory of that memorable moment
went sour some months later when, after the fighting in Chang-Ku-
Feng, the Army of the Far East regained two hills overlooking Possiet
Bay from the Japanese (the two hills turned out to be of enormous
strategic importance, though it had never been mentioned before).
The message from the C.C. detailing these glorious events did not
mention Blücher's name. Makeyev understood, and a chill came over
him. He felt himself compromised. Blücher, Blücher—it was his turn
to go down into subterranean darkness! Inconceivable! . . . What luck
that no snapshot had immortalized their last meeting!

Makeyev lived quite calmly through the proscriptions, because they
wrought havoc chiefly among the generation of power which had preceded his own and among generations even earlier. 'By and large,
socially the old generation is worn out . . . So much the worse for them,
this is no time for sentiment . . . Heroes yesterday, failures to-day—
it's the dialectic of history.' But his unspoken thoughts told him that
his own generation was rising to replace the generation which was
going out. Ordinary men became great men when their day arrived—
was that not justice? Although, when they had been in power, he had
known and admired a number of the defendants in the great trials, he
accepted their end with a sort of zeal. Incapable of comprehending
anything but the baldest arguments, he was not troubled by the
enormity of the accusations. (We have no time for subtleties!) And
what was more natural than to use lies to overwhelm an enemy who
must be put out of the way? The demands of mass psychology in a
backward country must be met. Called to rule by the subalterns of the
one and only Chief, integrated into the power behind the proscriptions,
Makeyev had never felt that he was threatened. But now he felt the
wind of the inevitable scythe that had mowed down Blücher. Had the
Marshal been relieved of his command? Arrested? Would he reappear?
He was not being tried, which perhaps meant that all was not over for

him. However that might be, no one ever mentioned his name now. Makeyev would have liked to forget it; but the name, the image of the man, pursued him—at work, in his moments of silence, in his sleep. He found himself fearing that, speaking at some meeting of district officials, he would suddenly utter the obsessing name in the middle of a sentence. And the more he put it out of his mind, the more it rose to his lips—to the point where he thought that, reading a message aloud, he had inserted Blücher's name among the names of the members of the Political Bureau ... 'Didn't I make a slip of the tongue?' he asked one of the Regional Committee members lightly. Inside, he was writhing with anguish.

'No indeed,' said the comrade he had addressed. 'Odd that you should think so.'

Makeyev looked at him, seized with a vague terror. 'He is making a fool of me ...' The two men blushed, equally embarrassed.

'You were most eloquent, Artyem Artyemich,' said the Committee member, to break the uncomfortable silence. 'You read the address to the Political Bureau with magnificent fervour ...'

Makeyev became completely confused. His thick lips moved silently. He made a wild effort to keep from saying, 'Blücher, Blücher, Blücher, do you hear me? I named Blücher!' The other became uneasy:

'Don't you feel well, Comrade Makeyev?'

'A touch of dizziness,' said Makeyev, swallowing saliva.

He got over the crisis, he conquered his obsession, Blücher did not reappear, it was a little more ended every day. There were further disappearances, but of less importance. Makeyev made up his mind to ignore them. 'Men like myself have to have hearts of stone. We build on corpses, but we build.'

That year the purges and personnel replacements in the Kurgansk district were not over until the middle of winter. Just before spring, one night in February, Tulayev was killed in Moscow. When Makeyev heard the news, he shouted for joy. Alia was playing solitaire, her body outlined in clinging silk. Makeyev threw down the red 'Confidential' envelope.

'There's one that deserved what he got! The fool! It had been coming to him for a long time. A plot? Not much—somebody whose life he was ruining let him have it on the head with a brick ... He certainly went out looking for it, with that character of his—a snarling dog ...'

'Who?' said Alia, without raising her head, because for the second time the cards had brought the queen of diamonds between herself and the king of hearts.

'Tulayev. I've just heard from Moscow that he has been murdered . . .'

'My God!' said Alia, preoccupied by the queen of hearts, doubtless a blonde woman.

Makeyev said sharply:

'I've told you a hundred times not to call on God like a peasant!'

The cards snapped under the pretty, red-nailed fingers. Irritation. The queen of diamonds confirmed the treacherous hints dropped by the wife of the president of the Soviet (Doroteya Guermanovna, a big, soft woman of German extraction who knew all the scandal of the city for the last ten years) . . . and the manicurist's skilful reticences . . . and the fatally precise information that had arrived in the form of an anonymous letter laboriously pieced together out of big letters cut from newspapers—at least four hundred of them had been pasted down one after the other to denounce the ticket girl of the Aurora Cinema, who had previously slept with the director of the municipal services department and who, a year ago, had become Artyem Artyemich's mistress, as witness the fact that she had had an abortion at the G.P.U. clinic last winter, being admitted on a personal recommendation, and then had been given a month's paid vacation, which she spent at the Rest House for Workers in Education, also on special recommendation, and as witness the fact that Comrade Makeyev had twice visited the Rest House during that period and had even spent the night there . . . The letter went on in this fashion for several pages, all in overlapping, ill-assorted letters which made absurd patterns. Alia looked at Makeyev out of eyes so intent that they became cruel.

'What is it?' asked the man, vaguely uneasy.

'Who was killed?' asked the woman, her face ugly with tension and distress.

'Tulayev, I told you, Tulayev—are you deaf?'

Alia came so close to him that she touched him, and stood pale and straight, her shoulders set, her lips trembling.

'And that blonde ticket girl—who's going to kill her? Tell me, you traitor, you liar!'

Makeyev had barely begun to realize what a serious shock the Party was in for: revamping the C.C., accounts to be settled in the bureaus, full-scale attacks on the Right, deadly accusations against the expelled

Left, counter-attacks—what counter-attacks? A vast, whirling wind out of the night drove the quiet daylight from the room, wrapped itself about him, made cold shivers run through his very marrow . . . Through those terrible, dark gusts, Alia's shaken words, Alia's poor shattered face, hardly reached him. 'Get out of here and leave me alone!' he shouted, beside himself.

He was incapable of thinking of big things and little things simultaneously. He shut himself up with his private secretary, to prepare the speech which he would deliver that evening at the extraordinary meeting of Party officials—a bludgeoning speech, shouted from the bottom of his lungs, punctuated with his clenched fist. He spoke as if he were fighting, then and there, single-handed, against the Enemies of the Party. Men who were Creatures of Darkness; the world Counterrevolution; Trotskyism, its brazen snout branded with the swastika; Fascism; the Mikado . . . 'Woe to the stinking vermin who have dared to raise a hand against our great Party! We shall wipe them out forever, even to the last generation! Eternal remembrance to our great, our wise comrade, Tulayev, iron Bolshevik, unswerving disciple of our beloved Chief, the greatest man of all the centuries! . . .' At five in the morning, dripping with sweat and surrounded by exhausted secretaries, Makeyev was still correcting the typescript of his speech, which a special messenger, starting two hours later, would carry to Moscow. When he went to bed, bright daylight flooded the city, the plains, the building yards, the caravan trails. Alia had just fallen into a doze after a night of torture. Feeling her husband's presence, she opened her eyes to the white ceiling, to reality, to her suffering. And, almost naked, she got quietly out of bed, and saw herself in the mirror: her hair in disorder, her breasts sagging, herself pale, faded, forsaken, humiliated, looking like an old woman—because of that blonde ticket girl at the Aurora. Did she know what she was doing? What did she want in the drawer where the trinkets were kept? She found a short bone-handled hunting knife there, and took it. She went back to the bed. Lying with the sheets thrown off and his dressing-gown open, Artyem was sound asleep, his mouth shut, his nostrils ringed with beads of sweat, his big body naked, covered with reddish hair, abandoned . . . Alia stared at him for a moment, as if it astonished her to recognize him, astonished her even more to discover something utterly unknown in him, something which incessantly escaped her, perhaps an unwonted presence, a soul that was kindled in him in sleep, like a secret light, and which his awakening extinguished. 'My God, my God, my God,' she repeated mentally, sensing that a power in her would raise the knife, clench her hand, stab down into that outstretched male body, the male body which she loved in the very depths of her hate. Where aim? Try to find the heart, well protected by an armour of bones and flesh, difficult to reach? Pierce the unprotected belly, where it is easy to make a mortal wound? Tear the penis lying in its fleece of hair—soft flesh, loathsome and touching? The idea—but it was not an idea, it was already the adumbration of an act—travelled darkly through her nerve centres . . . The dark current encountered another: fear. Alia turned her head, and saw that Makeyev had opened his eyes and was watching her with terrifying sagacity.

'Alia,' he said simply, 'drop that knife.'

She was paralysed. Sitting up in a single motion, he caught her wrist, opened her helpless little hand, flung the bone-handled knife across the room. Alia collapsed into shame and despair, great bright tears hung from her lashes . . . She felt like a naughty child caught doing something wrong; there was no help anywhere, and now he would cast her off like a sick dog . . . you drown sick dogs . . .

'You wanted to kill me?' he said. 'To kill Makeyev, secretary of the Regional Committee—and you a member of the Party? Kill the Builder Makeyev, you miserable creature? Kill me for a blonde ticket girl, fool that you are?'

Anger rose in him with every clearly spoken word.

'Yes,' said Alia feebly.

'Idiot! They'd have shut you up underground for six months—have you thought of that? Then one morning, about 2 a.m., they'd have taken you out behind the station and put a bullet there, right there!' (He hit her hard on the back of the neck.) 'Don't you know that? Do you want a divorce this morning?'

She said furiously:

'Yes.'

And at the same time, more softly, her long eyelashes lowered: 'No.'

'You are a liar and a traitor,' she repeated almost automatically, trying to collect her thoughts. Then she went on:

'Tulayev was killed for less, and you were glad. Yet you helped him to organize the famine—you've said so often enough! But perhaps he didn't lie to a woman, like you!'

They were such terrible words that Makeyev looked at his wife with panic in his eyes. He felt desperately weak. Only his fury saved him from collapsing. He burst out:

'Never! I never said or thought a word of your criminal ravings . . . You are unworthy of the Party . . . Bitch!'

He strode about the room, now this way, now that, waving his arms like a madman. Suddenly he came back to her, carrying a leather belt. He gripped the back of her neck with his left hand and struck with his right, beating, beating the almost naked body which writhed feebly under his hand, beating so hard that he panted . . . When the body stopped moving, when Alia's whimpering breathing seemed to have ceased, Makeyev turned away, pacified. He went for a wad of cotton, soaked it in eau-de-Cologne, came back, and began gently rubbing her face with it —her ravaged face which, in a few moments, had become ugly with a pitiful, little-girl ugliness . . . Then he went for ammonia, he dampened towels, he was as diligent and skilful as a good nurse . . . And, when Alia came to, she saw Makeyev's green eyes leaning over her, the pupils narrowed like a cat's eyes . . . Artyem kissed her face heavily, hotly, then turned away. 'Get some sleep, little fool. I'm going to work.'

Life became normal again for Makeyev, between a silent Alia and the queen of diamonds, whom, for safety's sake, he had sent to the construction yard for the new electric plant, between the plain and the forest, where she was put in charge of handling the mail. The yard operated twenty-four hours a day. The Secretary of the Regional Committee frequently appeared there to stimulate the efforts of the *élite* brigades, to oversee the execution of the weekly plans in person, to receive reports from the technical personnel, to countersign the daily telegrams to the Centre . . . He came back exhausted, under the clear stars. (Meanwhile, somewhere in the city, unknown hands, labouring in profound secrecy, obstinately cut alphabets of all dimensions from the papers, collected them, aligned them on notebook sheets: it would take at least five hundred characters for the contemplated letter. This patient labour was carried on in solitude, in silence, with every sense alert; the mutilated papers, weighted with a stone, went to the bottom of a well, for burning them would have made smoke—and where there's smoke there's fire, don't they say? The secret hands prepared the demonic alphabet, the unknown mind collected the evidence, the scattered clues, the infinitesimal elements of several hidden and un-avowable certainties . . .)

Makeyev was planning to go to Moscow to thrash out the question of material shortages with the directors of electrification; at the same time he would inform the C.C. and the Central Executive of the progress made during the last six months in road-improvements and irrigation (thanks to cheap convict labour); perhaps this progress would com-pensate for the dwindling supply of skilled labour, the crisis in live-stock, the poor condition of industrialized agriculture, the production slowdown in the railway workshops . . . With pleasure he received the brief message from the C.C. (*'Confidential. Urgent.'*) inviting him to attend a conference of regional secretaries from the South-west. Leav-ing two days early, Makeyev sat in his blue sleeping-car compartment, contentedly making abstracts of the reports from the regional Econ-omic Council. The specialists of the Central Plan Commission would find he was a man worth talking to! Endless fields of snow, dotted with ramshackle houses, fled past the windows; the wooded horizon was melancholy under the leaden sky, the light filled the white spaces with an immense expectancy. Makeyev looked at the rich black fields which an early thaw had scattered with standing pools that reflected the hurrying clouds. 'Indigent Russia, opulent Russia,' he murmured, because Lenin had quoted those two lines of Nekrassov's in 1918. The Makeyevs, by working those fields, made opulence come out of indigence.

At the station in Moscow, Makeyev had no difficulty in getting a C.C. car sent for him, and it was a big American car, strangely elon-gated and rounded—'streamlined,' explained the chauffeur, who was dressed much like a millionaire's chauffeur in a foreign film. Mak-eyev found that many things had changed for the better in the capital since he had been there seven months earlier. Life bustled through a grey transparency, over the new asphalt pavements which were relent-lessly cleared of snow day in and day out. The shop-windows made a good impression. At the Central Plan Commission, in a building made of reinforced concrete, glass, and steel, and containing from two to three hundred offices, Makeyev, in accordance with his rank, was received as an extremely important person by elegant officials who wore big spectacles and suits of British cut. He found no difficulty in obtaining what he wanted: materials, additional credits, the return of a dossier to the Projects department, authority to build an additional road. How could he have known that the materials did not exist, and that all these impressive personages no longer had anything but a sort of ghostly existence, since the P.B. had just decided 'in principle' upon a purge and complete reorganization of the Plan offices? Well satisfied, he became more important than ever. His plain fur coat, his plain fur cap contrasted with the careful attire of the technicians and made him look all the more the provincial builder. 'We who are clearing virgin soil . . .' He slipped little phrases like that into the conversation, and they did not ring false.

Of the few old friends whom he tried to find the second day, none could be reached. One was ill in a suburban hospital, too far from town; telephoning to two others, he received only evasive answers. On the second occasion, Makeyev got angry. 'Makeyev speaking, I tell you. Makeyev of the C.C., do you understand? I want to know where Foma is; I have a right to be told, I imagine . . .' The man at the other end of the wire answered, in a doubtful voice: 'He has been arrested . . .' Arrested? Foma, Bolshevik of 1904, loyal to the general line, former member of the Central Control Commission, member of Security's special college? Makeyev gasped for breath, a spasm passed over his face, for a moment he felt stunned. What was happening now?

He decided to spend the evening alone, at the opera. Entering the great government box (once the imperial box) soon after the curtain went up, he found no one there but an old couple, sitting at the left in the first row of chairs. Makeyev discreetly greeted Popov, one of the Party's directors of conscience, an untidy little old man with a vague profile and a yellowish straggling beard. He had on a grey tunic that sagged around the pockets. His companion looked amazingly like him; it seemed to Makeyev that she barely returned his greeting and even avoided looking at him. Popov crossed his arms on the velvet of the balustrade, coughed, thrust out his lips, entirely absorbed by the performance. Makeyev sat down at the other end of the row. The empty chairs increased the distance between himself and the Popovs; even if they had sat close together, the huge box would have surrounded them with solitude. Makeyev could not make himself take an interest either in the stage or the music, though music usually intoxicated him like a drug, filling his whole being with emotion, filling his mind with disconnected images, now violent, now plaintive, filling his throat with abortive cries, with sighs or a sort of wailing. He assured himself that all was well, that it was one of the finest spectacles in the world, even though it belonged to the culture of the old régime—but we are the legitimate heirs of that culture, we have conquered it. Then, too, those dancers, those lovely dancers—why should he not desire them? (Desire was another of his ways of forgetting.)

When the intermission began, the Popovs left so discreetly that only his increased solitude in the huge box made him aware that they had gone. For a moment he stood looking at the house, brilliant with lights and evening dresses and uniforms. 'Our Moscow, capital of the world.' Makeyev smiled. As he made his way to the lobby, an officer—spectacles, neat square-cut moustache, a little curved nose like an owl's beak—bowed to him most respectfully. Makeyev returned his bow, then stopped him with a gesture. The officer introduced himself:

'Captain Pakhomov, commanding the building police, happy to be of service to you, Comrade Makeyev.'

Flattered at being recognized, Makeyev felt like embracing him. His strange solitude vanished.

'Ah, so you have just arrived, Comrade Makeyev,' said Pakhomov slowly, as if he were thinking; 'then you haven't seen our new scene-shifting machines, bought in New York and installed last November. You ought to take a look at them—they made Meyerhold open his eyes! Shall I expect you after the third act, to show you the way?'

Before answering, Makeyev nonchalantly inquired:

'Tell me, Captain Pakhomov—the little dancer in the green turban, the one who's so graceful—who is she?'

Pakhomov's owl face and nocturnal eyes brightened a little:

'Very talented, Comrade Makeyev—getting a great deal of notice. Paulina Ananiyeva. I'll introduce you to her in her dressing-room, Comrade Makeyev—she will be very happy to meet you—oh, certainly . . .'

And now good riddance to you, Popov, you old moralist, you old crab—you and your antique wife who looks like a plucked turkey. What do you know about the life of strong men, builders, outdoor men, men who fight? Under floors, in cellars, rats gnaw at strange fodder— and you, you eat dossiers, complaints, circulars, theses, which the great Party throws at you in your office, and so it will go on until you are buried with greater honours than you ever knew in your miserable life! Makeyev leaned forward and almost turned his back on the disagreeable couple. Where should he take Paulina? To the Metropole bar? Paulina . . . nice name for a mistress. Paulina . . . Would she let herself be tempted to-night? Paulina . . . Makeyev's feeling, as he waited for the intermission, was almost blissful.

Captain Pakhomov was waiting for him at the turn in the great staircase. 'First, Comrade Makeyev, I'll show you the new machines; then we'll go to see Ananiyeva—she's expecting you . . .'

'Splendid, splendid . . .'

Makeyev followed the officer through a maze of corridors, each more brightly lighted than the last. Pushing back a curtain to his left, the officer pointed to mechanics busy around a winch; young men in blue blouses were sweeping the stage; a technician appeared, pushing a little searchlight on wheels. 'Fascinating, isn't it?' said the owl-faced officer. Makeyev, his head empty of everything except the expectation of a woman, said: 'The magic of the theatre, my dear comrade . . .' They went on. A metal door opened before them, closed behind them, they were in darkness. 'What's this?' the officer exclaimed. 'Stay where you are, just for a moment, Comrade Makeyev, I . . .' It was cold. The darkness lasted only a few seconds, but when a wretched little back-stage bulb came on, like the light in a forsaken waiting room or in the ante-chamber of a dilapidated Hell, Pakhomov was no longer there; instead, several black overcoats detached themselves from the opposite wall, someone rapidly advanced on Makeyev—a thick-set man with his overcoat collar turned up, his cap pulled down to his eyes, his hands in his pockets. Very close now, the voice of the unknown murmured, distinctly:

'Artyem Artyemich, we don't want any scenes. You are under arrest.'

Several overcoats surrounded him, pressed against him; skilful hands ran over him, pushed him about, fished out his revolver . . . Makeyev gave a violent start which almost freed him from all the hands, from all the shoulders, but they closed in, nailed him to the spot:

'We don't want any scenes, Comrade Makeyev,' the persuasive voice repeated. 'Everything will be all right, I am sure—there must be some misunderstanding. Just obey orders . . .' Then, to the others: 'No noise!'

Makeyev let himself be led, almost carried. They put on his overcoat, two men took him by the arms, others preceded and followed him and so they walked through formless semi-darkness, like a single creature clumsily moving a profusion of legs. The narrow corridor squeezed them together, they stumbled over each other. Behind a thin partition the orchestra began to play with miraculous sweetness. Somewhere in the meadows, beside a silvery lake, thousands of birds greeted the dawn, the light increased instant by instant, a song rose into it, a pure woman's voice sounded through the unearthly morning . . . 'Easy there, watch out for the steps,' someone whispered into Makeyev's ear . . . and there was no more dawn, no more song, there was nothing . . . nothing but the cold night, a black car, the unimaginable . . .

JOURNEY INTO DEFEAT

BEFORE REACHING Barcelona, Ivan Kondratiev underwent several standard transformations. First he was Mr. Murray Barron, of Cincinnati, Ohio, U.S.A., photographer for the World Photo Press, travelling from Stockholm to Paris by way of London ... He took a taxi to the Champs-Elysées, then, carrying his little brown valise, strolled about for a while between the Rue Marbeuf and the Grand Palais; he was seen to stop before the Clemenceau disguised as an old soldier who trudges along a block of stone at the corner in front of the Petit Palais. The bronze froze the old man's drive, and it was perfect: so a man walks when he is at the end of his resources, when all his strength is gone. 'For how much longer has your stubbornness saved a dying world, old man? Perhaps you only bored a deeper hole in the rock for the mine that will blow it up?'—'I messed things up for the bastards for fifty years,' the man of bronze muttered bitterly. Kondratiev looked at him with secret sympathy. Two hours later Mr. Murray Barron came out of a monastic-looking house near St.-Sulpice, still carrying his brown valise but now transformed into Mr. Waldemar Laytis, Latvian citizen, on a mission to Spain from his country's Red Cross. From Toulouse an Air-France plane, flying over landscapes bathed in happy light, the rusty summits of the Pyrenees, sleeping Figueras, the hills of Catalonia tanned like a beautiful skin, carried Mr. Waldemar Laytis to Barcelona. The officer representing the International Non-Intervention Board, a meticulous Swede, must have thought that the Red Cross organizations of the several Baltic States were displaying a laudable activity in the Peninsula: Mr. Laytis was certainly the fifth or sixth delegate they had dispatched to observe the effects of bombing on open cities. Ivan Kondratiev, noticing that the officer looked rather hard at his passport, merely made a mental note that the liaison office must be overdoing the trick. At the Prat airfield a podgy colonel, wearing glasses, complimented Mr. Laytis in unctuous tones, led him to a handsome car which displayed a few elegant shot scratches, and said to the driver: '*Vaya, amigo.*' Ivan Kondratiev, emissary of a strong and victorious revolution, felt that he was entering a very sickly one.

'The situation?'

'Fair. I mean, not entirely desperate . . . We are counting heavily on you. A Greek ship under British colours sunk last night off the Balearic Islands: munitions, bombings, artillery fire, the usual confusion . . . *No importa.* Rumours of concentrations in the Ebro region. *Es todo.*'

'Internal affairs? The Anarchists? The Trotskyists?'

'The Anarchists are ready to listen to reason—probably on the way out . . .'

'Since they will listen to reason,' Kondratiev said mildly.

'The Trotskyists are practically all in prison . . .'

'Very good. But you took a long time about it,' said Kondratiev severely, and something in him became tense.

Illuminated with sumptuous softness by a late-afternoon sun, a city opened before him, stamped with the same banally infernal seal as many other cities. The plaster of the low pink or red houses was scaling off; windows yawned, their glass gone; here and there were bricks smudged with black from fires, shop-windows barricaded with planks. Fifty patient chattering women waited at the door of a wrecked shop. Kondratiev recognized them by their earthy complexions, their drawn faces—he had seen them before, equally wretched, equally patient and talkative, on sunny days and grey days, at shop doors in Petrograd, Kiev, Odessa, Irkutsk, Vladivostok, Leipzig, Hamburg, Canton, Chang-sha, Wu-han. Women waiting for potatoes, sour bread, rice, the last sugar, must be as necessary to the social transformation as the speeches of leaders, the secret executions, the absurd passwords. Overhead expenses. The car jolted as if they were on a street in Central Asia. Villas among gardens. Through the trees, a view of a white façade pierced by great holes through which the blue sky showed . . .

'What percentage of houses damaged?'

'*No sé.* Not so many,' the podgy colonel answered nonchalantly; he

appeared to be chewing gum, but he was chewing nothing—it was a
nervous habit.

In the patio of a once-luxurious mansion in Sarria, Ivan Kondratiev smilingly distributed handshakes. The fountain seemed to be
softly laughing to itself, squat columns supported vaults under which
the cool shade was blue. A little stream trickled through a marble
channel, a faint, distant rapping of typewriters mingled with its silken
rustle, and left it unperturbed. Close-shaven and dressed in a brand-
new Republican uniform, Kondratiev had become General Rudin.
'Rudin?' exclaimed a high Foreign Affairs official. 'But haven't I met
you before? At Geneva, perhaps, at the League of Nations?' The
Russian unbent a little, but very little. 'I have never been in Geneva,
señor, but you may have encountered a person of the same name in one
of Turgenev's novels . . .' 'Of course,' said the high official. 'Turgenev
is almost a classic in Spain, you know . . .' 'I am delighted to hear it,'
Rudin answered politely. He was beginning to feel uncomfortable.

These Spaniards shocked him. They were likeable, childish, full of
ideas, plans, complaints, confidential information, unconcealed suspicions, secrets scattered to the four winds by warm, musical voices.
And not one of them had actually read Marx (a few had the effrontery
to say that they had, knowing so little about Marxism that they were
unaware that three sentences were enough to prove them liars), not
one of them would have made even a mediocre agitator in a second-
rate industrial centre like Zaporozhe. Furthermore, they considered
that Soviet *matériel* was arriving in insufficient quantities, that the
trucks were badly built. According to them, the situation was becoming untenable everywhere, but then the next minute they proposed a
plan for victory; some advocated a European war; Anarchists insisted
upon restoring discipline, establishing the sternest order, provoking
foreign intervention; *bourgeois* Republicans thought the Anarchists too
moderate and obliquely accused the Communists of being too con-
servative; the Syndicalists of the C.N.T. said that the Catalan U.G.T.
(Communist controlled) had been stuffed with at least a hundred
thousand counter-revolutionaries and semi-fascists; the leaders of the
Barcelona U.G.T. declared that they were ready to break with the
Valencia-Madrid U.G.T., they saw Anarchist intrigues everywhere;
the Communists despised every other party, at the same time treating
all the *bourgeois* parties with the greatest politeness; they seemed to
fear the phantom organization of the Amigos de Durutti, yet insisted.

that there was no such thing; neither were there any Trotskyists, but they were always being hunted down, they rose inexplicably from the most thoroughly trodden ashes in secret prisons; general staffs rejoiced over the death of some Lerida partisan shot from behind on the firing line, on his way to get rations for his comrades; a captain of the Karl Marx Division was congratulated on his loyalty when he skilfully invented a pretext for executing an old workman who belonged to the Partido Obrero de Unificacion Marxista—that pestilential organization. Accounts were never settled; it took years to get up a shaky case against generals who, in the U.S.S.R., would have been instantly shot without a trial; and, even so, there was never any certainty of finding a sufficient number of understanding judges who, after examining a set of false documents manufactured with incredible carelessness, would send the culprits to end their days in the moats of Montjuich at the shining hour when bird songs fill the new morning. 'It is our own staff of forgers who should have been shot to begin with,' said Rudin angrily as he looked through the dossier. 'Can't these fools understand that a false document must at least *look* like a real document? Stuff like this will never convince anybody but intellectuals who have already had their pay . . .'

'The forgers we had at the beginning have almost all been shot, but it didn't do any good,' replied the Bulgarian Yuvanov, in the extremely discreet voice which was one of his characteristics.

He explained, with profound irony, that, in this country of brilliant sunlight, where nothing is ever quite precise, where burning facts are modified in accordance with their degree of heat, forgeries never quite jelled; unexpected obstacles were always turning up; the dregs of the earth would suddenly be smitten with consciences that raged like the toothache, sentimental drunkards suddenly blabbed, the general lack of order would bring the authentic documents out of the general hodge-podge, the examining magistrates would blunder, the excise officer would blush and hide his face from an old friend who called him a swindler, and, to top it all, a deputy from the Independent Labour Party would arrive from London, dressed in a very old grey suit, thin, bony, ugly as only the British can be ugly, clamping his pipe between pure Stone Age jaws, and obstinately, automatically demanding: 'What has come of the investigation into the disappearance of Andrés Nín?' The ministers—a strange lot too!—would earnestly implore him, before a dozen people, to deny 'these calumnious rumours which outrage the Republic,' and when they were alone with him would clap him on the back and say: 'Those bastards got him, but what can we do about it? After all, we can't fight without the arms Russia is sending. Do you think we are safe ourselves?' Not one of these governmental dignitaries would have been worthy of a minor job in secret service, not even those who were Party members: they talked too much. A Communist minister, using a transparent pseudonym, wrote a newspaper article accusing a Socialist colleague of being sold to the London bankers . . . At a café the old Socialist commented on his skulking colleague's prose. His ponderous triple chin, his heavy jowls, and even his dark eyelids shook with laughter: 'Sold, *yo!* And the blind dupes have the gall to say so when they are sold to Moscow themselves—and paid with Spanish money, by the way!' The remark struck home. Yuvanov concluded his report: 'They are all incapable. The masses are magnificent, nevertheless.' He sighed: 'But what trouble they cause!'

Yuvanov's square shoulders were surmounted by the face of a dangerously serious fop: wavy hair plastered down on a thick skull, the crafty eyes of a lion tamer, a moustache carefully trimmed to meet the upper lip, accentuating it in bold black. Kondratiev felt an inexplicable antipathy to him, which grew more definite as they went over the list of visitors to be received. The Bulgarian several times indicated his disapproval by slightly shrugging his shoulders. And the three whom he wanted to strike from the list turned out to be the most interesting—at least it was from them that Kondratiev learned the most.

For several days he never left his two white, sparsely furnished rooms except to walk up and down in the patio consuming cigarettes— especially after dark, under the stars. The stenographers, relegated to the annexe, continued clattering at their typewriters. Not a sound came from the city, the bats circled noiselessly in the air. Wearied with reports on supplies, fronts, divisions, air units, plots, the personnel of the S.I.M., of the censorship bureau, of the navy, of the presidential secretariat, reports on the clergy, Party expenditures, personal cases, the C.N.T., the machinations of English spies, and so forth, Kondratiev became aware of the stars, which he had always wanted to study, but even the names of which he did not know. (Because, during the only periods in his life when he had had time to study and think—in sundry prisons—he had been debarred both from books on astronomy and from nocturnal walks.) Yet, properly considered, the stars in their multitudes have no names as they have no number, they have only their faint mysterious light—mysterious because of human ignorance. I shall die without ever knowing more about them. Such are men in this age, 'divided from themselves,' torn, as Marx put it—even the professional revolutionary in whom consciousness of the historical process attains its most practical lucidity. Divided from the stars, divided from themselves? Kondratiev refused to consider the strange formula which had come into his mind in the midst of useful thinking. As soon as you relax a little, your mind starts wandering, your old literary education revives, you could easily become sentimental, even though you are over fifty. He went in, returned to the artillery invoice, the annotated list of nominations for the Madrid Military Investigation Service, the photostats of the personal letters received by Don Manuel Azaña, President of the Republic, the abstract of the telephone conversations of Don Indalecio Prieto, Minister of War and the Navy, a most embarrassing person . . . By candlelight, during a power breakdown caused by a night bombing of the port, he received the first of the visitors whom Yuvanov had wanted to strike from the list, a Socialist lieutenant colonel, a lawyer before the Civil War, of *bourgeois* background—a tall, thin young man with a yellow face which his smile etched into ugly lines. He spoke intelligently, and his remarks were full of unequivocal reproaches.

'I have brought you a detailed report, my dear comrade.' (In the heat of conversation, he sometimes let fall a perfidious 'my dear friend.') 'In the Sierra we never had more than twelve cartridges per man . . . The Aragon front was not defended; it could have been made impregnable in two weeks; I sent out twenty-seven letters on the subject, six of them to your compatriots . . . Air arm entirely insufficient. In short, we are losing the war—make no mistake about that, my dear friend.'

'What do you mean?' interrupted Kondratiev, chilled by the precise statement.

'What I say, my dear comrade. If we are not to be given *matériel* to fight with, we must be allowed to treat. By negotiating now, between Spaniards, we might even yet avoid a total disaster—which it is not to your interest to court, I imagine, my dear friend.'

It was so brutally insolent that Kondratiev, feeling anger flare up in him, answered in a voice changed beyond recognition:

'. . . Your government's province to treat or to continue fighting. I consider your language unwarranted, comrade.'

The Socialist drew himself up, adjusted his khaki necktie, showed his yellow teeth in a wide smile.

'In that case excuse me, my dear comrade. Perhaps this is really all a farce which I fail to understand, but which is costing my people dearly. In any case, I have told you the absolute truth, General. Good-bye . . .'

He held out a long, supple, dry, simian hand, clicked his heels German fashion, bowed, and left . . . 'Defeatist,' Kondratiev thought angrily. 'A bad element . . . Yuvanov was right . . .' The first visitor on the following morning was a hirsute Syndicalist, with a very large nose compressed into a triangle, and eyes that alternately glowered or shone. His answers to Kondratiev's questions were delivered with a look of intense concentration. His two fat hands laid one on the other, he seemed to be waiting for something. At last, the silence having become embarrassing, Kondratiev began to rise, to indicate that the audience was over. At that moment the Syndicalist's face suddenly became animated, his two hands darted eagerly forward, he began talking very fast, fervidly, in clipped French, as if he wanted to convince Kondratiev of something mortally important:

'As for me, comrade, I love life. We Anarchists are the party of men who love life, the freedom of life, harmony . . . A free life! I'm no Marxist, I am anti-state and anti-political. I disagree with you about everything, from the bottom of my soul.'

'Do you think there can be such a thing as an Anarchist soul?' asked Kondratiev, amused.

'No. Blast the soul! But I am willing to be killed, like many before me, if it is for the Revolution. Even if we have to win the war first, as you people say, and have the Revolution only afterward—which seems to me a fatal mistake, because if people are to fight they need something to fight for . . . You think you can take us in with your nonsense about winning the war first—you'd be damn well taken in yourselves if we won it! But that is not what I have to say . . . I'm perfectly willing to get my skull broken open—but to lose the Revolution, the war, and my own skin at the same time is a little too much for me, damn it! And that is just what we are doing with all this skulduggery. You know what skulduggery is? For example: Twenty thousand men behind the lines, magnificently armed, all in new uniforms, guarding ten thousand anti-fascist revolutionaries, the best of the lot, in jails ... And your twenty thousand stinkers will run at the first alert, or go over to the enemy. For example: This policy of feeding Comorera—the shopkeepers making a good thing of the last potatoes and the proletarians pulling in their belts! For example: All this business about Poumists and Canallerists—I know them both, sectarians like all Marxists, but more honest than your lot.'

Across the table which separated them, his hands sought Kondratiev's, seized them, crushed them affectionately. His breath came nearer, his hirsute face with the shining eyes came nearer, he said:

'You were sent by your Chief? You can safely tell me. Gutierrez is a tomb for secrets. Listen! Doesn't your Chief know what is going on here, what his idiots, his toadies, his lame ducks have done? He wants us to win, doesn't he? He is sincere? If so, we can still be saved, we will be saved, won't we?'

Kondratiev answered slowly:

'I was sent by my Party's Central Committee. Our great Chief desires the good of the Spanish people. We have helped you, we shall continue to help you with all our strength.'

It was icy. Gutierrez drew back his hands, his hirsute face, the flame of his eyes; thought for a few moments, then burst out laughing.

'*Bueno*, Comrade Rudin. When you go to see the subway, remind yourself that Gutierrez, who loves life, will die there two or three months from now. We have made up our minds. We will go down into the tunnels with our machine pistols and fight our last battle, and it will cost the Francists dear, I assure you.'

Kondratiev would have liked to reassure him, to speak to him as a friend ... But he felt something inside him harden. When they parted, he could find only meaningless words, which he knew were meaningless. Gutierrez walked heavily out, rolling from side to side; their handshake had ended in a sort of shock.

And the third of the ill-omened visitors was shown in: Claus, noncommissioned officer in the International Brigade, seasoned militant in the German C.P., once involved in the Heinz Neumann deviation, sentenced in Bavaria, sentenced in Thuringia ... Kondratiev had first known him in Hamburg in 1923: three days and two nights of street fighting. A good shot, Claus, always cool. They were glad to see each other; they remained standing, face to face, their hands in their pockets—friends. 'You are really getting somewhere with building

Socialism back there? Better standard of living? How about the youth?' Kondratiev raised his voice, with a joy which he felt was artificial, to say that everything was flourishing. They discussed the defence of Madrid, professionally; the morale of the International Brigades (excellent). 'You remember Beimler—Hans Beimler?' said Claus. 'Of course,' Kondratiev answered. 'Is he with you?'

'Not any longer.'

'Killed?'

'Killed. In the front line, at the University City, but from behind, by our own people.' Claus's lips trembled, his voice trembled. 'That's why I wanted so much to see you. You'll make an investigation, I'm sure. An abominable crime. Killed because of some vague rumour or other, some nonsensical suspicion. That pimp-faced Bulgarian I saw on the way in here must know something. Question him.'

'I'll question him,' said Kondratiev. 'Is that all?'

'That's all.'

When Claus had gone, Kondratiev instructed his orderly to let no one else in, closed the door onto the patio, and for some minutes walked up and down the room, which seemed to have become as stifling as a cell. What answer was he to give these men? What was he to write to Moscow? The official declarations showed up in a sinister light each time they were confronted with the facts. Why did the D.C.A. not go into action until after the bombardments—too late? Why was the fleet inactive? Why was Hans Beimler killed? Why the lack of ammunition at the most advanced positions? Why had general staff officers gone over to the enemy? Why were the poor starving in the country? He was well aware that these definite questions screened a far greater evil, about which it was better not to think ... His meditation did not last long; Yuvanov knocked on the door. 'Time to leave for the conference of political commissars, Comrade Rudin.' Kondratiev nodded. And the investigation into the death of Hans Beimler, killed in action in the lunar landscape of Madrid's University City, was immediately closed.

'Beimler?' said Yuvanov indifferently. 'Ah, yes. Brave, a little on the rash side. Nothing mysterious about his death—these advance-post inspections cost us a man or two every day; he was warned not to go. His political behaviour had caused some dissatisfaction in the Brigade. Nothing serious—conversations with Trotskyists, which showed he rather condoned them, comments on the Moscow trials which showed he misunderstood them completely . . . I had all the details of his death from a reliable source. One of my friends was with him when he was hit . . .'

Kondratiev insisted:

'Did you go into it?'

'Go into what? The source of a bullet in a no man's land swept by thirty machine-guns?'

Ridiculous even to try, of course.

As the car started, Yuvanov resumed:

'Good news, Comrade Rudin! We have succeeded in arresting Stefan Stern. I've had him taken on board the *Kuban*. A real blow to the Trotskyist traitors . . . It is worth a victory, I assure you.'

'A victory? Do you really think so?'

Stern's name appeared in a great many reports on the activities of heretical groups. Kondratiev had paused over it a number of times. Secretary of a dissident group, it appeared; more a theoretician than an organizer; author of tracts and of a pamphlet on 'International Regrouping.' A Trotskyist engaged in a bitter polemic with Trotsky.

'Who arrested him?' Kondratiev went on. 'We? And you have had him put on board one of our ships? Were you acting under orders or on your own initiative?'

'I have the right not to answer that question,' Yuvanov answered firmly.

Not very long before, Stefan Stern had crossed the Pyrenees without a passport and without money, but carrying in his knapsack a precious typewritten manuscript: 'Theses on the Motive Forces of the Spanish Revolution.' The first dark, golden-armed girl he had seen at an inn near Puigcerda intoxicated him with a smile more golden than her arms and said: '*Aqui, camarada, empieza la verdadera revolución libertaria* [Here, comrade, begins the real libertarian revolution].' That was why she let him touch her breasts and kiss the little red curls on the back of her neck. She existed wholly in the flame of her tawny eyes, the whiteness of her teeth, the keen odour of her young flesh that knew the earth and beasts; in her arms was a bundle of freshly washed and wrung clothes, and the coolness of the well hung about her. A whiteness dyed the distant summits, beyond a tracery of apple boughs. '*Mi nombre es Nievo*,' she said, amused by the mingled excitement and shyness of the young foreigner, with his big, green, slightly slanting eyes and his forehead covered with disorderly rust-brown hair. And he understood: her name was 'Snow.' 'Snow, sunny Snow, pure Snow,' he murmured with a sort of exaltation, in a language which Snow did not understand. And though he went on caressing her distractedly, he seemed no longer to be thinking of her. The memory of that moment, a memory of simple, incredible happiness, never quite died in him. At that moment, life divided: the miseries of Prague and Vienna, the activities and schisms of small groups, the tasteless bread on which he had lived in little hotels that smelled of stale urine, in Paris, behind the Panthéon, the solitude of the man labouring with ideas—all that disappeared.

In Barcelona, at the end of a meeting, while the crowd sang in honour of those who were setting out for battle, under the huge portrait of Joaquin Maurin, killed in the Sierra (but actually alive, confined anonymously to an enemy prison), Stefan Stern met Annie, whose twenty-five years seemed hardly more than seventeen. Legs bare, arms bare, throat exposed, a heavy brief case dangling from one arm. A steadfast passion had brought her here from the faraway North. The theory of permanent revolution once understood, how could one live, why should one live, except to accomplish high things? If someone had reminded Annie of the great drawing-room at home, where her father, the shipowner, received the pastor, the burgomaster, the doctor, the president of the Charity Society; had reminded her of the sonatas which an earlier Annie, an obedient little girl with her hair in neat buns over her ears, played for the ladies on Sunday afternoons in that same drawing-room—Annie, according to her mood, would have made a wry face and declared that it was a nauseating *bourgeois* swamp, or, suddenly provocative, with a strident laugh that did not quite belong to her, would have said something like this: 'Shall I tell you how I learned love in a cave in Altamira with C.N.T. soldiers?' She had already worked with Stefan Stern occasionally, taking dictation from him; as they left the meeting with the surging crowd, he suddenly put his arm around her waist (he had not thought of it the moment before), drew her close, and simply said: 'You'll stay with me, Annie? I get so bored at night . . .' She looked at him out of the corner of her eye, divided between annoyance and a sort of joy, wanted to answer him angrily: 'Go get yourself a whore, Stefan—like me to lend you ten pesetas?' but she waited an instant, and then it was her joy which spoke, with a touch of bitter defiance:

'Do you want me, Stefan?'

'Damn right I do,' he said decisively, stopping and facing her, and he pushed his rusty curls back from his forehead. His eyes had a coppery glint.

'All right. Now take my arm,' she said.

Then they discussed the meeting, and Andrés Nín's speech: too muzzy on certain points, inadequate as regarded the central problem— 'He should have been much more forthright, not have given in an inch on the power of the committees,' said Stefan. 'You're right,' Annie answered eagerly. 'Kiss me; but please don't recite me any bad poetry . . .' They kissed awkwardly under the shadow of a palm in the Plaza de Cataluña, while a defence searchlight raked the sky, then stopped, pointing straight to the zenith like a sword of light. On the question of the revolutionary committees, they were in full agreement —they should not have been dissolved by the new government. From their agreement a warm friendship was born. After the days of May 1937, the abduction of Andrés Nín, the outlawing of the P.O.U.M., the disappearance of Kurt Landau, Stefan Stern lived with Annie at Gracia, in a one-story pink house surrounded by an abandoned commercial garden, where choice flowers, reverting to an astonishing wildness, grew in disorder, mingled with nettles and thistles and a strange plant with big velvety leaves . . . Annie's shoulders were straight, her neck was as straight as a rising stem. She carried her head high. It was narrow across the temples and her eyebrows were delicate and so pale that they were almost invisible. Her straw-blonde hair was drawn back from a smooth, hard little forehead, her slate-grey eyes looked at things coolly. Annie went marketing, cooked at the hearth or on an alcohol stove, washed the linen, corrected proofs, typed Stefan's letters and articles and theses. They lived almost in silence. Stefan would sometimes sit down across from Annie while her fingers danced on the typewriter keys, watch her with a wry smile, and simply say:

'Annie.'

She would answer: 'It's the message to the I.L.P., let me finish . . . Have you got an answer ready for the K.P.O.?'—'No, I haven't had time. I found a lot of points to raise in the Bulletin of the IVth.' There, as everywhere, error flourished, overwhelming the victorious doctrine of 1917, which he must try to preserve through to-day's troubles for the struggles of the future, because clearly only the doctrine was left to save before the last days would be upon them.

Comrades came every day, bringing news . . . Jaime told the oddest story—the story of three men who were being shaved at a barber shop during a bombardment and whose throats were cut simultaneously by the three barbers, who had jumped when a bomb exploded. Talk about film effects! A tram loaded with women carrying their morning groceries had suddenly gone up in flames for no reason; the breath of the conflagration stifled their cries in an enormous crackling; and the raging hell had left a metallic skeleton behind, to stand in the square under the shattered windows . . . 'The cars had to be detoured.' People who had failed to get their precious potatoes had walked slowly away, each towards his own life . . . Again the sirens bellowed, the women crowding around the shop door did not scatter, for fear of losing their turns and, with them, their quota of lentils. For death is only a possibility, but hunger is certain. When houses fell, people rushed into the ruins to pick up wood—something to boil the pot with. Bombs of a new pattern, manufactured in Saxony by conscientious scientists, let loose such cyclones that only the skeletons of big buildings remained standing, reigning over islands of silence that were like volcanic craters suddenly extinguished. No one survived under the ruins except, by a miracle, a little girl with short black curls, whom her companions found unconscious under fifteen feet of rubble in a sort of niche; their movements as they carried her away were inconceivably gentle, they were in ecstasies because they could hear her peaceful breathing. Perhaps she was only asleep? She came out of her faint the moment the full sunlight fell on her eyelids. She revived in the arms of half-naked, smoke-blackened beings whose eyes rolled with insane laughter; down they went into the heart of the city, into the banality of every day, from the summit of some unknown mountain . . . The old women insisted that they had seen a decapitated pigeon drop from the sky in front of the rescued girl; from the bird's pearl-grey neck jetted a copious red spray, like a red dew . . . 'You don't mean to say you believe in pious ravings like that?' You walked for a long time, beyond human endurance, through the cold darkness of a tunnel, skinning your fingers against sharp and slimy rock walls, stumbling over inert bodies which perhaps were corpses, perhaps exhausted people who would soon be corpses, you thought you were escaping, making your way up where it would be less dangerous, but there was not a house left unscathed, not a corner in a cellar where you could live—'Wait till someone dies,' people said, 'you won't have long to wait, Jesus!'

5*

Always their Jesus! The sea poured into a huge shelter excavated in rock, fire descended from heaven into prisons, one morning the morgue was filled with children in their Sunday clothes; the next, with militiamen in blue tunics, all beardless, all looking strangely like grown men; the day after that, with young mothers nursing dead babies; the next, with old women whose hands were hardened by half a century of toil— as if the Reaper enjoyed choosing his victims in successive series . . . The placards kept proclaiming, THEY SHALL NOT GET THROUGH—NO PASARAN!—but we, shall we get through the week? Shall we get through the winter? Get through, get on, *Only the dead Sleep sound in bed.* Hunger stalked millions, contending with them for the chick-peas and rancid oil and condensed milk that the Quakers sent, the soya chocolates sent by the Donetz unions, hunger moulded children's faces into the likenesses of little dying poets and murdered cherubs which the Friends of New Spain exhibited in windows on the Boulevard Haussmann in Paris. Refugees from the two Castilles, the Asturias, Galicia, Euzkadi, Malaga, Aragon, even families of dwarf Hurdanos, stubbornly survived day after day, contrary to all expectations, despite all the woes of Spain, despite all conceivable woes. Belief in the miracle of a revolutionary victory was still held by only a few hundred people, divided into several ideological families: Marxists, Liberals, Syndicalists, Marxist Liberals, Liberal Marxists, Left Socialists tending towards the extreme Left—most of them shut up in the Model Prison, hungrily eating the same beans, furiously raising their fists in the ritual salute, living in a devastating state of expectation, between assassination, execution at dawn, dysentery, escape, mutiny, insanity, the work of a single scientific and proletarian reason revealed by history . . .

'We'll soon see them escaping across the Pyrenees—all the fine soldiers and ministers and politicians and diplomats ready to sell themselves, fake Stalinized Socialists, fake Socialists got up as Communists, fake governmental Anarchists, fake brothers and pure totalitarians, fake Republicans sold out beforehand to the dictators—we shall see them making themselves scarce before the red flags—it will be a fine day of revenge, comrades. Patience!'

A festive sun lit this universe, which was simultaneously being born and ending, an ideally pure sea bathed it, and the Savoia bombers, arriving from Majorca to sow death in the lower districts of the port, hung between heaven and earth like floating gulls, in cloudless sunlight. No ammunition on the northern front; at Teruel, the federated divisions melted away in useless battles, like fat on the fire, but they were men, and men recruited by the C.N.T. in the name of Syndicalism and Anarchy, they were men in thousands who, setting out for the blast furnaces with some woman's tense farewell in their hearts, would never come back—or would come back on stretchers, in dirty noisy trains painted with red crosses and emitting a horrible smell of dressings, pus, chloroform, disinfectants, malignant fevers. Who wanted Teruel? Why Teruel? To destroy the last workers' divisions? Stefan Stern asked the question in his letters to his comrades from abroad, Annie's long fingers copied the letters on the typewriter, and already Teruel meant nothing but the past, the fighting moved towards the Ebro, crossed the Ebro, what could be the meaning of the slaughters ordered by Lister or El Campesino in accordance with some obscure plan? Why the premeditated retreat of the Karl Marx Division, if not to save it for a final fratricide behind the lines, to have it ready to shoot down the last men in the Lenin Division? Standing behind Annie, behind Annie's straight, strong neck, Stefan Stern could follow his own thoughts better through Annie's obedient mind, through Annie's fingers, the typewriter keys.

They sometimes talked with comrades from the clandestine Committee until late into the night, by candlelight, drinking a crude dark-red wine . . . President Negrin had delivered the gold reserve to the Russians, it had been sent to Odessa; the Communists held Madrid, with Miaja in supreme command (—just you watch: they'll give in at the last minute!), with Orlov and Gorev actually commanding, Cazorla in Security, and teams of inquisitors, secret prisons, they held everything in a tight net of intrigue, fear, blackmail, favour, discipline, devotion, faith. The Government, which had taken refuge in the monastery of Montserrat, a place surrounded by bristling rocks, could do nothing more. The Communists were making a bad job of holding the city, their organizers were already mortally hated.

'The day will soon come, I tell you, when they will get themselves torn to pieces in the streets by the people. Their nests of spies will be burned like monasteries. But I am very much afraid that it will be too late, after the last defeat, during the final rout.'

Stefan answered:

'They live by the most enormous and most revolting lie history has known since the cheat of Christianity—a lie which contains a great deal of truth ... They call their completed Revolution to witness, and it's true that it is completed; they fly the red flag, and so they appeal to the strongest and rightest instinct of the masses; they catch men by their faith, and then cheat them out of their faith, turn it into an instrument of power. Their most terrible strength lies in the fact that they themselves believe they are continuing the Revolution, while they are serving a new counter-revolution, a counter-revolution such as has never existed before, and set up in the very rooms where Lenin worked ... Think of it: a man with yellow eyes stole the Central Committee keys, walked in and sat down at old Ilich's desk, picked up the telephone, and said: "Proletarians, it's Me." And the same radio which the day before repeated: "Proletarians of all countries, unite," began shouting: "Listen to us, obey us, we can do anything, we are the Revolution ..." Perhaps he believes it, but in that case he is half insane, probably he only half believes it, because mediocrities reconcile their conviction with the situations in which they find themselves. Behind him, like a swarm of rats, rise the profiteers, the right-thinking cowards, the frightened, the new "ins," the careerists, the would-be careerists, the camp followers, those who praise the strong, those who are sold beforehand to any and every power, the old gang that seeks out power because power is the good old way of taking your neighbour's work and the fruits of his work, his wife if she's pretty, his house if it's comfortable. And the whole crowd begins howling, in the most unanimous chorus in the world: "Long live our beefsteak, long live our Chief, *we* are the Revolution, it is for us that the ragged armies won the victory, admire us, give us honours, jobs, money, glory to *Us*, woe to those who oppose *Us*!" What are the poor people to do? What are *we* to do? ... Marx and Bakunin lived in the age of simple problems; they never had enemies *behind* them.'

Jaime said: 'The worst thing is that people are fed up with everything. We'll swallow defeat, we'll swallow anything, they think, if only it will stop. They no longer know what the Republic is fighting for. They're not wrong. What Republic? For whom? They don't know that history never runs out of ideas, that the worst is always yet to come ... They think they have nothing more to lose ... And there is a direct relation between starvation to the present degree and the darkening of people's minds; when bellies are empty the little spiritual flame flickers and goes out ... By the way, I ran into an ugly-looking German on my

way here, I can't seem to place him. You haven't noticed anything?
The place is still safe?'

Annie and Stefan looked at each other searchingly. 'No, nothing . . .'

'You're taking every precaution? You don't go out?'

They counted up the number of comrades who knew the refuge:
seven.

'Seven,' said Annie musingly, 'is too many.'

They had omitted two, it was really nine. Absolutely trustworthy,
but *nine*. 'We must think about sending you to Paris,' Jaime concluded. 'There's where we need a good international secretary . . .'
Jaime readjusted his belt and the heavy pistol that hung from it, put
on his military cap, walked across the garden between them, stopped
at the door: 'Get up an outline of a moderate answer for the English—
they have a way of their own of understanding Marxism—they see it
through Positivism, Puritanism, Liberalism, "fair play," and whisky
and soda . . . And I think you had better sleep out on the hill to-night,
in any case, while I get some information from the Generalidad.' Jaime
left an unspoken anxiety behind him in the weedy garden where the
crickets raised their faint metallic chirping. At thirty-five, Stefan
Stern had survived the collapse of several worlds: the bankruptcy of a
proletariat reduced to impotence in Germany, Thermidor in Russia,
the fall of Socialist Vienna under Catholic canon, the dislocation of the
Internationals, emigrations, demoralizations, assassinations, Moscow
trials . . . After us, if we vanish without having had time to accomplish
our task or merely to bear witness, working-class consciousness will be
blanked out for a period of time that no one can calculate . . . A man
ends by concentrating a certain unique clarity in himself, a certain
irreplaceable experience. It has taken generations, innumerable sacrifices and defeats, mass movements, immense events, infinitely delicate
accidents of his personal destiny, to form him in twenty years—and he
stands at the mercy of a bullet fired by a brute. Stefan Stern felt that
he was that man, and he feared for himself, especially since a number
of others had ceased to exist. Two Executive Committees of the Party
thrown into prison successively, the members of the third, the best
who could be found among seven or eight thousand militants, thirty
thousand registered members, and sixty thousand sympathizers, were
mediocrities full of good will, of unintelligent faith, of confused ideas
which were often no more than elementary symbols . . . 'Annie, listen
to me. I am afraid of becoming a coward when I think of all that I

know, all that I understand, and that they don't know, don't understand . . .' Lacking time to think he put nothing clearly . . . 'Listen,
Annie. There are not more than fifty men on earth who understand
Einstein: If they were shot on the same night, it would be all over for a
century or two—or three, how do we know? A whole vision of the
universe would vanish into nothingness . . . Think of it: Bolshevism
raised millions of men above themselves, in Europe, in Asia, for ten
years. Now that the Russians have been shot, nobody can any longer
see from inside what was the thing by which all those men lived, the
thing which constituted their strength and their greatness; they will
become indecipherable and, after them, the world will fall below
them . . .' Annie did not know if he loved her; she would have been
willing to know that he did not love her, barely glimpsing love without
having time to pause there; she was indispensable to him in his work,
she brought a presence to his side, a proffered and reassuring body to
his arms. When she was there, he did not need to feel under his pillow
for his revolver in order to get to sleep.

The night that followed Jaime's warning they spent on the hill,
rolled up in blankets among the dense shrubbery. The moon was
shining. They stayed awake late, in a strange intimacy, happy to find
themselves suddenly brought infinitely close together by the limpid
sky. Dawn banished their fears, for the day broke bright and pure,
restoring their customary outlines to things, their familiar appearance
to plants, stones, insects, the distant mass of the city. As if blind
danger, having brushed against them, had withdrawn. 'Jaime must be
seeing things!' Stefan mocked. 'How can they have traced us here?
It's impossible to shadow anyone on the road without being seen . . .
Let's go in.' The house awaited them, unchanged. They washed at the
well; the water was icy. Then Annie took the milk jug and went running up the path to the farm, springing like a goat. At the farm Battista,
who was a sympathizer, sold her bread, milk, and cheeses, for friendship's sake. She did her errand happily; it took her about twenty
minutes. Why, when she came back, was the ancient wooden door in
the garden wall half open? As soon as she noticed it, four paces away,
the half-open door sent a little shock to her heart. Stefan was not in the
garden. At that hour he was usually shaving in front of a mirror hung
from the window latch, leaning over some open magazine on his desk
while he shaved. The mirror hung from the latch; his shaving brush,
white with suds, stood on the sill, with his razor beside it; there was an

open magazine on the table, the bath towel was draped over the back of the chair . . . 'Stefan,' Annie called, terrified. 'Stefan . . .' Nothing in the house answered her; but her whole being was irremediably aware that the house was empty. She rushed into the next room, where the bed was still made; to the well, through the garden paths, to the hidden door that gave on to the hill. It was closed . . . Annie whirled around, seized with a feeling of calamity, her eyes sunken, staring wildly, trying to see everything quickly, quickly, relentlessly quickly . . . 'It's impossible, it's impossible . . .' A core of anguish formed in her chest, she felt the violent beating of her heart, like troops on the march, reeling heavily. 'Oh, come back, Stefan! Stop playing with me, Stefan, I'm afraid, Stefan, I'm going to cry . . .' It was senseless to talk to him like that, she must act instantly, telephone . . . The telephone gave no sound; the wires were cut. Silence fell on the empty house in solid masses, like inconceivable clods of earth falling into an immense grave. Annie stared stupidly at the suds-filled shaving brush, the safety razor fringed with tiny bits of hair and soap. Wouldn't Stefan suddenly come up behind her, put his arms around her, say: 'I'm sorry if I've made you cry . . .' It was madness to think it. Sunlight poured down on the garden. Annie went up and down the paths, looking for impossible footprints in the grassy gravel. Six feet from the entrance something significant made her open her eyes wide: the end of a half-smoked cigar, crowned with its ash. Busy ants crossing the path made their way around the unfamiliar obstacle. For months there had been no cigarettes in the city, neither Jaime nor Stefan smoked, no one had smoked there for a long time, the cigar revealed the presence of rich, powerful foreigners—the Russians, my God! Annie set out at a run over the hot stony road to the city. The road burned, the heated air vibrated around the rocks. Several times she stopped to press both hands against her temples, where the blood was throbbing too fast. Then she set off for the city again, running over suddenly petrified lava.

Stefan began to recover consciousness a long minute before he opened his eyes. His vague feeling of nightmare lessened, he was going to wake, it would end; the feeling of nightmare returned, clearer and more overwhelming; no, perhaps it wasn't going to be the end, but a fresh beginning of the blackness, the entrance into a tunnel that might have no end. His shoulders rested on something hard, the curious feeling of well-being that comes with wakening spread through his limbs, conquering a cramp and a sense of fear. What had happened? Am I sick? Annie? Hey, Annie! His eyelids lifted heavily, then he felt afraid to open his eyes wide, he could not understand at first, because his whole being shrank from the terrible necessity of understanding, he *saw* nevertheless, for a fraction of a second, and, this time by an effort of will, closed his eyes again.

A man with a yellowish complexion, shaven skull, prominent cheek-bones, and receding temples was bending over him. Officer's insignia on his collar. A strange room, small and white, where other faces floated here and there in a hard light. Terror caught Stefan by the throat, terror like icy water flooded slowly to the ends of his limbs. Yet under that chill he continued to feel that his being was bathed in a comforting warmth. 'They must have given me an injection of mor-phine.' His eyelids clung together of themselves. To go back to sleep, to avoid this awakening, to go back to sleep . . .

'He is conscious again,' said the man with the receding temples. And then he said, or else he thought it very distinctly: 'He's faking now.'

Stefan felt a muscular hand grasp his wrist and take his pulse. He made an effort to collect himself; he must master the icy flood which devastated his being. He succeeded, though the chill did not go away. The memory of what had happened returned, with irremediable clear-ness. About nine in the morning, when he was getting ready to shave, Annie said: 'I'm going for food—don't open the door to anyone.' After the garden door closed on Annie, he walked for a while through the overgrown paths, feeling strangely depressed, finding no comfort in either the flowers or the fresh morning air. The hill beyond was already beginning to flame under the torrid sun. The white rooms were un-friendly; Stefan checked his Browning, slipped the magazine in and out; he tried to shake off his uneasiness, went to the typewriter, finally decided to shave as usual. 'Nerves, good God . . .' He was standing there wiping his face and trying to read a magazine that lay open on the desk, when the sand of the walk squeaked under an unfamiliar tread; the prearranged whistle sounded too—but how had whoever it was got the garden door open? Could it be Annie back already? But she wouldn't whistle. Stefan flung himself into the wild garden, pistol in hand. Someone was coming towards him, smiling—someone whom he did not recognize at first—a comrade who sometimes came in Jaime's place, but not often. Stefan did not like his big, flat face—it was like the face of a powerful ape. '*Salud!* I frightened you, did I? I have some urgent letters for you . . .' Reassured, Stefan held out his hand. 'Hello . . .' And that had been the beginning of unconsciousness, of nightmare, of sleep; he must have been hit on the head (an indistinct memory of a blow rose out of the forgotten past, a dull pain awoke in his forehead). The man—*comrade*, damn him!—had knocked him out, he had been dragged off, kidnapped—yes, obviously by the Russians. The icy water in his guts. Nausea. Annie. Annie, Annie! At that moment Stefan's collapse was complete.

'He is no longer unconscious,' said a calm voice, very close to him.

Stefan felt that they were looking at him, bending over him, with an attentiveness that was almost violent. He thought that he must open his eyes. 'They gave me a shot in the thigh. Ninety to a hundred I'm done for . . . Ninety to a hundred . . . I may as well admit it anyway . . .' Resolutely he opened his eyes.

He saw that he was lying on a couch in a comfortable ship's cabin. Light woodwork. Three attentive faces leaning towards him.

'Do you feel better?'

'I'm all right,' said Stefan. 'Who are you?'

'You have been arrested by the Military Investigation Bureau. Do you feel able to answer questions?'

So that was how these things were done. Stefan saw everything with a sort of remote detachment . . . He did not answer; he studied the three faces, his whole being tense in the effort to decipher them. One immediately dismissed itself as uninteresting and vague—doubtless the face of the ship's doctor, the man with the receding temples . . . In any case, it rose into the air, retreated in the direction of the wall, and vanished. A breath of salt air refreshed the cabin. The two other faces seemed the most real things in this half-reality. The younger was strong and square: the hair slick with pomade, the moustache neatly trimmed, the features strong, the velvety eyes unpleasantly insistent. An animal trainer, a brave and vain man whom beating tigers had turned into a fear-ridden coward . . . Or a white slaver . . . It was an animally hostile face that Stefan saw above the bright, striped tie. The other aroused his curiosity, then woke a wild gleam of hope in him. Fifty-five, thin grey strands of hair above a calm forehead, a mouth framed in bitter lines, tired eyelids, dark, sad, almost suffering eyes . . . 'Done for, absolutely done for'—through all he was able to

grasp and to think, Stefan heard the words sounding dully somewhere
inside him—'done for.' He moved his arms and legs, glad to find that
he was not fettered, slowly sat up, leaned against the wall, crossed his
legs, made an effort to smile, thought he had succeeded, but only produced a strange contorted expression, held out his hand towards the
dangerous one: 'Cigarette?'—'Yes,' said the other, surprised, and
began looking through his pockets . . . Then Stefan asked for a light.
He must be very, very calm, deathly calm. Deathly—it was certainly
the right word.

'Answer questions? After this illegal kidnapping? Without knowing
who you are—or knowing it only too well? Without guarantees of any
kind?'

The lion tamer's massive head swayed slightly over the tie: wide,
yellow teeth appeared . . . So the brute was trying to smile too. What
he muttered must have been intended to mean: 'We have ways of
making you answer.' Of course. With a low-tension electric current, a
human being can be made to twist and writhe, sent into convulsions,
driven insane, of course, and I know it. But Stefan saw a desperate
chance for salvation.

'. . . But I have a lot to tell you. I've got you, too.'

The sad-eyed man spoke, in French:

'Go ahead. Do you want a glass of wine first? Something to eat?'

Stefan was staking his life. He would strike with the truth as his
weapon. Rush in among them—the half that were implacable beasts,
ready for anything, the half that were genuine revolutionaries perverted
by a blind faith in a power that kept no faith. The two men before him
seemed representative. To trouble at least one of them might mean
salvation. He would have liked to observe their reactions as he spoke,
study their faces, but his weakness made him strangely vague, affected
his vision, made him speak excitedly and jerkily. 'I've got you. Do you
by any chance believe in the plots you invent? Do you think you are
winning victories, or saving something for your master in the midst of
your defeat? Do you know what you have done up to now?' He lost his
temper; he leaned towards them, his hands found the edge of the
couch, he had to grip it from time to time, with all his remaining
strength, to keep from falling over backward against the wall or forward onto the blue carpet which heaved like the sea, whose blueness
was beginning to make him dizzy. 'If you have only the shadow of a
soul, I'll get to it, I'll get hold of it, I'll make it bleed, your dirty little

soul. It will cry out despite you that I am right!' He spoke fiercely, violently, and he was persuasive, subtle, stubborn, without clearly knowing what he was saying; it came out of him as blood spurts out of a deep wound (the image flitted through his mind). 'What have you done, you vermin, with your faked trials? You have poisoned the most sacred possession of the proletariat, the spring of its self-confidence, which no defeat could take from us. When the Communards were stood up and shot in the old days, they felt clean, they fell proudly; but now you have dirtied them one with another, and with such dirt that the best of us cannot comprehend it . . . In this country you have vitiated everything, corrupted everything, lost everything. Look, look . . .' Stefan let go of the couch, the better to show them the defeat which he held out in his two bloodless hands, and he almost toppled over.

As he spoke, he watched the two men's faces. The younger man's remained impassive. The face of the man who might be fifty-five sank into a grey fog, disappeared, reappeared, deeply lined. Their hands assumed different expressions. The younger man's right hand, resting flat on the mahogany of a small table, lay like a sleeping animal. The older man's hands, tightly clasped, perhaps expressed a tense expectancy.

Stefan stopped, and heard the silence. Disconnected from him, his voice expired, leaving him extraordinarily alert in a ringing silence that became an eternity . . .

'Nothing that you have said,' calmly answered the big head with the pomaded hair, 'is of the slightest interest to us.'

The door opened and closed; someone helped the tottering Stefan to lie down again. I am done for, done for. On the bridge of the ship the two men who had just been listening to Stefan were walking up and down in silence. It was night, but not a dark night: a night that made one feel the presence of the stars, of summer, of the nearby land with its horde of living creatures and green things and flowers. The men stopped, then turned and faced each other. The younger, who was the sturdier of the two, had all the rigging of the ship behind him; the other, the one who might be fifty-five, leaned against the rail; behind him were the open sea, night, the sky.

'Comrade Yuvanov,' he said.

'Comrade Rudin?'

'I cannot understand why you had that young man kidnapped.

Another ugly business that will raise a fiendish row even in the Americas. He impresses me as a romanticist of the worst sort, a muddlehead, a Trotskyist, half an Anarchist, et cetera . . . We're pretty much at the end of our rope here . . . I advise you to have him taken ashore and set free as soon as possible, perhaps with some appropriate little stage business, before news of his disappearance gets around . . .'

'Impossible,' Yuvanov said curtly.

'Why impossible?'

In his anger, Kondratiev lowered his voice. His words almost whistled:

'Do you think I am going to let you get away with committing crimes under my eyes? Don't forget that I have a mandate from the Central Committee.'

'The Trotskyist viper in whose favour you are interceding, Comrade Rudin, is implicated in the plot which cost the life of our great comrade Tulayev.'

Ten years earlier that sentence out of a newspaper, spoken with such assurance, would have sent Kondratiev into a fit of laughter in which surprise, scorn, anger, derision, and even fear would have mingled; he would have slapped his thigh: Come now, you top everything—I can't help it, I admire you, your malicious idiocies really reach the point of genius! And indeed, somewhere inside him there was a chuckle, but sober cowardice instantly stifled it.

'I am not interceding for anyone,' he said. 'I merely gave you a piece of political advice . . .'

'I am a coward.' The ship pitched gently in the starry night. 'I am letting myself get bogged in their dirt . . .' The open sea was behind him, he felt as if he were leaning against the emptiness of it, against its immense freshness.

'Besides, Comrade Yuvanov, you have simply been taken in. I know the Tulayev case backward and forward. There's not a clue worth considering in the whole six thousand pages of the dossier, not a single one I tell you, that justifies indicting anybody . . .'

'With your permission, Comrade Rudin, I shall continue to be of a different opinion.'

Yuvanov bowed and left. Kondratiev became aware of the night horizon, where sea and sky mingled. Emptiness. From the emptiness there issued a confusion which was not yet oppressive, which was even attractive. Clouds split the constellations. He went down the rope ladder into the launch, which lay in the darkness against the *Kuban's* rounded hull . . . For a moment, suspended over the lapping water, he was suddenly alone between the huge black shape of the freighter, the waves, the almost invisible launch below: and he went down into the moving shadows alone—calm, and wholly master of himself.

In the launch the hand, a twenty-year-old Ukrainian, gave him a military salute. Acting upon a joy which he felt in his muscles, Kondratiev waved him away from the controls and started the engine himself. 'I haven't lost my hand for these things, brother. I'm an old sailor, you know.'

'Yes, Comrade Chief.'

The light launch skittered along the surface like a creature with wings —in fact, two great wings of white foam spread on either side. There are great red lions with golden wings at the entrance to a footbridge over a canal in Leningrad, there are . . . What else is there? There is the open sea! Oh, to plunge out into it, irretrievably, into the open sea, the open sea! The engine roared, the night, the sea, the emptiness, were intoxicating, it was good to dash straight ahead, not knowing where, joyously, endlessly, good as a gallop over the steppe . . . Nights like this (but the best ones were darker, because that meant less danger) long ago before Sebastopol, when we mounted guard on our peanut-shell boats against the squadrons of the Entente. And because we sang hymns of the World Revolution softly to ourselves, the admirals of the powerful squadrons were afraid of us. Past, past, it is all the past, and this moment, this marvellous moment, will be the past in an instant.

Kondratiev speeded up, heading for the horizon. How wonderful to be alive! He breathed deeply, he would have liked to shout for joy. A few motions would carry him out of the cockpit, a lunge would throw him forward, and he would dive through the beating wing of foam, and then—and then it would all be over in a few minutes, but they'd probably shoot the little Ukrainian.

'Where do you hail from, lad?'

'From Mariupol, Comrade Chief . . . From a fishermen's kolkhoze . . .'

'Married?'

'Not yet, Comrade Chief. When I get back.'

Kondratiev swung the launch around and headed for the city. The rock hill of Montjuich emerged from space, dense black against the transparent black of the sky. Kondratiev thought of the city which lay under that rock, a city torn by bombings, fallen asleep hungry, in danger, betrayed, forsaken, three-quarters lost already, a dead city still believing that it would live. He had not seen it, he would not see it, he would never know it. Conquered city, lost city, capital of defeated revolts, capital of a world in birth, of a lost world, which we took, which is dropping from our hands, is escaping us, rolling towards the tomb ... Because we, we who began the conquest, are at our last gasp, are empty, we have gone mad with suspicion, gone mad with power, we are madmen capable of shooting ourselves down in the end—and that is what we are doing. Too few minds able to think clearly, among the horde of Asiatics and Europeans whom a glorious calamity led to accomplish the first Socialist revolution. Lenin saw it from the very beginning, Lenin resisted so high and dark a destiny with all his power. In school language, you would have to put it that the working classes of the old world have not yet reached maturity, whereas the crisis of the régime has begun; what has happened is that the classes which are attempting to go against the stream of history are the most intelligent—ignobly intelligent—are the best educated, those which put the most highly developed practical consciousness in the service of the most profound lack of consciousness and of the greatest egotism ... At this point in his meditation, Kondratiev remembered Stefan Stern's contorted face, seemed to see it borne along on the great wings of foam ... 'Forgive me,' Kondratiev said to him fraternally. 'There is nothing more I can do for you, comrade. I understand you very well, I was like you once, we were all like you ... And I am still like you, since I am certainly done for, like you ...' He had not expected his thought to arrive at this conclusion, it surprised him. The phantom of Stefan, with his sweating forehead, his curly copper-red hair, his grimacing mouth, the steady flame of his eyes, mingled as in a dream with another phantom. And it was Bukharin, with his big, bulging forehead, his intelligent blue eyes, his ravaged face, still able to smile, questioning himself before the microphone of the Supreme Tribunal, a few days before his death—and Death was there already, almost visible, close to him, one hand on his shoulder, the other holding the pistol: it was not the Death Albrecht Dürer had seen and engraved, a skeleton with a grinning skull, wrapped in the homespun and armed with the scythe of the Middle Ages—no: it was death up-to-date, dressed as an officer of the Special Section for Secret Operations, with the Order of Lenin on his coat and his well-fed cheeks close-shaven ...

'For what reason am I to die?' Bukharin asked himself aloud, then spoke of the degeneration of the proletarian party . . . Kondratiev made an effort to shake off the nightmare.

'Take the controls,' he called to the sailor.

Sitting in the stern, suddenly tired, his hands crossed on his knee, the ghosts gone, he thought: Done for. The launch ploughed towards the city through that dark certainty. Done for like the city, the Revolution, the republic, done for like so many comrades . . . What could be more natural? A turn for each, a way for each . . . How had he managed not to be aware of it until now, how had he lived in the presence of that hidden revelation without divining it, without understanding it, imagining that he was doing things that were important or things that were unimportant, when actually there was nothing left to do? The launch came alongside in the dark port amid a chaos of scattered stone. A swinging lantern preceded Kondratiev into a low, ruined building, its roof full of holes, where militiamen were playing dice by the light of a candle . . . Part of a torn poster above them displayed emaciated women at last victorious over poverty, on the threshold of the future promised them by the C.N.T. . . . . At eleven o'clock Kondratiev had himself driven to a government building for a fruitless conversation with the officials in charge of munitions. Too much ammunition to yield, not enough to win. A member of the government had arranged a midnight supper for him. Kondratiev drank two large glasses of champagne with a minister of the Catalan Generalidad. The wine, sprung from French soil and impregnated with gentle and joyous sunlight, sent flakes of gold running through their veins. Kondratiev touched one of the bottles and, without in the least thinking what he was going to say, brought out:

'Why don't you keep this wine for the wounded, señor?'

The minister looked at him with a fixed half-smile. The Catalan statesman was tall, thin, and stooped: sixty, elegantly dressed; a severe face lighted by kind, shrewd eyes; a university professor. He shrugged his shoulders:

'You are absolutely right . . . And it is one of the small things we are now dying of . . . Too little ammunition, too much injustice . . .'

Kondratiev opened the second bottle. Ladies and gentlemen in broad plumed hats, hunting the stag to bay in the forests of another century, looked down on him from the tapestries. Again the old

Catalan university professor clinked glasses with him. An intimacy drew them together, they were disarmed before each other, as if they had left their hypocrisy in the cloakroom . . .

'We are beaten,' the minister said pleasantly. 'My books will be burned, my collections scattered, my school closed. If I escape, I shall be simply a refugee in Chile or Panama, speaking a language that no one will understand . . . With an insane wife, señor. There it is.' He did not know how it happened, but the most incongruous, the most outrageous question escaped him:

'My dear sir, have you any news of Señor Antonov-Ovseyenko, whom I esteem most highly?'

'No,' Kondratiev answered tonelessly.

'Is it true that . . . that he has been . . . that they . . . that . . .'

Kondratiev was so close to him that he saw the greenish streaks in the old man's dark pupils.

'. . . that he's been shot?' Kondratiev supplied quietly. 'We use the word quite frequently, you know. Well, it is probably true, but I don't know for certain.'

An odd silence—voicelessness or discouragement—fell between them.

'He has sometimes drunk my champagne with me in this very room,' the Catalan minister resumed confidentially.

'I shall probably end as he did,' Kondratiev answered, equally confidentially and almost gaily.

Before the half-open gold and white door they shook hands warmly, resuming their conventional roles but with more life than usual. One said: 'Have a good trip, *querido señor*.' The other, shifting from foot to foot, repeated his thanks for the warm reception he had been given. They felt that their farewells were taking too long, yet they felt too that, the moment their hands let go of each other, an invisible and fragile link, like a golden thread, would break, never to be restored between them.

Taking the bull by the horns, Kondratiev caught the plane for Toulouse the next morning. He must reach Moscow before the arrival of the secret reports which, distorting his slightest gestures, would show him interceding for a Trotskyist-Terrorist—what madness it all was! He must get there in time to propose the final measures which would turn the tide, a substantial shipment of arms, a purge of the services, immediate cessation of crimes behind the lines . . . He must arrange for an interview with the Chief before the enormous, crushing mechanism of government traps had been set in motion; he must see him face to face and stake his life on the risky trumps of a comradeship begun on the cold Siberian plains in 1906, of an absolute loyalty, of a controlled but cutting frankness, of the truth—after all, there is such a thing as truth.

At five thousand feet, in a sky that was pure light, the most sun-drenched catastrophe in history was no longer visible. The Civil War vanished at just the altitude at which the bomber pilots prepared to fight. The ground was like a map—so rich in colour, so full of geological, vegetable, marine, and human life that, looking at it, Kondratiev felt a sort of intoxication. When at last, flying over the forest of Lithuania, an undulating, dark mossiness which struck him as looking pre-human, he saw the Soviet countryside, so different from all others because of the uniform colouring of the vast kolkhoze fields, a definite anxiety pierced him to the marrow. He pitied the thatched roofs, humble as old women, assembled here and there in the hollows of almost black ploughlands, beside gloomy rivers. (Doubtless at bottom he pitied himself.)

The situation in Spain must have appeared so serious that the Chief received him on the day he arrived. Kondratiev waited only a few moments in the spacious ante-room, from whose huge windows, which flooded the room with white light, he could see a Moscow boulevard, trams, a double row of trees, people, windows, roofs, a building in course of demolition, the green domes of a spared church . . . 'Go in, please . . .' A white room, bare as a cold sky, high-ceilinged, with no decoration except a portrait of Vladimir Ilich, larger than life, wearing a cap, his hands in his pockets, standing in the Kremlin courtyard. The room was so huge that at first Kondratiev thought it empty; but behind the table at the far end of it, in the whitest, most desert, most solitary corner of that closed and naked solitude, someone rose, laid down a fountain pen, emerged from emptiness; someone crossed the carpet, which was the pale grey of shadowed snow, someone came to Kondratiev holding out both hands, someone, He, the Chief, the comrade of earlier days—was it real?

'Glad to see you, Ivan, how are you?'

Reality triumphed over the stunning effect of reality. Kondratiev pressed the two hands which were held out to him, held them, and real

warm tears gathered under his eyelids, only to dry instantly, his throat
contracted. The thunderbolt of a great joy electrified him:

'And you, Yossif? . . . You . . . How glad I am to see you . . . How
young you still are . . .'

The short greying hair still bristled vigorously; the broad, low,
deeply lined forehead, the small russet eyes, the stiff moustache, still
held such a compact charge of life that the flesh-and-blood man
shouldered away the image presented by his innumerable portraits.
He smiled, and there were smiling lines around his nose, under his
eyes, he emanated a reassuring warmth—would he be as warm and
kind as he looked? But how was it that all the mysterious dramas, the
trials, the terrible sentences pondered in the Political Bureau had not
exhausted him more?

'You too, Vania,' he said (yes—it was the old voice). 'You've stood
up well, you haven't aged much.'

They looked at each other, relaxed. How many years, old man!
Prague, London, Cracow years ago, that little room in Cracow where
we argued so fiercely all one evening about the expropriations in the
Caucasus; then we went and drank good beer in a *Keller*, with
Romanesque vaulting, under a monastery . . . The processions in
'seventeen, the congresses, the Polish campaign, the hotels in the little
towns we captured, where fleas devoured our exhausted revolutionary
councils. Their common memories came back in such a crowd that
not one became dominant: all were present, but silently and unob-
trusively, re-creating a friendship beyond expression, a friendship
which had never known words. The Chief reached into the pocket of
his tunic for his pipe. Together they walked across the carpet, towards
the tall bay windows at the farther end of the room, through the
whiteness . . .

'Well, Vania, what's the situation now, down there? Speak plainly,
you know me.'

'The situation,' Kondratiev began with a discouraged look and that
gesture of the hands which seems to let something drop, 'the situation . . .'

The Chief seemed not to have heard this beginning. His head bowed,
his fingers tamping tobacco into the bowl of his short pipe, he went on:

'You know, brother, veterans like you, members of the old Party,
must tell me the whole truth . . . the whole truth. Otherwise, who can I
get it from? I need it, I sometimes feel myself stifling. Everyone lies

and lies and lies! From top to bottom they all lie, it's diabolical . . . Nauseating . . . I live on the summit of an edifice of lies—do you know that? The statistics lie, of course. They are the sum total of the stupidities of the little officials at the base, the intrigues of the middle stratum of administrators, the imaginings, the servility, the sabotage, the immense stupidity of our directing cadres . . . When they bring me those extracts of mathematics, I sometimes have to hold myself down to keep from saying, Cholera! The plans lie, because nine times out of ten they are based on false data; the Plan executives lie because they haven't the courage to say what they can do and what they can't do; the most expert economists lie because they live in the moon, they're lunatics, I tell you! And then I feel like asking people why, even if they say nothing, their eyes lie. Do you know what I mean?'

Was he finding excuses for himself? He lighted his pipe furiously, put his hands in his pockets, squared his head and shoulders, stood firmly on the carpet in the harsh light. Kondratiev looked at him, studying him sympathetically, yet with a certain basic suspicion, considering. Should he risk it? He risked an unemphatic:

'Isn't it a little your own fault?'

The Chief shook his head; the minute wrinkles of a warm smile flickered about his nose, under his eyes . . .

'I'd like to see you in my place, old man—yes, that's something I'd like to see. Old Russia is a swamp—the farther you go, the more the ground gives, you sink in just when you least expect to . . . And then, the human rubbish! . . . To remake the hopeless human animal will take centuries. I haven't got centuries to work with, not I . . . Well, what's the latest news?'

'It's execrable. Three fronts barely holding out—a push, and collapse . . . They haven't even dug trenches in front of essential positions . . .'

'Why?'

'Lack of spades, bread, plans, officers, discipline, ammunition, of . . .'

'I see. Like the beginning of 'eighteen with us, eh?'

'Yes . . . On the surface . . . But without the Party, without Lenin'—Kondratiev hesitated for a fraction of a second, but it must have been perceptible—'without you . . . And it's not a beginning, it's an end—*the* end.'

'The experts have prophesied it—three to five weeks, don't they say?'

'It can last a long time, like a man taking a long time to die. It can be over to-morrow.'

'I need,' said the Chief, 'to keep the resistance going for a few weeks.'

Kondratiev did not answer. He thought: 'That is cruel. What's the use?'

The Chief seemed to divine his thought:

'We are certainly worth that,' he resumed. 'And now: Our Sormovo tanks?'

'Nothing to boast about. Armour plate passable . . .' Kondratiev remembered that the builders had been shot for sabotage, and felt a momentary embarrassment. 'Motors inadequate. Breakdowns in combat as high as thirty-five per cent . . .'

'Is that in your written report?'

'Yes.' Embarrassment. Kondratiev was thinking that he had laid the foundation for another trial, that his 'thirty-five per cent' would burn in phosphorescent characters in brains exhausted by night-long interrogations. He resumed:

'In point of defectiveness, the human *matériel* is the worst . . .'

'So I've been told. What is your explanation?'

'Perfectly simple. We fought, you and I, under other conditions. The machine pulverizes man. You know I am not a coward. Well, I wanted to see—I got into one of those machines, a No. 4, with three first-class men, a Catalan Anarchist . . .'

'. . . a Trotskyist, of course . . .'

The Chief had spoken with a smile, out of a cloud of smoke; his russet eyes twinkled through almost closed lids.

'Very likely—I didn't have time to go into it . . . You wouldn't have either . . . Two olive-skinned peasants, Andalusians, wonderful marksmen, like our Siberians or Letts used to be . . . Well, there we are, rolling along an excellent road, I try but can't imagine what it would be like if we were on bad terrain . . . There are four of us inside there, dripping sweat from head to foot, stifling, in the darkness, the noise, the stench of gasolene, we want to vomit, we're cut off from the world, if only it were over! There was panic in our guts, we weren't fighters any longer, we were poor half-crazed beasts squeezed together in a black, suffocating box . . . Instead of feeling protected and powerful, you feel reduced to nothing . . .'

'The remedy?'

'Better planned machines, special units, trained units. Just what we have not had in Spain.'

'Our planes?'

'Good, except for the old models . . . It was a mistake to unload so many old models on them . . .' The Chief gave a decided nod of approval. 'Our B 104 is inferior to the Messerschmitt, outclassed in speed.'

'The maker was sabotaging.'

Kondratiev hesitated before answering, for he had thought a great deal on the subject, convinced that the disappearance of the Aviation Experiment Centre's best engineers had unquestionably resulted in poorer quality products.

'Perhaps not . . . Perhaps it is only that German technique is still superior . . .'

The Chief said:

'He was sabotaging. It has been proved. He confessed it.'

The word *confessed* produced a distinct feeling of discomfort between them. The Chief felt it so clearly that he turned away, went to the table for a map of the Spanish fronts, and began asking detailed questions which could not really have been of any significance to him. At the point which things had reached, what could it matter to him whether Madrid's University City was more or less well supplied with artillery? On the other hand, he did not discuss the shipping of the gold reserves, probably having been already informed of it by special messenger. Kondratiev passed over the subject. The Chief made no reference to the changes in personnel suggested in Kondratiev's report . . . On a clock in the faraway bay window, Kondratiev read that the audience had already lasted more than an hour. The Chief walked up and down, he had tea brought, answered a secretary, '*Not until I call you* . . .' What was he expecting? Kondratiev became tensely expectant too. The Chief, his hands in his pockets, took him to the bay window from which there was a view of the roofs of Moscow. There was only a pane of glass between them and the city, the pale sky.

'And here at home, in this magnificent and heart-rending Moscow, what is not going right, do you think? What isn't jelling? Eh?'

'But you just said it, brother. Everyone lies and lies and lies. Servility, in short. Whence, a lack of oxygen. How build Socialism without oxygen?'

'Hmm . . . And is that all, in your opinion?'

Kondratiev saw himself driven to the wall. Should he speak? Should he risk it? Should he wriggle out of it like a coward? The tension in him prevented him from reading the Chief's face clearly, though it was only two feet away. Despite himself he was very direct, and therefore very clumsy. In a voice that was emphatic though he tried to make it casual:

'The older generation is getting scarce . . .'

The Chief put aside the outrageous allusion, pretending not to notice it:

'On the other hand, the younger generation is rising. Energetic, practical, American style . . . It's time the older generation had a rest . . .'

'May they rest with the saints'—the words of the Chant for the Dead in the liturgy . . .

Tensely, Kondratiev changed his tack:

'Yes, the younger generation, of course . . . Our youth is our pride . . .' ('My voice rings false, now I'm lying too . . .')

The Chief smiled curiously, as if he were laughing at someone who was not present. And then, in the most natural tone:

'Do you think I have many faults, Ivan?'

They were alone in the harsh white light, with the whole city before them, though not a sound from it reached them. In a sort of spacious courtyard below and some distance away, between a squat church with dilapidated towers and a little red-brick wall, Georgian horsemen were at sabre practice, galloping from one end of the courtyard to the other; about half-way they stooped almost to the ground to impale a piece of white cloth on their sabres . . .

'It is not for me to judge you,' said Kondratiev uncomfortably. 'You are the Party.' He observed that the phrase was well received. 'Me, I'm only an old militant'—with a sadness that had a shade of irony—'one of those who need a rest . . .'

The Chief waited like an impartial judge or an indifferent criminal. Impersonal, as real as things.

'I think,' said Kondratiev, 'that you were wrong in "liquidating" Nicolai Ivanovich.'

Liquidating: the old word that, out of both shame and cynicism, was used under the Red terror for 'execute.' The Chief took it without flinching, his face stone.

'He was a traitor. He admitted it. Perhaps you don't believe it?'

Silence. Whiteness.

'It is hard to believe.'

The Chief twisted his face into a mocking smile. His shoulders hunched massively, his brow darkened, his voice became thick.

'Certainly . . . We have had too many traitors . . . conscious or unconscious . . . no time to go into the psychology of it . . . I'm no novelist.' A pause. 'I'll wipe out every one of them, tirelessly, mercilessly, down even to the least of the least . . . It is hard, but it must be . . . Every one of them . . . There is the country, the future. I do what must be done. Like a machine.'

Nothing to answer?—or to cry out? Kondratiev was on the point of crying out. But the Chief did not give him time. He returned to a conversational tone:

'And in Spain—are the Trotskyists still intriguing?'

'Not to the extent that some fools insist. By the way, I want to talk to you about a matter that is of no great importance but which may have repercussions . . . Our people are doing some stupid and dangerous things . . .'

In a few sentences Kondratiev set forth the case of Stefan Stern. He tried to divine whether the Chief had already been told of it. Natural and impenetrable, the Chief listened attentively, made a note of the name, Stefan Stern, as if it were new to him. Was it really new to him?

'Right—I'll look into it . . . But about the Tulayev case, you are wrong. It was a plot.'

'Ah!'

'Perhaps, after all, it was a plot . . .' Kondratiev's mind gave a halting assent . . . 'How accommodating I'm being—the devil take me!'

'May I ask a question, Yossif?'

'Of course.'

The Chief's russet eyes still had their friendly look.

'Is the Political Bureau dissatisfied with me?'

That really meant: 'Are you dissatisfied with me, now that I have spoken to you freely?'

'What answer can I give you?' said the Chief slowly. 'I do not know. The course of events is unsatisfactory, there is no doubt of that—but there was not much you could do about it. You were in Barcelona only a few days, so your responsibility does not extend far . . . When every-

thing is going to the dogs, we have no one to congratulate, eh?
Ha-ha.'

He gave a little guttural laugh, which broke off abruptly.

'And now what shall we do with you? What work do you want?
Would you like to go to China? We have fine little armies there, a trifle
infected with certain diseases . . .' He gave himself time to think. 'But
probably you've had enough of war?'

'I've had enough of it, brother. No, thank you—so far as China is
concerned, spare me that, please. Always blood, blood—I am sick of
it . . .'

Precisely the words he ought not to have spoken, the words that had
been in his throat since the first minute of their meeting, the weightiest
words in their secret dialogue.

'I see,' said the Chief, and suddenly the bright daylight became
sinister. 'Well, what then? A job in production? In the diplomatic
corps? I'll think about it.'

They crossed the carpet diagonally. Sleepwalkers. The Chief took
Ivan Kondratiev's hand.

'I have enjoyed seeing you again, Ivan.'

Sincere. That spark deep in the eyes, that concentrated face—the
ageing of a strong man living without trust, without happiness, without
human contacts, in a laboratory solitude . . . He went on:

'Take a rest, old man. Have yourself looked after. At our age, after
our lives, it has to be done. You're right, the older generation is getting
scarce.'

'Do you remember when we hunted wild ducks on the tundra?'

'Everything, everything, old man, I remember everything. Go and
take a rest in the Caucasus. But I'll give you a piece of advice for down
there: let the sanatoriums look out for themselves, and you go climb
as many mountain trails as you can. That's what I'd like to do myself.'

Here there began, within them and between them, a secret dialogue,
which they both followed by divination, distinctly: 'Why don't *you*
go?' Kondratiev suggested. 'It would do you so much good, brother.'
—'Tempting, those out-of-the-way trails,' mocked the Chief. 'So I'll
be found one day with my head bashed in? I'm not such a fool as that
—I'm still needed . . .'—'I pity you, Yossif, you are the most threatened, the most captive of us all . . .'—'I don't want to be pitied. I forbid
you to pity me. You are nothing, I am the Chief.' They spoke none of
these words: they heard them, uttered them, only in a double *tête-à-*

tête—together corporeally and also together, incorporeally, one within the other.

'Good-bye.'

'Good-bye.'

Half-way across the huge ante-room Kondratiev encountered a short man with shell-rimmed glasses, a thick, curving nose, and a heavy brief case which almost dragged along the carpet: the new Prosecutor of the Supreme Tribunal, Rachevsky. He was going in the opposite direction. They exchanged reticent greetings.

EVERY MAN HAS HIS OWN WAY
OF DROWNING

FOR SIX MONTHS a dozen officials had been turning over the one hundred and fifty selected dossiers of the Tulayev case. Fleischman and Zvyeryeva, as 'examiners appointed to follow the most serious cases,' followed this one from hour to hour under the immediate supervision of Deputy High Commissar Gordeyev. Fleischman and Zvyeryeva, both formerly Chekists—that is, in the old heroic days—should have been under suspicion; they knew it, and hence they could be counted on to show the utmost zeal. The case ramified in every direction, linked itself to hundreds of others, mingled with them, disappeared in them, re-emerged like a dangerous little blue flame from under fire-blackened ruins. The examiners herded along a motley crowd of prisoners, all exhausted, all desperate, all despairing, all innocent in the old legal meaning of the word, all suspect and guilty in many ways; but it was in vain that the examiners herded them along, the examiners always ended up in some fantastic impasse. Common sense suggested dismissing the confessions of half a dozen lunatics who all told how they had murdered Comrade Tulayev. An American tourist, a woman who was almost beautiful and completely mad, though her self-control was an impenetrable weapon, declared: 'I know nothing about politics, I hate Trotsky, I am a Terrorist. Since childhood I have dreamed of being a Terrorist. I came to Moscow to become Comrade Tulayev's mistress and kill him. He was so jealous; he adored me. I should like to die for the U.S.S.R. I believe that the love of the people must be spurred by overwhelming emotions . . . I killed Comrade Tulayev, whom I loved more than my life, to avert the danger that threatened the Chief . . . I can't sleep for remorse—look at my eyes. I acted from love . . . I am happy to have accomplished my mission on earth . . . If I were free, I'd like to write my reminiscences for the papers . . . Shoot me! Shoot me!' During her periods of depression she sent her consul long messages (which of course were not transmitted), and she wrote to the examining judge: 'You cannot shoot me because I am an American.'—'Drunken trollop,' Gordeyev cursed, when he had spent three hours studying her case. Wasn't she simulating insanity? Hadn't she actually *thought* about committing a murder beforehand? Didn't her declarations contain some echo of plans ripened by others? What was to be done with her, mad as she was? An embassy was taking an interest in her, news agencies on the other side of the globe distributed pictures of her, described the tortures which they claimed the examiners were inflicting on her . . . Psychiatrists in uniform, still faithful to the rite of question-and-answer, applied suggestion, hypnotism, and psycho-analysis in turn, to persuade her to admit her innocence. She exhausted their patience. 'Well then,' Fleischman suggested, 'at least persuade her that she killed somebody else, anybody . . . Have you no imagination! Show her photographs of murder victims, give her details of sadistic attacks, and let her go to the devil! The witch!' But in her waking dream she would only consent to murder prominent people. Fleischman hated her, hated her voice, her accent, her yellowish-pink complexion . . . A young doctor assigned to the investigation spent hours with the mad woman, stroking her hands and knees while he made her repeat: 'I am innocent, I am innocent . . .' She repeated it perhaps two hundred times, gave a beatific smile, and said softly: 'How sweet you are . . . I've known for a long time that you love me . . . But it was I, I, I who killed Comrade Tulayev . . . He loved me as you do.' The same evening the young doctor made his report to Fleischman. A sort of bewilderment clouded his eyes and troubled his speech. 'Are you quite sure,' he asked at the end of the interview, with a strange seriousness, 'that she has no connection with the case?' Fleischman angrily crushed out his cigarette. 'Go take a shower, my boy—right away!' The young doctor was sent to rest his nerves in the forests of northern Pechora. Five sets of detailed confessions were thus classed as products of insanity—yet it took courage to dismiss them. Gordeyev sent the suspects back to the doctors. The doctors went mad in their turn . . . So much the worse for them! 'To the insane asylum under a strong

guard,' Fleischman proposed with his soft smile. Zvyeryeva smoothed
her dyed hair with her slim fingers, and answered: 'I consider them
extremely dangerous . . . Anti-social mania . . .' Face massages, creams,
and make-up kept her face an irritating, ageless mask of blurred
features and indistinct wrinkles. The hard, restless look in her eyes
aroused uneasiness. It was she who told Fleischman that Deputy High
Commissar Gordeyev expected them in his office at one-thirty for an
important conference. She added, in a significant tone: 'Prosecutor
Rachevsky will be there. He has had an interview with the Boss . . .'

'Then the crisis will soon be upon us,' Fleischman thought.

They conferred in Gordeyev's office on the thirteenth floor of a
tower that overlooks the principal streets of the city. Fleischman,
having taken a drink of brandy, felt well. Leaning towards the
window, he watched the human swarm in the street below, the line of
parked cars in front of the People's Commissariat for Foreign Affairs,
peered at the show windows of the book shops and co-operatives. To
wander around down there for a while, go into an antique shop, stare
into windows, follow a pretty girl—what a joy that would be! A hell
of a life! Even when you manage not to think of the danger. Stout,
decorated, with flabby jowls, tired eyelids, yellow blotches under his
eyes, thinning hair, he had lately begun to age quite obviously. He
thought: 'I shall be absolutely impotent in another year or two . . .'
no doubt because his eye had been caught by a group of students, with
their caps and books, who were rough-housing cheerfully as they
crossed the street between a black prison van, a shining diplomatic
Fiat, and a green bus.

Meanwhile, Prosecutor Rachevsky's eyes had fallen on a small landscape by Levitan which hung on the wall. A blue Ukrainian night, a
thatched roof, the ashy curve of a road, magic of the plains under dim
stars. Without looking away from that road into the unreal, he said:

'Comrades, I think it is time we produced results.'

'Obviously,' Gordeyev thought, warily. 'It's high time. But what
results, may I ask?' Gordeyev believed that he knew very well what
results, but he refrained from coming to a conclusion. The slightest
error in such a matter is like a mis-step by a man putting in rivets on a
skyscraper, three hundred feet above the pavement. Falling knows no
mercy. Impossible to get a definite directive. They left him to his own
devices, encouraged him, spied on him, and reserved the right to
reward him or disown him. What Prosecutor Rachevsky had said made

it likely that there would be a revelation, since he had been closeted with the Boss. Scales burst out at the other end of the apartment: Ninelle beginning her piano lesson.

'I am of the same opinion, Ignatii Ignatiyevich,' said Gordeyev with a broad, sugary smile.

Fleischman shrugged his shoulders.

'Certainly, let's get it over with. This preliminary investigation can't go on forever. But what would be the proper way to close it?' (He looked straight at Rachevsky.) 'The case is definitely political . . .'

Treacherously, or nonchalantly, he made a little pause before he went on:

'. . . though the crime, to tell the truth . . .'

To tell the truth, *what*? Fleischman turned to the window without finishing his sentence and stood there, intolerably fat, round-shouldered, his chin overflowing the collar of his tunic. Zvyeryeva, who never risked herself first, said starchily:

'You didn't finish your sentence, I believe?'

'On the contrary.'

Among the students grouped at the edge of the pavement, an amazingly blonde and beautiful girl was explaining something, gesturing vividly with both hands; at that distance her fingers seemed to hold the light, and she threw her head back a little to laugh more freely. Distant as a star, inaccessible and real as a star, her head did not feel Fleischman's dull eyes staring at it. The Deputy High Commissar for Security, the Prosecutor of the Supreme Tribunal, the Investigatress appointed to the most serious cases, waited for Fleischman to express his opinion. Aware of their expectation, he resumed firmly:

'The preliminary investigation must be closed.'

Turning until he almost faced them, he looked at the three, one after the other, giving each a pleasant nod, as if he had just said something most important—three repugnant, corrupt faces, composed of some horrible gelatinous substance . . . And I am ugly too, my complexion is greenish, I have a bestial jowl and puffy eyelids . . . We ought to be put out of the way . . . And now you are in a fine fix, my dear comrades, because that is all I intend to say. It's up to you to motivate our decision or to put it off, I've taken enough responsibility as it is . . . The students had gone, and so had the prison van and the bus . . . Other pedestrians passed, a baby carriage manœuvred across the street, under the heavy snouts of trucks. Of all that crowd in the street, not one knows the name of Tulayev . . . In this city, in this country of 170,000,000 inhabitants, not a single person really remembers Tulayev. Of the big, genial man with his moustaches, his clumsiness, his easy familiarity, his trite eloquence, his occasional drinking bouts, his sordid loyalty to the Party, who was ageing and growing ugly like all the rest of us, nothing remained but a handful of ashes in an urn and an uncordial and unvalued memory in the minds of a few exhausted and half-mad inquisitors. The only living beings for whom he had really been a man, the women whom, after an evening of drinking, he undressed to an accompaniment of throaty laughter, stammered endearments, obscene jokes, and bursts of taurine violence, would perhaps for a while preserve secret images of him completely different from the portraits of him which still hung in some offices because no one had thought to take them down. But did they know his name? Both memories and portraits would soon vanish . . . Nothing in the dossier, not a clue worth considering, nothing to implicate anyone. Tulayev had simply disappeared, carried off by the wind, the snow, the darkness, the bracing cold of a night of hard frost.

'Close the preliminary investigation?' said Zvyeryeva interrogatively.

The peculiar sensitivity of the official was always wide awake in her. Intuitions that were almost infallible gave her a presentiment of plans which were silently and doubtfully being matured in high places. With her chin in her hand, her shoulders hunched, her waved hair, her eyes that were gimlets, or rather less like gimlets than augurs, she was an incarnate question. Fleischman yawned behind his hand. Gordeyev, to cover his embarrassment, got brandy from a cupboard and began setting out small glasses. 'Martel or Armenian?' Prosecutor Rachevsky, realizing that no one would say anything more before he spoke, began:

'This case, which is indeed purely political, can have only a political solution . . . The results of the preliminary investigation are, in themselves, of only secondary interest to us . . . According to the criminologists of the old school, with whom in this case we are in agreement, the *quid prodest* . . .'

'Quite right,' said Zvyeryeva.

Prosecutor Rachevsky's face appeared to be sculptured in two opposite curves out of a resistant and unhealthy flesh. Concave in general effect from the bulging forehead to the grey bulbous chin, a curving nose, swollen at the base, with dark hairy nostrils, made it a strong face. In colour it was sanguine, with blotchy areas of violet. Large chestnut-brown eyes, like opaque marbles, gave it a dark expression. He had emerged but a few years since, during a terrible period, from the depths of a dismal destiny made up of obscure, difficult, and dangerous tasks, accomplished for no reward, with the plodding stubbornness of a beast of burden. Suddenly raised to greatness, he had stopped indulging in drinking bouts, for fear of talking too much. Because there had been times when, in the soothing warmth of a good drunk he had said of himself: 'I am a work horse . . . I pull the old harrow of justice. All I know is my furrow, ha-ha! I hear *Gee*, and I pull. A click of the tongue, and I stop. I am the beast of revolutionary duty, I am; get on, old beast—ha-ha!' Towards the friends who had heard him say such things, he felt an undying resentment afterwards. His rise dated from a sabotage trial—terrorism, treason—staged at Tashkent against men of the local government, his masters the day before. Without even an explicit order, he built up a complicated structure of false hypotheses and bits of fact, spread a net of tortuous dialectic over the laboriously worked-up declarations of a score of defendants, took it upon himself to dictate the implacable sentence which his superiors hesitated to communicate to him, delayed the transmission of the petitions for reprieve . . . Then he went to the Grand Theatre and spoke before three thousand workers. This episode decided his advancement. He wrapped perfectly clear thinking in halting phrases, which groped and tumbled over each other. Only his parentheses were more or less grammatical. Thus his voice shed a sort of fog over the minds of his hearers, yet through the fog certain threatening outlines became visible, always the same. 'You argue,' a defendant said to him one day, 'like a hypocritical bandit who talks to you with pacific gestures and all the time you see that he has a knife up his sleeve . . .'—'I scorn your insinuations,' the prosecutor answered calmly. 'And the whole room can see that my sleeves are tight-fitting.' In private conversation he lacked assurance. He found Zvyeryeva's encouragement so timely that he acknowledged it with a half-smile: the three caught a glimpse of his teeth, which were yellow and irregularly set. He discoursed:

'There is no occasion for me to set forth the theory of plots to you, comrades. The word, in law, can have either a restricted or a more general meaning, and, I will add, yet another, which accords much better with our revolutionary law, which we have restored to its original purity by rescuing it from the pernicious influence of the enemies of the people who had succeeded, here in Russia, in distorting its meaning to the extent of subjugating it to the outworn formulas of *bourgeois* law which rests upon a static establishment of fact whence it proceeds to seek out a formal guilt considered as effectual by virtue of pre-established definitions . . .'

The stream of words flowed for nearly an hour. Fleischman looked into the street, and felt disgust rising in him. What creatures without an ounce of talent make a career nowadays! Zvyeryeva blinked her eyes, pleased as a cat in the sun. Gordeyev mentally translated the discourse from the agitator's terms in which it was delivered into more intelligible ones, because somewhere in it, like a weasel crouched in a thicket, lay the Chief's directive. 'In short: we have lived at the heart of an immense and infinitely ramified plot, which we have succeeded in liquidating. Three fourths of the leaders of the previous periods of the revolution had ended by becoming corrupt; they had sold themselves to the enemy, or if not, it was the same thing, in the objective meaning of the word. Causes: the inner contradictions of the régime, the desire for power, pressure from surrounding capitalism, intrigues of foreign agents, the demoniac activity of Judas-Trotsky. The high foresight, the truly inspired foresight of the Chief has made it possible for us to thwart the machinations of innumerable enemies of the people who frequently held in their hands the levers which control the State. Henceforth no one must be considered above suspicion except for the entirely new men whom history and the genius of the Chief have summoned up for the salvation of the country . . . In three years, the battle for public security has been won, the conspiracy has been reduced to impotence; but in the prisons, in the concentration camps, in the street, men yet survive who are our last internal enemies, and the most dangerous because they are the last, even if they have done nothing, even if they are innocent according to formal law. Their defeat has taught them a more profound hatred and dissimulation, so dangerous that they are even capable of taking refuge in a temporary inactivity. Juridically innocent, they may have a feeling of impunity, believe that they are safe from the sword of justice. They prowl around us like hungry jackals at twilight, they are sometimes among us, hardly betray themselves by a look. By them and through them, hydra-headed conspiracy may be born anew. You know the news from the rural areas, with what we are faced in regard to harvests, there have been troubles in the Middle Volga, a recrudescence of banditism in Tadjikistan, a number of political crimes in Azerbaijan and in Georgia! Strange incidents have taken place in Mongolia in the field of religion; the president of the Jewish republic was a traitor, you know the role that Trotskyism has played in Spain; a conspiracy against the Chief's life was hatched in the suburbs of Barcelona, we have received an astounding dossier on the case! Our frontiers are threatened, we are perfectly aware of the deals between Berlin and Warsaw; the Japanese are concentrating troops in Jehol, they are building new forts in Korea, their agents have just manœuvred a breakdown of turbines at Krasnoyarsk . . .'

The prosecutor drank another brandy. Zvyeryeva said enthusiastically:

'Ignatii Ignatiyevich, you have the material for a tremendous indictment!'

The prosecutor thanked her by dropping his eyelids. 'Let us not, furthermore, conceal from ourselves that the preceding great trials were insufficiently prepared in certain respects, and hence have left the Party's cadres relatively disoriented. The conscience of the Party turns to us, asking for explanations which we can only furnish during the sessions of a trial which will be, as it were, complementary . . .'

'Complementary,' Zvyeryeva repeated. 'That is exactly what I was thinking.'

She beamed discreetly. The burden of doubt fell from Gordeyev's shoulders. Phew! 'I agree with you entirely, Ignatii Ignatiyevich,' he said loudly. 'Permit me to leave you for a moment; my little girl . . .' He hurried down the white hall, because Ninelle's scales had stopped and because he needed to take the precaution of a moment's solitude. He took Ninelle's bony buttocks between his flat hot hands. 'Well, darling, did your lesson go all right?' Sometimes he looked at the dark-haired child, with her green-flecked eyes, as he was no longer capable of looking at anyone else in the world. The music mistress was putting away her music, there was the snap of a brief case. 'And now,' Gordeyev thought, 'the traps are in the list of indictments . . . We'll have to dig up at least one genuine ex-Trotskyist, one genuine spy . . . Dangerous business . . .'

'Papa,' said Ninelle uncomfortably, 'you were so sweet and now you look angry . . .'

'Business, darling.'

He kissed her on both cheeks, quickly, but felt none of the happiness the pure caress should have given him—the ghosts of too many tortured men were astir in him, though he was not conscious of it. He returned to the conference. Fleischman sighed strangely: 'Music . . . what music . . .'

'What do you mean?' Zvyeryeva asked. Fleischman bent his pale forehead a little, thus spreading even more of his double chin over his tunic collar, and became stickily amiable: 'It's so long since I've heard any music . . . Don't you ever long for it?'

Zvyeryeva murmured something and looked bland.

'The list of indictments,' said Gordeyev . . .

No one answered him.

'The list of indictments,' repeated Prosecutor Rachevsky, firmly resolved to say no more.

Imagine a hippopotamus at the zoo suddenly sliding into his little concrete pool . . . Fleischman had the pleasant sensation of producing precisely the same effect as he brought out: 'It is for you, my esteemed comrades, to propose it . . .' Everyone has his responsibilities, so assume yours!

Erchov was gallingly aware that his preparation for the shock had been complete. Nothing surprised him, except not recognizing the place where he was taken. 'I had so many prisons to supervise, all more or less secret!' The Ex-High Commissar made the excuse to soothe his conscience. Yet this particular prison—new, modern, built of concrete, and located somewhere underground—should not have escaped his attention. The effort of memory which he made to recover some mention of it in the reports of the Prisons department or the Building department was unavailing. 'Perhaps it was under the sole jurisdiction of the Political Bureau?' He shrugged and abandoned the problem. The heating was adequate, the lighting soft. Cot, bedclothes, pillows, a swivel chair. Nothing else, nothing.—Even the fate of his wife troubled Erchov less than he had expected. 'We are all soldiers . . .' That meant: 'Our wives must expect to become widows . . .' Essentially, the transposition of another idea, which it was harder to admit: 'A dying soldier doesn't feel sorry for his wife . . .' Little elementary formulas like that satisfied his mind; there was nothing to be done about them, as there was nothing to be done about orders. He waited, going through his setting-up exercises every morning. He asked for a

daily shower and was granted it. He walked endlessly between the door
and the window, his head bowed, frowning. All his reflections ended in
a single word, a word that forced itself on him from outside, despite
his soundest arguments: 'Shot.' Suddenly he felt sorry for himself,
almost fainted. 'Shot.' He recovered without much effort, though he
turned pale (but he could not see that he was pale): 'Well, we're all
soldiers, aren't we? . . .' His male body, well rested, demanded a
woman, and he remembered Valia with anguish. But was it really Valia
he remembered, or was it his own bodily life, now over? If the burning
cigarette butt a man crushes underfoot could feel and think, it would
experience the same anguish. What could he do to get it over with
sooner?

Weeks passed, during which he was not allowed to see a glimpse of
the sky. Then came interrogation after interrogation—conducted in the
adjoining cell, so that a walk of thirty steps along a subterranean
corridor gave him no bearings on his prison. Men who were of high
rank, but whom he did not know, questioned him with a mixture of
deference and harsh insolence. 'Did you check on the use made of the
344,000 roubles allocated for reconstructing the offices of the prison
administration at Rybinsk?' Stupefied, Erchov answered: 'No.' A
smile which was perhaps sarcastic, perhaps pitying, creased the hollow
cheeks of the high official whose round spectacles gave him the look of
a deep-sea fish . . . And the session was over . . . At the next session:
'When you signed the appointment of Camp Commandant Illenkov,
did you know the past record of that enemy of the people?'—'Which
Illenkov?' The name must have been submitted to him in a long list.
'But this is ridiculous! Comrade, I . . .' —'Ridiculous?'said the other
in a threatening voice. 'On the contrary, it is most serious, it is a
matter of a crime against the security of the State committed by a high
official in the exercise of his office, and punishable, under Article . . . of
the Penal Code, by death . . .' This one was ageing—sandy hair,
coppery flecks in his face, his eyes hidden behind grey lenses. 'Then
you claim that you did not know, defendant Erchov?'—'No.'—'As you
please . . . But you are well aware that in our country confessing errors
and crimes is always a better choice than resisting . . . I am not telling
you anything new . . .' Another interrogation revolved around the
sending to China of an agent who had turned traitor. Erchov answered
sharply that the Organization Bureau of the Central Committee had
made the appointment. The thin inquisitor, whose long nose and dark

mouth made as it were a cross on his face, replied: 'You are making a clumsy attempt to elude your responsibilities . . .' Other subjects brought up were the price of Valia's furs, perfumes which he had taken for her from the stock of contraband articles, the execution of a confessed counter-revolutionary, a former officer in Baron Wrangel's army: 'No doubt you will claim that you did not know he was one of your most devoted agents?'—'I did not know it,' said Erchov, who, to tell the truth, remembered nothing. The meaninglessness of the inquiry restored his confidence a little—if they really had only these small things against him?—at the same time that it gave him a feeling of increasing danger. 'In any case, I shall probably be shot . . .' A sentence heard long ago at the War Academy haunted his memory: 'Within the radius of the explosion, the destruction of human life is instantaneous and complete . . .' We are all soldiers. He grew thin, his hands trembled. Write to the Chief? No, no, no . . .

Prisoners in solitary gradually sink into a state that is pure prolongation. If an event suddenly awakens them, it has the intensity of a dream. Erchov saw himself entering the spacious offices of the Central Committee. He advanced, almost as if he were floating, towards a group of half a dozen men seated around a table covered with a red cloth. Street sounds, oddly muffled, reached his ears. Erchov did not recognize a single face. The man at the right, ill-shaven, with a profile like a fat rodent, might be the new prosecutor, Rachevsky . . . Six official faces, abstract and impersonal, two uniforms . . . 'How weak I've become, I am afraid, terribly afraid . . . What shall I say to them? . . . What shall I try? I am going to hear everything, it will be over-whelming . . . It is not possible that they won't shoot me . . .' A heavy head seemed to lean towards him: slightly moonlike, slightly shining, entirely without hair, a tiny round nose, an absurdly small mouth. A eunuch's voice proceeded from it, saying almost amiably:

'Erchov, sit down.'

Erchov obeyed. There was one unoccupied chair behind the table. Tribunal? Six pairs of eyes studied him with great severity. Tired, pale, dressed in a tunic from which the insignia had been removed, he felt dirty. 'Erchov, you have belonged to the Party . . . Here, you must understand, all resistance is useless . . . Speak . . . Unburden yourself . . . Confess everything to us, we know it all already . . . Go down on your knees before the Party . . . There lies salvation, Erchov, there lies the only possible salvation . . . We are listening . . .' The man with the moonlike face, with the eunuch's voice, emphasized his invitation by a gesture. Erchov looked at him for a few seconds in bewilderment, then rose and said:

'Comrades . . .'

He must cry out his innocence, and he realized that he could not, that he felt obscurely guilty, justly condemned in advance, though he could not say why; and it was as impossible for him to confess anything whatever as to defend himself. All he could do was to pour out a flood of words before these unknown judges, words which he felt were lamentably confused. 'I have loyally served the Party and the Chief . . . ready to die . . . I have made mistakes, I admit . . . the 344,000 roubles for the Rybinsk Central, the nomination of Illenkov, yes, I agree . . . Believe me, comrades . . . I live only for the Party . . .'

The six did not listen to him, they rose as one man. Erchov came to attention. The Chief appeared, without a look towards him, silent, grey, his face hard and sad. The Chief sat down and bent his head over a sheet of paper, read it attentively. As one man, the six sat down again. There was a moment of absolute silence, even in the city. 'Go on,' the eunuch voice resumed, 'tell us about your part in the plot which cost the life of Comrade Tulayev . . .'

'. . . But that is absolutely insane,' Erchov cried. 'It is sheer madness, no, no, I mean it's I who am going mad . . . Give me a glass of water, I'm stifling . . .'

Then the Chief raised his wonderful and monstrous head, the head of all his numberless portraits, and said exactly what Erchov would have said in his place, what Erchov, in his despair, ought to be thinking himself:

'Erchov, you are a soldier . . . Not a hysterical woman. We ask the truth from you . . . The objective truth . . . This is not the place for scenes . . .'

The Chief's voice was so like his own inner voice that it restored Erchov to complete lucidity, and even to a sort of assurance. Later he remembered that he had argued coolly, gone over all the essential factors in the Tulayev case, quoted documents from memory . . . yet feeling clearly all the while that nothing could be of any use to him. Accused men who had disappeared long, long ago had argued in just the same fashion before him; and he had not been taken in, he knew what the wretches were concealing. Or he knew why words were superfluous. The Chief cut him off in the middle of a sentence.

'Enough. We are wasting our time with this cynical traitor . . . Have you sunk so low that you accuse *us*? Go!'

He was led away. He had only glimpsed the angry gleam in the russet eyes and the guillotine motion of a paper knife brought down on the table. Erchov spent that night walking up and down his cell—his mouth tasted bitter, his breathing was laboured. Impossible to hang himself, impossible to open his veins, ridiculous to fling himself at the wall headfirst, impossible to let himself die of starvation, he would be fed by force, through a tube (he had himself signed orders for cases of the sort). The Orientals say that you can die if you will to die, it is not the pistol that kills, it is the will . . . Mysticism. Literature. Materialists know very well how to kill, they do not know how to die at will. Poor creatures that we are!—Erchov understood everything now.

. . . Was it four weeks, or five, or six, that passed? What connection did measurements of time based on the rotation of the earth in space have with the fermentation of a brain between the concrete walls of a secret prison in the age of the rebuilding of the world? Erchov under-went twenty-hour interrogations without flinching. Amid a mass of questions which apparently had no connection with one another, there were three which were asked again and again: 'What did you do to prevent the arrest of your accomplice Kiril Rublev? What did you do to conceal the past of the Trotskyist Kondratiev on the eve of his mission to Spain? What messages did you give him for the Spanish Trotskyists?' Erchov explained that Kondratiev's personal dossier had been sent to him by the Political Bureau at the very last moment; that the dossier contained nothing unusual; that he had seen Kondratiev only for ten minutes and only to advise him about trustworthy agents . . . 'And who were these trustworthy agents?' When he returned to his cell after these interrogations, he slept like a stunned animal, but talked in his sleep, because the interrogation went on and on in his dreams.

During the sixteenth hour (but, for him, it could as well have been the hundredth; his mind dragged through weariness like an exhausted horse through mud) of his seventh or eighth interrogation, something fantastic happened. The door opened. Ricciotti walked in, quite simply, holding out his hand. 'Glad to see you, Maximka.'

'What's this? What? I'm so tired, damn it, that I don't know if I'm dreaming or awake. Where did you come from, brother?'

'Twenty hours of good sound sleep, Maximka, and everything will become clear, I promise you. I'll manage it for you.'

Ricciotti turned to the two examiners behind the big desk, as if he had been their superior: 'Leave us now, comrades . . . Tea, cigarettes, a little vodka, please . . .'

Erchov saw that, under the abundant white tangled hair, Ricciotti's face was bloodless like an old prisoner's, that his violet mouth was disagreeably lined, that his clothes were shapeless. The flame of intelligence in Ricciotti's eyes was still alight, but it shone through a cloud. Ricciotti forced a smile. 'Sit down, we have plenty of time . . . You're done in, eh?'

He explained:

'The cell I'm in is probably not far from yours. But in my case, the little formalities are all over . . . I sleep, I walk in the courtyard . . . I get jam with every meal, I even read the papers . . .' His eyelids blinked, he went through the gesture of snapping his fingers, soundlessly. 'Sickening, the papers . . . It's curious how different panegyrics look when you read them in an underground prison . . . We're going down like a ship that . . .' He pulled himself together. 'I'm getting a good rest, now, you see . . . Arrested about ten days after you . . .'

The tea, the cigarettes, and the vodka were brought in. Ricciotti opened the window curtains wide, on a great square courtyard in bright daylight. In the offices opposite, stenographers moved past the windows. Several young women, who must have been standing on a stair landing, were talking animatedly; you could even see their painted nails, see that one of them wore her hair just following the shape of her ears.

'It is strange,' said Erchov half aloud.

He swallowed down a big glass of steaming tea, then a stiff drink of vodka. He was like a man beginning to come out of a fog.

'My insides were cold . . . Do you understand what is going on, Ricciotti?'

'The whole thing. I'll explain it all to you. It is as clear as a chess game for beginners. Check and mate.'

His fingers gave a decisive little tap on the table.

'I committed suicide twice, Maximka. At the time of your arrest, I had an excellent Canadian passport, with which I could have cleared out . . . I learned what had happened to you, I expected it, I told myself that they would come for me within ten days—and I was right

. . . I began packing. But what was I to do in Europe, in America, in Constantinople? Write articles for their stinking press? Shake hands with crowds of *bourgeois* idiots, hide in dirty little hotels, or in palaces, and finally catch a bullet as I came out of the toilet? As for the West, I loathe it. And I loathe our world, this world here, too; but I love it more than I loathe it, I believe in it, I have all our poisons in my veins . . . And I am tired, I've had enough . . . I returned my Canadian passport to the Liaison office. It amazed me to walk through the streets of Moscow like a real living person. I looked at everything and told myself that it was for the last time. I took leave of women I didn't know, I suddenly felt like kissing children, I found an extraordinary charm in pavements scrawled over with chalk for a little girls' game, I stopped in front of house windows that interested me, I couldn't sleep, I went with whores, I got drunk. If by some chance they don't come for me, I asked myself, what will become of me? I'm good for nothing any more. I woke with a start, from sleep or drunkenness, to think up preposterous schemes which intoxicated me for half an hour: I'd go to Vyatka, get a job as foreman of a lumber-cutting gang under a false name . . . Become Kuzma, wood-cutter, illiterate, not a member of the Party, not a member of a union—why not? And it was not entirely impossible, but at bottom I did not believe it, I did not even want it myself . . . My second suicide was the Party cell meeting: The speaker sent by the Central Committee was obviously going to talk about you . . . The room was full, everyone in uniform, everyone green, green with fear, my friend, everyone silent, but waves of coughing and sniffling spreading over the room . . . I was afraid myself, yet I wanted to shout: "Cowards, you cowards, aren't you ashamed to be so afraid for your dirty little hides?" The speaker was discreet, his speech all slimy circumlocutions, he didn't mention your name until the end, and referred to "extremely serious professional errors . . . which might justify the gravest suspicions . . ." We didn't dare look at one another, I felt that everyone's face was sweating, that chills were running up and down everyone's spine. Because it wasn't *you* he was sparing when he talked about you. Even your wife . . . Arrests were still going on. After all, twenty-five members of your confidential entourage were there, all with their revolvers and all knowing very well what it was all about . . . When the speaker stopped, we dropped into a pocket of silence. The Central Committee's envoy himself dropped into it with us. Those who sat in the first row, under the Bureau's eyes, were the first to recover themselves, naturally; they began the applause, it became frenzied. "How many dead men are applauding their own end?" I asked myself, but I did as the rest did, to avoid calling attention to myself; we all applauded like that, under one another's eyes . . . Are you falling asleep? . . .'

'Yes . . . No, it's nothing, I'm awake . . . Go on.'

'Those who owed you the most, and who were consequently in the greatest danger, spoke of you with the greatest treachery . . . They asked themselves if the discreet C.P. orator was not setting a trap for them. It was pitiful. I got up on the platform, like the others, without much idea of what I was going to say, I began like everyone else with empty phrases about the Party's vigilance. A hundred asphyxiated faces looked up at me, open-mouthed; they impressed me as slimy and dried up, asleep and vicious, distorted by colic. The Bureau dozed on, what I might say to denounce you interested no one, it was an old story that wouldn't save me; and no one was thinking of anything but himself. And I found myself absolutely calm again, my friend, I had a tremendous desire to joke, I felt that my voice was clear and assured, I saw gelatinous faces moving feebly, I was beginning to make them uneasy. I calmly said unheard-of things, which froze the audience, the Bureau, the man from the Central Committee. (He was taking notes as fast as he could, he would have liked to sink into the ground.) I said that mistakes, under our overwhelming load of work, were inevitable, that I had known you for twelve years, that you were loyal, that you lived only for the Party and that everyone knew it, that we had very few men like you and a great many rats . . . The chill that rose around me might have come from the Great Ice Barrier. At the back of the room a strangled voice cried: "Shame!" It woke the terror-stricken ghosts: "Shame!"—"Shame on *you*," I said, stepping down from the platform, and I added: "You are fools if you think you're any better off than I am!" I walked the whole length of the room. They were all afraid I would come and sit down beside them, they shrank into their chairs as I approached—every one of my colleagues. I went out to the buffet, smoked a cigarette, and flirted with the waitress. I was satisfied, and I was trembling all over . . . I was arrested the next morning.'

'Yes, yes,' said Erchov vaguely. 'What were you going to say about my wife?'

'Valia? She had just written to the cell Bureau to say that she wanted a divorce . . . That she wanted to wash away the involuntary dishonour

of having, unknowingly, been the wife of an enemy of the people . . .
And so forth . . . You know the formulas. And she was right, she
wanted to live, Valia did.'

'It doesn't matter.'

In a lower voice, Erchov added:

'Perhaps she was right . . . What has become of her?'

Ricciotti made a vague gesture: 'I have no idea . . . In Kamchatka,
I suppose . . . Or the Altai . . .'

'And now?'

Through their weariness, they looked at each other, and the colourless daylight revealed in each of them the same bleak astonishment, the
same stricken and simple calm.

'Now,' Ricciotti answered, 'it is time to give in, Maximka. Resistance
serves no purpose . . . you know that better than anyone. You can force
yourself to suffer the tortures of the damned, but the end will be the
same, and furthermore it will be useless. Give in, I tell you.'

'Give in to what? Admit that I am an enemy of the people, a traitor,
that I killed Tulayev, and I don't know what else? Repeat that hodge-
podge which sounds as if it had been spouted by drunken epileptics?'

'Confess, brother. That or something else, anything they want you
to. In the first place, you'll sleep; in the second, you'll have a slim
chance . . . A very slim chance, almost no chance in my opinion, but
there's nothing left that anyone can do about it . . . Maximka, you are
a stronger man than I am, but I have better political judgment, you
must admit . . . That's how it is, I assure you. They need just that, and
they order it as they order a turbine destroyed . . . Neither the
engineers nor the workers discuss the order, and no one worries about
the lives it will cost . . . I had never even thought of it before . . . The
last trials did not produce the political results that were expected of
them, and the conviction now is that there must be a new demonstration and a new clean-up . . . You understand that they can't leave any
veterans anywhere . . . It is not up to us to decide if the Political
Bureau is wrong or not . . .'

'It is appallingly wrong,' said Erchov.

'Keep your mouth shut on the subject. No member of the Party has
a right to say such things. If you were sent against Japanese tanks as
the head of a division, you wouldn't argue, you'd go, even though you
knew that not a man would come back. Tulayev is only an accident or
an excuse. For my part, I am even convinced that there is nothing

behind the case, that he was killed by chance, if you please! You must see, nevertheless, that the Party cannot admit that it is impotent before a revolver shot fired from no one knows where, perhaps from the depths of the people's soul . . . The Chief has been in an impasse for a long time. Perhaps he's losing his mind. Perhaps he sees farther and better than all the rest of us. I don't believe he is a genius, I believe he has decided limitations, but we have no one else, and he has only himself. We have killed off all the others, allowed them to be killed off, that is; and he is the only one left, the only real one. He knows that when somebody shoots Tulayev, it is himself that was aimed at, because it can't be otherwise, there is no one but himself that anyone either *can* hate or *has* to hate . . .'

'You think so?'

Ricciotti said lightly:

'Only the rational is real, according to Hegel.'

'I cannot,' said Erchov, with an effort. 'It is beyond my strength . . .'

'Empty words. Neither you nor I have any strength left. And afterward?'

Half the offices in the building they could see through the window were closed and empty now. To the right, a few floors were lighted up, where people would be working all night . . . The green light through the window shades brightened the twilight. Erchov and Ricciotti were enjoying a singular freedom: they went and washed their faces in the toilet room, they were brought a reasonably good supper and plenty of cigarettes. They glimpsed faces that looked almost friendly . . . Erchov stretched out on the sofa, Ricciotti wandered around the room, straddled a chair:

'I know all that you are thinking, I have thought it all myself, I still think it. Point 1: There is no other solution, old man. Point 2: This way, we give ourselves a very slim chance, say one-half of one per cent. Point 3: I would rather die *for* the country than *against* it . . . I will admit to you that, at bottom, I no longer believe in the Party, but I believe in the country . . . This world belongs to us, we belong to it, even to the point of absurdity and abomination . . . But it is all neither so absurd nor so abominable as it seems at first sight. It is more by way of being barbarous and clumsy. We are performing a surgical operation with an axe. Our government holds the fort in situations that are catastrophic, and sacrifices its best divisions one after the other because it doesn't know anything else to do. Our turn has come.'

Erchov put his face in his hands.

'Stop, I can't follow you.'

He raised his head, he seemed able to think clearly again, he looked angry.

'Do you believe one-fifth of what you're telling me? What are they paying you to convince me?'

The same furious despair set them one against the other; their heads close together, they saw each other—unshaven for a week, their faces bloodless, their eyelids netted with wrinkles, their features blurred by a weariness without end. Ricciotti answered, without heat:

'No one is paying me anything, you idiot. But I don't want to die for nothing—do you understand that? That chance—one half of one per cent, of one thousand per cent, yes, of one thousand per cent—I mean to take it—do you understand that? I mean to try to live, cost what it may—and then, that's that! I am a human animal that wants to live despite everything, to kiss women, work, fight in China . . . Dare to tell me that you are any different! I want to try to save you, do you understand? I am logical. We used this move on others, now it's being used on us—they know the game! Things have overtaken us and we must keep going to the end. Don't you see that? We were made to serve this régime, it is all we have, we are its children, its ignoble children, all this is not a matter of chance—can I ever make you understand? I am loyal—don't you see? And you are loyal too, Maximka.' His voice broke, changed tone, acquired a shade of tenderness. 'That's all, Maximka. You are wrong to revile me. Think it over. Sit down.'

He took him by the shoulders and pushed him towards the sofa. Erchov let himself drop onto it limply.

Night had fallen, steps sounded in a distant corridor, mingled with the tapping of a typewriter. The scattered sounds, creeping into the silence, were poignant.

Erchov was still rebellious:

'Confess that I am complete traitor! That I was a party to a crime against which I have fought with all my strength! . . . Let me alone, you're mad!'

His comrade's voice came to him from very far away. There were icy distances between them, in which dark planets revolved slowly . . . There was nothing between them except a mahogany table, empty tea glasses, an empty carafe of vodka, five feet of dusty carpet.

'Better men than you and I have done it before us. Others will do it after us. No one can resist the machine. No one has the right, no one can resist the Party without going over to the enemy. Neither you nor I will ever go over to the enemy . . . And if you consider yourself innocent, you are absolutely wrong. We innocent? Who do you think you're fooling? Have you forgotten our trade? Can Comrade High Commissar for Security be innocent? Can the Grand Inquisitor be as pure as a lamb? Can he be the only person in the world who doesn't deserve the bullet in the neck which he distributed, like a rubber-stamp signature, at the rate of seven hundred per month on the average? Official figures—way off, of course. No one will ever know the real figures . . .'

'Shut up, will you?' cried Erchov. 'Have me taken back to my cell. I was a soldier, I obeyed orders—that's all! You are torturing me for no purpose . . .'

'No. Your torture is only beginning. Your torture is yet to come. I am trying to keep you from going through it. I am trying to save you . . . To save you, do you understand?'

'Have they promised you something?'

'They have us so in their hands that they don't need to promise us anything . . . We know what promises are worth . . . Popov has been to see me—you know, that blithering old fool . . . When his turn comes, I'll be very happy, even in the next world . . . He said to me: "The Party demands much of you, the Party promises nothing to anyone. The Political Bureau will decide in accordance with political necessities. The Party can also shoot you without trial . . ." Make up your mind, Maximka, I am as tired as you are.'

'Impossible,' said Erchov.

He covered his face with his hands and crumpled over. Perhaps he was crying. His breath came wheezily. There was a shattering interval.

'It would be a pleasure to blow out my own brains,' Erchov muttered.

'Of course,' said Ricciotti.

Time—sheer, colourless, deadly time stretching on and on—with nothing at the end. To sleep . . .

'One chance in a thousand,' Erchov muttered, out of a calm from which there was no appeal. 'Very well! You are right, brother. We have to stay in the game.'

Ricciotti pressed a frenzied finger on the bell push. Somewhere the bell rang commandingly . . . A young soldier of the special battalion

half opened the door. 'Tea, sandwiches, brandy! Quick!' Bluish daylight dimmed the lights in the windows of the Secret Service, which
was deserted at that hour. Before they parted, Erchov and Ricciotti
embraced each other. Smiling faces surrounded them. Someone said
to Erchov: 'Your wife is well. She is at Viatka, she has a job in the
communal government . . .' In his cell, Erchov was amazed to find
newspapers on the table. He had read nothing for months, his brain
had worked in a vacuum, at times it had been very hard. Exhausted,
he dropped onto the bed, unfolded a copy of *Pravda* to a benevolent
portrait of the Chief, looked at it for a long minute, laboriously, as if he
were trying to understand something, and fell asleep just as he lay,
with the printed image covering his face.

Telephones transmitted the important news. At 6.27 a.m. Zvyeryeva, who had herself been waked by her secretary, called Comrade
Popov by direct wire and informed him: 'Erchov has confessed . . .'
Lying in her big bed of gilded Karelian wood, she laid the receiver
down on the night table. A polished mirror, hung so that it tilted
towards the bed, sent her back an image of which she never tired:
herself. Her long, straight, dyed hair framed her face in an almost
perfect oval. 'I have a tragic mouth,' she thought, seeing the yellowish
curve of her lips, which expressed both shame and rancour. Complexion the colour of old wax, wrinkles painstakingly massaged—there
was nothing in that face human except the eyes. Soot-coloured, without lashes or brows, in everyday life their opaque darkness expressed
nothing but an ultimate dissimulation. But when she was alone with her
looking glass they expressed a ravenous bewilderment. Brusquely she
threw off the bedclothes. Because her breasts were ageing, she slept
in a black lace brassière. Her body appeared in the looking glass, still
pure in line, long, supple, lustreless, like the body of a slim Chinese
girl, 'like the Chinese slaves in the brothels at Harbin.' Her dry palms
followed the curve of her hips. She admired herself: 'My belly is tight
and cruel . . .' On the mount of Venus there was only an arid tuft;
below, the secret folds were sad and taut, like a forsaken mouth . . .
Towards those folds her hand glided, while her body arched, her eyes
clouded, the mirror expanded, became full of vague presences. She
caressed herself gently. Above her, in a loathsome emptiness, floated
the forms of men mingled with the forms of very young women
brutally possessed. Her own tranced face—the eyes half closed, the

mouth open—rose before her for an instant. 'Ah, I am beautiful, ah, I . . .' A violent trembling shook her from head to foot, and in it she sank into her solitude. 'Ah, when will I have . . .' The telephone squeaked. It was old Popov's insipid mumbling:

'My con-con-gratulations . . . The investigation has made a great step . . . Now, Comrade Zvyeryeva, get the Rublev dossier ready for me . . .'

'You shall have it this morning, Comrade Popov.'

For almost ten full years Makeyev's life had consisted in inflicting or swallowing humiliation. The only art of government that he knew was to abolish every objection by repression and humiliation. At first, when some comrade stood on the platform before an ironical audience, struggling to admit his errors of yesterday, to abjure his companions, his friendships, his own thoughts, Makeyev used to feel uncomfortable. 'Son of a bitch,' he would think, 'wouldn't you do better to let them beat you up?' After the arguments of 1927–28, he brought a scorn heavily weighted with mockery to bear on the great veterans who had recanted to avoid being expelled from the Party. In a confused way, he felt that he was called to share their heritage. His monumental scoffing influenced audiences against the militants of 1918, who, suddenly stripped of their haloes, stripped of their power, were seen to humiliate themselves before the Party—and in reality it was before mediocre men and women united by but one preoccupation: discipline. His whole head purple, Makeyev thundered: 'No, it is not enough! Less beating around the bush! Tell us about the criminal agitation you took part in at the factories!' His interruptions—like blows from a blackjack full in the face—contributed largely to opening the path of power before him. He followed it as he had risen to it: persecuting his vanquished comrades; insisting on their repeating—over and over, and each time in blunter and more revolting terms—the same abjurations, because it was the only way left them to withdraw their claims to power (which, it seemed, was always about to fall into their hands, because actually they were free from the errors of the present); insisting that his subordinates should take the responsibility for his own errors, because he, Makeyev, was of more value to the Party than they were; hurrying to humiliate himself in turn, when someone bigger than himself demanded it. Prison plunged him into an animal desperation. In his dark, low cell he was like a steer which the slaughterer's hammer has not hit hard enough. His powerful muscles became flabby, his hairy chest caved in, a beard the colour of weather-beaten straw grew up to his eyes, he became a big, bent *mujik*, round-shouldered, with sad and timid eyes . . . Time passed, Makeyev was forgotten, no one answered his protestations of loyalty. He himself did not dare to claim an innocence which was as imprudent as it was doubtful, if not more so. The reality of the outside world came to an end, he could no longer picture his wife to himself, even at the moments when a sexual frenzy seized him and prostrated him on his cot, his flesh throbbing, an edge of foam in the corners of his mouth . . . When his questioning began, he felt a great relief. Everything would come out all right, it was only a broken career, it couldn't call for more than a few years in an Arctic concentration camp, and even there you can show that you are zealous, that you have a sense of organization, there are rewards to be won . . . There are women too . . . He was called upon to agree that he had carried the May directives too far and, on the other hand, had consciously neglected to apply those of September; to admit that he was responsible for the decrease in sown fields in the region; to admit that he had appointed to the agricultural directorate officials who had since been sentenced as counter-revolutionaries (he had denounced them himself); to admit that he had diverted for his personal use, specifically for the purchase of furniture, monies earmarked for a Rest House for Agricultural Workers . . . The point was arguable, but he did not argue, he agreed, it was all true, it could be true, it must be true . . . as you see, comrades, if the Party demands it, I am more than ready to take everything on myself . . . A good sign: none of the accusations rated capital punishment. He was allowed to read old illustrated magazines.

Wakened one night from the deepest of sleep, led to his interrogation by a different route—lifts, courtyards, well-lighted basements—Makeyev suddenly found himself facing new dangers. A terrible severity made everything clear:

'Makeyev, you admit that it was you who organized the famine in the district which the Central Committee entrusted to you . . .'

Makeyev made a sign of assent. But the formula was startlingly disquieting—it was reminiscent of recent trials . . . But what else could they ask of him? Of what could he reasonably accuse himself if not of that? No one at Kurgansk would doubt his guilt. And the Political Bureau would be freed of responsibility.

'The time has come for you to make us a fuller confession. What you are hiding from us shows what an indomitable enemy of the Party you have become. We know everything. We have proof of everything, Makeyev, irrefutable proof. Your accomplices have confessed. Tell us what part you played in the plot which cost the life of Comrade Tulayev . . .'

Makeyev bowed his head—or, more precisely, his strength failed him and his head dropped on his chest. His shoulders sagged, as if, while he had listened to the examiner's words, the very substance of his body had drained away. A black hole, a black hole before him, a vault, a grave, and there was nothing more he could say. He could neither speak nor move, he stared stupidly at the polished floor.

'Answer to the accusation, Makeyev! . . . Do you feel ill?'

If they had beaten him they could have got nothing from him, his big body appeared to have no more substance than a sack of rags. He was led away, doctored; a shave gave him back something of his usual appearance. He talked to himself ceaselessly. His head looked like a skull—high, conical, with prominent jawbones and carnivorous teeth. One night when he had recovered from the first nervous shock, he was led out to be questioned again. He walked totteringly, his heart sank, what little strength he had left failed him the nearer he came to the door . . .

'Makeyev, we have an overwhelming deposition against you in the Tulayev case—your wife's statement . . .'

'Impossible.'

The curiously unreal image of the woman who had been real to him in another life, one of those former lives which had become unreal, brought a flash of firmness into his face. His teeth gleamed balefully.

'Impossible. Or else she is lying because you have tortured her.'

'It is not for you to accuse us, criminal. You still deny the charge?'

'I deny it.'

'Then listen and be abashed. When you learned that Comrade Tulayev had been assassinated, you exclaimed that you had expected it, that it served him right, that it was he, and not you, who had organized the famine in the district . . . I have your actual words, do I need to read them to you? Is it true?'

'It is false,' Makeyev murmured. 'It is all false.'

And the memory emerged mysteriously from his inner darkness. Alia, her face miserably swollen from crying . . . She held the queen of hearts in a trembling hand, she was shouting, but her wheezy breath-less voice could hardly be heard: 'And you, traitor and liar, when will someone kill you?' What could she have thought, what could they have suggested to her, the poor simpleton? Was she denouncing him to save him or to ruin him?

'It is true,' he said. 'I ought to explain to you that it is more false than true, false, false . . .'

'That would be wholly useless, Makeyev. If you have the remotest chance of salvation, it lies in a complete and sincere confession . . .'

The urgent memory of his wife had revived him. He became like himself again, grew sarcastic:

'Like the others, you mean?'

'To what are you alluding, Makeyev? What is it that you presume to think, counter-revolutionary Makeyev, traitor to the Party, murderer of the Party?'

'Nothing.'

Again he collapsed.

'In any case, this may be your last interrogation. It may be your last day. A decision may be reached this very evening, Makeyev—did you hear me? Take the prisoner back to his cell.'

. . . At Kurgansk the man was taken from the prison in a van. Some-times he was informed of his sentence, sometimes he was left in doubt —and that was better, because occasionally men who had no doubts left had to be carried, tied, helped along, gagged. The others walked like broken-down automatons, but they walked. A few miles from the station, at a place where the tracks make a shining curve under the stars, the van stopped. The man was led towards the underbrush . . . Makeyev attended the execution of four railwaymen who had stolen parcel-post packages. Traffic was being disorganized by such larcenies. At the regional Committee, Makeyev had demanded capital punish-ment for the proletarians turned brigands. The bastards! He held a grudge against them for forcing him into a hideous severity. The four still hoped for a transfer. 'They won't dare shoot workers for so little . . .' seven thousand roubles' worth of merchandise . . . Their last hope vanished in the underbrush, under an ugly yellow moon whose sickly light filtered through little leaves. Standing at a turn in the path, Makeyev watched to see how the men would behave. The first walked straight on, his head held high, his step firm, charging forward towards the open grave ('the stuff of a revolutionary . . .'). The second stumbled over roots, jerked epileptically, hung his head—he looked as if he were plunged in deep thought, but when he came nearer Makeyev saw that, for all his fifty years, the man was crying silently. The third was like a drunken man with sudden intervals of clearheadedness. He dragged along, then ran a few steps (they were going in single file, followed by several men with rifles). The last, a lad of twenty, had to be supported. He recognized Makeyev, fell to his knees, and cried: 'Comrade Makeyev, beloved father, pardon us, have mercy on us, we are workers . . .' Makeyev sprang back, his foot struck a root, he felt a stab of pain, the silent soldiers dragged the boy on . . . At that moment the first of the four turned his head and said calmly, in a voice perfectly distinct in the moonlit silence: 'Keep quiet, Sacha, they are not men any more, they are hyenas . . . We ought to spit in his dirty face . . .' Four reports, quite close together, reached Makeyev in his car. A cloud darkened the moon, the driver almost drove the car into the ditch. Makeyev went straight to bed, put his arms around his sleeping wife, and lay so for a long time, his eyes open on darkness. Alia's warmth and her regular breathing calmed him. Since it was easy for him not to think he was able to escape from himself. The next morning, seeing a brief notice of the execution in the paper, he was almost glad to feel that he was 'an iron Bolshevik' . . .

Makeyev lived but little by his memories; rather, his memories lived a life of their own, an insidious and awkward life, in him. That one had appeared on the luminous screen of consciousness while he was being led towards his cell, towards . . . And, horribly, it brings another with it: In those days, Makeyev felt that he belonged to a different race from that of men who walked such paths at night, under the yellow moon, towards graves dug by soldiers of the Special Battalion. No conceivable event could cast him down from the summits of power, make him in turn one of the disinherited. Even disgraces would leave him in the files of the Central Committee. Nothing short of expulsion from the Party, and that was impossible . . . He was loyal, body and soul! Adaptable, too, and he knew very well that the Central Committee was always right, that the Political Bureau was always right, that the Chief was always right, because might is right; the errors of power compel recognition, become Truth; just pay the overhead, and a wrong solution becomes the right solution . . . In the little lift cage Makeyev was pressed against the wall by the massive torso of a non-commissioned officer who might be forty and who looked like him—

that is to say, who looked like the Makeyev of former days. The same rugged head and chin, the same stubborn eyes, the same broad shoulders. (But neither of them was aware of the resemblance at the time.) The guard fixed his prisoner with an anonymous eye. Man-pincers, man-revolver, man-password, man-might—and Makeyev was in the power of such men, from henceforth he belonged to the other race . . . He had a momentary vision of himself walking through a wood, under a patchwork of yellow moonlight and leaf shadows, with rifles following him at the ready . . . And the same man was waiting for Makeyev at a turn in the path, he was dressed in leather, his hands were in his pockets; and when Makeyev should be no more, the same man would go calmly home and climb into a wide, warm bed, beside a sleeping woman with burning breasts . . . The same man, or another, but with the same anonymous eyes, would come for Makeyev, perhaps that very night . . .

Yet another sombre image rose from the past. At the Party club a new film in honour of Soviet aviation, *Aerograd*, was being shown. In the Siberian forest, in the Far East, bearded peasants who had been Red partisans were standing up against Japanese agents . . . There were two old trappers who were like brothers, and one of them discovered that the other was a traitor. Face to face under the great grim trees, in the murmuring taiga, the patriot disarmed the traitor: 'Walk ahead!' The other walked, bent towards the ground, feeling himself sentenced to death. Again and again, the two almost identical faces alternated on the screen—the face of an old bearded man, stricken with terror, and the face of his comrade, his like, who had judged him, who cried to him: 'Prepare yourself! In the name of the Soviet people . . .' and who raised his carbine . . . Around them the maternal forest, the inescapable forest. Close-up: the enormous face of the guilty man baying at death . . . It disappeared at last in the welcome roar of a shot. Makeyev gave the signal for applause . . . The lift stopped, Makeyev would have liked to bay at death. Yet he walked uprightly enough. When he reached his cell he sent for a sheet of paper. Wrote:

'I cease all resistance in the face of the Party. I am ready to sign a complete and sincere confession . . .'

Signed it: *Makeyev*. The *M* was still strong, the other letters looked crushed.

Kiril Rublev refused to answer his examiners' questions. ('If they need me, they will give in. If they only intend to get rid of me, I am shortening the formalities . . .') A high official came to inquire into his demands. 'I do not wish to be treated worse in a Socialist prison than in a prison under the old régime . . . After all, citizen, I am one of the founders of the Soviet State.' (As he spoke, he thought: 'I am being ironical despite myself . . . Integral humour . . .') 'I want books and paper . . .' He was given books from the prison library and note-books with numbered pages . . . 'Now, leave me in peace for three weeks . . .' He needed the time to clarify his thought. A man feels singularly free when all is lost, he can at last think in a strictly objective fashion—to the extent, that is, to which he overcomes the fear which, in a living being, is a primordial force comparable to the sex instinct . . . Both the instinct and the force are almost insurmountable; it is a matter of inner training. Nothing more to lose. A few gymnastic exercises in the morning: naked, loose-limbed, sharp-faced, he found it amusing to imitate the supple movement of the reaper in the wheat field—the upper body and both arms swinging vigorously forward and to the side. Then he walked a little, thinking; sat down and wrote. Interrupted himself to meditate on another theme: on death, from the only rational point of view, that of the natural sciences: a field of poppies. The thought of Dora often tormented him, more often than it ought. 'We had been prepared for so long, Dora . . .' All her life, all their life, their real life, seventeen years, since the hardships and enthusiasms of the Revolution, Dora had been strong, under a defenceless gentleness, a scrupulous gentleness that was full of hesitancies and doubts. There are plants like that, plants which under their delicate tracery of leaves have such a resistance and vitality that they survive storms, that, seeing them, we divine the existence of a true and admirable strength entirely different from the mixture of instantaneous ardour and brutality which is commonly called strength. Kiril talked to Dora as if she had been present. They knew each other so well, they had so many thoughts in common, that when he wrote she sometimes foresaw the sentence or the page that was to follow. 'I thought you would go on like that, Kiril,' she would say; and looking up, he would see her, pale and pretty, her hair brushed away from her forehead and drawn into tresses that lay piled above either temple. 'Why, you're absolutely right!' he would marvel. 'How well you read me, Dora!' In the joy of their mutual understanding they sometimes kissed each other over his manuscripts. Those were the days of the

Cold, of the Typhoid, of the Famine, of the Terror, of the War
Fronts which were always being broken through but which never quite
gave in, the days of Lenin and Trotsky, the good days. 'What luck if
we had died together then, Dora!' This conversation between them
took place fifteen years later, when they were struggling in the grip of
nightmare as suffocating miners struggle in a doomed mine. 'We even
missed the chance, you remember: you had typhoid, and one day the
bullets made a perfect half-circle around me . . .'—'I was delirious,'
said Dora, 'I was delirious and I saw everything, I understood everything, I had the key to things, and it was I who kept the bullets from
your head by moving my hand, and I touched your hair . . . My
hallucination was so real that I almost believed it, Kiril. Afterward I
had a terrible period of doubt—what was I good for if I could not keep
the bullets away from you, had I a right to love you more than the
Revolution, for I knew very well that I loved you more than anything
in the world, that if you disappeared I could not go on living, even for
the Revolution . . . And you scolded me when I told you, you talked to
me so well in my delirium, that was the first time I came to really know
you . . .' Kiril put both his hands on Dora's hips and looked into her
eyes; they smiled only with their eyes now, and they were very pale,
very much older, very much troubled. 'Have I changed much since?'
he asked in a strangely young voice. 'You are amazingly the same,'
Dora answered, stroking his cheeks. 'Amazingly . . . But as for me,
who have always told myself that you must go on living because the
world would be a lesser place if you were not in it, and that I must go
on living with you . . . I begin to believe that we missed that chance to
die, really I do . . . Perhaps there are whole periods when, for men of a
certain kind, it is no longer worth while to live . . .' Kiril answered
slowly: 'Whole periods, you say? You are right. But since, in the
present state of our knowledge, no one can foresee the duration or the
succession of periods, and since we must try to be present at the
moment when history needs us . . .' He would have talked like that in
his course on 'Chartism and the Development of Capitalism in England' . . . Now he squeezed into the right-hand corner of his cell,
directly against the wall; and, raising his Ivan the Terrible profile
towards the window at the precise angle which allowed him to see a
lozenge of sky a foot square, he murmured: 'Well, Dora, well, Dora,
now the end has come . . .'

His manuscript progressed. In a swift hand, a little unsteady at the beginning of each day's first paragraph, but firm after twenty lines, he went over the history of the last fifteen years, wasting no words, with the concision of an economist, quoted figures from the secret statistics (the correct ones), analysed the decisions and acts of those in power. He achieved a terrifying objectivity, which spared nothing. The confused battles for the democratization of the Party; the first debates of the Communist Academy on the subject of industrialization; the real figures on goods shortages, on the value of the rouble, on wages; the growing tension of the relations between the rural masses, a weakling industry, and the State; the N.E.P. crisis; the effects of the world crisis on Soviet economy, shut up within its own borders; the gold crisis; the solutions imposed by a power which was at once far-sighted (in matters of danger which threatened it directly) and blinded by its instinct for self-preservation; the degeneration of the Party, the end of its intellectual life; the birth of the authoritarian system; the beginnings of collectivization, conceived as an expedient to avoid the bankruptcy of the directing group; the famine which spread over the country like a leprosy . . . Rublev knew the minutes of the meetings of the Political Bureau, he quoted the most forbidden passages from them (passages probably now destroyed); he showed the General Secretary daily encroaching upon all powers; he followed the intrigue in the lobbies of the Central Committee; against it as a background, the figure of the Chief began to appear, still hesitantly, between resignation, arrest, the violent scene at the end of which two equally pale members of the P.B. faced each other among the overturned chairs and one said: 'I will kill myself so that my corpse will denounce you! But as for you, the *mujiks* will rip your guts out one day, and more power to them—but the country, the Revolution . . .' And the other, his face closed as the grave, murmured: 'Calm yourself, Nicolas Ivanovich. If you will accept my resignation I tender it . . .' It was not accepted, there were no more successors.

When he had written page after page, written freely, as he had not written for more than ten years, Kiril Rublev would walk up and down his cell, smoking. 'Well, Dora, what do you think of it?' Dora invisibly turned over the written sheets. 'Good,' she said. 'Firm and clear. Yourself. Go on, Kiril.' Then he returned to that other necessary meditation, his meditation on the poppy field.

Early morning. A field of red flowers on a gentle slope, undulating like flesh. Each flower is a flame, and so frail that a mere touch makes the petals fall. How many flowers are there? Impossible to count them. Every instant one withers, another opens. If you were to cut down the tallest ones, those that had made the best growth—whether because they sprang from more vigorous seed or because they had found some elements unequally distributed through the soil—neither the appearance nor the nature nor the future of the field would be changed. Shall I give a name, shall I vow a love, to one flower among them all? It seems to be a fact that each flower exists in itself, is unique and solitary in its particular kind, different from all the others, and that, once destroyed, that flower will never be born again . . . It seems so, but are we sure? From instant to instant, the flower changes, it ceases to be like itself, something in it dies and is reborn. The flower of this instant is no longer the flower of the instant before. Is the difference between its successive selves, in time, really less than the present difference between itself and many others which closely resemble it, which are perhaps what it was an hour before, what it will be an hour hence?

A rigorous investigation thus abolished in reverie the boundaries between the momentary and the enduring, the individual and the species, the concrete and the conceptual, life and death. Death was completely absorbed into that marvellous field of poppies, sprung perhaps from a mass grave, perhaps fed by decomposed human flesh . . . A different and vaster problem. Studying it, would one not likewise see the boundaries between species abolished? 'But that would no longer be scientific,' Rublev answered himself, who considered that, outside of purely experimental syntheses, philosophy does not exist or is only 'the theoretical mask of an idealism which is theological in origin.'

As he was brave, lyrical, and a little tired of living, the poppies helped him to grow accustomed to a death which was not far distant, and which had been the death of so many of his comrades that it was no longer strange or too terrifying. Besides, he knew that men were seldom executed while an investigation was in process. So the threat— or the hope—was not immediate. When he should have to go to sleep with the thought of being waked only to be shot, his nerves would undergo another trial . . . (But weren't there executions in the day-time too?)

Zvyeryeva sent for him. She tried to give the examination the tone of a familiar conversation.

'You're writing, Comrade Rublev?'

'Yes, I am writing.'

'A message to the Central Committee, I take it?'

'Not exactly. I don't really know whether we still have a Central Committee in the sense in which we used the term in the old Party.'

Zvyeryeva was surprised. Everything that was known about Kiril Rublev suggested that he was 'in line,' docile—not without inward reservations—disciplined; and inward reservations strengthen acceptances in practice. The investigation was in danger of failing.

'I don't quite understand you, Comrade Rublev. You know, I believe, what the Party expects of you?'

Prison had made the less change in his appearance because he had always worn a beard. He did not look depressed, though he looked tired: dark circles under his eyes. The face of a vigorous saint, with a big bony nose, such as are to be seen in certain icons of the Novgorod school. Zvyeryeva tried to decipher him. He spoke calmly:

'The Party . . . I know more or less what is expected of me . . . But what Party? What is now called the Party has changed so much . . . But you certainly cannot understand me . . .'

'And why, Comrade Rublev, should you think that I cannot understand you? On the contrary, I . . .'

'Don't go on,' Rublev interrupted. 'What is on your tongue is an official phrase that no longer means anything . . . I mean to say that you and I probably belong to different human species. I say it without the slightest animosity, I assure you.'

What might be offensive in his remark was lessened by his objective tone and the polite look he gave her.

'May I ask you, Comrade Rublev, what you are writing, and to whom, and for what purpose?'

Rublev shook his head and smiled, as if one of his students had asked him an intentionally embarrassing question.

'Comrade Examining Judge, I am thinking of writing a study on the machine-smashing movement in England at the beginning of the nineteenth century . . . Please don't protest, I am seriously thinking of it.'

He waited to see what effect his joke would produce. Zvyeryeva was observing him too. Small, shrewd eyes.

'I am writing for the future. One day the archives will open. Perhaps my memorial will be found in them. The work of the historians who are studying our period will thereby be lightened. I regard that as much more important than what you are probably commissioned to ask me . . . Now, citizen, permit me to ask a question in turn: Of what, precisely, am I accused?'

'You will learn that before long. Are you satisfied with your living conditions? The food?'

'Passable. Sometimes not enough sugar in the preserves. But many Soviet proletarians, who are accused of nothing, are less well fed than you and I are, citizen.'

Zvyeryeva said dryly:

'The session is over.'

Rublev returned to his cell in excellent humour. 'I sent that hideous cat running, Dora. If one had to explain oneself to such creatures . . . Let them send me someone better, or let them shoot me without any explanations . . .' The field of poppies appeared on a distant slope, through a veil of rain. 'My poor Dora . . . Am I not even now tearing their entire scaffolding down?' Dora would be glad. She would say: 'I am certain that I shall not survive you long, Kiril. Show me the way.'

Rublev did not always turn around when the door opened. This time, after he had distinctly heard the door close, he had the feeling of a presence behind him. He went on writing—he did not intend to let his nerves get the better of him.

'Good day, Rublev,' said a drawling voice.

It was Popov. Grey cap, old overcoat, bulging brief bag under his arm, just the same as ever. (They had not seen each other for years.)

'Good day, Popov, sit down.'

Rublev gave him the chair, closed his notebook, which lay open on the table, and stretched out on the bed. Popov examined the cell—bare, yellow, stifling, surrounded by silence. He obviously found it unpleasant.

'Well, well,' said Rublev, 'so they've locked you up too! Welcome, brother, you have more than deserved it.'

He laughed to himself, heartily. Popov threw his cap on the table, dropped his overcoat, spat several times into a grey handkerchief. 'Toothache. The devil take . . . But you are mistaken, Rublev, I have not been arrested yet . . .'

Rublev flung his two long legs into the air in a jubilant caper. And, talking to himself and laughing uncontrollably: 'Old Popov said *not yet. Not yet!* Freud would give three roubles spot cash for that *lapsus linguae* . . . Seriously, Popov, did you hear yourself say *not yet? Not yet!*'

'I said *not yet?*' Popov stammered. 'Not yet what? What can it matter? What do you mean by . . . by picking on words like that? What is that I am *not yet?*'

'. . . arrested, arrested, arrested, not yet arrested!' Rublev cried, with wild mockery in his eyes, in the reddish tangle of his eyebrows, in his bristling beard.

Wall, window with dirty panes, iron grating . . . Popov stared at them stupidly. This insane reception staggered him. He let silence grow between them until it became almost uncomfortable. Rublev crossed his arms under his neck.

'Rublev, I have come to decide your fate with you. We expect much of you . . . We know what an intensely critical mind you have . . . but we know too that you are loyal to the Party . . . The men of the older generation, like myself, know you . . . I have brought you some documents . . . Read them . . . We have confidence in you . . . Only, if you don't mind, let's change places—I'd rather lie down . . . My health, you know—rheumatism, myocarditis, polyneuritis, et cetera . . . You're lucky to be healthy, Rublev . . .'

Spilled water spreads, but the very obstacles it encounters give it a definite outline. So Popov regained the advantage. They changed places, Popov lay down on the cot, and he really looked like a sick old man—his teeth grey, his skin muddy, his few strands of hair a sorry white and absurdly ruffled. 'Will you hand me my brief bag, please, Rublev? You don't mind if I smoke?' He extracted a sheaf of papers from his bag. 'There, read those . . . Don't hurry . . . We have plenty of time . . . It is serious, everything is extremely serious.' His short sentences ended in little coughs. Rublev settled down to read. *Résumé of the reports of the military attachés at . . . Report on the construction of strategic roads in Poland . . . Fuel Reserves . . . The London Conversations . . .* Long minutes passed.

'War?' said Rublev at last, wholly serious.

'Very probably war, next year . . . mmmm . . . Did you see the figures on transport?'

'Yes.'

'We still have a slight chance of shifting the war towards the West . . .'

'Not for long.'

'Not for long . . .'

They discussed the danger as if one of them were calling on the other at his house. How long would it take to mobilize? Cover troops? There would have to be a second oil refinery, in the Far East, and the Komsomolsk road system would have to be developed at top speed. Was the new railroad in Yakutia really finished? How did it stand up under winter conditions?

'We count on the probability of extremely high troop losses . . .' said Popov in a clear voice. 'All those young fellows . . .' thought Rublev. He had always enjoyed watching parades of athletes; his eyes, as he walked through the streets, would follow the strapping young men from different parts of Russia: Siberians with broad noses and horizontal eyes set deep under stern foreheads, Asiatics with broad, flat faces, and certain Mongols with delicate features, products of fine races civilized long before white civilization. Their young women went through life with them, shoulder to shoulder (he was perhaps visualizing these images from recollections of films), and all together they moved through crumbling cities, under the bombers; and our new square reinforced-concrete buildings, the work of so many famished proletarians, became burning skeletons, and all those young men, all those young women, millions of them, splattered with blood, filled hideous pits, hospital trains, ambulances stinking of gangrene and chloroform—we shall certainly have a shortage of anæsthetics . . . Slowly, there in the hospitals, they continued their transformation into corpses . . . 'I must stop thinking in images,' he said, 'it becomes unbearable.'

'Unbearable indeed,' Popov answered.

Rublev nearly cried out: 'You still here! What are you doing here?'

But Popov attacked first:

'We count on losses which may reach several millions of men during the first year . . . That is why . . . mmmm . . . the Political Bureau has adopted the . . . mmm . . . unpopular measure . . . forbidding abortion . . . Millions of women are suffering under it . . . We no longer count in anything less than millions . . . We must have millions of children, and have them now, to replace the millions of young men who will perish . . . mmmm . . . and you, meanwhile, sit here writing . . . may the devil take . . . take what you are writing, Rublev . . .

mmmm . . . and all this paltry business of your resisting the Party . . .
Knee and jaw at once . . .'

'What jaw?'

'The upper . . . Pain here, pain there . . . Rublev, the Party asks
you, the Party orders you . . . *I* am not the Party.'

'Asks what? Orders what?'

'You know as well as I do . . . It is not for me to go into details . . .
You can arrange things with the examining judges . . . they know the
scenario . . . that's what they're paid for . . . mmm . . . some of them
even believe it, the young ones, the stupid ones . . . mmm . . . they're
the most useful . . . I pity the suspects who fall into their clutches . . .
mmm . . . You still resist? . . . You'll be made to stand up in front
of a roomful of people—all the diplomats, the official spies, the foreign
correspondents, the ones we pay, the ones who are on more than one
payroll, the scum of the earth, all hungry for just that, you will be put
in front of the microphone, and you'll say, for example, that you are
morally responsible for the assassination of Comrade Tulayev . . .
That, or something else . . . mmm . . . how should I know what?
You will say it because the Prosecutor, Rachevsky, will make you say
it, word by word and not once but ten times over . . . mmm . . . he's
patient, Rachevsky, like a mule . . . a filthy mule . . . You will say
whatever they want you to say, because you know the situation . . .
because you have no choice: obey or betray . . . Or we will call upon
you to stand in front of the same microphone and dishonour the
Supreme Tribunal, the Party, the Chief, the U.S.S.R.—everything at
once, to proclaim . . . the devil take me . . . my knee . . . to proclaim
what you call your innocence . . . and what a pretty spectacle your
innocence will make at that moment! . . .'

It had grown dark. Rublev walked up and down his cell in silence.
The voice that sometimes rose out of Popov's mutterings, sometimes
was lost in them, showered him with little muddy words; he did not
hear them all, but he had the feeling that he was walking on spit, and
little grey splatterings of spit kept raining around him, and there was
nothing to say in answer, or what he could say in answer was of no
use . . . 'And it is on the eve of war, in this hour of danger, that you
have destroyed the cadres of the country, decapitated the army, the
Party, industry—you immitigable idiots and criminals . . .' If he cried
that, Popov would answer: 'My knee . . . mmm . . . perhaps you are
right, but what good does it do you to be right? It is we who are the

power, and even we can do nothing about it. You are being asked for your own head now; and you aren't going to announce the fact before the international *bourgeoisie*, are you? Even to avenge your precious little head, which will soon be cracked open like a nut . . . mmmm . . .'
A despicable person—but what way was there out of this infernal circle, what way?

Dressed in an old tunic and shapeless trousers, his hands crossed on his chest, Popov continued his monologue, with short pauses. Rublev stopped beside him as if he were seeing him for the first time. And now he addressed him in the familiar form—sadly at first:

'Popov, old man, you look like Lenin . . . It is striking . . . Don't move, let your hands stay just as they are . . . Not like Ilich alive, not a bit . . . You look like his embalmed body . . . the way a rag doll looks like a living being . . .' He studied him with an attention that was at once dreamy and intense. 'You look like him in grey crumbling stone, or after the fashion of a sow bug . . . the bumps on your fore-head, your miserable little beard, poor, poor old man . . .'

There was sincere pity in his voice. On his side, Popov was watching him with the most intense attention. Rublev read something in his eyes which was at once veiled and unmistakable: danger.

'. . . poor bastard that you are, poor old wreck . . . Cynical and foul-smelling . . . Ah!'

With a look of despairing disgust, Rublev turned away and went to the door. The cell seemed too small for him. He thought aloud:

'And this graveyard maggot has brought me word of the war . . .'

Popov's muttering and spluttering began behind him again—spite-fully perhaps?

'Ilich said that there's always some use around a house for a cleaning rag . . . mmmm . . . a slightly dirty rag, naturally, since it is in the nature of cleaning rags to be slightly dirty . . . I am willing . . . I am no individualist . . . mmmm . . . It is written in the Bible that a living dog is better than a dead lion . . .'

Popov rose, put away the papers he had brought, and laboriously got into his overcoat. Rublev stood with his hands in his pockets, not offer-ing to help him. He murmured, for himself:

'Living dog, or plague-bearing, half-dead rat?'

Popov had to pass in front of him to get the guard to open the door. They did not take leave of each other. Before he crossed the threshold, Popov shoved his cap on his head with a quick gesture, visor tilted up

and at a slight angle. At seventeen, just before his first taste of prison
in the days of the first revolutionary enthusiasm, he had enjoyed giving
himself the same sort of underworld air. Framed in the metal doorway,
he turned, his chest brushing against the square double tooth of the
lock, and looked straight at Rublev with eyes that were clear and still
vigorous.

'Good-bye, Rublev. I don't need your answer . . . I know what I
needed to know . . . mmmm . . . Basically, we understand each other
perfectly . . .' He lowered his voice because of the uniforms outside
the door. 'It is hard, certainly . . . mmmm . . . for me too . . . But . . .
mmm . . . the Party has confidence in you . . .'

'Go to hell!'

Popov took two strides back into the cell and, without any stammer-
ing, as if the hideous fog of his life had cleared around him, asked:

'What answer shall I take from you to the Central Committee?'

And Rublev, erect too, said firmly:

'That I have lived my whole life only for the Party. Sick and
degraded though it may be, our Party. That I have neither thought nor
conscience outside of the Party. That I am loyal to the Party, whatever
it may be, whatever it may do. That if I must perish, crushed by my
Party, I consent . . . But that I warn the villains who are killing us that
they are killing the Party . . .'

'Good-bye, Comrade Rublev.'

The door closed, the well-oiled bolt slipped gently into the socket.
The darkness was almost complete. Rublev rained smashing blows on
the sepulchral door. Muffled steps hurried along the corridor, the
wicket opened.

'What is it, citizen?'

Rublev thought that he roared, but actually his voice was only an
angry breath:

'Turn on the light!'

'Sh . . . sh . . . There you are, citizen.' The electric bulb went
on.

Rublev shook the pillow on which his visitor's head had left a
hollow. 'He is unspeakable, Dora, he is filthy. It would be a pleasure to
drop him over a cliff, into a well, into a black abyss, provided that he
would stay under forever and neither his cap nor his brief bag would
float to the surface of any water ever again . . . One would go away
afterward with a feeling of relief, the night air would seem purer . . .

Dora, Dora . . .' But—as Rublev very well knew—it was Popov's flabby hands which were pushing *him* insidiously towards the black abyss . . . 'Dialectics of the relation between social forces in periods of reaction . . .'

THE BRINK OF NOTHING

DEPORTEE RYZHIK presented insoluble problems to numerous offices. What could one think of an engine driver who had escaped unscathed from thirty telescoped locomotives? Of his fellow combatants, not one had survived. Prison had providentially protected him for over ten years, from 1928 on. A series of pure chances, such as save a single soldier out of a destroyed battalion, kept him out of the way of the great trials, of the secret investigations, and even of the 'prison conspiracy'! At time of the latter, Ryzhik was living absolutely alone, under surveillance from the highest quarters, on a kolkhoze in the middle Yenisei; during the progress of the investigation, which should have disclosed him to be a political witness of the most dangerous sort, one of those who are instantly inculpated because of their moral solidarity with the guilty, he was in solitary confinement near the Black Sea, under absolutely secret orders! Yet his dossier left the directors of purges with no excuse. But the very outrageousness of his situation saved him, from the moment when prudence advised not paying too much attention to him for fear of involving too many people in responsibility. The offices finally became accustomed to this strange case; certain heads of bureaus began obscurely to feel that the old Trotskyist was under some high and secret protection. They had vaguely heard of similar cases, precedents.

Through Prosecutor Rachevsky, the Acting High Commissar for Security, Gordeyev, and Popov (delegated by the Central Committee to supervise 'judicial inquiries into the most serious cases'), the Bureaus received an order to add to the dossier of the Erchov-Makeyev-Rublev case (assassination of Comrade Tulayev) that of an influential Trotskyist (which meant a genuine Trotskyist), whatever his attitude might be. Rachevsky, contrary to Fleischman's opinion, held that to make the case more convincing to foreigners, one of the accused might this time be allowed to deny all guilt. The Prosecutor undertook to confound him by testimony which could easily be worked up. Popov casually added that the verdict might take into consideration the doubt raised by his denials, it would produce a good effect, if the Political Bureau considered it worth while. Zvyeryeva volunteered to bring together the secondary testimony which would overwhelm the denials of the as yet unknown defendant. 'We have such a mass of material,' she said, 'and the conspiracy had so many ramifications, that no resistance is possible. The guilt of these counter-revolutionary vermin is collective . . .' A search of the files brought to light a number of dossiers, only one of which perfectly suited the end in view: Ryzhik's. Popov studied it with the caution of an expert faced with an infernal machine of unknown construction. The successive accidents which explained the survival of the old Oppositionist were revealed to him in their strict concatenation. Ryzhik: erstwhile worker in the Hendrikson Pipe and Tube Works, St. Petersburg, member of the Party since 1906, deported to the Lena in 1914, returned from Siberia in April 1917; had several conversations with Lenin immediately after the conference of April '17; member of the Petrograd Committee during the Civil War; defended the Workers' Opposition before the Petrograd Committee in '20, but did not vote for it. Commissar of a division during the march on Warsaw, worked at that time with Smilga, of the C.C., Rakovsky, head of the government of Ukrainia, Tukhachevsky, commandant of the army, three enemies of the people too tardily punished in 1937 . . . expelled from the Party in '27, arrested in '28, deported to Minusinsk, Siberia, in July '29, condemned by the secret collegium of Security to three years of penal internment, sent to the isolator of Tobolsk, there became the leader of the so-called 'Intransigents' tendency, which published a manuscript magazine entitled *The Leninist* (four issues attached). In 1932, the secret collegium gave him an additional sentence of two years (upon decision of the Political Bureau), to which he answered: 'Ten years if it amuses you, for I very much doubt if you will remain in power more than six months with your blind starvation policy.' Author, during this same period, of an 'Open Letter on the Famine and the Terror,' addressed to the C.C. Refuted the theory of state capitalism and maintained that of Soviet bonapartism. Liberated in '34 after an eighteen-day hunger strike. Deported to Chernoe, arrested at Chernoe with Elkin, Kostrov, and others (the 'deportees' Trotskyist centre' cases). Transferred to Butirky prison, Moscow, refused to answer questions, went on two hunger strikes, transferred to the special infirmary (cardiac deficiency) . . . 'To be deported to the most distant regions . . . No letters . . .' More than a hundred names appeared in the 244 pages of the dossier and they were the terrifying names of men cut down by the sword of the Party. Sixty-six—a bad age, either the will stiffens for the last time or it suddenly collapses. Popov decided: 'Have him transferred to Moscow . . . See that he travels under good conditions . . .' Rachevsky and Gordeyev answered:

'Certainly.'

Incomparable dawns rose for Ryzhik from the profound indifference of desert lands. He lived in the last of the five houses which made up the hamlet of Dyra (Dirty Hole), at the junction of two icy rivers lost in solitude. The houses were built of unhewn logs which had come down in the spring drives. The landscape had neither bounds nor landmarks. At first, when he still wrote letters, Ryzhik had named the place the Brink of Nothing . . . He felt that he was at the extreme limit of the human world, at the very verge of an immense tomb. Most of the letters he wrote never reached any destination, of course, and none came from anywhere. To write from here was to shout into emptiness —which he sometimes did, to hear his own voice; and the sound of it intoxicated him with such violent grief that he would begin yelling insults at the triumphant counter-revolution: 'Criminals! Drinkers of proletarian blood! Thermidorians!' The stony plain sent him back only a vague, murmuring echo, but birds of which he had been unaware flew up in terror and their panic spread from one to another until the whole sky was alive with them—and Ryzhik's absurd rage dissolved, he began swinging his arms in circles, trotted straight ahead until he had to stop for lack of breath, his heart beating violently, his eyes moist.

There in Dyra five families of fishermen—Old Believers, of Great Russian ancestry, but more than half adjusted to Ostiak ways of life— wore out a destiny from which there was no escape. The men were stocky and bearded, the women squat, with flat faces, bad teeth, small bright eyes under heavy lids. They spoke little, laughed not at all, they smelled of fish fat, they worked unhurriedly, cleaning the nets which their grandfathers had brought in the days of the Emperor Alexander, drying fish, preparing tasteless foods for the winter months, weaving wickerwork, mending faded clothes made of cloth from the previous century. From the end of September, a bleak whiteness blanketed the flat landscape to the horizon.

Ryzhik shared the house of a childless couple, who disliked him because he never crossed himself, pretending not to see the icon. So taciturn were these two dull-eyed beings that a silence as of an unfertile field seemed to emanate from them. They lived in the smoke from a dilapidated stove, fed by scrawny brushwood. Ryzhik occupied a nook which had a tiny dormer window three-quarters covered over with boards and stuffed with rags, because most of the glass was gone. Ryzhik's chief treasure was a small cast-iron stove, which had been left by some previous deportee. The chimney ran to one of the upper corners of the window. Thus Ryzhik could have a little fire, provided that he would get wood for it himself in the coppice on the other side of the Bezdolnya ('the Forsaken') and two miles upstream. Another envied treasure was his clock, which people sometimes came from the neighbouring houses to see. When a Nyenets hunter crossed those plains, the people explained to him that there was a man living among them who was being punished, and that he owned a machine that made time, a machine that sang all by itself, without ever stopping, sang for invisible time. And in fact the obstinate nibbling of the clock devoured a silence as of eternity. Ryzhik loved it, having lived almost a year without it, in pure time, pure motionless madness, earlier than creation. To escape from the silent house, Ryzhik would set off across the waste. Whitish rocks broke the soil; the eye clung hungrily to the few puny, bristling shrubs, part rust-coloured, part an acid green. Ryzhik would shout to them: 'Time does not exist! Nothing exists!' Space, beyond the limits of human time, swallowed the small, unusual sound of his voice—not even the birds were frightened. Perhaps there were no birds beyond time? On the occasion of a great Socialist victory, the Yeniseisk colony of deportees succeeded in sending him presents, among which he found a concealed message: 'To you whose fidelity is a pattern to us all, to you, one of the last survivors of the Old Guard, to you who have lived only for the cause of the international proletariat . . .' The carton also contained unbelievable treasures: three ounces of tea and the little clock, procurable for ten roubles in city co-operatives. That it gained an hour in twenty-four when he forgot to hang his penknife on the weight that made it run, was really of no importance. But Ryzhik and Pakhomov never tired of their joke. It consisted in one of them asking the other: 'What time is it?' 'Four . . .' 'With or without the penknife?'—'With the clog,' Ryzhik once answered very seriously, for he had been reading last month's *Pravda*. Bearing their half century of masterless servitude, Ryzhik's host and his wife—he stroking his rough beard, she with her hands clasped in her sleeves—had come to look at the wonder and they had spoken in its presence, saying only one word, but a profound word, risen from the depths of their souls (and how had they come to know that word?):

'Beautiful,' he said, shaking his head.

'Beautiful,' his wife repeated.

'When the two hands are here,' Ryzhik explained to them, 'in the daytime it means that it's noon, at night it means that it's midnight.'

'By God's grace,' said the man.

'By God's grace,' said the woman.

They crossed themselves and left, shuffling awkwardly, like a pair of penguins.

As Pakhomov was in Security, he lived in the most comfortable room (requisitioned) in the best of the five houses. It stood two-thirds of a mile away, in front of the hamlet's three fir trees. The only representative of the government in a region almost as extensive as a state of old Europe, he was decidedly well off: among his possessions were a sofa, a samovar, a chess-board, an accordion, some odd volumes of Lenin, last month's papers, tobacco, vodka. What more does a man need? Leo Nikolayevich Tolstoy, although a nobleman and a mystic (that is to say, benighted), carefully calculated just how much ground a man, with all his avidity, required: A little short of six feet long, by sixteen inches wide, by a yard deep, for a shipshape grave . . . 'Right?' Pakhomov would ask, sure of assent. He had a wry humour, in which there was nothing malicious. If, coming to the end of the snowy track that led to the house on which a sign: POST OFFICE—CO-OPERATIVE hung askew, he saw a tired team—reindeer or shaggy horses—he joked with them fondly: 'Be glad you're alive, you are useful creatures!' Deputed to watch Ryzhik, he had conceived a reserved but warm affection for his deportee, an affection which kindled a timid little light in his prying eyes. He would say to him: 'Orders are orders, brother. We do as the service tells us. We are not expected to understand, all we have to do is obey. Me—I'm a very small man. The Party is the Party, it is not for me to judge men of your stamp. I have a conscience, a very small conscience, because man is an animal that has a conscience. I can see that you are pure. I can see that you are dying for the world Revolution, and if you are wrong, if it doesn't come, if Socialism has to be built in a single country with our little bones, then, naturally, you are dangerous, you have to be isolated, that's all, and here we are, in this backwater that might as well be the North Pole, each doing his duty—and, as long as I have to be here, I am glad I'm here with you.' He never got thoroughly drunk, perhaps to keep alert, perhaps out of respect for Ryzhik, who, because he dreaded arteriosclerosis, drank little—just enough to keep his courage up. Ryzhik explained it to Pakhomov: 'I want to be able to think for a while yet.' 'Quite right,' said Pakhomov. Tired of the bare walls of his lodging, Ryzhik often took refuge in his guardian's room. Pakhomov's face always wore an expression of suspicious humility, as if his features and his wrinkles had frozen at a moment when he wanted to cry and would not let himself. His complexion was reddish and rough, his eyes russet, his nose flat and turned up; he never quite smiled, his lips opened on rusty stumps of teeth. 'Like some music?' he asked when Ryzhik had stretched out on the sofa. 'Have a swallow of vodka . . .' Before he drank, Ryzhik munched a pickled cucumber. 'Play.' Pakhomov drew heart-rending wails from his accordion, and also bright notes that made one want to dance. 'Listen to this, it's for the girls back home!' He dedicated his passionate music to the girls of a faraway region. 'Dance, girls, dance again! Come on, Mafa, Nadia, Tania, Varia, Tanka, Vassilissa, dance, little golden-eyes! Hip-hop, hip-hop!' The room filled with movement, with joyous phantoms, with nostalgia. Next door, bowed in their perpetual semi-darkness, an old woman untangled fish nets with rheumatic fingers, a young woman with a round Ostiak face full of an animal gentleness busied herself at the fire; the little girls left their work to hold each other awkwardly and spin around between the table and the stove; the black-bearded face of St. Vasili, lit from above by a little lamp, sternly judged the strange joy which yet had made its entrance there without sin . . . Through the old woman's hands, through the young woman's hands, the blood flowed with new vigour, but neither said a word, there was more discomfort than anything else in the feeling. In the fenced yard, the reindeer raised their heads, fear was born in their glassy eyes. And suddenly they began running from fir tree to fir tree, from the trees

to the house. Endless white space absorbed the magical music.—Ryzhik
listened with a colourless smile. Pakhomov drew the fullest tones from
his instrument, as if he wanted to send one yet stronger cry, and yet
another, into emptiness—and having drawn it forth, he flung his
instrument on the bed. Silence fell implacably, like a weight, on space,
the reindeer, the house, the women, the children. (The old woman,
mending broken cords on her knees, asked herself if his music did not
come of the Evil One? For a long time her lips continued to move,
repeating an exorcism, but she had forgotten why.)

'The world will be a good place to live in, in a hundred years,'
Pakhomov once said at such a moment.

'A hundred years?' Ryzhik calculated. 'I'm not sure a hundred years
will be enough.'

From time to time they took guns and went hunting on the farther
side of the Bezdolnya. The landscape was strangely simple. Rounded
and almost white rocks rose out of the ground in groups, as far as the
eye could see. You vaguely felt that they were a people of giants surprised by a flood, frozen and petrified. Dwarfed trees spread their
slender network of branches. To find themselves lost after an hour's
tramping and climbing would have been easy. It was difficult to
manage skis, and they encountered few animals, and those few were
wary, hard to surprise, they had to run them down, track them, lie in
wait for them for hours, lying half buried in the snow. The two men
passed a flask of vodka back and forth. Ryzhik stared admiringly at the
pale blue sky. At times he would even say to his companion, inexplicably: 'Look at that sky, brother. It will soon be full of black stars.'

The words brought them together again after a long silence; Pakhomov felt no surprise. He said:

'Yes, brother. The Great Bear and the Pole Star will be black. Yes.
I've seen just that in a dream.'

There was nothing more they could say to each other, even with
their eyes. Frozen stiff, after an exhausting journey, they brought
down a flame-coloured fox, and the dead beast's slim muzzle, contorted in a feminine rictus as it lay on the snow, made them uncomfortable. They did not express their feeling. Joylessly they started
back. Two hours later, as they glided down a white slope in the livid
twilight towards the red ball of the sun, Pakhomov let Ryzhik catch up
with him. His expression showed that he had something to say. He
murmured:

'Man is an evil beast, brother.'

Ryzhik forged ahead without answering. The skis bore him through a sort of irreality. More hours passed. Their weariness became terrible, Ryzhik was on the verge of collapse, the cold crept into his guts. In his turn, he let his companion catch up with him, and said:

'Nevertheless, brother . . .'

He had to gather strength to finish his sentence, he had almost no breath left:

'. . . we will transform man.'

At the same moment he thought: 'This has been my last hunt. Too old. Farewell, beasts that I shall not kill. You are one of the fascinating and cruel faces of life, and life is passing away. What must be done will be done by others. Farewell.'

Ryzhik spent several days lying on his furs by the warm stove, under the nibbling clock. Pakhomov came to keep him company. They played cards—an elementary game which consisted in cheating. Pakhomov usually won. 'Of course,' he said. 'I have a low streak in me.' So life passed during the long, nocturnal winter. The reddish ball of the sun dragged along the horizon. Mail arrived by sleigh once a month. A little ahead of schedule, Pakhomov wrote reports for his superiors on the deportee under his surveillance. 'What am I to write them about you, old man?'—'Write them,' said Ryzhik, 'that I consign the bureaucratic counter-revolution to hell.'

'They know that already,' Pakhomov answered. 'But you ought not to tell me about it. I am doing my duty. There's no call for you to make me angry.'

The day always comes when things end. No one can predict it, though everyone knows that come it must. The silence, the whiteness, the eternal North, will go on endlessly, that is to say until the end of the world—and perhaps even after that, who knows? But Pakhomov came into the hovel where Ryzhik sat rereading old newspapers in a nightmare as diffuse as a fog. Redder than usual, the Security man, beard twisted, eyes sparkling:

'We're leaving here, old man. We're through with this dirty hole. Get your stuff together. I have orders to take you to the city. We're in luck.'

Ryzhik turned a petrified face towards him, with eyes that were terribly cold.

'What's the matter?' Pakhomov asked kindly. 'Aren't you glad?'

Ryzhik shrugged his shoulders. Glad? Glad to die? Here or somewhere else? He felt that there was hardly enough strength left in him for change, for struggle, for the mere thought of struggle; that he no longer genuinely felt fear or hope or defiance, that his courage had become a sort of inertia . . .

The five households watched them set out on a day of low-hanging clouds pierced by feeble glimmers of silver. The universe seemed forgotten. The smallest children, muffled in furs, were brought out in their mothers' arms. Thirty short figures dotted the dull whiteness around the sleigh. The men gave advice and looked to see that the reindeer were properly harnessed. Now that they were about to vanish, Pakhomov and Ryzhik became more real than they had been the day before; discovering them roused a slight emotion. It was as if they were going to die. They were setting off for the unknown, one guarding the other, for freedom or for prison, God alone knew. Eyno, the Nyenets, the Samoyed, who had come for furs and fish, took them in his sleigh. Dressed in wolf-skins, his face bony and brown, with slit eyes and scanty beard, he looked like a Mongol Christ. Green and red ribbons decorated his boots, his gloves, his cap. He pushed the last yellow strands of his beard carefully into his collar, studied the whole extent of the heavens and the earth in one sweeping look, roused the reindeer with a click of his tongue. Ryzhik and Pakhomov stretched out side by side, wrapped in furs. They carried a store of dried bread, dried fish, vodka, matches, and alcohol in tablet form to make a fire. The reindeer gave a little leap and stopped. 'Go with God!' said someone. Pakhomov answered, with a laugh: 'Our kind gets along better without.'

Ryzhik shook all the hands that were held out to him. They were of all ages. There were old hands, rough and calloused, strong hands, tiny hands, delicately formed. 'Good-bye, good-bye, comrades!' Men and women who did not love him said: 'Good-bye, Comrade Ryzhik, a good journey to you!' and they looked at him with new, kindly eyes. The new eyes followed the sleigh all the way to the horizon. The reindeer leaped forward into space; a sleeping forest appeared in the distance, recognizable by its purplish shadows. Above, the sky cleared in silvery lacework. Eyno leaned forward, watching his animals. A haze of snow surrounded the sleigh, shimmering with rainbows.

'It's good to get away,' Pakhomov repeated joyously. 'I've had my bellyful of this hole. I can't wait to see a city!'

Ryzhik was thinking that the people of Dyra probably would never get away. That he himself would never return here, nor to Chernoe, nor to the cities he had known, nor, above all, to the days of strength and victory. There are moments in life when a man may hope everything, even in the depths of defeat. He lives behind the bars of a county jail, and he knows that the Revolution is coming; that, under the gallows, the world lies before him. The future is inexhaustible. Once a solitary man has exhausted his future, every departure becomes the last. Almost at the end of his journey—his cross-checkings made it clear enough. His mind had long been made up, he felt himself available. The chill in his stomach bothered him. He drank a swallow of vodka, covered his face with furs, and gave himself up to torpor, then to sleep.

He did not wake again until night. The sleigh was gliding swiftly over the nothingness which was the world. The night had a greenish transparency. In the sky reigned stars which as they twinkled changed from lightning blue to a soft glacial green. They filled the sky; he felt that convulsions raged beneath their apparent immobility, that they were ready to fall, ready to burst on the earth in tremendous flames. They enchanted the silence; the snow-crystal world reflected their infinitesimal and sovereign light. The one absolute truth was in them. The plain undulated, the barely visible horizon heaved like a sea and the stars caressed it. Eyno kept watch, crouched forward; his shoulders swayed to the rhythm of their journey, to the rhythm of the revolving world; they hid and then revealed entire constellations. Ryzhik saw that his companion was not asleep either. His eyes open as never before, his eyeballs glinting gold, he breathed in the magical phosphorescence of the night.

'Everything all right, Pakhomov?'

'Yes. I'm fine. I don't regret anything. It's marvellous.'

'Marvellous.'

The gliding sleigh lulled them in a common warmth. A slight chill stung their lips and nostrils. Freed of weight, of boredom, of nightmare, freed of themselves, they floated in the luminous night. The least stars, those that they had thought almost invisible, were perfect; and each was inexpressibly unique, though it had neither name nor form in the vast glitter.

'I feel as if I were drunk,' Pakhomov murmured.

'My head is clear,' Ryzhik answered, 'and it's exactly the same thing.'

He thought: 'It is the universe that is clear.' It lasted several minutes or several hours. Around the brightest stars appeared huge shining circles, visibly immaterial. 'We are beyond substance,' murmured one. 'Beyond joy,' murmured another. The reindeer trotted briskly over the snow; it looked as if they were hurrying to meet the stars on the horizon. The sleigh sped dizzily down slopes, then climbed again with a vigour that was like a song. Pakhomov and Ryzhik fell asleep, and the wonder continued in their dreams, continued when they woke to find dawn breaking. Pillars of pearly light rose to the zenith. Ryzhik remembered that in his dream he had felt himself dying. It had been neither frightening nor bitter, it was as simple as the end of night; and all lights, the brightness of the stars, the brightness of suns, the brightness of Northern Lights, the more remote brightness of love, continued to pour endlessly down upon the world, nothing was really lost. Pakhomov turned to him and said, strangely:

'Ryzhik, brother, there are the cities . . . It is incomprehensible.'

And Ryzhik answered: 'There are the executioners,' just at the moment when unknown colours flooded the sky.

'Why do you insult me?' asked Pakhomov, after a long silence during which the sky and the earth became one sheet of white.

'I was not thinking of you, brother, I was only thinking of the truth,' said Ryzhik.

It seemed to him that Pakhomov was weeping without tears, his face almost black, although they were being carried through an unbelievable whiteness. If it is your black soul, poor Pakhomov, rising into your face, let it suffer from the cold daylight, and if it dies, die with it— what have you to lose?

They made a halt under the high red sun, to drink tea, stretch their legs, and let the reindeer search for their diet of moss under the snow. After lighting the stove and bringing the kettle to a boil, Pakhomov suddenly squared up as if to fight. Ryzhik stood before him, legs apart, hands in his pockets, straight, firm, silently happy.

'How do you know, Comrade Ryzhik, that I have that yellow envelope?'

'What yellow envelope?'

Looking straight into each other's eyes, alone in the midst of the magnificent wilderness, in the cold, the light, with the good hot tea they were about to share, they could tell no lies . . . Thirty paces away, they heard Eyno talking to his team. Perhaps he was humming.

'Then you don't know?' asked Pakhomov blankly.

'Are you going out of your head, brother?'

They drank tea in little sips. The liquid sunshine flooded through them. Pakhomov spoke heavily:

'The yellow secret-service envelope—it is sewed into my tunic. I put that tunic under me when I go to sleep. I have never been parted from it. The yellow envelope—it is there against my chest . . . I wasn't told what's in it, I haven't the right to open it except if I receive an order in writing or code . . . But I know that it contains the order to shoot you . . . You understand—in case of mobilization, in case of counter-revolution, if the powers decide that you must not go on living . . . It has often kept me awake, that envelope. I thought of it when we drank together . . . When I watched you starting off towards the Bezdolnya for firewood . . . When I played gipsy songs to you . . . When a black dot appeared on the horizon, I said to myself, "The damned mail, what is it bringing me, small man that I am?" You understand, I'm a man who does his duty. Now I've told you.'

'I never even thought of it,' said Ryzhik. 'Though I certainly should have suspected it.'

They played a strange game of chess. Little by little, the chess-board was buried under a dust of beautifully wrought crystals. Ryzhik and Pakhomov strode up and down on the rock, which at that point had only a light covering of snow. Their boots left rounded marks in it, like the prints of gigantic beasts. They moved a piece, and walked away, thinking or dreaming, drawn by horizons which, a few minutes later, they would renounce. Eyno came and crouched by the board, playing both sides in his mind at once. His face had a look of concentration, his lips moved. Slowly the reindeer came wandering back, from far away, and they too looked on with their great opaque eyes, watching the mysterious game, until miniature snow squalls, trailing along the ground, finally buried it in crystal whiteness. The black and white chessmen had ceased to exist except in the abstract, but through the abstract the small, strict powers of the mind continued their combat. Pakhomov lost, as usual, full of admiration for Ryzhik's ingenious strategy.

'It is not my fault if I won,' Ryzhik said to him. 'You have a lot to lose yet, before you will understand.'

Pakhomov did not answer.

The dazzling journey brought them to landscapes covered with

starved bushes. Blotches of green grass emerged from the snow. The
same emotion seized all three men when they saw in the grass the ruts
of a wagon road. Eyno muttered an incantation against bad luck. The
reindeer began to trot jerkily. The sky was dull, a leaden sky.

Ryzhik felt his sadness return, the sadness which was the texture of
his life and which he despised. Eyno left them at a kolkhoze where they
procured horses. Life there must have been a picture in earthy colours,
washed over by the dawns which poured azure on the world. The roads
wandered away into woods filled with birds. Brooks ran through singing coppices; the light was reflected from the water-spangled soil, rock,
and roots. They forded rivers on which clouds floated. They travelled
through this region in peasant carts, whose drivers hardly ever spoke a
word and, full of suspicion, came out of their torpor only when they
had drunk a little vodka. Then they hummed endless songs.

Parting came to Ryzhik and Pakhomov in the single street of a
straggling market town, among large dark houses standing well apart,
on the threshold of the building which housed both the Soviet and
Security, a wood-and-brick building with broad shutters. 'Well,' said
Pakhomov, 'our journey together is over. I have orders to turn you
over to the Security post. The railroad is only about sixty miles from
here. I wish you luck, brother. Don't hold a grudge against me.'
Ryzhik pretended an interest in the street, in order not to hear the last
words. They clasped hands. 'Good-bye, Comrade Pakhomov, I wish
you understanding, dangerous though it be . . .' In the Security office
two young fellows in uniform were playing dominoes on a dirty table.
The unlighted stove sent out a wretched chill. One of the two glanced
at the papers which Pakhomov had brought. 'State criminal,' he said to
his companion, and both of them looked at Ryzhik hostilely. Ryzhik
felt the white hair on his temples bristle, an aggressive smile uncovered
his purplish gums, and he said:

'You can read, I suppose. That means: Old Bolshevik, faithful to
Lenin's work.'

'An old story. Plenty of enemies of the people have used the same
camouflage. Come, citizen.'

Without another word, they led him to a small dark room at the end
of the hall, closed the door on him, and padlocked it. It was hardly
more than a cupboard, it stank of cat urine, the air was heavy with
mould. But from behind the wooden wall came children's voices.
Ryzhik heard them with delight. He made himself as comfortable as

possible, his back against the wall, his legs stretched out. His old tired flesh groaned despite itself and wished that it could lie down on clean straw . . . A little girl's voice, refreshing as a trickle of water over the rocks of the taiga, came from the other side of the world, solemnly reading Nekrassov's *Uncle Vlass*, no doubt to other children:

'*With his bottomless sorrow—tall, straight, his face tanned—old Vlass walks unhurried—through cities and villages.*

'*Far places call him, he goes—he has seen Moscow, our mother—the sweep of the Caspian—and the imperial Neva.*

'*He goes, carrying the Sacred Book—he goes, talking to himself—he goes and his iron-shod stick—makes a little sound on the ground.*'

'I have seen all that too,' Ryzhik thought. 'Trudge on, old Vlass, we are not through trudging . . . Only, our sacred books are not the same . . .'

And, before he sank under weariness and discouragement, he remembered another line of Nekrassov's: 'Oh my Muse, scourged to blood . . .'

Nothing but worry and work, these transfers! There are no prisons within the Arctic Circle; jails appear with civilization. District Soviets sometimes have at their disposal an abandoned house that no one wants because it has brought people bad luck or because it would need too much repairing to make it habitable. The windows are boarded up with old planks on which you can still read TAHAK-TRUST, and they let in wind, cold, dampness, the abominable blood-sucking midges. There are almost always one or two wrong letters in the chalked inscription on the door: RURAL PRISON. Sometimes the tumble-down hovel bristles with barbed wire; and when it lodges an assassin, an escaped prisoner who wears glasses and has been recaptured in the forest, a horse thief, the director of a kolkhoze the order for whose arrest came from a high source, the door is guarded by a sentry, a Young Communist of seventeen—preferably one who is good for nothing—with an old rifle slung from his shoulder—a rifle which is good for nothing either, be it understood . . . On the other hand, there are freight cars armoured with scrap iron and big nails; excrement has dribbled under the door; they are shabbily sinister; they have the look of an old, disinterred coffin . . . The extraordinary thing is that you can always hear sounds coming from them—the groaning of sick men, vague moans, even songs! Are they never emptied? They never reach the end of their journey. It would take forest fires, showers of meteors, cities overthrown, to abolish their kind . . . Through a green path which the white bark of birches brightened like laughter, two naked sabres conducted Ryzhik towards one of these cars, which stood on a siding among fir trees. Ryzhik laboriously climbed in, and the rickety door was padlocked behind him. His heart was pounding from the effort he had made; the semi-darkness, the stench which was like a fox's earth, stifled him. He stumbled over bodies, groped for the opposite wall with both hands outstretched, found it by the light from a crack, through which he could see the peaceful bluish landscape of firs, stowed his sack, and crouched in stale straw. He became aware of movement around him, saw a score of young, bony faces supported by half-naked, emaciated bodies. 'Ah,' said Ryzhik, recovering his breath. 'Greetings, *chpana*! Greetings, comrade tramps!' And he began by making a well-calculated statement of principles to the children of the roads, the oldest of whom might be sixteen: 'If anything disappears from my bag, I'll bloody the noses of the first two of you I can lay my hands on. I'm like that—nothing mean about me. Be that as it may, I have six pounds of dry bread, three cans of meat, two smoked herrings, and some sugar—government rations—which we will share fraternally but with discipline. The watchword is "conscious"!' The twenty ragged children smacked their tongues joyously before giving a feeble 'Hurrah!' 'My last ovation,' thought Ryzhik. 'At least it's sincere . . .' The children's shaven skulls were like the heads of plucked birds. Some of them had scars that went down to the bone; a sort of fever burned in them all. They sat down in an orderly circle, to talk to the enigmatic old man. Several began delousing themselves. They crunched the lice between their teeth, Kirghiz fashion, muttering: 'You eat me and I eat you'—which is said to comfort the soul. They were being sent to the regional Tribunal for having looted the commissary of a penal 'colony for rehabilitation through work.' They had been travelling in the same car for twelve days, the first six without ever getting out of it, and had been fed nine times. 'We used to relieve ourselves under the door, Uncle, but at Slavianka an inspector came by, our delegates complained to him in the name of hygiene and the new life, so now they come and let us out twice a day . . . No danger that we'll escape into a forest as thick as this one—did you see it?' The same inspector—an ace—had got them fed immediately. 'Except for him, some of us would be dead, sure thing. Must have been through the same mill himself, he looked like an old hand—otherwise it would never have happened . . .' They looked forward to the prison to which they were bound as to salvation, but they wouldn't get there in much less than a week, because of the munitions trains that had to be let by . . . a modern prison, with heat, clothes, radios, cinema, baths twice a month, if you could believe what you heard. It was worth the trip, and the older ones, once they had been sentenced, might have the luck to stay there.

A ray of moonlight fell through the slit in the roof. It fell on bony shoulders, was reflected in human eyes that were like the eyes of wildcats. Ryzhik portioned out some of his dry bread and divided two herrings into seventeen pieces. He could hear the children's mouths salivating. The joy of the feast brightened the beautiful moonbeam. 'How good I feel!' exclaimed the one who was called 'the Evangelist' because he had been adopted for a time by Baptist or Mennonite peasants (then they had been deported themselves). He purred with satisfaction, lying stretched out at full length on the floor. The ashy light touched only the top of his forehead; below, Ryzhik saw his little dark eyes gleaming. The Evangelist told a good transfer story: Grichathe-Pockmarked, a little boy from Tyumen, died just like that, without a word, rolled up in his corner. Nobody cared until he began to stink, and they decided to keep it quiet as long as possible so that they could share his rations. The fourth day they couldn't stand it any longer—but they'd had that much more to eat—talk about a show! . . .

Kot-the-Tomcat, the Pimp—face tilted up, mouth open, showing carnivorous teeth—studied Ryzhik benevolently and almost guessed: 'Uncle, you an engineer or an enemy of the people?'

'And what do you call an enemy of the people?'

Answers began coming out of an embarrassed silence. 'Men that derail trains . . . The Mikado's agents . . . The people that start fires underground in the Donetz . . . Kirov's assassins . . . They poisoned Maxim Gorki . . .'—'I knew one once—president of a kolkhoze, he killed the horses by putting spells on them . . . He knew a trick to bring drought . . .'—'I knew one too, a rat, he was head of the penal colony, he sold our rations in the market . . .'—'Me too, me too . . .' They all knew wretches who were responsible, enemies of the people, robbers, torturers, fomenters of famines, despoilers of prisoners—it's right to shoot them, shooting's not bad enough for them, they ought to have their eyes put out first, be emasculated with a bit of string, the way the Koreans do, 'I'd make them do some telegraphing, I would! A bit of a buttonhole right here—see, Murlyka?—in the middle of his belly and you get hold of his guts, they unwind like a spool of thread, you hook them onto the ceiling, there are yards of them, more than you know what to do with, and the man squirms around and you tell him the best thing he can do is telegraph to his fools of a father and mother, may the devil roast them . . .' The invigorating thought of torture aroused them all, made them forget Ryzhik, the pale, square-jawed old man, whose face grew hard as he listened.

'Little brothers,' Ryzhik said at last, 'I'm an old partisan from the days of the Civil War, and I tell you I have seen much innocent blood spilled . . .'

From the darkness, through which the shaft of moonlight pierced like a dagger, a discordant chorus answered him: 'Innocent blood, you're right about that . . .' They had known plenty of bastards, but they had known even more victims. And sometimes the bastards were victims too—what could you make of it all? They discussed it late into the night, until the moonbeam withdrew into the innocent sky—but principally among themselves, because Ryzhik lay down with his head on his sack and fell asleep. Bony bodies huddled against him. 'You're big, you have clothes on, you stay warm . . .' The slumber of the moon-drenched forest finally impregnated the old man and the grown-up children with such vast quiet that it seemed to cure all ills.

Ryzhik shunted from prison to prison, so tired that he could no longer think. 'I am a stone carried along by a dirty flood . . .' Where did his will-power end, where did his indifference begin? At certain dark moments he was so weak that he could have wept: This is what it means to be old, your strength goes, your mind flickers like the yellow lanterns trainmen carry up and down the tracks at unknown stations . . . His sore gums indicated the beginning of scurvy, his joints ached, after resting he could hardly straighten up his tall body, it was so stiff with rheumatism. Ten minutes of walking exhausted him. Shut up in a huge barracks with fifty human spectres, some of whom were peasants (officially: 'special colonists'), others old offenders, he felt almost glad when his fur cap and his sack were stolen. In the sack was the clock from the brink of silence. Ryzhik came out of there with his hands in his pockets and his head bare, bitterly erect. Perhaps he was no longer waiting for anything but the chance to spit his disgust for the last time into the face of some anonymous sub-torturer who was not worth the effort? Perhaps he had lost even that useless passion? Police, jailers, examiners, high officials—all climbers who had climbed aboard at the eleventh hour, ignorant, their heads stuffed with printed formulas—what did they know about the Revolution, had they ever known anything about it? Between him and their kind, no common language remained. And anything written vanished into secret files which would never open until the earth, shaken to its bowels, should gape under the palatial government buildings. What use would anyone have for the last cry of the last Oppositionist, crushed ur.der the machine like a rabbit under a tank? He dreamed stupidly of a bed with sheets, a quilt, a pillow for his head—such things existed. What has our civilization invented that is better? Socialism itself will not improve the modern bed. To lie down, to fall asleep, never to wake again . . . The rest are all dead, all of them, all of them! How much time will this country need before our new proletariat begins to become conscious of itself? Impossible to force it into maturity. You can't hurry the germination of seeds under the ground. You can kill it, though . . . Yet (reassuring thought!) you can't kill it everywhere or kill it always or kill it completely . . .

He was tormented by lice. In the glass doors of railroad carriages he saw himself looking exactly like an old tramp still in fairly vigorous health. Now he was in a third-class compartment, surrounded by a non-commissioned officer and several soldiers in heavy boots. It was pleasant to see people again. But people hardly noticed him—'You see so many prisoners.' This one might be a great criminal, since he was so heavily escorted, yet he didn't look it, could he be a believer, a priest, a man under persecution? A peasant woman with a child in her arms asked the noncom for permission to give the prisoner some milk and a few eggs, because he looked ill—'in a Christian spirit, citizen.'—'It is strictly forbidden, citizen,' said the soldier. 'Go along, citizen, or I'll have you put off the train . . .'—'Thank you a thousand times, citizen,' said Ryzhik to the peasant woman, in a strong deep voice which made every head in the corridor turn. The noncom, blushing crimson, intervened: 'Citizen, you are strictly forbidden to speak to anyone . . .'

'To hell with that,' Ryzhik said quietly.

'Shut up!'

One of the soldiers, who was lying in the upper berth, dropped a blanket over him. A great pushing and tussling followed, and when Ryzhik got rid of the blanket he saw that the corridor had been cleared. Three soldiers blocked the compartment doorway. They were looking at him with rage and terror. Across from him, the noncom intently watched his every movement, ready to fling himself on him to gag him, to manacle him (even to kill him?)—anything to prevent him from uttering another word.

'Idiot,' said Ryzhik, looking straight at him. He felt no anger—only a desire to laugh, which was overcome by nausea.

Calmly, his elbows resting on the window sill, he watched the fields fly past. Grey and sterile they looked at first, but they were not really so, for soon he could see the first green shoots of wheat. As far as the horizon, and beyond it, the plains were sown with seeds of vegetable gold, weak but invincible. Towards evening, smoke-stacks appeared in the distance, belching black smoke. A big factory was alight with concentrated red flame. He was in the Ural industrial district. He recognized the outlines of mountains. 'I came through here on horseback in 1921, it was a wilderness . . . What an accomplishment!' The little local prison was clean, well lighted, painted sea green like a hospital. Ryzhik took a bath, was given clean linen, cigarettes, a passably good hot meal . . . His body felt small pleasures of its own, independently of his mind —the pleasure of swallowing hot soup and finding the flavour of onion in it, the pleasure of being washed clean, the pleasure of stretching itself comfortably on the new mattress . . . 'Now,' murmured his mind, 'we are back in Europe, it's the last lap . . .' A great surprise awaited him. The dimly lighted cell to which he was taken contained two beds, and on one of them a man lay sleeping. The noise of the bolts being opened and closed wakened him. 'Welcome,' he said in a friendly voice.

Ryzhik sat down on the other bed. Through the dimness, the two prisoners looked at each other with instantaneous sympathy. 'Political?' Ryzhik asked. 'Just like yourself, my dear comrade,' replied the man who had been asleep. 'I know already, you see—I've acquired an infallible nose for that sort of thing . . . Isolator—most likely Verkhne-Uralsk or Tobolsk, possibly Suzdal or Yaroslavl? One of the four, I am certain. After that, the Far North. Right?' He was a short man with a little beard; his wrinkled face looked like a baked apple, but was lighted by kindly round owl eyes. His long fingers—the sort of fingers a wizard might have—drummed on the blanket. Ryzhik nodded his assent, though he felt a little hesitant about trusting this stranger. 'The devil take me! How have you managed to keep yourself alive all this time?'

'I really don't know,' said Ryzhik. 'But I don't think I have much time left.'

The other hummed:

> 'Life fleets like the wave,
> Pour me the wine of comfort . . .

'But in fact all this unpleasant business is not as fleeting as they say. Allow me to introduce myself: Makarenko, Boguslav Petrovich, professor of agricultural chemistry at the University of Kharkov, member of the Party since 1922, expelled in '34—Ukrainian deviation—Skrypnik's suicide, and so on . . .'

Ryzhik introduced himself in turn: '. . . former member of the Petrograd Committee, former deputy member of the C.C. . . . Left Opposition . . .' The little man's blankets rose like wings, he jumped out of bed—night-shirt, waxy body, hairy legs. His absurd face puckered with smiles and tears. He waved his arms, embraced Ryzhik, tore himself away from him, came back, finally stood in the middle of the cell jerking like a puppet.

'You! Amazing! Your death was discussed last year in every prison . . . Dead from a hunger strike . . . Your political testament was discussed . . . I read it—not bad at all, although . . . You! I'll be damned! Well, I congratulate you! It's terrific.'

'I *did* go on a hunger strike,' said Ryzhik, 'and changed my mind at the last moment because I believed that the régime would be going into its crisis almost immediately . . . I did not want to desert.'

'Naturally . . . Magnificent! Amazing!'

His eyes misty, Makarenko lit a cigarette, swallowed smoke, coughed, walked up and down the concrete floor barefoot.

'I have had only one other meeting as strange as this. It was in the prison at Kansk. An old Trotskyist—think of it!—on his way from a secret isolator, who knew nothing about the trials, nothing about the executions, who had no suspicions whatever, can you image that? He asked me for news of Zinoviev, of Kamenev, of Bukharin, of Stetsky . . . "Are they writing? Does their stuff get printed in the papers?" At first I said "Yes, yes"—I didn't want to kill him. "What are they writing?" I played dumb—theory is not in my line, and so on ... At last I said to him: "Prepare for a shock, esteemed comrade, and don't think I have gone mad: They are all dead, they were all shot, from the first to the last, and they confessed." "What could they possibly have confessed?" ... He started calling me a liar and a *provocateur*, he even went for my throat—oh God, what a day! A few days later he was shot himself, fortunately, on an order telegraphed from the Centre. I still feel relieved for him when I think of it ... But you—it's amazing!'

'Amazing,' Ryzhik repeated, and leaned against the wall. His head suddenly felt heavy.

He began to shiver. Makarenko wrapped himself in his blanket. His long fingers played with the air.

'Our meeting is absolutely extraordinary ... An inconceivable piece of negligence on the part of the services, a fantastic success commanded by the stars ... the stars which are no longer in their courses. We are living through an apocalypse of Socialism, Comrade Ryzhik ... Why are you alive, why am I—I ask you! Why? Magnificent! Staggering! I wish I might live for a century so that I could understand ...'

'I understand,' said Ryzhik.

'The Left theses, of course ... I am a Marxist too. But shut your eyes for a minute, listen to the earth, listen to your nerves ... Do you think I am talking nonsense?'

'No.'

Ryzhik clearly deciphered the hieroglyphics (perhaps he was the only person in the world to decipher them, and it gave him an agonizing feeling of vertigo)—the hieroglyphics which had been branded with red-hot iron into the very flesh of the country. He knew, almost by heart, the falsified reports of the three great trials; he knew all the available details of the minor trials in Kharkov, Sverdlovsk, Novosibirsk, Tashkent, Krasnoyarsk, trials of which the world had never heard. Between the hundreds of thousands of lines of the published texts, weighted down with innumerable lies, he saw other hieroglyphics, equally bloody but pitilessly clear. And each hieroglyphic was human: a name, a human face with changing expressions, a voice, a portion of living history stretching over a quarter century and more. Such and such an answer of Zinoviev's at the trial in August '37 was connected with a sentence spoken in '32 in the courtyard of an isolator, with a speech full of double meanings (seemingly cowardly, but unyielding with a tortuous, calculating devotion), delivered before the Central Committee in '26; and the thought behind that speech was connected with such and such a declaration by the president of the International, made in '25, with such and such a remark at a dinner in '23 when the democratization of the dictatorship was first being discussed ... Beyond that, the thread of the idea ran back to the Twelfth Congress, to the discussion on the role of syndicates in '20, to the theories of war Communism debated by the Central Committee during the first famine, to differences of opinion just before and just after the insurrection, to brief articles commenting on the theses of Rosa Luxembourg, the objections of Yuri Martov, Bogdanov's heresy ... If he had credited himself with the slightest poetic faculty, Ryzhik would have allowed himself to become intoxicated by the spectacle of that powerful collective brain, that brain which brought together thousands of brains to perform its work during a quarter of a century, now destroyed in a few years by the backlash of its very victory, now perhaps reflected only in his own mind as in a thousand-faceted mirror ... All snuffed out, those brains; all disfigured, those faces, all smeared with blood. Even ideas were swept into a convulsive dance of death, texts suddenly meant the opposite of what they stated, a madness carried away men, books, the history that was supposed to have been made once and for all; and now there was nothing but aberration and buffoonery—one man beating his breast and crying, 'I was paid by Japan,' another moaning, 'I wanted to assassinate the Chief whom I worship,' yet another accompanying a scornful 'Come now!' with a shrug that suddenly opened a hundred windows on an asphyxiated world ... Ryzhik could have produced a set of biographies, with an appendix of documents and photographs, covering the public, private, and ideological lives of five hundred men who had been executed, three hundred who had disappeared. What could a Makarenko add to such a detailed picture? So long as he had retained the slightest hope of surviving usefully, Ryzhik had continued his investigations. From sheer force of habit, he asked questions: 'What happened in the prisons? Whom did you meet? Tell me, Comrade Makarenko ... Give me your story, Comrade Makarenko ...'

'The November seventh and May first celebrations gradually died out during those black years. A deadly certainty lighted the prisons, as with the blaze of salvoes at dawn. You know of the suicides, the hunger strikes, the final, despicable—and useless—betrayals, which were suicides too. Men opened their veins with nails, broke bottles and ate the glass, flung themselves on guards so that they would be shot down . . . you have heard of all that. The custom of calling on the dead in the isolator courtyards. On the eves of the great anniversaries, the comrades formed a circle during the exercise period; a voice hoarse with distress and defiance called out the names, the greatest first, the rest in alphabetical order—and there were names for every letter of the alphabet. And each man present answered in turn: "Dead for the Revolution!" then we would begin singing the hymn to the dead "fallen gloriously in the sacred struggle," but we could not often sing it through because the guards would be summoned and come running like mad dogs; the comrades made a chain to receive them, and so, arm linked in arm, they held together through the scuffle; under the blows and the curses and the icy water from the fire pumps, they went on shouting in rhythm: "Glory be to them, glory be to them!" '

'Enough,' said Ryzhik, 'I can see what came next.'

'These demonstrations died out within eighteen months, although the prisons were more jammed than ever. Those who maintained the tradition of the old struggles disappeared underground or into Kamchatka, we never knew exactly; the few survivors were lost in the new crowds. There were even opposing demonstrations—prisoners shouting, "Long live the Party, long live our Chief, long live the Father of his Country!" It did them no good, they were doused with icy water too.'

'And now the prisons are quiet?'

'They are thinking, Comrade Ryzhik.'

Ryzhik formulated 'theoretical conclusions, the chief thing being not to lose our heads, not to let our Marxist objectivity be perverted by this nightmare.'

'Obviously,' said Makarenko in a tone which perhaps meant exactly the contrary.

'First: Despite its internal regression, our state remains a factor of progress in the world because it constitutes an economic organism which is superior to the old capitalist states. Second: I maintain that, despite the worst appearances, there is no justification for classifying our state with fascist régimes. Terror is not enough to determine the nature of a régime, what is basically significant is property relations. The bureaucracy, dominated by its own political police, is obliged to maintain the economic régime established by the Revolution of

October '17; it can only increase an inequality which, in its own despite, becomes a factor in the education of the masses . . . Third: The old revolutionary proletariat ends with us. A new proletariat, of peasant origin, is developing in new factories. It needs time to reach a certain degree of consciousness and, by its own experience, to over-come the totalitarian education it has received. To fear that war will interrupt its development and liberate the confused counter-revolu-tionary tendencies of the peasantry . . . Do you agree, Makarenko?'

Lying on his bunk, Makarenko nervously tugged at his little beard. His owl eyes were dimly phosphorescent.

'Of course,' he said, 'on the whole . . . Ryzhik, I give you my word of honour that I shall never forget you . . . See here, you must try to get a few hours' sleep . . .'

Awakened at dawn, Ryzhik had a few moments in which to say good-bye to his companion of the night: they kissed each other. A detachment of special troops surrounded Ryzhik in the open truck, so that no one should see him; but there was no one in the street. At the station he found a well-equipped Prisons Service van awaiting him. He surmised that he was probably on the main line to Moscow. The basket of provisions which was put on the seat beside him contained luxurious foods that he had long forgotten—sausage and cream cheese. He could think of little else, because he was very hungry; his strength was ebbing. He decided to eat as little as possible, only enough to sustain himself; and, because he was something of a gourmet, to confine himself to the more delectable and uncommon viands. Lying on the wooden seat amid the clattering of the express train, he savoured them pleasurably and thought, without the least feeling of fear, and indeed with a certain relief, that he was soon to die. It was a restful journey. Of Moscow, Ryzhik saw only a freight station by night. Distant arc lights lit the network of rails, a vague red halo hid the city. The police van travelled through sleeping streets, in which Ryzhik heard only the hum of the motor, drunkards quarrelling drearily, the magical chimes of a clock letting a few musical, shattering notes fall into the silence. 3 a.m. Some indefinable atmosphere enabled him to recognize one of the courtyards of the Butirky prison. He was taken into a small building which had been recently made over and then into a cell painted grey up to six feet from the floor, as cells were painted under the old régime—why? There were sheets on the cots, the electric bulb in the ceiling gave a weak light. It is nothing, it is only the real Brink of Nothing . . .

He was taken to be examined early in the morning. It was only a few steps down the corridor. The doors of the adjoining cells stood open— an unoccupied building. In one of these cells, which was furnished with a table and three chairs, Ryzhik immediately recognized Zvyer-yeva, whom he had known for twenty years, since the days of the Petrograd Cheka, the Kaas plot, the Arkadi case, the Pulkovo battles, the commercial manœuvrings at the beginning of the N.E.P. Hys-terical, crooked to the marrow, devoured by unsatisfied desires, had she outlived so many valiant men? 'I might have known it,' Ryzhik thought. 'The last touch!' It brought a wry smile to his face. He did not greet her. Beside her, a round face with oily, carefully parted hair. 'The dirty bureaucrat who keeps tabs on you, you old whore?' Ryzhik said nothing, sat down, and looked at her calmly.

'You recognize me, I suppose,' said Zvyeryeva quietly, with a sort of sadness.

Shrug.

'I hope that your transfer was effected under not too uncomfortable conditions . . . I had given orders. The Political Bureau does not forget your service records . . .'

Another shrug, but less pronounced.

'We consider your period of deportation finished . . .'

He did not stir. His face became ironical.

'The Party expects you to display a courage which will be your own salvation . . .'

'Aren't you ashamed of yourself?' said Ryzhik with disgust. 'Look at yourself in a mirror to-night—I am sure you will vomit. If it were possible to die of vomiting, you would die . . .'

He had spoken in an undertone: a voice from a tomb. White hair, pale face, shaggy beard—weak as an invalid and hard as an old light-ning-blasted tree. For the baby-faced high official with the pomaded hair, he had only a brief look, a scornful curl of the nostrils.

'I should not allow myself to become angry—you are not worth it. You are below shame. At most, you are worth the proletarian bullet that will shoot you one day if your masters do not liquidate you beforehand, to-morrow for example . . .'

'In your own interest, citizen, I beg you to restrain yourself. Here insult and violence serve no purpose. I am doing my duty. You are

8

charged with a capital crime, I offer you a way to exonerate yourself . . .'

'Enough. Take due note of this: I am irrevocably resolved neither to enter into any conversation with you nor to answer any questions. That is my last word.'

He looked away—at the ceiling, at nothingness. Zvyeryeva put up her hand and patted her hair into place. Gordeyev took out a handsome lacquered cigarette-case, with a design of a troika dashing through snow, and held it out towards Ryzhik:

'You have suffered a great deal, Comrade Ryzhik, we understand you . . .'

His answer was a look so scornful that he lost his composure, pocketed the cigarette-case, looked at Zvyeryeva for help, only to find her as abashed as himself. Ryzhik half smiled at them, calmly insulting.

'We have ways of making the most hardened criminals talk . . .'

Ryzhik spat heavily on the floor, rose, muttered, 'What stinking vermin!' for his own ears, turned his back on them, opened the door, and said to the three waiting special service men: 'Take me to my cell!' and returned to his cell.

No sooner was he gone than Gordeyev took the offensive. 'You should have prepared this examination in advance, Comrade Zvyeryeva.' Thus he declined all responsibility for the set-back. Zvyeryeva stared stupidly at her painted fingernails. Half of the trial swept away? 'With your permission,' she said, 'I will break him. I have no doubt of his guilt. His attitude alone . . .' Her words placed Gordeyev face to face with his responsibility again. 'If you do not give me *carte blanche* to force this man whose confession we must have, it will be you who has scuttled the trial . . .'

'We'll see,' Gordeyev murmured evasively.

Ryzhik threw himself on the cot. He was shaking all over. He could feel his heart beating heavily in his chest. Thoughts in shreds, like rags scorched in a fierce fire, fragments of broken syllogisms whose edges momentarily glittered and hurt, swirled in his brain—yet he felt no need to put them in order. Everything was probed, weighed, concluded, finished. This tempest within him had arisen despite himself. It began to die away when he noticed his daily ration on the table—the black bread, the mess tin of soup, two lumps of sugar . . . He was hungry. Tempted to get up and smell the soup (sour cabbage and fish, no doubt!), he restrained himself. For a moment he felt a desire to eat for the last time, the last time! . . . It would do him good . . . No. Get it over with! It was that act of will which restored him to complete self-control, which brought him to a decision, irrevocably. A stone slides down a slope, reaches the edge of a precipice, drops—there is no comparison between the slight impulse which first set it in motion and the depths to which it falls. Calmed, Ryzhik shut his eyes, to think. Several days would probably pass before these vermin made their intentions clear. How long shall I hold out? At thirty-five, a man can still be somewhat active between the fifteenth and the eighteenth days of a hunger strike, provided that he drinks several glasses of water each day. At sixty-six, in my present condition—chronic undernourishment, fatigue, will to non-resistance—I shall go into the final phase in a week . . . Without water, a hunger strike brings death in from six to ten days, but is extremely difficult to keep up after the third day because of hallucinations. Ryzhik decided to drink in order to suffer less and to keep his mind clear, but to drink as little as possible in order to shorten the process. The great difficulty would be to cheat the vigilance of his guards in the matter of destroying his rations. At all costs he must avoid the loathsome business of forced feeding . . . The flushing apparatus of the toilet worked well; Ryzhik found no difficulty until it came to destroying the bread, which he had to crumble up, and it took a long time, the smell of fermented rye rose into his nostrils, the feeling of that doughy substance which was life itself entered into his fingers, into his nerves. In a few days it would be a trial which his weakening fingers, his overstrained nerves, would find it more and more difficult to surmount. The thought that that filthy creature Zvyeryeva and the vermin with the greased hair had not foreseen this made Ryzhik burst out laughing. (And the guard on duty, who had orders to look at him every ten minutes through the bull's-eye glass in the door, saw his pasty face lit up by a great laugh and instantly transmitted his report to the assistant warden in charge of Corridor II: 'The prisoner in Cell 4 is lying on his back, laughing and talking to himself . . .') Usually a hunger striker remains lying down, since every movement means an expenditure of strength . . . Ryzhik decided to walk as much as he could.

Not an inscription on the freshly repainted walls. Ryzhik sent for the assistant warden and asked for books. 'Presently, citizen.' Later he came back and said: 'You must make your request to the examining judge at your next hearing . . .' 'I shall read no more,' thought Ryzhik, surprised that his farewell to books left him so indifferent. What were needed to-day were books like thunderbolts, full of an irrefutable historical algebra, full of merciless indictments, books which should judge these days, every line of which should breathe implacable intelligence, be printed in pure fire. Such books would be born later. Ryzhik tried to call to mind books which, for him, were connected with his sense of being alive. The greyish newsprint of the papers left him only a memory of insipidity. From a very distant past there came back to him with great intensity the image of a young man stifling in his cell, pulling himself up on the window grating to a position from which he saw three rows of barred windows in a yellow façade, a courtyard in which other prisoners were sawing wood, a beautiful sky which he longed to drink . . . That faraway prisoner (myself, a self which I really don't know if it is alive or dead, a self which is actually more of a stranger to me than many of the men who were shot last year) one day received certain books which made him joyfully renounce the call of the sky— Buckle's *History of Civilization*, and a collection of decorous *Popular Tales* which he looked through with irritation. But towards the middle of the volume the type changed, and it was *Historical Materialism* by G. V. Plekhanov. Until then, he thought, that young man had been nothing but primitive vigour, instincts, trained muscles which effort tempted, he had felt like a colt in the fields; and the sordid street, the workshop, fines, lack of money, worn-out shoes, prison, had held him like a tethered animal. He suddenly discovered a new capacity for living, something inexpressibly greater than what was commonly called life. He read the same pages over and over, pacing up and down his cell, so happy to understand that he wanted to run and shout, that he wrote to Tania: 'Forgive me if I hope I shall stay here long enough to finish these books. At last I know why I love you . . .' What is consciousness? Does it appear in us like a star in the pale twilight sky, invisibly, undeniably? He who, the day before, had lived in a fog now saw the truth. 'It is *that*, it is contact with truth.' Truth was simple, near as a young woman you take in your arms and say 'Darling!' and then you discover her eyes, where light and darkness blend. He possessed truth forever. In November '17 another Ryzhik—yet was it the same?—went to a great printing plant in Vassili-Ostrov with the Red Guard, and requisitioned it in the name of the Party. Before the great machines which produce books and papers he exclaimed: 'Now, comrades, the days of falsehood are done! Mankind will print nothing but the truth!' The owner of the plant, a fat, pale, yellow-lipped gentleman, cruelly put in: 'That, gentlemen, I defy you to do!' and Ryzhik wanted to kill him on the spot, but we were not bringing barbarism, we were putting an end to war and murder, we were bringing proletarian justice. 'We shall see, citizen; in any case, I inform you that there are no more gentlemen, now or henceforth . . .' The man he had been in those days was over forty, a hard age for a worker, but he felt himself an adolescent again: 'Coming into power,' he said, 'has made us all twenty years younger . . .'

The first three days that he spent without food caused him hardly any suffering. Was he not drinking too much water? His hunger was only an intestinal torment, which he appraised with detachment. Headaches forced him to lie down, then they passed off, but attacks of giddiness suddenly sent him staggering to the wall in the midst of his walking. His ears hummed like the sound in a sea shell. He brooded more than he thought, but both his broodings and his thoughts on the subject of death were absurdly superficial. 'A purely negative concept, a minus sign; only life exists . . .' It was obviously true, it was horrifyingly false. The truth and the falsehood were both stupid . . . Lying under the blanket and his heavy winter overcoat, he felt cold. 'It is the warmth of life leaving me . . .' He shivered for a long time, shaking like a leaf in a gale—no, it was more like an electric bell vibrating, ting-ting-ting-ting . . . Great bands of colour, like Northern Lights, filled his eyes; he also saw dark lights fringed with fire: flashes, discs, extinguished planets . . . Perhaps man can glimpse many mysterious things when his cerebral substance begins to disintegrate? Is it not made of the same matter as the worlds? A sumptuous warmth flowed into his limbs, he rose, economizing his movements, to force his aching fingers to crumble the black rye, which must be destroyed, destroyed at all costs, comrades, despite its intoxicating smell.

The day came when he no longer had the strength to get up. His jaws were decomposing, they would burst like an abscess—what a relief, to burst like a great bubble of flesh, a great bubble of transparent soap in which he recognized his face, an absurd, grimacing sun. He laughed. The glands under his ears were swelling, painful as aching teeth . . . A nurse came, addressed him affectionately by the first name he used to have, and he sat up to tell her to go away, but he recognized her: 'You, you, you have been dead for so long, and here you are, and it is I who am dying, because it must be, darling. Let's take a little walk, shall we?' They followed the Neva as far as the Summer Garden, walking through the white night. 'I am thirsty, thirsty, darling, incredibly thirsty . . . I am delirious . . . it's all right so long as they don't notice it too soon. A big glass of beer, my friend, quick!' His hand shook so as it reached for the glass that the glass rolled over the floor tinkling like little bells, and beautiful blue and gold spotted cows with wide, transparent horns breasted the grass in a Karelian field; the birches grew taller second by second, waving leaves that signalled, better than hands could do: Here is the stream, here is the pure spring, drink, you splendid beasts! Ryzhik lay down on the grass to drink, drink, drink . . .

'Do you feel ill, citizen? What is the matter?'

The warden laid a hand on his forehead, a cool, refreshing hand, an immense hand of clouds and snow . . . The day's ration untouched on the floor, a fragment of bread in the toilet bowl, those enormous eyes glittering from dark sockets, that long body trembling so that the cot shook, the prisoner's fetid breath . . . The warden understood instantly (and saw himself ruined: what criminal negligence!):

'Arkhipov!'

Arkhipov, soldier in the special battalion, walked in with a heavy tread; it echoed in Ryzhik's head like clods of earth on his coffin—that's odd, is it so simple to have died, but where are the comets?

'Arkhipov, pour a little water into his mouth—gently . . .'

The warden spoke over the telephone: 'Comrade Chief, I report: Prisoner 4 is dying . . .' From telephone to telephone, the death of Prisoner 4, who was still alive, travelled through Moscow, spreading panic as it went; it hummed in the Kremlin receiver, it raised a shrill little voice in the telephones of Government House, the Central Committee, the Commissariat for Internal Affairs, it assumed a man's voice, simulating firmness, to announce itself in a villa surrounded by idyllic silence in the heart of the Moskva woods; there its aggressive murmur outweighed other murmurs which were announcing a skirmish on the Chinese-Mongolian frontier and a serious breakdown in the Chelyabinsk factory. 'Ryzhik dying?' said the Chief in the low voice of his repressed angers. 'I order him saved!'

Ryzhik was quenching his thirst with a delicious water that was mingled snow and sunshine. 'Together, together,' he said joyfully, because all his comrades, arm in arm as at the revolutionary funerals of long ago, the Older Generation, the men of energy and will, were pulling him over the ice . . . Suddenly a crevasse opened at their feet, clean-cut as a lightning flash; at the bottom of it plashed dark smooth glinting water. Ryzhik cried: 'Comrades, look out!' A tearing pain, that was like a lightning flash too, flickered in his chest. He heard brief explosions under the ice . . . Arkhipov, soldier of the special battalion, saw the prisoner's smile writhe over his teeth, their chattering stopped at the edge of the glass. The delirious eyes ceased to see.

'Citizen, citizen!'

Nothing moved in the heavy face with its bristling white beard. Arkhipov slowly put the glass on the table, fell back a step, came to attention, and froze in terror and pity.

No one even noticed him when the important people came hurrying in—the doctor in his white smock, an officer of very high rank with perfumed hair, a little woman in uniform, so pale that she had no lips, a little old man in a frayed overcoat, to whom the officer himself, for all his general's insignia, spoke only with a bow . . . The doctor waved his stethoscope courteously: 'Excuse me, comrades, science can do no more here . . .' and assumed an ostentatiously annoyed air, because he felt that he was safe: Why was I called in so late? No one knew what to say. Arkhipov, the soldier, remembered that in churches they chant for the dead, in tones of supplication: 'Forgive him, Lord!' An atheist, as a man should be in our day, he instantly reproached himself for the recollection, but the liturgical chant continued to surge into his memory despite himself. Was it so wrong after all? No one would know. 'Forgive him, Lord! Forgive us!' For a moment the silence of the prison fell upon them all. The important people were calculating the consequences: responsibility to be established, the investigation to be begun over again from a different angle, the Chief to be told—what was the Tulayev case to be tied to now?

'In whose charge was the prisoner?' Popov asked, without looking at anyone—because he knew very well.

'In Comrade Zvyeryeva's,' answered the Deputy High Commissar for Security, Gordeyev.

'Did you have him given a medical examination when he arrived, Comrade Zvyeryeva? Have you been receiving daily reports on his condition and his attitude?'

'I thought . . . No . . .'

Popov's reproach burst out:

'Do you hear that, Gordeyev, do you hear that?'

Swept on by his anger, he was the first to hurry out of the cell. He almost ran, feebly, like an overlarge puppet; but it was he who dragged along the imposing Gordeyev by an invisible thread. Zvyeryeva was the last to leave. As she passed Arkhipov, the soldier, she felt that he gave her a look of hatred.

THE ROAD TO GOLD

SINCE HIS return from Spain, Kondratiev had been living in a sort of vacuum. Reality fled him. His room, on the fifteenth floor of Government House, was a chaos of neglect. Books piled up on the little desk, open one on top of another. Newspapers cluttered the couch on which he suddenly flung himself, his eyes on the ceiling, his mind empty, with a faint feeling of panic in his heart. The bed seemed always unmade, but in some strange fashion it no longer looked like the bed of a living man, and Kondratiev did not like to look at it, did not like to undress and lie down in it, did not like to sleep . . . To think that to-morrow he would have to wake again, see the same white ceiling, the same rather elaborate hotel curtains, the same ash-tray full of unfinished cigarettes, forgotten almost as soon as they were begun, the same snapshots, once cherished, now almost meaningless . . . Astonishing, how images fade away! He could bear nothing in his apartment except the window which looked out on the great Palace of the Soviets (in course of construction), the curve of the Moskva, the superimposed towers and buildings of the Kremlin, the square barracks of the last tyrannies (before our own), the domes of the ancient churches, the white tower of Ivan the Terrible . . . There were always people walking by the river, an official's car overtook a shaky brickmaker's cart from the previous century—the perpetual coming and going, as of busy ants with draft animals and motors, fascinated him. So the ants imagine they have something to do, that there is a meaning to their minute existences? A meaning other than statistical? But what has got into me to give me these morbid ideas? Have I not lived consciously, steadfastly? Am I becoming neurotic? He knew very well that he was not becoming neurotic, but his only way of escaping from the sickness of that room was the window. The sharp-pointed towers preserved the severity of ancient stone, the sky was vast, the feeling of an immense city flowed into him, bringing comfort. Nothing could end, what did a man's end matter? Kondratiev went out, took a tram to the end of the line in a suburb where no man of his rank ever went, wandered through wretched streets bordered by empty lots and wooden houses with blue or green blinds. There were pumps at the corners. His pace slackened before windows behind which a warm domesticity appeared to reign, because they had clean crisp curtains, flowers on the inner sill, little casseroles set among the flowerpots to cool. If he had dared, he would have stayed there to watch the people live: People live, that's odd, they live simply, this vacuum does not exist for them, they could not imagine that there are men who walk through a vacuum, right beside them, in a wholly different world, men who will never know any other road. Shake it off, my lad, you're getting sick! He forced himself to show up at the Combustibles Trust, since he was supposed to be in charge of carrying out the special plans of the Central Bureau for Military Supplies. Other men did the work, and they looked at him strangely, with the usual respect, but why did they have that distant and rather frightened attitude? His secretary, Tamara Leontiyevna, came into the glass-partitioned office too silently, her mute lips were outlined in too harsh a red, her eyes looked frightened, and why did she lower her voice like that when she answered him, and never smile? The thought came to him for a moment that perhaps he was like that himself, and that his expression, his coldness, his own anxiety (it was really anxiety) were apparent at first glance. Can I be contagious? He went to the wash-room to look at himself in the mirror and stood there before himself for a long moment, almost without thinking, in a forsaken immobility. Absurd, really, how interesting we are to ourselves! That tired man is myself, that sallow face, that ugly mouth, those rust-red lips tinged with grey, myself, myself, myself, that human apparition, that phantom in flesh! The eyes recalled to him other Kondratievs, whose disappearance roused no regrets in the Kondratiev he now was. Ridiculous to have lived so much, only to have come to this! Shall I be very different when I am dead? They probably don't take the trouble to close the eyes of executed men, I shall stare like this forever, that is to say for a little while, until the tissues decompose or are cremated. He shrugged his shoulders, washed his hands, lathering them automatically, too long, combed his hair, lit a cigarette, drifted into reverie. What am I doing here? He smoked in front of the mirror, looking at nothing, thinking of nothing. He went back to his office. Tamara Leontiyevna was waiting for him, pretending to read over the day's mail. 'Please sign . . .' Why didn't she call him 'comrade,' or, more intimately, 'Ivan Nicolayevich'? She avoided his eyes, apparently she didn't want him to see her hands, the nakedness of her simple, delicate hands. The nails were not painted; she kept them hidden behind papers. Would not people fear a dying man's eyes in the same way? 'Stop hiding your hands, Tamara Leontiyevna,' Kondratiev said angrily, and immediately excused himself, frowning and gruff: 'I mean it's all the same to me, hide them if you like, excuse me; we cannot send this letter to the Malakhovo Collieries, it is not at all what I told you to write!' He did not hear her explanations, but answered with relief: 'That's it, that's it—write the letter over again from that angle . . .' The astonishment in the brown eyes, which were so close to him, malignly close, questioning or terrified, gave him a slight shock, and he signed the letter, assuming an off-hand air: 'After all, it will do as it is . . . I shan't come in to-morrow . . .'—'Very well, Ivan Nikolayevich,' his secretary answered, in a voice that sounded kind and natural . . . 'Very well, Tamara Leontiyevna,' he repeated gaily, and dismissed her with a pleasant nod, at least he thought he did, but in reality his face remained terribly sad. Left alone, he lit a cigarette and watched it burn itself out between his fingers as they rested on the desk.

The directors avoided him, he himself avoided the bureau heads, who were always preoccupied by insignificant matters. The president of the Trust came out of his office just as Kondratiev rang for the lift. They had to go down together in the dark mahogany box, whose mirrors multiplied their two bulky reflections. They spoke to each other almost as usual, but the president did not offer Kondratiev a lift in his car, he bolted into it after a hasty handshake which was so unpleasant that, a moment afterward, Kondratiev rubbed his hands together to get rid of the feeling of it. How could that fat, hog-jowled creature have guessed? How had Kondratiev guessed himself? There was no reasonable answer to the question, but Kondratiev *knew*, and the others, everyone with whom he came into contact, *knew* too. At a lecture at the Agronomic Institute, the lecturer, a very gifted and very ambitious young man, whose name was being mentioned for the post

of assistant director of the Transbaikalian Forests Trust, discreetly
escaped by the back door, quite obviously in order not to have to talk
for a few minutes to Kondratiev, whose protégé he had been. Kondratiev had sat down alone in a corner of the room, and no one had
come to sit beside him. To avoid his comrades' curt, embarrassed
greetings, he had joined some half-grown girl students after the
lecture—only they *did not know*, it was obvious, they still looked at him
pleasantly and naturally, they still saw in him an important personage,
an old Party man, they even rather admired him because, rumour had
it, he was close to the Chief, he had been to Spain on a mission, he was
a man of a special breed, a convict under the old régime, a hero of the
Civil War, with a baggy suit, an awkwardly knotted necktie, kindly and
tired eyes (really quite a handsome man); but why has the girl from the
Polytechnic—the one we saw the other night at the Grand Theatre—
left him? The two girls wondered as he moved slowly away, square-
shouldered, walking heavily. 'He must have a bad disposition,' said
one, 'did you notice the wrinkles on his forehead and the way he
frowns? God knows what is in his mind . . .' There was nothing in his
mind except: 'How do they all know, how do I know myself, but do I
really know, isn't it that people read a neurotic anxiety in my face?'

A bus full of people whom he did not see carried him to Sokolniki
Park. There he walked in the solitary darkness, under great cold trees,
went into a tavern where workmen who looked like tramps, and thugs
who looked like workmen, were drinking beer and smoking. From a
corner came angry outbursts of an interminable quarrel: 'You're a rat,
brother, and I don't see why you won't admit it. Don't get mad, I
admit I'm just as much of a rat myself . . .' From another part of the
room a youthful voice called: 'That's the truth, citizen!' and the
drunken man answered: 'You bet it's the truth, we're all rats . . .'
Then he got up—thick-set, red-haired, shiny-faced, in coarse coolie
clothes not suitable for the time of year—and led away his staggering
companion: 'Let's go, brother, we're still Christians and I'm not going
to break open anybody's head to-day . . . And if they don't know
they're rats, better not tell them and make them sore . . .' He saw
Kondratiev, a strong, sad-faced stranger in a European tailored suit,
staring vaguely into space, his elbows on the wet table. The drunken
man stopped, puzzled. Then, speaking to himself: 'Is he a rat too?
Hard to say . . . Excuse me, citizen, I'm only looking for the truth.'
Kondratiev showed his teeth in an amused half-smile: 'I am almost

like you, citizen, but it is not easy to judge . . .' He had spoken in an earnest voice, which produced an effect. He felt that he had drawn too much attention to himself; he got up and left. In the darkness outside, a sinister-looking man wearing a cap turned a flashlight on him, abruptly asked for his papers, and, seeing the Central Committee pass, fell back as if to disappear into the shadows: 'Excuse me, comrade, duty . . .' 'Get along,' Kondratiev grumbled, 'and be quick about it.' The sinister-looking man, on the edge of absolute darkness, gave him a military salute, raising his hand to a shapeless cap. And Kondratiev, resuming his walk along the dark path with a lighter step, knew two incontrovertible facts: that doubt was no longer possible, it was not worth going over the fragments of evidence; *and that he would fight.*

He knew, and everyone who came into contact with him must know, because the subtle revelation proceeded from himself, that a dossier, KONDRATIEV, I. N., was making its way from office to office, in the illimitable domain of the most secret secrecy, leaving unspeakable anxiety in its wake. Confidential messengers laid the sealed envelope on the desks of the General Secretariat's secret service; there, attentive hands picked it up, opened it, jotted notes on the new document added by the High Commissar for Security; the open envelope made its way through doors which were exactly like any doors anywhere, in the limited region where all secrets revealed themselves, naked, silent, often mortal, mortally simple. The Chief looked over the sheets for a moment—he must have the same old grey fleshy face, the low, deeply lined forehead, the small russet eyes with the uncompromising look, the hard look, of a forsaken man. 'You are alone, brother, absolutely alone, with all the poisoned documents that you have ordered into existence. Where are they leading you? You know where they lead us, but you cannot know where they are leading *you*. You will drown at the end of the road, brother, I pity you. Terrible days are coming, and you will be alone with millions of lying faces, alone with huge portraits of yourself placarded over the fronts of buildings, alone with ghosts whose skulls show the round hole of a bullet, alone at the summit of the pyramid of their bones, alone with this country which has forsaken itself, which has been betrayed by you, you who are loyal as we too are loyal, you who are mad with loyalty, mad with suspicions, mad with jealousies you have repressed all your life . . . Your life has been black, you alone see yourself approximately as you are, weak, weak, weak, driven mad by problems, weak and loyal, and evil because,

under the armour that you will never take off, in which you will die,
taut with will, you are feeble, you are nothing. That is your tragedy.
You would like to destroy all the mirrors in the world, so that you
would never see yourself in them again, and our eyes are your mirrors
and you destroy them, you have had heads shot open to destroy the
eyes in which you saw yourself, in which you judged yourself, just as
you are, irremediably . . . Do my eyes trouble you, brother? Look me
in the face, drop all the documents manufactured by our machine for
crushing men. I do not reproach you with anything, I assess all the
wrong you have done, but I see all your solitude and I think of to-
morrow. No one can raise the dead nor save what has been lost, what is
already dying, we cannot slow down this slide towards the abyss, jam
the machine. I am without hate, brother, I am without fear, I am like
you, I fear only for you, because of the country. You are neither great
nor intelligent, but you are strong and loyal like all those who were
better men than you and whom you have made to disappear. History
has played us this rotten trick: we have only you. That is what my
eyes say to you, you can kill me, you will only be the more defenceless,
the more a nullity, and perhaps you will not forget me, as you have not
forgotten the others . . . When you have killed us all, brother, you will
be the last, brother, the last of us all, the last for yourself, and falsehood, danger, the weight of the machine you have set up will stifle
you . . .'

The Chief raised his head slowly, because everything about him was
heavy, and he was not terrifying, he was old, his hair getting white, his
eyelids swollen, and he asked, simply, in a voice as heavy as the bones
of his shoulders: 'What is to be done?'

'What is to be done?' Kondratiev repeated aloud in the chilly darkness. He strode quickly towards a vaguely swaying red dot in the
middle of the road. Stars rose above the brick buildings of Spartacus
Place; to the right, the dark square, with its sickly trees.

'What is to be done, old man? I do not ask you to confess . . . If you
were to begin confessing, everything would go to pieces. You have
your own way of holding a world in your hands: saying nothing . . .'

A few steps beyond the little red lantern, from a tar vat that was
doubtless still warm, tousled heads protruded side by side, each with a
glowing cigarette; and from the vat came a murmur of excited voices.
His hands in his pockets, his head bowed, Kondratiev stopped in the
face of his problem, because a rope barred the road, because of the red

lantern marking the spot where the pavement had been torn up. He could see perfectly well, but he looked only within himself and far beyond himself. From the warm vat, heads were raised, turned towards the stranger, who did not look like a policeman, besides everyone knows that those loafers are never around at 3 a.m. So he must be a drunk, with pockets to be emptied, Hi there, Yeromka-the-Sly, it's your turn and you're the specialist on that kind of citizen, he looks rugged, watch out ... Yeromka straightened up, thin as a girl, but all steel, his knife ready in his rags, and through the darkness he looked at the man—fifty-five, square-shouldered and square-jawed, well-dressed, mumbling away to himself. 'Hi, uncle!' said Yeromka, in a hissing voice, which could perfectly well be heard where it ought to be heard but which was then swallowed up in the darkness. ' 'Smatter, uncle? Drunk?' Kondratiev became aware of the group of children, and, cheerfully:

'Greetings! Not too cold?'

Not drunk, strangely cordial, an assured voice: suspicious. Yeromka slowly pulled himself out of the vat and came forward, limping a little (a trick he had to make himself look weaker than he was; iron wire, acrobat, broken puppet with metal joints—he suggested them all). Separated only by the rope and the red lantern, Yeromka and Kondratiev studied each other in the darkness and the silence. 'Here are our children, here are our abandoned children, Yossif, I present our children to you,' Kondratiev thought, and it brought a dark smile to his dark lips. 'They have knives in their lousy rags, that is all we have known how to give them. I know that it is not our fault. And you, you have all the revolvers of your special troops, and you haven't known how to give yourself anything either, you who had all our wealth in your hands ...' Yeromka looked him up and down, studying him with his dangerous eyes, which looked like a girl's. He said: 'Uncle, get along, you haven't lost anything here . . . We're holding our local conference here, see? We're busy; get along.'—'Right,' said Kondratiev, 'I'll be going. Greetings to the conference.'—'A lunatic,' Yeromka reported to the tight circle of his comrades in the vat, 'nothing to worry about, go ahead, Timocha . . .' Kondratiev walked on towards the towers of the three railway stations: October, Yaroslavl, Kazan—the station of the Revolution, the station of the city where we had eighteen shot and three hundred and fifty captured together, the station of Kazan, where, on a fire-ship, with Trotsky and Raskolnikov, we set fire to the White fleet . . . It is astonishing how we were victorious, how we are victorious, how we are abandoned and conquered (Yaroslavl suggests nothing now but a secret prison), like those little thugs who are perhaps conferring on a crime or on the best way to organize begging and thefts in the region of the three stations—but they live, they fight, they are right to beg and kill and steal and hold conferences, they are fighting . . . Kondratiev talked to himself heatedly, waving his open hand just as he used to on the platform.

When he reached home the cocks were crowing in far-off courtyards, it must be in streets that had a provincial look, with little houses of wood and brick, overcrowded and disorderly, with old-fashioned trees in wretched little gardens, piles of refuse in the corners, and in each room a family slept warmly, with the children at the foot of the bed, under patchwork quilts made of little squares of bright-coloured cloth sewed together. There were icons in the ceiling corners, and children's drawings pinned to the yellowed wall-paper, and poverty-stricken victuals on the window sills. Kondratiev envied these people, sleeping the sleep of their lives, husband and wife side by side, in the animal odour of their mingled bodies. His room was cool, clean, and empty; the ash-tray, the writing paper, the calendar, the telephone, the books from the Institute of Plan Economy—they all seemed useless, nothing in the room was alive. He looked at his bed with gloomy apprehension. To lie down once again between sheets (sheets like a shroud), to struggle with a useless and powerless thought, to know that presently there will come the utterly black hour of lucidity in a pure void, when life has no more meaning; and if life is no longer anything but that vain anguish, that vacillating consciousness of 'what is the use,' how could he flee himself? The searching eyes rested for a moment on the Browning that lay on the bed table . . . Kondratiev came back from the window to the alcove, picked up the Browning, happily felt the weight of it in his hand. What happens inside us to make us feel suddenly and absurdly strong again? He heard himself mutter: 'Certainly.' Morning brightened at the window, the street along the Moskva was still deserted, a sentry's bayonet moved between the crenellations of the outer Kremlin wall, a wash of pale gold touched the faded dome on the tower of Ivan the Terrible, it was a barely perceptible light, but already it was victorious, it was almost pink, the sky was turning pink, there was no boundary line between the pink of dawn and the blue of the vanishing night, in which the last stars were about to be extinguished.

'They are the strongest stars, and they are going out because they are outshone . . .' An extraordinary freshness radiated from the landscape of sky and city, and the feeling of a power as limitless as that sky came from the stones, the pavement, the walls, the building yards, the carts which appeared and moved slowly along the street, following the pink-and-blue river. Millions of indestructible, patient, tireless beings were going to rise from sleep and from the stones, because the sky was bright, were going to set out again on their millions of roads, which all led to the future. 'Well, comrades,' Kondratiev said to them, 'I have made my decision. I am going to fight. The Revolution needs a clean conscience . . .' The words almost plunged him back into despair. A man's conscience, his own, worn and paralysed—what use was it any longer, clean or not? Broad daylight brought forth clear ideas. 'Though I am alone, though I am the last, I have only my life to give, I give it, and I say NO. Too many have died in falsehood and madness, I will not further demoralize what is left to us of the Party . . . NO. Somewhere on earth there are young people whom I do not know but whose dawning consciousness I must try to save. NO.' When one thinks clearly, things become as limpid as the sky of morning; one must not think as intellectuals think, the brain must feel that it is acting . . . Though it was quite cold, he undressed in front of the open window so that he could watch the growing light. 'I shan't be able to sleep . . .' It was his last gleam of thought, he was asleep already. Enormous stars of pure fire, some copper-coloured, others transparent blue, yet others reddish, peopled the night of his dream. They moved mysteriously, or rather they swayed; the diamond-studded spiral of a nebula appeared out of darkness, filled with an inexplicable light, it grew larger, Look, look, the eternal worlds!—to whom did he say that? There was a presence too; but who was it, who? The nebula filled the sky, overflowed onto the earth, now it was only a great, bright sun-flower, in a little courtyard under a closed window, Tamara Leon-tiyevna's hands made a signal, there were stone stairs, very wide, which they climbed at a run, and an amber torrent glided in the opposite direction, and in the eddies of the torrent big fish jumped, as salmon jump when they go up the rivers . . .

When he shaved, about noon, Kondratiev found fragments of his dream floating in his mind; they did him good. Old crones would say . . . But what would a psycho-analyst say? To hell with psycho-analysts! The summons from the Party Committee aroused no emotion in him. And in fact it turned out to be nothing—merely a matter of an unimportant mission, a celebration over which he was to preside, at Serpukhov, on the occasion of the presentation of a flag to a tank battalion by the workers in the Ilich factory. 'The tank boys are splendid, Ivan Nikolayevich,' said the Secretary of the Committee, 'but there has been some trouble in this battalion, a suicide or two, an incapable political instructor, we need a good speech . . . Talk about the Chief, say that you have seen him . . .' To avoid any misunderstanding, he was given an outline of topics. 'Count on me for a good speech,' said Kondratiev. 'And I'll say a few well-chosen words to the fellow who tried to commit suicide and failed!' He thought of the unknown lad with love and anger. At twenty-five, with this country to be served, aren't you crazy, my boy? He went to the buffet to buy the most expensive cigarettes, a luxury which he rarely allowed himself. A delegation of working women from the Zamoskvoryechie were having tea with the Director of Production Cadres and the women organizers of the Women's Section. Several tables had been drawn together. Geraniums made vivid spots of red above the tablecloths; other and more beautiful spots of red were provided by the kerchiefs on young foreheads. One of the organizers whispered: 'There's Kondratiev, deputy member of the C.C. . . .' and several faces turned towards the ageing man, who was opening a box of cigarettes. The words 'Central Committee' made the circuit of the tables. The ageing man was a part of power, of the past, of loyalty, of secrecy. The buzz of conversation subsided, the Director of Production Cadres called in his loud, cordial voice: 'Hi, Kondratiev, come and take tea with the rising generation from the Zamoskvoryechie!' At that moment Popov, his cap on his grey head, came hobbling up to put both hands on Kondratiev's shoulders. 'Good old brother, what a time since we've met! How goes it?'

'Not too badly. And you? How's your health?'

'Nothing to boast about. I'm overworked. And the devil take the Anthropological Institute for not yet having invented a way to make us young again!'

They looked into each other's eyes and smiled cordially. Together they sat down at the textile workers' big table. Chairs were cheerfully shifted. Some of the women wore insignia, there were several charming faces with broad cheek-bones and big eyes, welcoming faces. A young woman immediately asked for their opinion: 'Decide between us,

comrades, we are discussing the production index. I was saying that
the new rationalization has not been pushed far enough . . .' She was so
full of what she had to say that she raised both hands and blushed, and
since she had a very fair complexion, full lips, eyes that were the grey
green of leaves in frosty weather, and a red kerchief over her hair, she
became almost beautiful, though she was only commonplace, a
daughter of the soil transformed into a daughter of the factory with a
passion for machines and figures . . . 'I am listening, comrade,' said
Kondratiev, rather amused, but at the same time pleased. 'Don't pay
any attention to her,' interrupted another woman, who had a thin stern
face under tightly rolled dark hair. 'Efremovna, you always exaggerate,
the quota was more than met—to the extent of 104 per cent, but we
had twenty-seven loom breakdowns, that is what really set us back . . .'
Old working-women, wearing decorations, became excited: No, no,
no, that was not it either! Popov's hands, earthy as an old peasant's,
called for silence and he explained that old Party members . . . mmm
. . . were not qualified in matters of the textile industry, hum, mmm,
it is you young people who are qualified, with the engineers, however,
mmm, the Plan directives demand good will, mmm, I was saying,
resolution, mmm, we must be a country of iron, with a will of iron . . .
mmm. 'Right! Right!' said old and young voices, and there was a murmured chorus: 'Will of iron, will of iron . . .' Kondratiev looked at their
faces one after the other, estimating how much of what they said was
official, how much sincere, certainly the greater part of it was sincere,
and a conventional phrase is sincere too, basically. A will of iron, yes.
His face hardened as he looked at Popov's grey profile. We shall see!

A moment later Popov and Kondratiev found themselves alone,
sitting in deep leather arm-chairs in an office. 'Let's talk a little, Kondratiev, shall we?'—'Certainly . . .' The conversation drifted on. Kondratiev became suspicious. What did the old man have in mind? What
was he trying to get at with his puerilities? He is in the Political
Bureau's confidence, he performs certain duties . . . Was it really by
chance that we met here? Finally, after discussing Paris, the French
C.P., and the agent who directed it—not up to snuff, mmm, I believe
he will be replaced—Popov asked:

'. . . and what impression . . . mmm . . . would you say the trials
produced abroad? Mmmmm . . .'

'Ah,' thought Kondratiev, 'so that's what you've been getting at?'
He felt as well, as calm, as he had that morning in his cool, dawn-

flooded room, when he had held the Browning a foot from an available, vigorous, courageous brain, while the pink light outshone the last stars, the brightest stars, reduced to white points absorbed by the sky. A strange question, which was never asked, a dangerous question. You ask it, brother? Perhaps you were waiting here just to ask me that question? And now you're going to make your report, eh, old rat? And it is my head that I stake when I answer you? Very well, I'm on.

'The impression? Deplorable, couldn't be more demoralizing. Nobody could make head or tail of them. No one believed in them ... Not even the best paid of our paid agents believed in them ...'

Popov's little eyes looked terrified. 'Shh, speak lower . . . No, it is impossible . . .'

'It is the truth, brother. Reports that tell you otherwise lie abominably, idiotically ... I'd like to send the General Secretariat a memorandum on the subject . . . to supplement the one I prepared on some stupid crimes committed in Spain . . .'

Have you got what you wanted, old Popov? Now you know what I think. Not me—you can't make anything out of me—that is, you can always make a corpse out of me, but that's all. Nothing doing, I'm not budging, the dossier can go where it pleases, I'm not budging, that's settled.

He had only thought it, but Popov understood it perfectly, thanks to Kondratiev's tone, his firm jaw, his unflinching eyes. Popov rubbed his hands softly and studied the floor:

'Well, then . . . mmmm . . . It's very important, what you've just told me . . . Don't write that memorandum—no, better not . . . I . . . mmm . . . I'll bring it up . . . mmm . . .' Pause. 'You're being sent to Serpukhov, for a celebration?'

'For a celebration, yes.'

The answer had been made with such sarcastic sternness that Popov suppressed a grimace. 'I wish I could go myself . . . mmm. This damned rheumatism . . .' He fled.

Better than any of the other insiders, Popov knew the secret journeyings of the Kondratiev dossier, enlarged during the last few days by several embarrassing documents: Report of the doctor attached to the Odessa secret service concerning the death of prisoner N. (picture attached) on board the *Kuban*, the day before the freighter docked: cerebral hæmorrhage apparently due to a constitutional weakness and overstrained nerves, and perhaps accelerated by emotion. Other documents disclosed the identity of prisoner N., which had been twice dissembled, with the result that you began to doubt whether he really was the Trotskyist Stefan Stern, though the fact was attested by two agents home from Barcelona, but their testimony might be doubted because they were obviously frightened and had denounced each other. Stefan Stern disappeared in these dubious documents as completely as he had disappeared at the secret service morgue in Odessa, when an official at the military hospital ordered the preparation for export of 'a male skeleton in perfect condition, delivered by the autopsy service under the number A4-27.' What idiot had included even that document in the K. dossier? The report from an agent of Hungarian origin (suspect because he had known Bela Kun) contradicted the information in the Yuvanov report on the Trotskyist conspiracy in Barcelona, the role of Stefan Stern, and the possibility that K. was a traitor, since it revealed the identity of an air force captain with whom Stefan Stern was supposed to have had two secret meetings and whom the Yuvanov documents confused with 'Rudin' (K.). An attached document, included by mistake, but extremely useful, showed that Agent Yuvanov had been taken ill on board, had misused his authority to leave the ship at Marseilles, and was now marking time in a hospital at Aix-en-Provence . . . Kondratiev's memorandum, directed against Yuvanov, thus became incriminating—which was perhaps the meaning of a blue-pencil mark beside a discreet note by Gordeyev, which opened the door to two accusations, one of which excluded the other . . . In any case, the original minutes showed beyond doubt that it was not true that Kondratiev had voted for the Opposition in 1927 as member of the Foreign Commerce party cell; on this point the Archives secret service had made a gross error by confusing Kondratenko, Appollon Nicolaye-vich, an enemy of the people executed in 1936, with Kondratiev, Ivan Nicolayevich! Attached: a note dictated by the Chief demanding a severe inquiry into 'this criminal confusion of names' . . . The implication was that the Chief . . . ? The Chief said nothing when he handed the dossier to Popov, he did not commit himself, his brow was dark, deeply lined, his eyes expressionless; he appeared not to have made up his mind, but he probably wanted a good trial demonstrating the connection between Tulayev's assassins and the Trotskyists in Spain, a trial the reports of which could be translated into several languages with fine prefaces written by some of those foreign jurists who will prove anything for you, sometimes even for little or no compensation.

Through these documents, which were like a series of nets, ran the life line of Ivan Kondratiev, a strong line which neither prison in Orel nor exile to Yakutia nor a jail term in Berlin for possessing explosives had snapped, a line which seemed to vanish, on the eve of the Revolution, in the swamp of private life, somewhere in Central Siberia, where, having married, Kondratiev the agronomist allowed himself to be forgotten, although he kept up an occasional correspondence with the regional Committee. 'No revolutionist without a revolution,' he would say in those days, cheerfully shrugging his shoulders. 'Perhaps we shall amount to nothing, and I shall end my life testing seeds and publishing little monographs on fodder parasites! But if the Revolution comes, you'll see whether I have settled down or not!' They did see— when he transformed himself into a cavalryman, put himself at the head of the Middle Yenisei partisans, and, with old fowling pieces for armament and plough horses for mounts, swept down as far as Turkestan in pursuit of the national and imperial bandits, made his way back to Baikal, attacked a train bearing the flags of three Powers, capturing Japanese, British, and Czech officers, checkmated them on several occasions, almost cut off Admiral Koltchak's retreat . . .

Popov said:

'I ran across an old magazine the other day and reread your recollections . . .'

'What recollections? I've never written anything.'

'Yes, you have. The case of the archdeacon, in 'nineteen or 'twenty . . .'

'Of course. Those numbers of the *Party Historical Review* have obviously been withdrawn from circulation?'

'Obviously.'

He was giving blow for blow! It must mean that he was either boiling with rage inside or had made a disconcerting decision . . . The case of Archdeacon Arkhangelsky, in 'nineteen or 'twenty: Taken prisoner during the rout of the Whites, whom he blessed before battle. A hale old man, bearded and hairy, with a healthy complexion, at once a mystic and a charlatan, who carried in his knapsack a packet of obscene postcards, a copy of the Gospels with the pages yellowed by his tobacco-stained fingers, and the Apocalypse annotated in the margins with symbols and exclamations: *God forgive us! May the hurricane cleanse this infamous world! I have sinned, I have sinned, miserable slave that I am, criminal a thousand times damned! Lord, save me!* Before a village Soviet, Kondratiev opposed shooting him: 'They are all the same . . . In this part of the country everyone is a good Christian . . . We don't want to exasperate them . . . We need hostages for exchanges . . .' He took him onto a barge with seventy partisans, of whom ten were women. And so they set off down a river which flowed between deep forests, from which, at dawn or twilight, rifles fired devastatingly accurate bullets at the men who were above decks manoeuvring the craft. They had to travel at night and, by day, moor their craft against some small island or anchor in shallow water. The wounded lay in rows below decks, they never stopped groaning and bleeding, cursing and praying, they were hungry, the men chewed the leather of their belts which had been cut in pieces and boiled, the nightly fishing yielded only a small catch which had to be divided among the weakest, who devoured them raw, guts and all, under the avid eyes of the stronger men . . . They were nearing the rapids, they had to fight, they could not fight; through the long days they felt as if they were in a stinking coffin, not a head dared show itself above deck, Kondratiev watched the banks through peep-holes, the implacable forest rose above purple or copper-red or golden-yellow rocks, the sky was white, the water white and cold, it was a mortally hostile universe. Night brought respite, fresh air, the stars, but climbing the ladder had become more and more tiring. Then the secret counsels began, and Kondratiev knew what was said at them: Surrender is the only thing left, we must hand over the Bolshevik—let them shoot him, it's only one man, and what does one man more or less matter? Surrender or we will all end up like the three astern there, who don't groan any more . . . The next to the last night, before they reached the rapids, a revolver shot like a whipcrack was heard on deck, then the sound of a heavy body falling into the water, which at that point was shallow. No one moved. Kondratiev came down the ladder, lighted a torch, and said: 'Comrades, come this way, all of you . . . I declare the meeting open . . .' Tottering spectres gathered around him, death's-heads, shaggy manes of hair, with eye sockets in which a dull spark still gleamed. They let themselves slowly down onto the boards against which the lapping of the black, cold water could be heard. 'Comrades, to-morrow at dawn, we fight our last battle . . . Innokentievka is four versts away, in Innokentievka there are bread and cattle . . .'—'What, fight now?' someone growled. 'Fool! Can't you see that we're no better than corpses?' Kondratiev was sheer dizzy nausea, chattering teeth,

resolve. He pretended not to have heard; slowly brought out the most
terrible oath he knew, his mouth foaming. Then: 'In the name of the
risen People, I have shot that vermin in a cassock, that libertine, that
bearded Satan, may his black soul go straight to his master . . .' The
dying men instantly understood that there was no forgiveness for them
now. A silence like the tomb held them for several seconds, then moans
drowned a murmur of curses, and Kondratiev saw a troop of mad
ghosts coming towards him, he thought that they would crush him,
but a tall, tottering body fell weakly on him, feverish eyes glittered
close to his own, skeleton arms that were strangely strong embraced
him fraternally, a warm cadaverous breath whispered into his face:
'You did right, brother, right! Dirty dogs all of them, I say, all of
them!' Kondratiev summoned the leaders of the detachments to a
'general staff counsel,' to prepare the next morning's operation. From
under his mattress he brought out the last sack of dry black bread, and
himself divided the surprise ration. He had hidden this last reserve for
the moment of supreme effort. Each man received two pieces which he
could hold in the palm of his hand. Dying men demanded their share—
wasted rations. While the leaders deliberated in the torchlight, the only
sound was crusts crumbling under the attack of sore jaws . . . Of this
episode from a distant past, the two men had at the moment only a
documentary memory. They continued to measure each other, as it
were gropingly . . .

Kondratiev said:

'I have almost forgotten about it . . . I never suspected then that
the value of human life would fall so low among us twenty years after
our victory.'

It was not an aggressive remark, but Popov knew very well that it
was the most cogent comment possible. Kondratiev smiled.

'Yes . . . At dawn we marched for a long time over wet sand . . .
It was a green, silent dawn . . . We felt monstrously strong—as strong
as dead men, I thought. And we did not have to fight; day broke on
bitter foliage which we chewed as we marched on—forward with wild
joy . . . Yes, old man.'

'Now that you are over fifty,' Popov thought, 'how much of that
strength can you have left?'

Afterwards Kondratiev was in charge of river transport, when
abandoned barges rotted along the banks; he harangued crafty and discouraged fishermen in forgotten settlements, got together teams of

young men, appointed captains seventeen years old, whom he put in command of rafts, created a School of River Navigation which principally taught political economy, became the chief organizer of a district, quarrelled with the Plan Commission, asked to be put in charge of the Far Northern Fur Depots, was sent to China on a mission to the Red Dragons of Szechwan . . . Not a man to flinch, Popov thought; psychologically a soldier rather than an ideologist. Ideologists, being susceptible to the supple and complex dialectics of our period, give in more easily; whereas seven times out of ten, the only thing to do with a soldier, once things get started, is to shoot him and say nothing. Even if he finally promises that he will behave before the judges and the audience, you're never sure, and what's to be done then? Experiences, secret investigations, closed trials, trials that might be opened, memories, dossiers—these things and many more, formless, jumbled, instantly clear when clarity was needed, lived for a moment in Popov's brain while he considered imponderables . . . Kondratiev had forgotten his own life for the moment, but he almost divined all the rest, and he wore a hard half-smile that was like an insult, he sat straight and massive in his chair. Popov sensed a great aggressiveness in him. Nothing could be got from him, it was most annoying. Ryzhik's death had scuttled fifty per cent of the trial; Kondratiev, the ideal defendant, was scuttling the other fifty per cent—what was he to say to the Chief? Something had to be said . . . Could he wriggle out of it, leave the job to the Prosecutor, Rachevsky? A donkey, Rachevsky, with nothing in his head but dragging off one cartload of culprits after another . . . He would pile blunder on blunder—and to kill him afterwards, like the stupid beast he was, would help nothing . . . Popov, feeling that he had been silent a few seconds too long, raised his head just in time to receive a blow straight from the shoulder.

'Have I made myself clear?' Kondratiev asked, without raising his voice. 'I have told you a great deal in a few words, I believe . . . And, as you know, I never go back on what I have said . . .'

Why was he so insistent? Could he know? How? Impossible that he should know. 'Certainly, certainly,' Popov muttered. 'I . . . we know you, Ivan Nicolayevich . . . We appreciate you . . .'

'Delighted,' said Kondratiev—absolutely insufferable. And what he did not say, but thought, Popov understood: 'And I know you too.'

'Well, so you're going to Serpukhov?'

'To-morrow, by car.'

Popov could think of nothing more to say. He put on his falsest smile of cordiality, his face was never greyer, his soul never shabbier. A telephone call delivered him. 'Good-bye, Kondratiev . . . I have to hurry . . . Too bad . . . We ought to see each other oftener . . . Hard life, mmm . . . It's good to have a frank little talk . . .'

'Good indeed!'

Kondratiev followed him to the door with unseeing eyes. 'Tell them that I'll yell at the top of my lungs, that I'll yell for all those who didn't dare yell, that I'll yell by myself, that I'll yell underground, that I don't give a damn for a bullet in my head, that I don't give a damn for you or for myself, because someone has got to yell at last, or everything is done for . . . But what has come over me, where do I get all this energy from? From my youth, from that dawn at Innokentievka, from Spain? What does it matter? I'm going to yell.'

That day at Serpukhov passed in a region of lucidity that bordered on dream. How could Kondratiev feel sure that he would not be arrested that night, nor in the C.C. car, which was driven by a Security man? He knew it, and he smoked calmly, he admired the birches, the russet and grey of fields under flying clouds. He did not go to call on the local Committee before the function, as he should have done: Let me see as few administrative faces as possible (though there must still be some decent people among these provincial bureaucrats). He dismissed the astonished chauffeur in the middle of a street, stopped in front of the display windows of co-operative groceries and stationery stores, immediately discovered little placards reading 'Samples,' 'Empty' (the latter on biscuit boxes . . .), 'No notebooks'; set off again, wandered through the streets, read the newspaper posted at the door of the Industrial Survey Commission, a paper exactly like the papers of all provincial towns of the same size, no doubt supplied with news by the daily circulars sent out by the C.C.'s Regional Press Bureau. He read only the local items, knowing in advance the entire contents of the first two pages, and he at once found the oddities that he had expected. The editor of the local column wrote that 'Comrade President of the "Triumph of Socialism" Kolkhoze, despite repeated warnings from the Party Committee, persists in his pernicious anti-cow ideological deviation, contrary to the instructions of the Commissariat for Kolkhozes . . .' Anti-cow! What a wonderful neologism! God almighty! These specimens of illiterate prose made him angry and sad at once . . . 'Comrade Andriuchenko would not allow cows to be harnessed for ploughing! Must we recall to him the decision of the recent conference, unanimously voted after the most convincing report by Veterinary Trochkin?' Somewhere under the immense sky of the steppes, Kondratiev remembered, he had once seen a cow drawing a cart on which there was nothing but a white coffin and a heap of paper flowers; a peasant woman and two small children followed it. Well—if a cow can pull a poor devil's coffin to a cemetery on the horizon, why shouldn't a cow pull a plough? The director of the dairy can always be sent to court afterwards, if milk production falls below the Plan quota . . . We lost between sixteen and seventeen million horses during the period of collectivization—between fifty and fifty-two per cent. So much the worse for the Russian cow—since obviously we can't make the members of the C.C. pull ploughs! There was nothing in the rest of the paper. Nicholas I had his official architects design models of churches and schools, to be followed by builders throughout the Empire . . . For our part, we have this press in uniform, edited by fools who think up 'anti-cow ideological deviations.' It is a slow process, the rise of a people, especially when you put such heavy burdens on their shoulders and so many shackles on their bodies . . . Kondratiev thought of the complex relation between tradition and the mistakes for which we ourselves are responsible. A tall young man in the black leather uniform of the Tank School came hurrying out of a shop, turned, suddenly found himself face to face with Kondratiev; and surprise and hostility appeared in his fresh young cold-eyed face. 'Eyes which are determined to reveal nothing . . .'

'You, Sacha!' Kondratiev exclaimed softly, and he felt that, from that instant, he too would force himself to reveal nothing—nothing.

'Yes, Ivan Nicolayevich, it is I,' said the young man, so embarrassed that he blushed slightly.

Kondratiev almost said, idiotically: 'Nice day, isn't it?' but that evasion was not permissible . . . A virile face, regular features, the high forehead and wide nostrils of a great Russian—a handsome face under the leather helmet.

'You make quite a fine-looking warrior, Sacha. How's your work getting on?'

Sacha sternly broke the ice, with unbelievable calm, as if he were speaking of perfectly commonplace things:

'I thought that I would be thrown out of the school when my father

was arrested . . . But I wasn't. Is it because I am one of the top
students, or is there a directive that forbids throwing the sons of
executed men out of special units? What do you think, Ivan Nicolayevich?'

'I don't know,' said Kondratiev, and looked at the pavement.

The toes of his boots were dirty. A red, half-crushed worm writhed
in the muddy space between two paving blocks. There was a pin on the
pavement too, and a few inches from it, a blob of spit. Kondratiev
raised his eyes again and looked straight into Sacha's face.

'What is your own opinion?'

'For a while I told myself that everyone knew my father was
innocent, but obviously that doesn't count. And besides, the Political
Commissar advised me to change my name. I refused.'

'You were wrong, Sacha. It will be a great handicap to you.'

They had nothing more to say to each other, nothing whatever.

'Are we going to have war?' Sacha asked in the same unemotional
voice.

'Probably.'

Sacha's face barely lit up with a restrained smile.

Kondratiev smiled broadly. He thought: Don't say a word, lad. I
know. The enemy first.

'Do you need any books?'

'Yes, Ivan Nicolayevich. I want German books on tank tactics . . .
We shall have to meet superior tactics . . .'

'But our morale will be superior . . .'

'Right,' said Sacha dryly.

'I will try to get the books for you . . . Good luck, Sacha.'

'Good luck to you too,' the young man said.

Was there really that strange little gleam in his eyes, that implication
in his tone, that restrained vigour in his handshake?

'He would have every right to hate me,' Kondratiev thought, 'to
despise me, and yet he must understand me, know that I too . . .' A
girl was waiting for Sacha in front of the wax figures of the 'Scehera-
zade' Hairdressers' Syndicate Co-op ('permanents thirty roubles'—
one third of a working woman's monthly wage). Kondratiev made
more serious calculations. According to the no longer up-to-date
statistics of the C.C. Bulletins, we have eliminated to date between
sixty-two and seventy per cent of Communist officials, administrators, and officers—and that in less than three years. In other words,

out of some two hundred thousand men representing the Party cadres, between 124,000 and 140,000 Bolsheviks. It is impossible, on the basis of the published data, to determine the proportion between men executed and men interned in concentration camps, but to judge from personal experience . . . It is true that the proportion of men executed is particularly high in government circles, which doubtless gives me a wrong perspective . . .

A few minutes before the hour set for his speech, he found himself under the white colonnade of Red Army House. Worried secretaries came running to meet him . . . the secretary of the Executive Committee, the secretary of the General Staff, the secretary of the local Commandant, and yet others—almost all dressed in uniforms so new that they looked as if they had been polished, with yellow knee leathers, shining holsters, shining faces too, and obsequious handshakes; and they made an impressive escort as he mounted the great marble stairway and young officers threw out their chest to salute him, magnificently immobile. 'How many minutes before I am to speak?' was the only question he asked. Two secretaries answered simultaneously, their freshly shaven faces bowing eagerly. 'Seven minutes, Comrade Kondratiev . . .' A voice which respect made almost hoarse ventured: 'Will you take a glass of wine?' and added in a humble and casual tone: 'We have a remark-a-ble Tsinondali . . .' Kondratiev nodded and forced a smile. It was as if he were walking surrounded by perfectly constructed manikins. The group entered a sort of drawing-room and buffet in one. Two heavily framed pictures faced each other from cream-coloured walls, on either side of the edibles: one represented Marshal Klimentii Efremovich Voroshilov on a rearing charger, his naked sabre pointing to a murky spot on the horizon; red flags surrounded by bayonets hurried to overtake him under a sky of dark clouds. The horse was painted with extraordinary care, the nostrils and the dark eye, to which a high-light lent animation, were even more successfully rendered than the details of the saddle; the rider had a round, slightly foreshortened head which might have come out of a popular picture book; but the stars on his collar glittered. The other large portrait showed the Chief, in a white tunic, delivering a speech from a platform, and he was pure painted wood, his smile a grimace, the platform looked like an empty buffet, the Chief like a Caucasian waiter saying, in his pungent accent: 'Nothing left, citizen . . .' On the other hand, the real buffet gleamed white and opulent, with caviar,

Volga sturgeons, smoked salmon, glazed eels, game, fruits from the Crimea and Turkestan. 'Gifts of our native soil,' Kondratiev joked cheerfully, as he went to the buffet to receive the offered glass of Tsinondali from the plump hands of a dazzled blonde. His joke, the bitterness of which no one divined, was greeted by obliging little laughs, not very loud because no one knew whether it was really permissible to laugh in the presence of such an eminent personage. Behind the waitress who had been given the honour of serving him (photogenic, fifty-rouble permanent, and decorated with the Medal of Honour of Labour), Kondratiev saw a broad red ribbon garlanding a small photograph—of himself. Gilt letters proclaimed: WELCOME TO COMRADE KONDRATIEV, DEPUTY MEMBER OF THE CENTRAL COMMITTEE . . . Where the devil had they unearthed that old snapshot, the bootlickers? Kondratiev slowly drank the Caucasian wine, waved away smiles and sandwiches with a stern hand, remembered that he had barely glanced at the printed outline of his speech, supplied by the Division for Army Propaganda. 'Excuse me, comrades . . .' His escort instantly fell back, leaving him in the centre of a six-foot circle of emptiness. He drew several crumpled sheets from his pocket. An enormous white-eyed sturgeon pointed its minute carnivorous teeth at him. The bulbs in the chandeliers were reflected in the amber jelly. The printed speech discussed the international situation, the battle against the enemies of the people, technical training, the invincibility of the Army, patriotic feeling, loyalty to 'our inspired Chief, guide of peoples, unique strategist.' Idiots! they've given me the standard speech for Morale Office representatives with the rank of general! . . . 'The Chief of our great Party and of our invincible Army, animated by a will of iron against the enemies of the Fatherland, is at the same time filled with a profound and incomparable love for the workers and all upright citizens. "Think of man!" That unforgettable phrase, which he propounded at the XIXth Conference, should be graven in letters of fire in the consciousness of every commander of a unit, of every political commissar, of every . . .' Kondratiev thrust the dead clichés back into his trousers pocket. Scowling, he looked around for someone. A dozen faces offered themselves, hastily assuming dutiful smiles: We are here, absolutely at your disposal, Comrade Deputy Member of the C.C.! He asked:

'You have had some suicides?'

An officer with cropped hair answered, speaking very quickly:

'Only one. Personal reasons. Two attempts—both men have acknowledged their misconduct, and reports on them are good.'

All this took place completely outside reality, in a world as insubstantial and superficial as an airy vision. Then suddenly reality forced itself upon him; it was a painted wooden lectern, on which he laid his heavy, blue-veined, hairy hand, a hand which had a life of its own. He became aware of it, looked at it for a long moment, observed too the minute details of the wood, and out of that real wood, out of that hand, there came to him a simple decision: He would face the entire reality of the moment, three hundred strange faces, different yet alike, each one of them silently triumphing over uniformity. Attentive, anonymous, moulded in a flesh that suggested metal, what did they expect of him? What was he to say to them that would be basically true? Already he heard his own voice, heard it with nervous displeasure, because it was speaking vain words, words he had glimpsed in the printed speech, words long known by heart, read a thousand times in editorials, the sort of words of which Trotsky once said that when you spoke them you felt as if you were chewing cotton batting . . . Why have I come here? Why have they come here? Because we are trained to obedience. Nothing is left of us but obedience. They do not know it yet. They do not suspect that my obedience is deadly. Everything that I say to them, even if it is as true as the whiteness of snow, becomes spectral and false because of obedience. I speak, they listen, some of them perhaps try to understand me, and we do not exist: we obey. A voice within him answered: To obey is still to exist. And he continued the debate: It is to exist as numbers and machines . . . He went on delivering the prepared speech. He saw Russians with shaved heads, the strong race which we formed by freeing the serfs, then by breaking their will, then by teaching them to resist us unendingly, thereby creating within them a new will, despite ourselves and against ourselves. In one of the front rows sat a Mongolian, arms crossed, small head held erect, looking sternly into Kondratiev's face. Eyes eager to the point of cruelty. He was weighing every word. It was as if he had distinctly murmured: 'You are on the wrong track, comrade, all that you are saying is useless, I assure you . . . Stop speaking, or find words that are alive . . . After all, we are alive . . .' Kondratiev answered him with such assurance that his voice changed. Behind him there was a stir among the secretaries, who, with the garrison commander, made up the presidium. No longer were they hearing the familiar phrases to which they were accustomed at functions of this sort; it made them physically uneasy—with the sort of uneasiness that is produced by an error of command in field manœuvres . . . The line of tanks suddenly sags, breaks, all is confusion, the commanders are reduced to humiliating rages. The Political Commissar of the Tank School stiffened against his dismay, reached for his automatic pencil, and began taking notes so hurriedly that the letters overlapped on the page . . . He could not grasp the phrases which he heard being uttered by the orator—who was a member of the Central Committee, of the Central Committee, of the Central Committee—was it possible? The orator was saying:

'. . . we are covered with crimes and errors, yes, we have forgotten the essential in order to live from hour to hour, and yet we are justified before the universe, before the future, before our magnificent and miserable fatherland, which is not the Union of Socialist Soviet Republics, which is not Russia, which is the Revolution . . . did you hear me? . . . the Revolution, outside of any definite territory . . . the mutilated, universal, human Revolution . . . Be well assured that, in the battle which will break on us to-morrow, all our forces will be dead within three months . . . And you are our forces . . . You must understand why . . . The world is going to split in two . . .' Should he be stopped? Was it not a crime to let him say such things? The Political Commissar is responsible for all that is said by a speaker at the school, but has he the right to stop the Central Committee's orator? The Commandant, the fool, would certainly not understand a word of it, he was probably hearing only a murmur of periods; the head of the school had turned purple and was concentrating his attention on an ash-tray . . . The orator was saying (the commissar caught only snatches of his fiery discourse, and could not establish a connection between them):

'. . . the old Party members of my generation have all perished . . . most of them in confusion, in despair, in error . . . servilely . . . They had roused the world . . . all in the service of truth . . . Never forget . . . Socialism . . . Revolution . . . to-morrow, the battle for Europe amid world crisis . . . Yesterday, Barcelona, the beginning . . . we arrived too late, too sapped by our errors . . . our forgetfulness of the international proletariat, of mankind . . . too late, wretches that we are . . .' The orator spoke of the Aragon front, of the arms which did not arrive—why? He shouted the '*why*' in a tone of defiance, and did not answer it—a reference to what? He proclaimed the 'heroism of the Anarchists . . .' He said (and the commissar, transfixed, could not take his eyes from him), he said:

'. . . Perhaps, young men, I shall never speak again . . . I have not come here, in the name of the Central Committee of our great Party, that iron cohort . . .'

Iron cohort? Hadn't the phrase been coined by Bukharin, enemy of the people, agent of a foreign intelligence service?

'. . . to bring you the copybook phrases which Lenin called our Communist lie, "Comm-lie"! I ask you to look at reality, be it baffling or base, with the courage of your youth, I tell you to think freely, to condemn us in your consciences—we, the older generation, who could not do better; I tell you to go beyond us as you judge us . . . I urge you to feel that you are free men under your armour of discipline . . . to judge, to think out everything for yourselves. Socialism is not an organization of machines, a mechanizing of human beings—it is an organization of clear-thinking and resolute men, who know how to wait, to give way and to recover their ground . . . Then you shall see how great we are, one and all—we who are the last, you who are the first, of to-morrow . . . Live forward . . . Among you there are some who have thought of deserting, for hanging yourself or putting a bullet in your brain is deserting . . . I understand them thoroughly, I have considered doing the same thing myself—otherwise I should not have the right to speak to them . . . I tell them to see this vast country before them, this vast future . . . I tell them . . . A pitiful creature, the man who thinks only of his own life, his own death, he has understood nothing . . . and let him go, it is the best thing he can do, let him go with our pity . . .' The orator continued his incoherencies with such persuasive power that for a time the Political Commissar lost his own self-control, and regained it only when he heard Kondratiev speaking of the Chief in very strange terms: 'The most solitary man among us all, the man who can turn to no one, overwhelmed by his superhuman task, by the burden of our common faults in this backward country where the new consciousness is feeble and sickly . . . corrupted by suspicion . . .' But he ended with reassuring words: 'the inspired guide,' the 'pilot's immovable hand,' the 'continuer of Lenin' . . . When he stopped speaking, the entire audience hovered in painful indecision. The presidium did not give the signal for applause, the three hundred listeners waited for more. The young Mongolian rose

9

and clapped passionately, it set off a tumult of irregular and as it were galvanic applause, in which there were islands of silence. Kondratiev saw Sacha standing at the back of the hall—he was not applauding, his hair was rumpled . . . Facing off stage, the Political Commissar was making fervid signals, an orchestra struck up 'Be There War To-morrow,' the audience took up the virile refrain in chorus, three work-ing women, wearing decorations and the uniform of Chemical Avia-tion, filed onto the platform, one of them carrying the new school flag, in red silk richly embroidered with gold . . .

Forced smiles displayed above new uniforms surrounded Kon-dratiev during the ball. The garrison commander, who had understood not a word of the speech but whose good humour was fortified by a slight degree of intoxication, displayed all the grace of a bear gorged on sweetmeats. The sandwiches which he offered Kondratiev—going to fetch them from the buffet, three rooms away—he recommended in coy phrases and with languishing looks: 'Just taste this adorable caviar, my dear comrade . . . ah, life, life !' When, tray in hand, he made his way through the circle of dancers, his face beaming, his boots so highly polished that they reflected the fluttering silks of the women's dresses, he seemed grotesquely on the point of falling over backward, but he forged ahead despite his stoutness, with the amazing lightness of a steppe horseman. The head of the school, a ruddy bulldog whose very small blue eyes remained cold and steely through everything, neither moved nor spoke. His legs crossed, his face frozen into a grimacing Oriental smile, he sat beside the Central Committee's delegate, pondering fragments of incomprehensible sentences, which he clearly saw might be terrible, and which hung over him like an obscure menace, however loyal he might be. 'We are covered with crimes and yet we are justified before the universe . . . Your elders have nearly all perished servilely, servilely . . .' It was so incredible that he stopped pondering to scrutinize Kondratiev out of the corner of his eye—was he, in fact, the genuine Kondratiev, deputy member of the C.C. ? Or was he some enemy of the people who had abused the con-fidence of the bureaus, forging official documents with the help of foreign agents, to bring a message of defeat into the heart of the Red Army ? Suspicion gripped him so intensely that he rose and went to the buffet to look at the beribboned portrait of Comrade Kon-dratiev. The picture left no room for doubt, but the enemy's artifices are inexhaustible—plots, trials, even marshals turned traitors, had more than demonstrated it. The impostor might be made up; intelligence services use chance resemblances with consummate skill; the photograph might be a forgery! Comrade Bulkin, who had recently been promoted to lieutenant colonel, and who had seen three of his superiors disappear (probably shot) in three years, was completely panic-stricken. His first thought was to order the exits guarded and to alert the secret service. What a responsibility! Sweat stood on his forehead. Beyond the tangoing couples he saw the city's Chief of Security talking very earnestly with Kondratiev—perhaps he had actually penetrated his disguise, was questioning him without seeming to? Lieutenant Colonel Bulkin, built like a bulldog, his conical forehead drawn into horizontal wrinkles which expressed his state of tension, wandered through the rooms looking for the Political Commissar and finally found him, equally preoccupied at the door of the telephone booth—direct wire to the capital. 'Saveliev, my friend,' said Bulkin, taking him by the arm, 'I don't know what's happening . . . I hardly dare to think . . . I . . . Are you sure he is really the speaker from the Central Committee?'

'What, Filon Platonovich?'

It was not an answer. They talked for a moment in terrified whispers, then walked the length of the room to examine Kondratiev again. Kondratiev was sitting with his legs crossed, smoking, feeling thoroughly at ease, pleased by the dancers, among whom there were not a few pretty girls and not a few young men made of excellent human material . . . The sight of him nailed the two men to the spot with respect. Bulkin, the less intelligent of the two, gave a long sigh and murmured confidentially: 'Don't you think, Comrade Saveliev, that this may augur a change in policy by the C.C. . . . may indicate a new line for the political education of subalterns?'

Commissar Saveliev asked himself if he had not been out of his head when he had telephoned a brief summary of Kondratiev's speech to Moscow, though he had been extremely circumspect in what he had said. In any case, when he took leave of the C.C. envoy he must tell the comrade that 'the precious directives contained in his most interesting report would henceforth form the basis of our educational work . . .' Aloud he concluded: 'It is possible, Filon Platonovich; but until we receive supplementary instructions, I believe we should refrain from any initiatives . . .'

Kondratiev rose and walked away, trying to escape from the obsequious circle of officials. He succeeded for only a very short time, having, by some unlikely chance, found himself alone at the door of the great room. It was alive with movement and music. The faces of a dancing couple emerged before him, one charming, with eyes that smiled like pure spring, the other firm-featured and, as it were, illuminated by a restrained light: Sacha. Sacha held back his partner and they danced slowly round and round in one spot so that the young man could lean towards Kondratiev:

'Thank you, Ivan Nicolayevich, for what you said to us . . .'

The rhythmical revolution brought the other face towards Kondratiev, a face framed in chestnut braids caught in a knot at the neck, a smooth forehead, golden eyebrows; again the movement carried it away, and here was Sacha, his lips colourless, his eyes intense and veiled. Through the music, Sacha said softly, without apparent emotion:

'Ivan Nicolayevich, I believe you will soon be arrested.'

'I believe so too,' Kondratiev said simply, waving them an affectionate good-bye.

He was impatient to escape from this irritating gathering, these too-well-fed heads with rudimentary minds, these insignia of command, these girls with too carefully dressed hair who were nothing but young sex organs under gaudy silks, these young men who were uneasy despite themselves, incapable of really thinking because discipline forbade it, and who bore their lives almost joyously to imminent sacrifices which they did not understand . . . Perhaps it is a very good thing that we cannot wholly rule our minds and that they force on us ideas and images which we would ignobly prefer to dismiss; thus truth makes its way in spite of egotism and unconsciousness. In the great, brightly-lit room, to the rhythm of a waltz, Kondratiev had suddenly remembered a morning inspection by the Ebro. A useless inspection, like so many others. The General Staffs could no longer do anything to better the situation. For a moment they looked professionally at the enemy positions on reddish hills dotted with bushes like a leopard's hide. The morning was fresh as the beginning of the world, blue mists dissolved on the slopes of the sierra, the purity of the sky increased from moment to moment, the rays of the sun rose into it, prodigiously straight, prodigiously visible, fanning out just above the glittering curve of the river which separated the armies . . . Kondratiev knew that the orders neither could nor would be carried out, that the men

who would give them, these colonels, some of whom looked like mechanics exhausted by too many sleepless nights, others like elegant
gentlemen (which indeed they doubtless were) who had left their
ministries for a week-end at the front and were all ready to set off for
Paris on secret missions by plane and Pullman—that all these leaders
of defeat, at once heroic and contemptible, had ceased to have any
illusions about themselves . . . Kondratiev turned his back on them
and, following a goat track strewn with white pebbles, climbed back
up the hill alone, towards the battalion commander's shelter. At a turn
in the path a muffled, rhythmical sound drew him to a nearby ridge;
on its summit, thistles grew, thorny and solitary, springing from a
stony soil, and the tough thickets of them, spared by yesterday's bombardment, speared up into the sky. Just below that miniature landscape
of desolation, a squad of militiamen were at work, silently filling a wide
grave in which lay the corpses of other militiamen. The living and the
dead were dressed in the same clothes, they had almost the same faces:
those of the dead, taking on the colour of the soil, more harrowing than
terrible, with their partly open mouths, their swollen lips, mysterious
in their bloodlessness; those of the living, famished and concentrated,
bent towards the ground, oily with sweat, unseeing, as if the morning
light knew them not. The men were working fast and in unison; their
shovels threw up a single stream of earth, which fell with a muffled
sound. No officer was in command of them. Not one of them turned to
look at Kondratiev, probably not one of them was aware of his
presence. Embarrassed to be there behind them, completely useless,
Kondratiev went back down the slope, making an effort to keep the
pebbles from rolling under his feet . . . Now, in the same way, he stole
away from the ball-room, and no one turned to look at him—he was as
distant from these young dancing soldiers as he had been from the
grave-digging militiamen in Spain. And just as there in Spain, here
too the General Staff overtook him, danced attendance on him, asked
his advice—here on the great marble staircase. He had to make his way
down surrounded by commissars, commandants, declining their in-
vitations. Those of the highest rank offered to put him up for the night,
offered to take him to the manœuvres in the morning, to show him the
factories, the school, the barracks, the library, the swimming pool, the
disciplinary section, the motorized cavalry, the model hospitals, the
travelling printing press . . . He smiled, thanked them, spoke familiarly
to people he did not know, even joked, in spite of his violent desire to

shout at them: 'Enough! Shut up, will you? I don't belong to the species "general staff"—can't you tell it from my face?' Not one of these puppets suspected that he would be arrested one of these days, they all saw him only through the gigantic shadow of the Central Committee's stamp of approval . . .

He slept in the C.C. Lincoln. Somewhere on the road, just before dawn, a jolt waked him. The landscape was beginning to emerge from darkness—black fields under pale stars. A few hours later Kondratiev saw the same dark desolation in a woman's face, in the depths of Tamara Leontiyevna's eyes. She had come into his office at the Combustibles Trust to report. He felt in a good humour, he made a healthy man's ordinary gesture, he took her arm with a smile, and instantly he felt a vague terror enter into him. 'This matter of the Donetz Syndicate is in fine shape, it will be all settled in twenty-four hours, but what's the trouble, Tamara Leontiyevna, are you ill? You shouldn't have come in this morning if you didn't feel well . . .'—'I would have come at any cost,' the girl murmured, her lips pale, 'excuse me, I have, I have to warn you . . .' She was desperate, finding no words. Then: 'Go away, Ivan Nicolayevich, leave at once and never come back. I involuntarily overheard a telephone conversation between the Director and . . . I don't know who . . . I don't want to know, I have no right to know, I have no right to tell you either, what am I doing, my God!' Kondratiev took her hands—they were as cold as ice. 'There, there, I know all about it, Tamara Leontiyevna, calm yourself . . . You think that I am going to be arrested?' She barely nodded. 'Go away, quick, quick!'

'No indeed,' he said. 'Not under any circumstances.'

He freed himself from her, became again the distant assistant director in charge of special plans:

'I am much obliged to you, Tamara Leontiyevna, please have the documents on the Yuzovka Refineries ready by two o'clock. Meanwhile, get the General Secretary of the Party on the telephone for me. Use my name, and insist on getting through to the General Secretary's office. At once, if you please.'

Could this light be the light of the last day? One chance in a thousand that he would be granted an audience . . . And once there? The beautiful fish, armed all over with scales each one of which reflects the whole light of an asphyxiating universe, struggles in the net, struggles in utter impossibility, suffocating—but I am ready. He smoked furiously, taking two puffs from a cigarette, then crushing it out on the edge of the desk and flinging it on the floor. He instantly lighted another, and his jaws clenched, he forgot himself in his director's chair, in this absurd office, ante-chamber to a place of unforseeable tortures. Tamara Leontiyevna came back without knocking. 'I didn't call you,' he said crossly, 'leave me alone . . . Ah, yes, put the call on my line here . . .' To escape—perhaps there actually was a slight possibility that he could? 'What now? The Gorlovka Refineries?'— 'No, no,' said Tamara Leontiyevna, 'I asked for an audience for you. *He* expects you at three sharp at the Central Committee . . .'

What, what! You did that? But who gave you permission? You are mad, it is not true! I tell you, you are mad! 'I heard HIS VOICE,' Tamara went on, 'HE came to the telephone HIMSELF, I assure you . . .' She spoke of him with terrified reverence. Kondratiev turned to stone—the great fish beginning to die.

'Very well,' he said dryly. 'Keep after the reports on the Donetz, Gorlovka, and so on . . . And if you have a headache, take aspirin.'

Ten minutes to three, the great reception of the General Secretariat. Two presidents of Federated Republics were conversing in low tones. Other presidents of Republics had disappeared, it was said, after leaving here . . . Three o'clock. The void. Steps in the void.

'Go in, please . . .'

Go into the void.

The Chief was standing in the attenuated whiteness of the huge office. Tensely collected. He received Kondratiev without a gesture of welcome. His tawny eyes were impenetrable. He murmured: 'Greetings' in an indifferent voice. Kondratiev felt no fear; his feeling was more one of surprise at finding himself almost impassive. Good—now we are face to face, you, the Chief, and I who do not know whether I am a living man or a dead one—leaving out of account a certain period of minor importance. Well?

The Chief took two or three steps towards him, without holding out his hand. The Chief looked him up and down, from head to foot, slowly, harshly. Kondratiev heard the question, too serious to be spoken: Enemy? and he answered in the same fashion, without opening his lips: Enemy, I? Are you mad?

The Chief quietly asked:

'So you are a traitor too?'

Quietly, from the depths of an assured calm, Kondratiev answered:
'I am not a traitor either.'

Each syllable of the terrible sentence stood out like a block of ice in
Arctic whiteness. There was no going back on such words. A few more
seconds, and all would be over. For such words in this place, one
should be annihilated on the spot, instantaneously. Kondratiev finished
them firmly:

'And you must know it.'

Would he not summon someone, give orders in a voice so furious
that it would sound stifled? The Chief's hands, still hanging at his
sides, sketched several little incoherent movements. Were they looking
for the bell? Take this creature out of here, arrest him, do away with
him! What he says is a thousand times worse than treason! A calm and
completely disarmed resolve forced Kondratiev to speak:

'Don't get angry, it will do no good. All this is very painful to me . . .
Listen . . . You can believe me, or you can not believe me, I hardly
care, the truth will still be the truth. And it is that, despite everything . . .'

Despite EVERYTHING?

'. . . I am loyal to you . . . There are many things that escape me.
There are too many that I understand. I am in agony. I think of the
country, of the Revolution, of you, yes, of you—I think of *them* . . .
Of them above all, I tell you frankly. Their end has left me with an
almost unbearable regret: what men they were! What men! History
takes millenniums to produce men so great! Incorruptible, intelligent,
formed by thirty or forty decisive years, and pure, pure! Let me speak,
you know that I am right. You are like them yourself, that is your
essential worth . . .'

(So Cain and Abel, born of the same womb under the same stars . . .)

The Chief swept away invisible obstacles with both hands. With no
apparent emotion, looking away, and even giving himself an air of
detachment, he said:

'Not another word on this subject, Kondratiev. What had to be had
to be. The Party and the country have followed me . . . It is not for you
to judge . . . You are an intellectual . . .' A malevolent smile appeared
in his leaden face. 'I, as you know, have never been one . . .'

Kondratiev shrugged his shoulders.

'What has that to do with us? . . . This is hardly the moment to
discuss the failings of the intelligentsia . . . The intelligentsia did a lot

of useful work, though, eh? . . . We shall soon be at war . . . Accounts will be settled, all the dirty old accounts, you know it better than I do . . . Perhaps we shall all perish, even to the last—and drag you down with us. Let us put the best face on things: you will be the last of the last. You will hold out an hour longer than we do, thanks to us, on our bones. Russia is short of men, men whose brains know what ours know, what theirs knew . . . Who have studied Marx, known Lenin, lived through October, gone through all the rest, the best of it and the worst! How many of us are left? You know the figure, you are one of them yourself . . . And the earth is going to begin shaking, as when all volcanoes come to life at once, from continent to continent. We shall be under the ground at the dark hour—and you will be alone. That's it.'

Kondratiev went on, in the same melancholy, persuasive tone:

'You will be alone under the avalanche, with the country in its last agony behind you and a host of enemies around you . . . No one will forgive us for having begun Socialism with so much senseless barbarity . . . That your shoulders are strong, I know . . . As strong as ours: ours carried you . . . Only—we have the place of the individual in history . . . not a very big place, especially when a man has isolated himself at the peak of power . . . I hope that your portraits, as big as buildings, have not given you any illusions on the subject?'

The simplicity of his speech performed a miracle. They walked up and down together over the white carpet. Which led the other? They stopped before the Mercator's projection: oceans, continents, frontiers, industries, green spaces, our sixth part of the earth, primitive, power-ful, threatened . . . A heavy red line, in the ice-floe region, indicated the great Arctic road . . . The Chief studied the relief of the Ural Mountains: Magnitogorsk, our new pride, blast furnaces as well equipped as Pittsburgh's. That's what counts! The Chief half turned to Kondratiev, his gestures were clearer, his voice more relaxed. His eyes grew less impenetrable:

'Always the writer! You ought to go in for psychology . . .'

An amused gesture of his forefinger completed the word: twisting and untwisting an imaginary skein . . . The Chief smiled:

'In our day, old man, Chekhov and Tolstoy would be genuine counter-revolutionaries . . . Yet I like writers, though I don't have time to read them . . . Some of them are useful . . . I see that they are very well paid . . . One novel sometimes brings them in more than several proletarian lives. Is that just or not? It is something we need . . . But I don't need your psychologizing, Kondratiev.'

A rather strange pause followed. The Chief filled his pipe. Kondratiev looked at the map. The dead can no longer fill their pipes or feel proud of Magnitogorsk, which they built! There was nothing more to add, everything had been set forth under an impersonal light which permitted neither manœuvring nor fear. The consequences would be what they must be: irrevocable.

The Chief said:

'Do you know that you have been denounced? That you are accused of treason?'

'Naturally! What should all those vermin do but denounce me? That's what they live on. They gobble denunciations day and night . . .'

'What they affirm seems not unlikely . . .'

'Of course! They know how to cook these things up. In our day what is easier? But whatever stinking nonsense they may have sent you . . .'

'I know. I have gone into it. A piece of stupidity, or worse, in Spain . . . You were wrong to get yourself mixed up in it, there's no doubt of that . . . I know better than anyone how many vile things and stupid things have been done there . . . That fool of a prosecutor wanted to have you arrested . . . Once let them get started and they'd arrest all Moscow. He is a brute we shall have to get rid of someday. A sort of maniac.

'Enough of that. I have made my decision. You will leave for eastern Siberia, you will receive your appointment to-morrow morning. Do not lose a day . . . Zolotaya Dolina, the Valley of Gold—do you know what it is? Our Klondike, production increasing from forty to fifty per cent every year . . . Splendid technicians, a few cases of sabotage as is to be expected . . .'

Pleased with himself, the Chief began to laugh. He was not good at joking, and the fact sometimes made him aggressive. He would have liked to be jovial. His laugh was always a little forced.

'We need a man there who has character—sinew, enthusiasm, the Marxist instinct for gold . . .'

'I loathe gold,' said Kondratiev, almost angrily.

Life? Exile in the mountains of Yakutia, in the white brushland, among secret placers, unknown to the universe? His whole being had prepared itself for a catastrophe, hardened itself by expecting it, accustomed itself to bitterly wishing for it, as a man seized with vertigo above a chasm knows that a double within him longs for the relief of falling. And now? You let me off after what I came here to say to you? Are you trying to make a fool of me? Am I not going to disappear at the first corner I come to after I leave here? It is too late to restore our confidence, you have killed too many of us, I no longer believe in you, I don't want any of your missions which turn out to be traps! You will never forget what I have said to you, and if you let me off to-day, it will be to order my arrest six months from now, when remorse and suspicion have gone to your head . . . 'No, Yossif, I thank you for granting me life, I believe in you, I came here to find my salvation, you are great despite everything, you are sometimes blind when you strike, you are perfidious, you are eaten by bloody jealousies, but you are still the leader of the Revolution, we have no one but you, I thank you.' But Kondratiev restrained both protest and effusion. There was no pause. The Chief laughed again:

'I told you that you were always the writer. As for me, I have no feeling about gold one way or the other . . . Excuse me—this is audience day. Get the dossier on Gold from the secretariat, study it. Your reports you will send to me directly. I count on you. A good journey, brother!'

'Right. Keep in good health! Good-bye.'

The audience had lasted fourteen minutes . . . A secretary handed him a leather brief case on which, in letters of gold, stood the magical words: *East Siberian Gold Trust*. He passed blue uniforms without seeing them. The daylight seemed pellucid. He walked for a while, mingling with the people in the street and thinking of nothing. A physical happiness grew in him, but his mind did not share it. He also felt a sadness which was like a sense of uselessness. He sat down on a bench in a square, before disinherited trees and lawns of a green which meant nothing. An old woman was watching her grandchildren making mud pies. Farther away rolled long yellow trams; their clatter rebounded from the front of a recently constructed office building of glass, steel, and reinforced concrete. Eight floors of offices: a hundred and forty compartments, each containing the same portrait of the Chief, the same adding machines, the same glasses of tea on directors' and accountants' desks, the same worried lives . . . A beggar woman passed, leading several small children. 'For the love of Christ . . .' she said, holding out a pretty brown hand. Kondratiev put a handful of small change into it. On each of the little coins, he remembered, you could read the words: Proletarians of all countries, unite! He passed his hand over his forehead. Could the nightmare be over? Yes, over, for a time at least—my small, personal nightmare. But all the rest goes on, nothing is clarified, no dawn rises on the tombs, we have no real hope for to-morrow, we must still travel through darkness, ice, fire . . . Stefan Stern is doubtless dead. For his sake, I must hope so. Kiril Rublev has disappeared; with him the line of our theoreticians of the great days is extinguished . . . In our schools of higher education we have nothing left but teachers as contemptible as they are insipid, armed with an inquisitorial dialectic that is three-fourths dead. As usual, names and faces crowded into his memory. What a peaceful motion—the motion of those militiamen by the Ebro, covering their comrades in that mass grave with heavy shovelfuls of earth! The same men, in the grave and beside the grave—buried and buriers the same. They were covering *themselves* with earth, yet they had not lost heart to live and fight. The thing is to keep on, comrades, obviously. To wash gold-bearing sand. Kondratiev opened the Gold Trust brief case. Only the maps interested him, because of their peculiar magic—an algebra of the earth. With the map of the Vitim district open on his knees, Kondratiev looked at the hatchings which signified elevations, patches of green which indicated forests, the blue of watercourses . . . No villages, stern solitudes, brush on rock, cold streams which absorbed the colours of sky and stone, shining mosses clothing rock, the low, tenacious vegetation of the taiga, indifferent skies. Among the gaunt splendours of that world, man feels himself delivered over to a glacial freedom which has no human meaning. The nights glitter, they have an inhuman significance, sometimes their brightness sends the weary sleeper to sleep forever. Bodaibo is doubtless only an administrative settlement surrounded by clearings, in the heart of the forested wilderness, under a metallic brightness like a perpetual lightning bolt. 'I'll take Tamara Leontiyevna with me,' Kondratiev thought, 'she'll come. I'll say to her: You are as straight as the young birches in those mountains, you are young, I need you, we shall fight for gold, do you understand?' Kondratiev's eyes turned from the map to pursue a joy beyond visible things. And he discovered a pair of worn-out shoes, laced with string, a dusty trouser cuff. The man had on only one sock, which hung around his ankle like a dirty rag. His feet expressed violence and resignation, a desperate determination—to do what? To walk through the city as through a jungle, seeking the pittance of food, the knowledge, the ideas, by which to live the next day, blind to the stars which the electric signs drive back into their immensities. Kondratiev slowly turned to look at his neighbour on the bench, a young man whose hands clutched an open notebook full of equations. He had stopped reading, his grey eyes were exploring the square with intense and idle attention. On the hunt, always prey to the same desolate bitterness? 'In this distress and apathy, no one whose hand I can take,' says the poet, but the wandering Maxim the Bitter, Gorki, amends: 'no one whose jaw I can break . . .' An obstinate forehead under the visor of the cap, which he wears tipped back, guttersnipe fashion. Irregular features, tormented from within by an anæmic violence; chalky complexion. Clear eyes—not an alcoholic. Movements still lithe and flexible. Were he ever to sleep on the naked soil of the Siberias, no glitter of stars would kill him, because his desperate determination would never go to sleep. Kondratiev forgot him for the moment.

Such should be those who prowl the taiga around the Upper Angara, in Vitim, around Chara, in the Zolotaya Dolina, the Valley of Gold. They follow wild beasts by invisible signs, they foretell the storm, they fear the bear, they say 'thou' to him, as to an elder brother whom it is wise to respect. It is they who come to the solitary posts, bringing silvery furs and bulging leather purses filled with grains of gold—for the war chest of the Socialist Republic. A minor official, silent because he has lost the habit of speech, who lives alone with his wife, his dog, his machine pistol and the birds of the air, in an isba of heavy blackened logs, weighs the grains of gold, counts roubles, sells vodka, matches, gunpowder, tobacco, the precious empty bottle, makes notes on the work card issued by the Gold-Seekers' Co-operative. He smiles and swallows a glass of vodka, does some figuring, says to the man from the taiga: 'Comrade, it's not enough. You are eight per cent behind your Plan quota . . . Won't do. Make it up, or I can't sell you any more vodka . . .' He says it in a toneless voice, and adds: 'Palmyra, bring us tea . . .' because his wife is named Palmyra, but he has no idea that it is the magical name of a vanished city in another world, a world of sand and palms and sun . . . Those hunters, those prospectors, those gold washers, those engineers, Yakuts, Buriats, Mongols, Tungus, Oirads, Great Russians from the capitals, Young Communists, Party members initiated into the sorceries of shamans, those clerks half mad with solitude, their wives, their little Yakut girls from obscure villages who sell themselves in a dark corner of the house for a pinch of yellow grains or a packet of cigarettes, the Trust's inspectors, ambushed on the road by sawed-off shotguns, the engineers who know the latest statistics from the Transvaal and the new methods of hydraulic drilling to work deep-lying auriferous strata—all of them, all of them live a magnificent life under the twofold sign of the Plan and of glittering nights, in the vanguard of forward-marching mankind, in communion with the Milky Way!—The preamble to the *Report on Socialist Emulation and Sabotage in the Zolotaya Dolina Gold Placers* contained these lines: '... As our great Comrade Tulayev, traitorously assassinated by Trotskyist terrorists in the service of world imperialism, recently said, workers in gold production form an élite contingent at the spearhead of the Socialist army. They fight Wall Street and the City with capitalism's own weapons ...' Ah, Tulayev, the stupid fool, and this verbiage of public prosecutors intoxicated with vileness ... Prosaically put, but, so far as gold was concerned, true enough ... The icy winds of the North carry violet snow-laden clouds down to that country. Behind them whiteness covers the universe, which has relapsed into a sort of void. Before them flee such multitudes of birds that they hide the sky. At sunset faraway flocks of white birds trace gilded snakes in the upper air. The Plan must be carried out before winter.

Kondratiev rediscovered the string-laced shoes of the poverty-stricken walker.

'Student?'

'Technology, third year.'

Kondratiev was thinking of too many things at once. Of the winter, of Tamara Leontiyevna, who would come, of life beginning again, of the prisoners in the prison where he had expected to end this day, of the dead, of Moscow, of the Valley of Gold. Without looking at the young man—and what did that thin, bitter face matter to him, after all?—he said:

'Do you want to fight with winter, with the wilderness, with solitude, with the earth, with night? To fight—understand? I am the head of an enterprise. I offer you work in the Siberian brush.'

Without taking time to reflect, the student answered:

'If you really mean it, I accept. I have nothing to lose.'

'Neither have I,' Kondratiev murmured cheerfully.

LET PURITY BE TREASON

On his desk Prosecutor Rachevsky found a foreign newspaper which announced (the item was carefully circled in red pencil) the imminent trial of Comrade Tulayev's assassins. 'From our special correspondent: Informed circles are discussing . . .—the principal defendants—the former High Commissar for Security, Erchov; the historian Kiril Rublev, former member of the Central Committee; the Regional Secretary for Kurgansk, Artyem Makeyev; an immediate agent of Trotsky's, whose name is still a secret . . .—are said to have made complete confessions . . .—it is hoped that this trial will cast light on certain points which the preceding trials left obscure . . .' The Foreign Affairs Commissariat's press bureau added a request for information concerning the source of this item. Originally emanating from the Supreme Court, the request had been officially communicated by the press bureau itself . . . Calamity. Towards noon the Prosecutor learned that the audience for which he had been asking for several days was granted.

The Chief received him in a small ante-room, before a glass-covered table. The audience lasted three minutes and forty-five seconds. The Chief seemed preoccupied. 'Good day. Sit down. Well?' Discommoded by his thick glasses, Rachevsky could not see the Chief well. The lenses broke his image into absorbing details: wrinkles at the corners of his eyes, bushy black eyebrows in which there was a sprinkling of white hairs . . . Leaning slightly forward, his two hands resting on the edge of the table (because he did not dare to gesticulate), the Prosecutor made his report. He did not know quite what he was saying, but professional habit made him brief and precise: 1. Complete confessions from the principal defendants; 2. The unexpected death of the person who appeared to be the soul of the conspiracy, the Trotskyist Ryzhik, a death due to the unpardonable negligence of Comrade Zvyeryeva, who had been in charge of the preliminary investigation; 3. The very strong presumptive evidence collected against Ryzhik, whose guilt, if proven, would show the connection between the conspirators and foreign powers . . . In principle, a doubt must be admitted until Kondratiev should be questioned . . . However . . .

The Chief interrupted:

'I have investigated the Kondratiev matter. It is of no further interest to you.'

The Prosecutor bowed, choking. 'Ah, so much the better. Thank you . . .' Why was he saying thank you? He felt as if he were falling, falling straight down. It was thus that one would fall from the skyscrapers of some inconceivable city, past oblongs of window, oblongs, oblongs, five hundred stories . . .

'Go on.'

Go on with what? The Prosecutor gropingly returned to the 'complete confessions of the principal defendants . . .'

'They have confessed? And you have no doubts?'

A thousand floors, the pavement below him. His head hitting the pavement at meteor speed.

'. . . No,' said Rachevsky.

'Then apply the Soviet law. You are the Prosecutor.'

The Chief rose, his hands in his pockets. 'Good-bye, Comrade Prosecutor.' Rachevsky walked away like an automaton. No question presented itself to him. In the car he gave himself up to stupor—the stupor of a man stunned. 'I will see no one,' he told his secretary, 'leave me to myself . . .' He sat down at his desk. The huge office offered nothing to hold his eyes (the life-size portrait of the Chief was behind the Prosecutor's chair). 'I am so tired,' he said to himself, and put his head in his hands. 'When all is said and done, there is only one way out for me: to shoot myself . . .' The idea came to him of itself: there it was in his mind, quite simply. A telephone buzzed—direct wire from the Commissariat for the Interior. As he took up the receiver, Rachevsky became aware what a languor there was in his limbs. There was absolutely nothing in him but that one idea, reduced to an impersonal force, without emotion, without images, without argument, obvious. 'Hello . . .' It was Gordeyev, inquiring into 'this deplorable indiscretion which has communicated a so-called rumour to certain European newspapers . . . Do you know anything about it, Ignatii Ignatiyevich?' Excessively polite, Gordeyev—using circumlocutions to avoid saying: 'I am making an investigation.' Rachevsky began by spluttering. 'What indiscretion? What did you say? An English newspaper? But all communications of that nature go through the Foreign Affairs press bureau . . .' Gordeyev insisted: 'I think you don't quite understand, my dear Ignatii Ignatiyevich . . . Allow me to read you this paragraph: *From our special correspondent* . . .' Rachevsky hastily interrupted: 'Ah, yes, I know . . . My secretariat issued a verbal communication . . . at the suggestion of Comrade Popov . . .' Gordeyev appeared to be embarrassed by the unexpected precision of this answer. 'Right, right,' he said, lowering his voice. 'The point is'—his voice rose an octave: Perhaps there was someone with Gordeyev? Perhaps their telephone conversation was being recorded?—'have you a written memorandum from Comrade Popov?'—'No, but I am sure he remembers it very well . . .'—'Thank you very much. Excuse me now, Ignatii Ignatiyevich . . .'

When he was under great pressure of work, Rachevsky often slept at Government House. There he had the use of a small, plainly furnished apartment, which was crammed with dossiers. He did a great deal of work himself, since he did not know how to use secretaries and trusted no one. Sixty cases of sabotage, treason, espionage, which he must look into before he went to bed, were scattered over various articles of furniture. The most secret were in a small safe at the head of his bed. Rachevsky stopped in front of the safe and, to shake off his sluggishness, elaborately wiped his glasses. 'Obviously, obviously.' His usual supper was brought in, and he devoured it standing by the window, without being aware of the suburban view, in which innumerable golden sparks were kindling into light. 'It is the only thing to do, the only thing . . .' Of the thing as such, he thought hardly at all. Present within him, it offered no real difficulty. To blow out his brains—what could be simpler? No one suspects how simple it is. He was a rudimentary man, who feared neither pain nor death since he had been present at a number of executions. There is probably no real pain, only a shock of infinitesimal duration. And materialists like ourselves have no need to fear nothingness. He longed for sleep and for darkness, which gives the best idea of nothingness, which does not exist. Let me be, let me be! He would write nothing. It would be better for his children. As he was thinking of his children, Masha called him on the telephone: 'You won't be home to-night, Papa?'—'No.'—'Papa, I got *very good* to-day in history and political economy . . . Tiopka got a cut finger cutting out decalcomanias, Niura bandaged it the way it says to in the First Aid Manual. Mama's headache is better. All well on the Interior Front! Sleep well, Comrade Papa-Prosecutor!'—'Sleep well, all of you,' Rachevsky answered.

Oh, God. He opened the cupboard in the little bureau, took out a bottle of brandy and drank from it. His eyes dilated, a warmth ran through him, it was good. He slammed the bottle down and it rocked back and forth on the table. Will you fall or won't you? It did not fall. He banged at the table on either side of the bottle, but keeping one hand open, ready to catch the bottle if it should start to fall. 'You won't fall, damn you—ha-ha-ha-ha!' He was laughing and hiccuping. 'A-bullet-in-the-brain—poo-poo-poo-poo! A-bullet-in-the-bottle—poo-poo-poo-poo!' Leaning so far to one side that he almost toppled over, he tried to get his fingers on a blue dossier which lay on a stand against the wall. The effort made him groan. 'So you won't let me catch you, damn you . . . damn you!' He worked his fingers to the edge of the dossier, drew it towards him craftily, caught it in the air while other papers showered onto the carpet, put it on the table, flung his glasses into a corner over his shoulder, licked his forefinger and, drawing it clumsily along under the words on the cover, began spelling them out: *Sa-bo-tage in the Chemical Industry, Armolinsk Case.* The syllables overlapped, ran after each other, and each letter, written in black ink in a big round hand, was fringed with fire. His finger captured the syllables, but they got away like mice, like rats, like the little lizards which, when he was a boy in Turkestan, he used to catch with a noose made from a blade of grass—ha ha ha! 'I was always a specialist in nooses!' He tore the dossier across and then across again. Come here, bottle, come here, damn you—hurrah! He drank till he lost breath, the desire to laugh, consciousness . . .

When he arrived at his office on the afternoon of the next day, Popov was waiting for him, surrounded by the department heads, whom he dismissed with a wave. Popov looked bored, yellow, and ill. The Prosecutor sat down under the great portrait of the Chief, opened his brief case, assumed a pleasant look, but a headache pressed down on his eyelids, his mouth was woolly, he breathed laboriously. 'Had a bad night, Comrade Popov, attack of asthma, my heart, I don't know what to make of it, haven't had time to see a doctor . . . At your service!'

Popov asked softly:

'Have you read the papers, Ignatii Ignatiyevich?'

'Haven't had time.'

He had not read his mail either, since the unopened envelopes lay there on his desk. Popov rubbed his hands. 'So . . . so . . . Well, Comrade Rachevsky, it is just as well that I should tell you the news . . .' It couldn't be easy, because he looked in his pockets for a newspaper, opened it, found an item towards the middle of the third page. 'There, read that, Ignatii Ignatiyevich . . . In any case, everything has been arranged, I saw to it this morning . . .'

'*By decision of . . . and so on . . . Comrade Rachevsky, I.I., Prosecutor to the Supreme Tribunal, is relieved of his functions . . . in view of his appointment to another post . . .*'

'It stands to reason,' said Rachevsky, without emotion, for he saw quite a different reason.

Weakly, using both hands, he pushed the heavy brief case towards Popov. 'There you are.'

To an accompaniment of hand-rubbing, little coughs, and vaguely pleasant smiles—none of which had any meaning—Popov said: 'You understand, do you not, Ignatii Ignatiyevich? . . . You have carried out a task . . . a superhuman task . . . Mistakes were inevitable . . . We have thought of a post which will give you a chance to take some rest . . . Your appointment is'—from the depths of his torpor, Rachevsky pricked up his ears—'is . . . Director of the Tourist Bureau . . . with two months' leave in advance . . . which, as a friend, I advise you to spend at Sochi . . . or at Suk-Su—they are our two best rest houses . . . Blue sea, flowers, Alupka, Alushta, views, Ignatii Ignatiyevich! You will come back renewed . . . ten years younger . . . and tourist travel, you know, is far from a negligible matter!'

Former Prosecutor Rachevsky appeared to wake up. He gesticulated. The thick lenses of his glasses flashed lightning. A laugh made a horizontal gash in his concave face.

'Delighted! Travel, touring, the dream of my life! Little birds in the woods! Cherry trees in flower! The Svanetia highway! Yalta! Our Riviera! Thank you, thank you!' His two gnarled, hairy hands seized Popov's flabby ones. Popov drew back a little, his eyes uneasy, his smile fading.

The office staff saw them come out, arm in arm like the good old friends they were. Rachevsky showed all his yellow teeth in a smile, and Popov appeared to be telling him a good story. Together they got into a Central Committee car. Rachevsky had the driver stop for a moment in Maxim Gorki Street in front of a large grocery store. He came back from the store with a package which he carefully placed in Popov's lap. He was his old serious self again. 'Look, old man!' The neck of an uncorked bottle protruded from the wrapping. 'Drink, my friend, drink first,' Rachevsky said amiably, and his arm went around Popov's puny shoulders. 'No, thank you,' said Popov coldly, 'furthermore, I advise you . . .' Rachevsky burst out:

'You advise me, my dear friend! How nice of you!'

And he drank greedily, his head thrown back, the bottle held high in a firm hand, then licked his lips. 'Long live tourist travel, Comrade Popov! Do you know what I regret? I regret having begun my life by hanging lizards!' After that he said nothing, but he unwrapped the bottle to see how much was left in it. Popov took him all the way home —his house was in the outer suburbs. 'How is your family, Ignatii Ignatiyevich?'—'All right, very well,' he said. 'This news will make them terribly happy. And yours?' Was he sneering?—'My daughter is in Paris,' said Popov, with a hint of uneasiness. He watched the former Prosecutor get out of the car in front of a villa surrounded by faded shrubs. Rachevsky stepped heavily into a muddy puddle, which made him laugh and swear. The bottle protruded from his overcoat pocket, he felt it with a hand that was like a big crab. 'Good-bye, old man,' he said cheerfully, or sarcastically, and ran towards the gate of the little garden.

'He's done for,' Popov thought. And what of it? He was never good for much.

Paris was not at all as Xenia had vaguely imagined it. Only at moments and by chance did she find it resembling the twofold city she had expected—the capital of a decaying world, the capital of workers' risings . . . It had all been built so many centuries ago, and so much rain, so much daylight, so much darkness, had impregnated the old stones, that the idea of a unique achievement forced itself upon her mind. Turbid yet bluish, the Seine flowed between scattered, ancient trees, between stone quays whose exact colour was indeterminable. The stone seemed to have no consistency, the water, polluted by the huge city, could be neither ill-tasting nor dangerous—and nowhere else could drowned bodies evoke more simple tears. The tragedy of Paris was clothed in a worn, almost fragile splendour. It became a delight to stop before a bookstall, under the skeleton of a tree, and take in the prospect with one sweeping look: the books before her (hardly alive, yet not quite dead, soiled with the finger-prints of unknown hands), the stones of the Louvre across the river, the Belle Jardinière's sign farther on, beside a square full of antlike motion, the arching span and the equestrian statue of the Pont-Neuf, with, below it, that strange little triangular park almost at water level, and then, among the distant rooftops, the dark, fretted spire of the Sainte Chapelle. The sordid old quarters, seared with the leprosy of a civilization, attracted and horri-fied Xenia; they called for dynamite; where they had stood there should rise great blocks of houses into which air and sunlight should stream. Yet it would be pleasant to live there, even the poverty-stricken life of the little hotels, of lodgings partitioned off in very old houses, reached by dark stairways, but whose pots of flowers on a window-sill were as surprising as a smile on the face of a sick child. Exploring districts of ancient poverty and humiliation through the late after-noons, Xenia conceived a strange tenderness for these abandoned cities within the giant city, far from the wide avenues, the royal quays, the nobly architectural squares, the triumphal arches, the opulent boulevards . . . At the end of a sloping street, the high, creamy cupolas of Sacré-Cœur caught all the evening light. It gilded even their soul-less ugliness. In this street, women, infinitely remote from all pity, whether Christian or atheist, watched at the doors or from behind dirty windowpanes, in the poisonous half-darkness of shabby rooms. Seen across the width of the street, with their shawls drawn tight or their arms crossed over dressing-gowns, they looked pretty; but close to, they all had the same ravaged faces, lithographs in make-up, crudely and melodramatically drawn. 'They are women and I am a woman . . .' Xenia found it difficult to judge this truth. 'What have we in common, what is the difference between us?' It was so easy to answer herself: 'I am the daughter of a people which has accomplished the Socialist revolution and they are the victims of age-old capitalist exploitation'—so easy that it became almost an empty formula. Were there not such women in certain streets in Moscow too? What was she to think? Curious eyes followed the obviously foreign girl in her white jacket and white beret as she went up the steep street—what on earth could she be looking for in this quarter? Not her happiness—that was certain—nor 'bizness,' nor a man—so what, then?—vice?—a neat little package, though, d'ya see those ankles, I had ankles like that when I was seventeen, no kidding! Xenia passed a dreary-looking Oriental, like a Crimean Tatar, who was peering furtively into windows and doorways, and she saw that he was driven by a kind of hunger more pitiful and keener than hunger. The most wretched little shops, next door to the brothels, displayed flyspecked chocolate bars, cigarette papers, cheeses, imported fruits. Xenia remembered the poverty of our co-operatives in the Moscow suburbs. How could it be?—are they so rich that even their poverty can wallow in a sort of abundance? The fetid horror of these sloughs spread over a base and hoggish ease full of food and drink, of charming dress prints, of sentimental love-making and sexual irritants.

Xenia made her way back to the Left Bank. The Châtelet marked the end of a commercial city whose bustle was purely elemental— bellies and guts to be fed. The animality of the crowds sought its ends on the spot. The Tour St.-Jacques, surrounded by a sorry oasis of greenery and two-*sou* chairs, was only a useless poem in stone. 'A vestige of the theocratic age,' Xenia thought, 'and this city is in the mercantile age . . .' She had only to cross a bridge and—between the Préfecture, the Conciergerie, and the Palais de Justice—she would reach the administrative age. The prisons dated back seven hundred years, their round towers, facing the Seine, were so nobly proportioned that they made you forget their ancient torture chambers. The courts nourished a people of scribes, but there was a flower market there too.

Another bridge over the same waters, and books lived on the stalls, students walked bareheaded with notebooks under their arms, in the cafés you glimpsed faces bent over texts which were simultaneously the Pandects of Justinian, Cæsar's *Commentaries*, Sigmund Freud's *Book of Dreams*, and surrealist poems. Life surged along the café terraces towards a garden laid out in quiet lines; and the garden ended, among *bourgeois* apartment houses, in an airy bronze globe supported by human figures, like a thought bound to the earth, metallic but transparent, terrestrial but proudly aloof. Xenia preferred to go home through this square, where the sky was wider than elsewhere. The printed fabrics which the Ivanovo-Voznesensk Textile Trust wanted required little of her time—one conference a week on submitted samples. She let herself live, an unimaginable thing, but so easy.

To stop before a sixteenth-century doorway in the Rue St. Honoré and remember that Robespierre and Saint-Just had passed it on their way to the guillotine, to discover beside it a shop window displaying cloths from the Levant, to ask the price of a bottle of perfume, to wander through the Eiffel Tower gardens ... Was it beautiful or ugly, that metal skeleton which rose so high into the sky above Paris? Lyric in any case, moving, unique in the world! What æsthetic emotion was involved in the feeling with which Xenia saw it from the heights of Ménilmontant, on the horizon of the city? Sukhov explained that our Palace of the Soviets would raise a steel statue of the Chief yet higher into the sky above Moscow, would be of another order of greatness and symbolism! Their little Eiffel Tower, an outmoded monument to industrial technique at the end of the nineteenth century, made him laugh. 'How can you find that thing interesting?' (The word moving was not in his vocabulary.) 'You may be a poet,' Xenia answered, 'but you have less intuition about certain things than a plant has'; and since he had no idea what she meant, he laughed, sure of his superiority ... So Xenia preferred to go out alone.

Having waked late, about nine o'clock, Xenia dressed, then opened her window, which looked out on the intersection of the Boulevard Raspail and the Boulevard de Montparnasse. Happy to be alive, she contemplated the scene as if it were a landscape—houses, cafés with their chairs still upside down on the tables, and pavements. A subway station: *Métro Vavin*. The oyster and shellfish stand, still closed; the woman who kept the news-stand, unfolding her camp-stool ... Nothing changed from one day to another. Xenia ate breakfast in the hotel café, and it was a pleasant interlude. The matutinal rites of the establishment brought her a feeling of peaceful security. How could these people live without anxiety, without enthusiasm for the future, without thinking of others and of themselves with anguish, pity, sternness? From whence did they draw this plenitude in a sort of emptiness? Hardly had Xenia (already falling a victim, she too, to the beginning of a habit) sat down at her usual table close to the curtains behind which the boulevard was visible in shades of stone, uncon-cernedly beginning its daily life over again—hardly had she settled herself there, before Madame Delaporte came silently in, like a large and very dignified cat. Cashier of the café-restaurant for twenty-three years, Madame Delaporte quite simply felt herself the queen of a realm from which uneasiness was banished—like a Queen Wilhelmina of Holland reigning over fields of tulips. Even the unpaid bills of several old clients inspired confidence too. The house extends credit, sir—why not? That Dr. Poivrier, who owned a house in the Rue d'Assas besides holding stock in the Bon Marché, owed five hundred francs—why, it was money in the bank! Madame Delaporte considered that the respectable and regular clientele which patronized the establishment was her own handiwork. If Leonardo da Vinci had painted the Gioconda, Madame Delaporte had created that clientele. Other, less privileged women have children who grow up and marry, who get divorced, whose children fall ill, whose businesses fail, and all the rest of it, in short! 'As for me, sir, I have this establishment, it is my home, and as long as I am here, things will be as they should be!' Madame Delaporte would bring out the last words with a modest assurance which left no doubts in her hearer's mind. She began the morning by opening the cash drawer, then put within easy reach her knitting, her spectacles, a book from the lending library, the illustrated magazine in which, at slack times, she would read, with a pitying and sceptical half-smile, Aunt Solange's advice to 'Myosotis, eighteen years old,' 'Blondinette, Lyons,' 'Unhappy Rose': 'Do you think he really loves me?' Madame Delaporte patted her hair with her fingers to make sure that each prettily waved grey strand was properly in place. Then she took her first comprehensive look at the café. Unchanging order still reigned. Monsieur Martin, the waiter, was just putting the last ash-trays on the last tables; then, with an excess of conscientiousness, he rubbed at the blurred outline of a wet stain until the wood shone irreproachably. He smiled at Xenia, and Madame Delaporte smiled at her too. Together the two friendly voices wished her good morning: 'Everything to your liking, mademoiselle?' The phrases seemed to be uttered by things themselves—things happy to exist, and sociable by nature. Between ten and ten-fifteen the first regular client, Monsieur Taillandier, came in, to lean on the counter by the cash register and take a coffee with kirsch. Cashier and client exchanged remarks which varied so little that Xenia thought she knew them by heart . . . For twelve years Madame Delaporte had been taking medicines for various stomach ailments—flatulence, acidity . . . Monsieur Taillandier was preoccupied by his diet for arthritis. 'There you are, madame—both coffee and kirsch are on my forbidden list, and yet—you see . . . I don't

deny myself the pleasure of them, not I, madame! What doctors say
has to be taken with a grain of salt; the only guide I trust is my
instinct! Why, in 'twenty-four, when I was with my regiment . . .'—
'As for me, monsieur'—at this point Madame Delaporte's long knitting
needles began their ballet—'I have tried the most expensive preparations, I have consulted the greatest specialists without a thought for
the cost, I beg you to believe me, yes, monsieur . . . Well, I have come
back to plain, homely remedies; what does me the most good is a herb
tea that a herbalist in the Marais compounds for me, and you can see
that I don't look too badly after all . . .' Sometimes at about this time
the elegant Monsieur Gimbre arrived. He knew all about the races:
'Be sure to bet on Nautilus II! And in the next race, Cleopatra!'
Peremptory on this subject, Monsieur Gimbre sometimes ventured
into politics if he could find anyone to sustain a dialogue with him; he
spoke disapprovingly of the Czechoslovaks, whom he even pretended
to confuse with the Kurdo-Syriacs, and revealed the exact prices of the
châteaux Léon Blum had bought. Xenia looked at him over her newspaper. His self-importance, his contemptible viewpoint, irritated her,
and she asked herself: What meaning can the life of such a creature
have? Full of tact, Madame Delaporte quickly managed to change the
subject. 'Is Normandy still your sales territory, Monsieur Taillandier?'
and the discussion immediately turned to Norman cooking. 'Ah, yes,'
the cashier sighed inexplicably. Monsieur Taillandier left, Monsieur
Gimbre shut himself up in the telephone booth, Monsieur Martin, the
waiter, took his stand in front of the open door between the grass plots,
whence, without appearing to, he could watch the modistes across the
way, Chez Monique. An old, grey, terribly egotistic tomcat glided
among the tables without deigning to see anyone. Madame Delaporte
called him discreetly: 'Here, here, Mitron.' Mitron went his own way,
probably flattered by the attention. 'Ungrateful beast!' Madame Delaporte would murmur, and if Xenia looked up, she would go on:
'Animals, mademoiselle, are just as ungrateful as people. If you take
my advice you won't trust either!' It was a minute and peaceful
universe, where people lived without discussing Plan quotas, without
fearing purges, without devoting themselves to the future, without
considering the problems of Socialism. That morning Madame Delaporte had been just about to launch one of her usual aphorisms when,
instead, she dropped her knitting, climbed down from her high stool,
drew the waiter's attention by a nod, and, her face full of interest,

advanced towards the corner where Xenia, her elbows on the table, sat before coffee, croissants, and a newspaper.

What was strange about Xenia was her immobility. Her chin in one hand, 'white as a shroud' (Madame Delaporte remarked later), her eyebrows raised, her eyes staring, she ought to have seen the cashier approaching, but she did not see her, did not see her set off hurriedly in the opposite direction, did not hear her say to the waiter: 'Quick, quick, Martin, a Marie Brizard—no, better an anisette, but do hurry— she's out of her senses, my God!' . . . Madame Delaporte herself carried the anisette to the table and set it in front of Xenia, who did not stir . . . 'Mademoiselle, my child, what is it?' A hand laid gently on her white beret and her hair recalled Xenia to present reality. She looked at Madame Delaporte, blinking back her tears; she bit her lips, she said something in Russian. ('What can I do? Oh, what can I do?') There were affectionate questions on Madame Delaporte's lips: 'Lovesick, child? Has he been cross to you? Is he unfaithful?' but that hard waxen face, with its concentrated bewilderment, did not look like lovesickness, it must be something much worse, something unheard of and incomprehensible . . . did one ever know with these Russians?

'Thank you,' said Xenia.

A wild smile disfigured her childish face. She swallowed the anisette, rose, her eyes dry again, and, without thinking of touching up her powder, left the café almost at a run, crossed the boulevard, dodging buses, and disappeared down the subway stairs . . . The open paper, the untouched coffee and croissants on the table, bore witness to some very unusual trouble. Monsieur Martin and Madame Delaporte bent over the paper together. 'Without my glasses I can't see, Monsieur Martin—do you find anything? An accident, a crime?' After a moment Monsieur Martin answered: 'All I see is the announcement of a trial in Moscow . . . You know, Madame Delaporte, they shoot people there in a wink, and for nothing at all . . .'

'A trial?' said Madame Delaporte incredulously. 'Do you think that can be it? In any case, I pity the poor girl. I feel very strange, Monsieur Martin. Give me an anisette, please—or no, better a Marie Brizard. It is as if I had seen bad luck . . .'

In the luminous field of her consciousness Xenia saw but two clear ideas: 'We cannot let Kiril Rublev be shot . . . Perhaps there is only a week left to save him, a week . . .' She let the train carry her, she let the crowd guide her through the subterranean corridors of St.-Lazare, she read the names of unknown stations. Her thought went no further than the idea that obsessed it. Suddenly, on the wall of a station, she saw a huge and monstrous advertisement representing a bull's head, black and wide-horned, with one eye alive and the other pierced by an enormous square wound in which the blood was as red as fire. A beast shot dead, an atrocious vision. Fleeing the picture, which reappeared in station after station, Xenia found herself on the pavement in front of the Trois Quartiers opposite the Madeleine, irresolutely talking to herself.

What was she to do? An elderly gentleman took off his hat to her, he had gold teeth, he was saying something in a honeyed voice, he seemed embarrassed. He said 'graceful' and Xenia heard 'grace.' To write instantly, to telegraph: Grace, grace for Kiril Rublev, grace! The gentleman saw her sharp, childish face light up, he was preparing to look ravished, but Xenia stamped her foot, she saw him, his thin but carefully parted hair, his piglike eyes, and she did what she used to do when she was a child, in her worst furies, she spat . . . The gentleman fled, Xenia entered a noisy café. 'Letter-paper, please . . . Yes, coffee, and quickly.' The waiter brought her a yellow envelope, a sheet of cross-ruled paper. Write to the Chief, only he would save Kiril Rublev. 'You who are dear and great and just, our beloved Chief . . . Comrade!' Xenia's impulse failed. 'Dear'—but was she not, even as she wrote, overcoming a sort of hatred? It was a terrible thought. 'Great'— but what did he not permit? 'Just'—and Rublev was going to be tried, to be killed, Rublev who was like a saint . . . and these trials are certainly decided on by the Political Bureau! She reflected. To save Rublev, why should she not humiliate herself, why should she not lie? Only, the letter would not arrive in time—and even if it arrived, would he read it, *He* who received thousands of letters a day, which were opened by a secretary? Whom could she beg to intervene? The Consul General, Nikifor Antonich, stupid, unfeeling, soulless coward that he was? The First Secretary of the Legation, Willi, who was teaching her bridge, took her to Tabarin, seeing in her only Popov's pretty daughter? He spied on the ambassador, he was the perfect climber, was Willi, and he too had no soul. Other faces came to her, and they all suddenly looked repulsive. That very evening, as soon as the newspaper paragraph was confirmed, the Party would meet, the secretary would propose telegraphing a unanimous resolution demanding the supreme penalty for Kiril Rublev, Erchov, Makeyev, traitors, assassins, enemies of the people, scum of humanity. Willi would vote Yes, Nikifor Antonich would vote Yes, the rest would all vote Yes ... 'May my hand wither if I raise it with yours, you wretches!' No one to beg for help, no one to whom she could talk, no one! The Rublevs perish alone, alone! What was she to do?

It came to her: Father! Father, help me! You have known Rublev all your life, Father, you will save him, you can save him. You will go to the Chief, you will tell him ... She lit a cigarette: the match flame was a star of good omen in her fingers. Almost radiant, Xenia began writing her telegram in a post office. The first word she put on paper extinguished her confidence. She tore up the first blank, and felt her face become tense. Above the desk a poster explained: '*By a monthly payment of fifty francs for twenty-five years, you can assure yourself of a peaceful old age ...*' Xenia burst out laughing. Her fountain pen had run dry, she looked around. A magic hand held out a yellow pen with a gold band. Xenia wrote decisively:

Father, Kiril must be saved Stop You have known Kiril for twenty years Stop He is a saint Stop Innocent Stop Innocent Stop If you do not save him there will be a crime upon our heads Stop Father you will save him ...

Where had that absurd yellow fountain pen come from? Xenia did not know what to do with it, but a hand took it from her; a gentleman, of whom she saw nothing but his Charlie Chaplin moustache, said something agreeable to her which she did not hear. Go to the devil! At the counter the clerk, a young woman with thick lips heavily rouged, counted the words in Xenia's telegram. She looked straight into Xenia's eyes and said:

'I hope you will succeed, mademoiselle.'

A knot of sobs in her throat, Xenia answered:

'It is almost impossible.'

The brown, gold-flecked eyes on the other side of the counter looked at her in terror, but their expression enlightened Xenia—she recovered herself: 'No, everything is possible, thank you, thank you.' The Boulevard Haussmann vibrated under a pale sun. At a corner a crowd had gathered to look up at a second-floor window in which slender, swaying mannequins appeared one by one, displaying the season's dresses ...
Xenia knew that she would find Sukhov at the Marbeuf. Though she

did not think about it, he inspired in her the physical confidence which a young woman has in the male who desires her. Poet, secretary of a section of the Poets' Syndicate, he wrote prosaic, impersonal poems which were printed in the newspapers and which the State Publishing House collected in small volumes: *Drums, Step by Step, Guard the Frontier* . . . He repeated Maiakovsky's epigrams: 'Notre-Dame? It would make a magnificent cinema.' Associated with Security, he visited the cells of young officials on missions abroad, recited them his verses in the virile voice of a town crier, and wrote confidential reports on the behaviour of his auditors in their capitalist surroundings. When Sukhov and Xenia were alone in a garden, he put his arm around her. The grass, the smell of earth made him amorous, made him want to run, to gallop, Xenia said. She let him embrace her and was pleased, though she insisted to him that she felt no more than friendship for him, 'and if you want to write to me, let it be in prose, please!' No—he was writing nothing. She refused him her lips, she refused to go to a hotel in the Porte Doré district with him to begin 'an adventure *à la française*'—'which perhaps, Xeniuchka, would make me as lyrical as old Pushkin! You ought to love me for poetry's sake!' Sukhov kissed her hands. 'You get prettier every day, you have a little Champs-Elysées air about you now that fascinates me, Xeniuchka . . . But you don't look well. Come closer.' He squeezed her into a corner of the bench, knee to knee, put his arm around her waist, looked her up and down with eyes that were like a fine stallion's. But what Xenia said froze him. He drew away. And, severely: 'Xeniuchka, don't do anything foolish. Keep out of this business. If Rublev has been arrested, then he is guilty. If he has confessed, you cannot make a denial for him. If he is guilty, he no longer exists for anyone. That is my point of view, and there is no other.' Xenia was already looking for someone else to help her. Sukhov took her hand. The contact aroused such intense disgust in her that she suppressed it and remained inert. Was I mad that I thought of *him* to save a Rublev? 'Are you leaving so soon, Xeniuchka, you're not angry, are you?'

'What an idea! I'm busy. No, don't come with me.'

You are nothing but a brute, Sukhov, just fit to turn out poems for rotary presses. Your loud linen waistcoat is grotesque, your double crepe-rubber soles give me the horrors. Xenia was refreshed by her irritation. 'Taxi . . . Anywhere . . . Bois de Boulogne . . . No, Buttes-Chaumont . . .' The Buttes-Chaumont floated in a green haze. On fine summer mornings the trees and shrubs in Petrovsky Park look like that. Xenia looked at the leaves. Leaves, calm me. Leaning over the pool, she saw that she looked as if she had been crying for a long time. Absurd ducklings came running towards her . . . An insane nightmare —there had been nothing in that accursed paper, it was impossible. She powdered her face, rouged her lips, took a deep breath. What a frightful dream! The next instant her distress overpowered her again —but she remembered a name: Passereau. How could she have failed to remember it sooner? Passereau is a great man. Passereau had an audience with the Chief. Together, Passereau and Father will save Rublev.

It was about three o'clock when Xenia called on Professor Passereau, famous in two hemispheres, President of the Congress for the Defence of Culture, corresponding member of the Moscow Academy of Sciences, whom even Popov did not refuse to visit when he made an inspection trip to Paris. A servant took in her name, the door of the drawing-room opened at once (Xenia had a glimpse of provincial furniture, walls decorated with water-colours), and Professor Passereau advanced to take her most affectionately by the shoulders. 'Mademoiselle! How happy I am to see you! In Paris for a while? Do you know, mademoiselle, that you are adorable? The daughter of my old friend will forgive the compliment, I am sure . . . Come in, come in!' He took her arm, seated her on the sofa in his study, smiled at her with every inch of his frank, military-looking face. None of the city's noises penetrated here. Various pieces of precision apparatus, under glass bells, occupied the corners of the room. A cluster of green leaves filled the door that gave on the garden. A large portrait in a gold frame appeared to attract Xenia's attention. The professor explained: 'Count Montessus de Ballore, mademoiselle, the man of genius who deciphered the enigma of earthquakes. . . .'

'But you too,' said Xenia enthusiastically, 'you have . . .'

'Oh, I—that was much easier. Once the trail has been blazed in scientific matters, all one has to do is to follow it . . .'

Xenia allowed herself to be distracted, because she shrank from her problem. 'Yours is a magnificent and mysterious science, is it not?' The professor laughed: 'Magnificent, if you insist, like all science. But not mysterious. We are hot on the track of mystery, mademoiselle, and it will not elude us!' The professor opened a file. 'See—here are the co-ordinates for the Messina earthquake of 1908; no more mystery

there. When I demonstrated them before the Tokio Congress . . .' But
he saw that Xenia's lips were trembling. 'Mademoiselle . . . What is it?
Bad news of your father? . . . Are you in trouble? Tell me . . .'

'Kiril Rublev,' Xenia stammered.

'Rublev, the historian? . . . The Rublev of the Communist Academy,
you mean? I've heard of him, I believe I even met him once . . . at a
banquet . . . a friend of your father, is he not?'

Xenia felt ashamed of the tears she was holding back, ashamed of her
absurd feeling of humiliation, ashamed perhaps of what was about to
take place. Her throat became dry, she felt that she was an enemy here.

'Kiril Rublev will be shot before the week is over if we do not intervene instantly.'

Professor Passereau appeared to shrink into his chair. She saw that
he had a potbelly, old-fashioned ornaments dangling from his watch
chain, an old-fashioned waistcoat. 'Ah,' he said. 'Ah, what you tell me
is terrible . . .' Xenia explained the dispatch from Moscow, published
that morning, the abominable phrase concerning the 'complete confessions,' the assassination of Tulayev a year since . . . The professor
stressed the point: 'There was an assassination?'—'Yes, but to make
Rublev responsible for it is as mad as . . .'—'I understand, I understand . . .' She had nothing more to say. The glittering and preposterous seismographic machines occupied an inordinate space in the
silence. There was no earthquake anywhere.

'Well, mademoiselle, I beg you to believe that you have my deepest
sympathy . . . I assure you . . . It is terrible . . . Revolutions devour
their children—we French have learned that only too well . . . the
Girondins, Danton, Hébert, Robespierre, Babeuf . . . It is the implacable movement of history . . .' Xenia heard only fragments of what
he was saying. Her mind distilled the essence of his sentences, the
fragments fitted together to compose a different discourse for her. 'A
sort of fatality, mademoiselle . . . I am an old materialist myself, and
yet, in the presence of these trials, I think of the fatality of antique
tragedy . . .' ('Hurry up and get it over,' Xenia thought sternly.)
'. . . before which we are powerless . . .

'Besides, are you quite sure that partisan passion, the spirit of
conspiracy, have not proved too much of a temptation to an old revolutionary whom . . . I admire, with you, of whom I too think with
distress . . .' The professor made an allusion to Dostoevsky's *The
Possessed* . . .

'If he brings in the Slavic soul,' Xenia said to herself, 'I will make a scene . . . And your own soul, you puppet?' Her despair changed into a sort of hate. If she could throw a brick at those idiotic seismographs, go at them with a blacksmith's hammer, or even with the old axe of the Russian countryside . . .

'In short, mademoiselle, it seems to me that all hope is not lost. If Rublev is innocent, the Supreme Tribunal will accord him justice . . .'

'Do you mean to say you believe that?'

Professor Passereau tore yesterday's sheet from the calendar. This young woman in white, with her beret askew, her hostile mouth and eyes, her uneasy hands, was a strange being, vaguely dangerous, swept into his peaceful study by a sort of hurricane. If his imagination had been literary, Passereau would have compared her to a stormy petrel, and she made him uncomfortable.

'You must telegraph to Moscow at once,' said Xenia resolutely. 'Have your League telegraph this afternoon. That you stand guarantee for Rublev, that you proclaim his innocence. Rublev belongs to science!'

Professor Passereau sighed deeply. The door opened, a visiting card was handed to him on a tray. He looked at his watch and said: 'Ask the gentleman to wait for a moment . . .' Whatever be the tragedies that convulse distant lands, we have our usual obligations. The intervention of the visiting card gave him back all his eloquence.

'Mademoiselle, never doubt that I . . . I am more moved than I can express . . . But please note that I have met Rublev, whom I respect, only once in my life, at a reception . . . How can I stand guarantee for him in such a complex situation? That he is a scientist of great ability, I do not doubt, and, like you, I hope with all my heart that he will be preserved to science . . . For the justice of your country I have a respect which is absolute . . . I believe in the goodness of men, even in our age . . . If Rublev—I state it purely as a hypothesis—is guilty to any degree, the magnanimity of the Chief of your Party will, I am sure, leave him every hope of escaping punishment . . . Personally, my most fervent wishes accompany him, and you too, mademoiselle—I share your emotion, but I really do not see what I could do . . . I have made it a principle never to interfere in the internal affairs of your country, it is a matter of conscience with me . . . The League Committee meets only once a month, the date of the next meeting is the twenty-seventh, three weeks hence, and I have no power to call a meeting earlier, since I am only vice-president . . . Furthermore, the League has, properly speaking, but one object—to fight fascism. A proposal to take a step contrary to our by-laws, even coming from me, would be likely to arouse the most intense objection . . . If we insisted, we might well open a breach in the heart of an organization which has, nevertheless, a noble mission to accomplish. Our present campaigns in favour of Carlos Prestes, Thaelmann, the persecuted Jews, might thereby suffer. You follow me, mademoiselle?'

'I am afraid I do!' said Xenia brutally. 'So you refuse to take any steps?'

'I am extremely sorry, mademoiselle—but you greatly overestimate my influence . . . Believe me . . . Come, consider the situation! What could I do?'

Xenia's clear eyes looked at him coldly.

'And the execution of a Rublev will not rob you of any sleep, I take it?'

Professor Passereau answered sadly:

'You are most unjust, mademoiselle. But, old man that I am, I understand you . . .'

She did not look at him again, did not give him her hand. She was walking down the middle-class street; her face was set. No one passed. 'His science is vile, his instruments are vile, his brown study is vile! And Kiril Rublev is lost, we are all lost, there is no way out any more, no way out!'

In the editorial office of a weekly which was almost extreme Left, another professor, a man of thirty-five, listened to her as if her news moved him to profound grief. Was he not going to tear his hair, wring his hands? He did nothing of the sort. He had never heard of Rublev, but these Russian catastrophes haunted him day and night. 'They are Shakespearean tragedies . . . Mademoiselle, I have cried my indignation in this very paper. "Mercy!" I cried, "in the name of our love and devotion to the Russian Revolution." I was not heard, I aroused reactions which must likewise be accepted in good faith, I tendered my resignation to our managing committee . . . To-day, the political situation makes it impossible for such an article to appear. We represent the average opinion of an audience which belongs to numerous parties; the ministerial crisis, of which the papers have not yet got wind, imperils all our work of the last few years . . . A conflict with the Com-

munists at this moment might have the most disastrous results . . .
And should we save Dublev ?'

'Rublev,' Xenia corrected.

'Yes, Rublev—should we save him ? My unfortunate experience does
not permit me to believe so . . . I really cannot see how . . . At most,
I could try calling on your ambassador at once and expressing my
concern to him . . .'

'At least do that,' murmured Xenia, completely discouraged, for she
was thinking: 'They won't do anything, no one will do anything, they
don't even understand . . .' She felt like beating her head against the
wall . . . She swept through several other editorial offices, so hastily,
borne along by such a desperate and exasperated grief, that later she
had only a confused memory of where she had gone. An old intellectual
with a soiled necktie became almost rude in the presence of her
insistence. 'Well then, go and see the Trotskyists! We have our
sources of information, our minds are made up. All revolutions have
produced traitors, who may appear to be, who may in fact be, admirable personally. I admit it. All revolutions have committed great
injustices in particular cases. You have to take them by and large!' He
picked up a paper cutter and hacked furiously at the wrapping of a
morning paper. 'Our task, here, is to fight reaction!' Somewhere else,
an old lady with a carelessly powdered, lined face was so touched that
she called Xenia 'my dear child.' 'If I really had any influence with the
editor, my dear child, ah, believe me, I . . . In any case I will try to slip
in a paragraph emphasizing the importance of your friend's work—
Uplev, did you say, or Rulev? Here, write it down for me, clearly.
A musician, you said? Ah, a historian, yes, yes, a historian . . .' The
old lady wrapped a faded silk scarf around her throat. 'What days we
live in, my dear child! It is frightening to think of it!' She leaned
forward, sincerely moved: 'Tell me—excuse me if I am indiscreet—
but a woman—are you in love with Kiril Rublev? Such a beautiful
name, Kiril . . .'

'No, no, I'm not in love with him,' said Xenia, in great distress and
finding it as difficult to restrain her tears as her anger.

For no reason, she stopped in front of an American book and
stationery shop in the Avenue de l'Opéra. Photographic cut-outs of
pretty little nudes posed above ash-trays, not far from maps of partitioned Czechoslovakia. The books had a well-to-do look. They raised
great problems, they were idiotic. *The Mystery of the Moonless Night*,

The Masked Stranger, Pity Poor Women! It all emanated the luxurious futility of well-fed, well-bathed, well-perfumed people who wanted to expose themselves to a little shudder of fear or pity before going to sleep in silk sheets. Is it possible that this present age goes on, without their ever learning fear and pity in their own flesh, in their own nerves? In another white-and-gilt display, sea horses in an aquarium promised luck to the purchasers of jewels. Luck in love, luck in business, with our brooches, rings, necklaces—the latest thing—the astral sea horse. She must flee! Xenia rested at the other end of Paris, on a bench, in a grey landscape of hospital windows and chalky walls. Every few minutes the monstrous thunder of a train crossing a bridge penetrated to the depths of her nerves. Home again, dead tired—where had she been, how could she sleep? The next morning she had to overcome a feeling of nausea as she dressed, her hands trembled when she rouged her lips, she got down after Madame Delaporte had come in, sat at her usual table without noticing the curious and pitying looks that greeted her, put her chin in her hands, stared at the Boulevard Raspail . . . Madame Delaporte herself came and touched her on the shoulder: 'Telephone, mademoiselle . . . No better?'—'Oh yes,' said Xenia, 'it's nothing . . .' In the telephone booth a man's voice, velvety and assured, a voice like doom, spoke in Russian:

'Krantz speaking . . . I am aware of all your . . . imprudent and criminal proceedings . . . I insist that you cease them immediately . . . Do you understand? The consequences can be serious, and not only for yourself . . .'

Xenia hung up without answering. Willi, First Secretary of the Embassy, entered the café—grey raglan overcoat, immaculate felt hat, the well-dressed man, English style; just the type for ash-trays decorated with naked women, a copy of *Esquire*, yellow pigskin gloves, she'd like to throw them all in his face at once, the climber! Fake gentleman, fake Communist, fake diplomat, fake, fake! He took off his hat, bowed: 'Xenia Vassilievna, I have a telegram for you . . .' While she opened the blue envelope, he watched her attentively. Tired, nervous, resolved. He must be careful.

The telegram was from Popov:

MOTHER ILL WE BOTH BEG YOU RETURN IMMEDIATELY . . .

'I have reserved a place for you on Wednesday's plane . . .'

'I am not going,' said Xenia.

Without being asked, he sat down at the other side of her table. Leaning towards one another, they looked like a pair of lovers who had quarrelled and were making up. Madame Delaporte understood it all now.

'Krantz has instructed me to tell you, Xenia Vassilievna, that you must go home . . . You have been most imprudent, Xenia Vassilievna, allow me to tell you so, as your friend . . . We all belong to the Party . . .'

It was not the thing to say. Willi began again:

'Krantz is a fine sort . . . He's worried about you. Worried about your father . . . You are seriously compromising your father . . . He's an old man, your father . . . And you can do nothing here, you will get nowhere, absolutely nowhere . . . You're up against a blank wall.'

That was more like it. Xenia's white face lost a little of its hardness.

'Between ourselves, I believe that when you get back you will be arrested . . . But it will not be serious, Krantz will intervene, he has promised me . . . Your father can stand guarantee for you . . . You have no need to be afraid.'

That reference to being afraid had worked . . . Xenia said:

'You think I am afraid?'

'Not in the least! I am talking to you as a comrade, as a friend . . .'

'I will go back when I have done what I have to do. Tell that to Krantz. Tell him that if Rublev is shot, I will go through the streets protesting . . . That I will write to every paper . . .'

'There will be no trial, Xenia Vassilievna, we have received information on the subject. We are not issuing a denial, as we consider that the sooner that unfortunate announcement is forgotten, the better. Krantz does not even know if Rublev has really been arrested. If he has been, the publicity you might stir up for him could only harm him . . . And it horrifies me to hear you say such things. It is not like you. You are incapable of treason. You will say nothing to anyone, no matter what happens. To whom would you protest? To this hostile world around us? To this *bourgeois* Paris, to these fascist papers which calumniate us? To the Trotskyist agents of the fascists? What more could you accomplish than to stir up a little counter-revolutionary scandal for the delectation of a few anti-Soviet publications? Xenia Vassilievna, I promise to forget what you have said. Here is your ticket. The plane leaves Le Bourget at 9.45 a.m. Wednesday. I shall be there. Have you money?'

'Yes.'

It was not true, Xenia was uneasily aware. When she had paid her hotel bill she would have almost nothing left. She pushed away the ticket: 'Take it, if you don't want me to tear it up in front of you.' Willi calmly put it into his wallet. 'Think it over, Xenia Vassilievna, I shall come back to see you to-morrow morning.' Madame Delaporte was disappointed when they parted with no sign of affection. 'She must be terribly jealous, Russian women are tigresses once they get started . . .'—'Either tigresses or profligates—none of these foreigners have any sense of decency . . .' Through the curtains Xenia observed that before Willi got into his Chrysler he looked towards the head of the boulevard, where a beige overcoat was strolling up and down. Already shadowed. They will force me to go. They stop at nothing. To hell with them! But . . .

She counted what money she had left. Three hundred francs. Should she go to the Foreign Commerce Bureau? They would refuse her an advance. Would they even let her go? Could she sell her wrist-watch, her Leica? She packed her suitcase, put a pair of pyjamas and some odds and ends in her brief case, and set off down the Rue Vavin without looking back—she was sure she was being followed. And at the Luxembourg she caught a glimpse of the beige overcoat, fifty yards behind her. 'Now I am a traitor too, like Rublev . . . And my father is a traitor because I am his daughter . . .' How could she rise above this flood of thoughts, this shame, this indignation, this anger? It was exactly like the ice breaking up on the Neva: the enormous floes, like shattered stars, must collide and battle and destroy one another until the moment when they would disappear under the quiet sea swell. She must undergo her thought, follow it to its uttermost limits, until the unforeseeable but inevitable moment when all would be over, one way or another. The moment will come, can it come, can it fail to come? It seemed to Xenia that her torture would never end. But what would end, then? Life? Would they shoot me? Why? What have I done? What has Rublev done? A terrible possibility. Stay here? Without money? Look for work? What work? Where could she live? Why live? Children were sailing boats in the great circular fountain. In this French world, life is as calm and insipid as children's games, people live only for themselves! To live for myself—how ridiculous! Expelled from the Party, I could no longer look a worker in the face, I could explain nothing to anyone, no one would understand. Willi, the beast, had just said: 'Well, I grant you—perhaps they are crimes, we know nothing about it. Our duty is to trust, with our eyes shut. Because there is nothing else for either of us to do. To accuse, to protest, never results in anything but serving the enemy. I would rather be shot by mistake myself. Neither the crimes nor the mistakes alter our duty . . .' It is true. On his lips they are parroted phrases, because he will always manage to risk nothing. But they are true. What would Rublev himself do, what would he say? The faintest shadow of treason would never enter his mind . . .

At the St.-Michel subway station Xenia shook off the detective in the beige overcoat. She wandered on through Paris, stopping sometimes to look at her reflection in shop windows: bedraggled silhouette, rumpled jacket, pale face and sunken eyes—it was not in order to feel sorry for herself, but to see that she was ugly, I want to be ugly, I must be ugly! The women she passed—self-centred, carefully dressed, pleased because they had chosen some hideous bauble to dangle from the lapel of a tailored jacket or the neck of a bodice—were merely human animals satisfied to breathe, but the sight of them made her want to stop living . . . At nightfall Xenia found herself on the edge of a brightly lit square. She was exhausted from walking. Cascades of electric light flowed over the dome of a huge cinema, the flood of barbaric brilliance surrounded two enormous faces, joined in the most meaningless of kisses, as revolting in their beatitude as in their utter anonymity. The other corner of the square, flaming with red and gold, sent a love song pouring frantically out of loudspeakers, to an accompaniment of little strident cries and clicking heels. For Xenia the whole effect resolved itself into a long and insistent caterwauling whose human intonation made it a thing of shame. Men and women were drinking at the bar, and they suggested strange insects, cruel to their own kind, collected in an overheated vivarium. Between these two conflagrations—the theatre and the café—a wide street mounted into a darkness starred with signs: HOTEL, HOTEL, HOTEL. Xenia started up it, turned in at the first door, and asked for a room for the night. The little old bespectacled man whom she woke from a drowse seemed inseparable from the keyboard and the counter between which his tobacco-reeking person was wedged. 'It will be fifteen francs,' he said, laying his cloudy spectacles on the paper he had been reading. His staring rabbit eyes blinked. 'Funny, I don't recognize you. Could you be Paula, from the Passage Clichy? Don't you always go to the

Hotel du Morbihan? You're a foreigner? Just a minute . . .' He stooped, disappeared, popped out from under a board, disappeared again down the corridor . . . And the proprietor himself appeared, his shirt sleeves rolled up, exposing thick butcher's arms. He seemed to be surrounded by a greasy fog. He looked Xenia over, as if he were going to sell her, hunted for something under the counter, finally said: 'All right, fill out the form. Have you your papers?' Xenia held out her diplomatic passport. 'Alone? Right . . . I'll give you Number 11, it'll be thirty francs, the bathroom is right next door . . .' Huge, bull-necked, he preceded Xenia up the stairs, swinging a bunch of keys between his fat fingers. Cold, dimly lighted by two shaded lamps set on two night tables, Room No. 11 reminded Xenia of a detective story. In that corner over there was the ironbound chest in which the murdered girl's body was found, cut up in pieces. The corner smelled of phenol. After she put out the lamps, the blue neon signs in the street filled the room from mirror to ceiling with luminous arabesques. Among them Xenia quickly discovered visions familiar to her childhood: the wolf, the fish, the witch's spinning wheel, the profile of Ivan the Terrible, the enchanted tree. She was so tired from thinking and walking that she went to sleep immediately. The murdered girl timidly raised the lid of the chest, stood up, stretched her bruised limbs. 'Don't be afraid,' Xenia said to her, 'I know we are innocent.' She had hair like a naiad's, and calm eyes like wild daisies. 'We'll read the story of the Golden Fish together, listen to that music . . .' Xenia took her into her bed to warm her . . . Downstairs, behind the desk, the proprietor of the Two Moons Hotel was conversing by telephone with Monsieur Lambert, assistant police commissioner of the district.

Life begins anew every morning. Too young to despair, Xenia felt that she had shaken off her nightmare. If there was no trial, Rublev would live. It was impossible that they should kill him—he was so great, so simple, so pure, and Popov knew it, the Chief must know it. Xenia felt happy, she dressed, she looked in the mirror and found herself pretty again. But where did I think the murder chest was yesterday? She was glad she had not felt afraid. There was a little knock, she opened the door. A broad-shouldered figure, a broad, sad face appeared in the half-light of the hall. Neither familiar nor un-familiar, a vague fleshy face. The visitor introduced himself, in a thick, velvety voice:

'Krantz.'

He entered, looked the room over, took in everything. Xenia covered up the unmade bed.

'Xenia, I have come for you on your father's behalf. A car is waiting at the door for you. Come.'

'And if I don't wish to?'

'I give you my word that you shall do as you please. You have not been a traitor, you will never be a traitor. I am not here to use force on you. The Party trusts in you as it trusts in me. Come.'

In the car Xenia rebelled. Half facing her and pretending to be busy with his pipe, Krantz felt the storm coming. The car was going down the Rue de Rivoli. Jeanne d'Arc, with her gilt dull and peeling off, but still very beautiful, brandished a childish sword on her little pedestal. 'I want to get out,' Xenia said firmly, and she half rose. Krantz caught her arm and forced her to sit down.

'You shall get out if you wish, Xenia Vassilievna, I promise you; but not as simply as that.'

He lowered the window on Xenia's side. The Vendôme Column disappeared down a perspective of arches, in the pale light.

'Do not be impulsive, I beg of you. Whatever you do, do it deliberately. We shall pass a number of policemen on the way. We are not going fast. You can call out if you wish, I will not stop you. You, a Soviet citizen, will put yourself under the protection of the French police . . . I will be asked for my papers. You will go your way. Afternoon extras will announce your escape—that is, your treason. Throw your little handful of mud on the embassy, on your father, on our Party, on our country. I will take Wednesday's plane alone and I will pay for you—with Popov. You know the law: close relatives of traitors must at least be deported to the most distant parts of the Union.'

He drew away a little, admired the white meerschaum mermaid which formed the bowl of his handsome pipe, opened his tobacco pouch, said to the driver:

'Fedia, be so good as to slow down whenever you pass a policeman.'

'At your orders, Comrade Chief.'

Xenia's hands clenched painfully. She looked at the policemen's short capes almost with hatred. She said:

'How strong you are, Comrade Krantz, and how despicable!'

'Neither as strong nor as despicable as you think. I am loyal. And you too, Xenia Vassilievna, you must be loyal, no matter what happens.'

They took Wednesday's plane from Le Bourget together. The Eiffel Tower dwindled, glued to the earth, the severe design of the gardens opened around it, the Arc de Triomphe was only a block of stone at the centre of radiating avenues. The marvel of Paris vanished under clouds, leaving Xenia regretting a world which she had scarcely touched and had not understood, which perhaps she would never understand. 'I have accomplished nothing towards saving Rublev, I will fight for him in Moscow, if only we arrive in time! I will make my father act, I will ask for an audience with the Chief. He has known us for so many years that he will not refuse to listen to me, and if he listens to me, Rublev will be saved.' In her waking dream Xenia imagined her interview with the Chief. Confidently, without fear and without humility, well knowing that she was nothing and he the incarnation of the Party for which we must all live and die, she would be brief and direct, for his minutes were precious. He had all the problems of a sixth of the world to solve every day; she must speak to him with her whole soul, that she might convince him in a few moments . . . Krantz considerately left her to her thoughts. He occupied his time reading, alternating between stupid magazines and military reviews in several languages. The poem of the clouds unrolled above the moving earth. Rivers flowing from their distant springs enchanted the eye. They dined almost gaily in Warsaw. It seemed an even more elegant and luxurious city than Paris, but from the sky you saw that it was surrounded and, as it were, menaced by a poverty-stricken terrain. Presently, through rents in the clouds, appeared great sombre forests . . . 'We are nearly home,' Xenia murmured, flooded with a joy so poignant that she felt a momentary sympathy for her travelling companion. Krantz leaned towards the porthole; he looked tired. With gloomy satisfaction he said: 'We're already over kolkhoze land—see, there are no more small strips . . .' Infinite fields of an indefinable colour, something between ochre and greyish brown. 'We shall reach Minsk in twenty minutes . . .' From under the *French Infantry Review* he drew a copy of *Vogue* and turned the glossy pages.

'Xenia Vassilievna, I must ask you to excuse me. My instructions are definite. I request you to regard yourself as under arrest. From Minsk on, your journey will be managed by Security . . . Don't be too uneasy, I hope that it will all come out all right.'

On the cover of the magazine, elegant faces, eyeless under wide hat-brims, displayed lips rouged in different shades to match their complexions. Fifteen hundred feet below, between newly ploughed fields, peasants dressed in earth-coloured rags followed a heavily loaded cart. You could see them urging on the exhausted horse, pushing at the cart when the wheels sank into the mud.

'So I can do nothing for Rublev,' thought Xenia desolately. They could do nothing for anyone in the world, those peasants with their bogged wagon, and no one in the world could do anything for them. They disappeared, the bare ground gradually approached.

Since he had received his daughter's criminally insane telegram, Comrade Popov had been in a state between uneasiness and prostration, besides being really tortured by his rheumatism. There was no mistaking the coldness people showed him. The new Prosecutor, Atkin, who was investigating his predecessor's activities, carried his veiled insolence to the point of twice excusing himself when Popov invited him or went to call on him. Stopping in at the General Secretariat to test the atmosphere, Popov found only preoccupied faces which gave him an impression of hypocrisy. No one came hurrying to meet him. Gordeyev, who usually consulted him on current matters, did not show himself for several days. But he came on the fourth day, about six in the evening, having learned that Popov was not well and was staying at home. The Popovs lived in a C.C. villa in Bykovo Forest. Gordeyev arrived in uniform. Popov received him in a dressing-gown; he walked across the room to meet him, supporting himself on a cane. Gordeyev began by asking about his rheumatism, offered to send him a doctor who was said to be exceptionally good, did not insist, accepted a glass of brandy. The furniture, the carpets, everything in the quiet room, which gave the impression of being dusty without being so, was slightly antiquated. Gordeyev coughed to clear his throat.

'I have news of your daughter for you. She is very well ... She ... She is under arrest. She did some foolish things in Paris—have you heard about it?'

'Yes, yes,' said Popov, utterly crushed. 'I can imagine, it's possible ... I received a telegram, but is it serious, do you think?'

Coward that he was, what he most wanted to know was whether it was serious for himself.

Gordeyev looked doubtfully at his finger-nails, then at the faded half-tints of the room, the black firs outside the window. 'What shall I say? I do not know yet. Everything will depend on the inquiry.

Theoretically it can be quite serious: attempted desertion in a foreign country, during a mission, activities contrary to the interests of the Union ... Those are the terms of the law, but I certainly hope that, in actual fact, it is only a matter of ill-advised, or let us say unconsidered, acts, which are reprehensible rather than culpable ...'

Shivering into himself, Popov became so old that he lost all substance.

'The difficulty, er, Comrade Popov, is that ... I find it most awkward to explain it to you ... Help me ...'

He wanted help, the creature!

'It puts you, Comrade Popov, in a delicate situation. Aside from the fact that the relevant articles of the Code—which, of course, we shall not apply in all their rigour, without definite orders from above—that the law provides for ... for measures ... concerning the relatives of guilty parties, you certainly know that Comrade Atkin has opened an inquiry ... which is being kept secret ... into the case of Rachevsky. We have established that Rachevsky—it is incredible, but it is a fact —Rachevsky destroyed the dossier on the Aktyubinsk sabotage affair ... We have sought for the source of the most unfortunate indiscretion which caused the announcement abroad of a new trial ... We even thought it might be a manœuvre on the part of foreign agents! Rachevsky, with whom it is very difficult to talk since he appears to be always drunk, admits that he ordered the preparation of a dispatch on the subject, but he claims that he acted on verbal instructions from you ... As soon as he is arrested, I shall question him myself, you may be sure, and I shall not allow him to elude his responsibilities ... The coincidence between this fact and the charge that hangs over your daughter remains, however—how shall I put it?—most unfortunate ...'

Popov answered nothing. Twinges of pain shot through his limbs. Gordeyev tried to read him: a man at his last gasp, or an old fox who would still find a way out? Difficult to decide, but the former hypothesis seemed more likely. Popov's silence invited him to come to a conclusion. Popov was looking at him with the piercing eyes of a beast tracked to its lair.

'You can have no doubt, Comrade Popov, of my personal feelings ...'

The other did not flinch: Either he doubted them or he didn't give a damn for them, or else he felt too badly to consider them of the slightest importance. What his feelings were, Gordeyev did not feel called upon to say.

'It has been decided . . . provisionally . . . to ask you to remain at home and to make no telephone calls . . .'

'Except to the Chief of the Party?'

'It is painful to me to insist: To anyone whomsoever. It is not impossible, in any case, that your line has been cut.'

When Gordeyev was gone, Popov did not stir. The room grew darker. Rain began falling on the firs. Shadows lengthened across the forest roads. There in his arm-chair, Popov became one with the darkness of things. His wife entered—stooped, grey-haired, walking noiselessly, she too a shadow.

'Shall I turn on the light, Vassili? How do you feel?'

Old Popov answered in a very low voice:

'All right. Xenia is under arrest. We are both under arrest, you and I. I am infinitely tired. Don't turn on the light.'

10

AND STILL THE FLOES CAME DOWN...

THE LIFE of the 'Road to the Future' kolkhoze was really like an obstacle race. Definitely set up in 1931, after two purges of the village —marked by the deportation (God knows where!) of the well-to-do families and a few poor families who had shown a wrong spirit—by the following year the kolkhoze was without cattle and horses, since the farmers had contrived to destroy their livestock rather than turn it over to collective enterprise. The fodder shortage, carelessness, and epizootic diseases carried off the last horses just at the moment when a Machine and Tractor Station (M.T.S.) was finally set up at Molchansk. The arrest of the township veterinary, probably guilty because he belonged to the Baptist sect, caused no improvement. The difficulties of travel by road between Molchansk and the regional centre immediately caused the M.T.S. to suffer from lack of motor fuel and parts for repairs. Situated on the Syeroglazaya (the Grey-eyed River), the old village of Pogoryeloye (so named to perpetuate the memory of ancient fires), being one of the farthest villages from the M.T.S., was one of the last to be served. The village, consequently, was without motors; and the *mujiks* put little effort into sowing fields which they no longer considered to be their own, under the supervision of the president of a Communist kolkhoze, a workman from the bicycle factory at Penza who had been mobilized by the Party and sent by the Regional Centre. They strongly suspected that the State would take almost all of the harvest away from them. Three harvests were short. Famine came nearer and nearer, a considerable group of men took refuge in the woods, where they were fed by relatives whom, this time, the authorities did not dare to deport. The famine carried off the small children, half the old men, and even a few adults. A president of the kolkhoze was drowned in the Syeroglazaya with a stone around his neck. The new law, several times revised by the C.C., restored a precarious peace by re-establishing family properties in the collective enterprise. The kolkhoze was inspected by a good agronomist and received selected seed and chemical fertilizers, there was an unusually hot and wet summer, and magnificent wheat flourished despite the rages and quarrels of men; there was a shortage of hands at harvest-time, and half the crop rotted in the fields. The bicycle-factory worker, tried for carelessness, incapacity, and abuse of power, was sentenced to three years at hard labour. 'I hope my successor has a very good time,' he said simply. The management of the kolkhoze passed to President Vaniuchkin, a native of the village and a Communist recently demobilized from military service. In 1934–35 the kolkhoze rose from the depths of famine to a state of convalescence, thanks to the new C.C. directives, to the beneficent rhythm of rain and snow, to mild seasons, to the energy of the Young Communists, and—in the opinion of the old women and two or three bearded Believers—thanks to the return of the man of God, Father Guerassim, amnestied after three years of deportation. The seasonal crisis continued nevertheless, although it could not be denied that the sowing cycle, the selected seed, and the use of machines markedly increased the productivity of the soil. To retrieve the situation 'definitely,' there appeared on the scene, first, Agronomist Kostiukin, a curious character; then a militant from the Young Communists, who had been sent by the Regional Committee, and whom everyone was soon familiarly calling 'Kostia.' Not long before the autumn sowing, Agronomist Kostiukin observed that a parasite had attacked the seed (a part of which had been previously stolen). The M. and T. Station delivered only one tractor instead of the two which had been promised and the three which were absolutely necessary; and for the one and only tractor there was no gasolene. When the gasolene arrived, there was a break-down. The ploughing was done with horses, laboriously and late, but since the horses now could not be used to bring supplies from the township co-operatives to the kolkhoze with any regularity, the kolkhoze suffered from a shortage of manufactured articles. Half the trucks in the district were immobilized by lack of gasolene. The women began muttering that we were heading for a new famine and that it would be the just punishment for our sins.

It is a flat, slightly rolling country, severe in line under the clouds, among which you can distinctly see troops of white archangels pursuing one another from horizon to horizon. By the soft roads, muddy or dusty according to the season, Molchansk, the township, is some thirty-eight miles away; the railroad station is ten miles from the township; the nearest large city, the regional centre, a hundred miles by rail. In short, a rather privileged location with regard to means of communication. The sixty-five houses (several of them unoccupied) are made of logs or planks, roofed with grey thatch, set in a half circle on a hill at a bend in the river: surrounded by little yards, they straggle out like a procession of tottering old women. Their windows look out on the clouds, the soft grey water, the fields on the farther shore, the sombre mauve line of the forests on the horizon. On the paths that lead down to the river there are always children or young women carrying water in battered little casks hung from the two ends of a yoke which they carry on their shoulders. To keep the motion from spilling too much of the water, you float a disc of wood in each cask.

Noon. The rusty fields are hot under the sun. They are hungry for seed. You cannot look at them without thinking of it. Give us seed or you will go hungry. Hurry, the bright days will soon be over, hurry, the earth is waiting . . . The silence of the fields is a continual lament . . . Flakes of white cloud wander lazily across an indifferent sky. Two mechanics are exchanging advice and despairing oaths over a disabled tractor behind the house. President Vaniuchkin yawns furiously. The waiting fields cause him pain, the thought of the Plan harasses him, it keeps him awake at night, he has nothing to drink, the stock of vodka being exhausted. The messengers he sends to Molchansk come back covered with dust, exhausted and crestfallen, bringing slips of paper with pencilled messages: 'Hold out, Comrade Vaniuchkin. The first available truck will go to you. Communist greetings. Petrikov.' It means exactly nothing. I'd like to see what he'll do with the first available truck, when every kolkhoze in the township is hounding him for the same thing! Besides: Will there be a first available truck? The only piece of furniture in his office was a bare table, littered with papers which were turning yellow like dead leaves. The open windows gave onto the fields. At the other end of the room a portrait of the Chief contemplated a sooty samovar perched on the stove. Under it slumped sacks, piled one on another like exhausted animals and not one containing the prescribed amount of seed. It was contrary to the instructions of the regional Directorate for Kolkhozes, and Kostia, checking the weight of the sacks, emphasized the fact with a sneer. 'It's not worth putting a crick in my back to find out whether somebody's been sending out short-weight sacks, Yefim Bogdanovich! If you think the *mujiks* won't know it just because they haven't a pair of scales! You don't know them, the devils, they can weigh a sack by looking at it— and you'll see what a howl they'll set up . . .'

Vaniuchkin chewed on an extinguished cigarette:

'And what do you think you can do about it, know-it-all? All right, we'll make a little trip to the township tribunal. It's not up to me . . .'

And they saw Agronomist Kostiukin coming across the fields in their direction, walking with a springy stride, his long arms swinging as if they were flapping in the wind. 'Here he comes again!'

'Like me to tell you everything he's going to say to you, Yefim Bogdanovich?' Kostia proposed sarcastically.

'Shut up!'

Kostiukin entered. His yellow cap was pulled down over his eyes; drops of sweat stood on his sharp red nose; there were wisps of straw in his beard. He began complaining immediately. 'We're five days behind the Plan.' No trucks to bring the clean seed that had been promised from Molchansk. The M. and T. Station had given their word, but they would not keep it. 'You've seen how they keep their promises, haven't you?' As for the spare parts for emergency repairs, the Station would not receive them for ten days, in view of the congestion on the railroad—'I'm sure of that. And there we are! It's all up with the sowing plan . . . just as I told you it would be. We'll be short forty per cent if everything goes well. Fifty or sixty if the frost . . .'

Vaniuchkin's small red face, which looked like a clenched fist flattened by a collision, wrinkled in circles. He looked at the agronomist with hatred, as if he wanted to cry at him: 'Are you happy now?' Agronomist Kostiukin gesticulated too much: when he talked he looked as if he were catching flies; his watery eyes became too bright; his tart voice sank and sank. But just when you thought it would become quite inaudible, it revived harshly. The kolkhoze directors were rather afraid of him, because he was always making scenes and prophesying misfortunes, and his very clear-sightedness seemed to evoke the calamities it foresaw. And what was one to think of him? Released from a concentration camp, an ex-saboteur who had once allowed a whole crop to rot in the fields—for lack of hands to harvest it, if you believed his story! He had been released before his time was up, on account of his admirable work on the penitentiary farms, he had been mentioned in the newspapers for an essay he had written on new methods of clearing land in cold regions, finally he had been awarded the Labour Medal of Honour for having set up an ingenious irrigation system for the Votiak kolkhozes during a dry season . . . In short, then: an extremely able technician, a counter-revolutionary who perhaps might have sincerely repented or who might equally well be remarkably clever and remarkably well camouflaged. You had to be on your guard with him; however, he had a right to be respected, you had to listen to him—and consequently be doubly on your guard. President Vaniuchkin, himself a former seasonal mason and former *élite* infantryman, whose knowledge of agriculture had been derived from one of the short courses established for the executive personnel of collective farms, really did not know which way to turn. Kostiukin continued: The peasants saw everything. 'At it again, working in order to die of starvation this winter!' Who is sabotaging? They wanted to write to the regional centre, denounce the township. 'We must call a meeting, explain things.' Kostia was chewing his nails. He asked:

'How far from here to the township?'

'Thirty-four miles by the plain.'

The agronomist and Kostia instantly understood each other: they had had the same idea. Seed, provisions, matches, the calicoes that the women had been promised—why shouldn't the people of the kolkhoze bring them from Molchansk on their own backs? It could be done in three or four days if the able-bodied women and the sixteen-year-old boys were mobilized to relieve the bearers. Days and nights of work would count double. We'll promise a special distribution of soap, cigarettes, and sewing thread by the Co-op. If the Co-op objects, Vaniuchkin, I'll go to the Party Committee, I'll say, 'Either that or the Plan is sunk!' They can't refuse—we know what they have on hand. They'd prefer to keep the things for the Party cadres, the technicians, and so on—naturally; but they'll have to give in, we'll all go to see them together! They might even let us have some needles; we know they've received some, though they'll deny it. The agronomist and Kostia flung the firm sentences back and forth as if they had been throwing stones. Kostiukin wriggled in his grey blouse, the pockets of which were stuffed with papers. Kostia took him by the elbows, they were face to face: the young, energetic profile, the old, sharp-nosed face with the cracked lips half open, the gaps in the rows of teeth. 'We'll call a meeting. We can mobilize as many as a hundred and fifty bearers if the Iziumka people come!'

'Shall we get the priest to speak?' President Vaniuchkin proposed.

'If the devil himself would make us a good stirring speech, I'd ask him,' Kostia cried. 'We'd see his cloven hoofs sticking out through his boots, there'd be a smell of burning, he'd dart out his flaming tongue— to accomplish the sowing plan, citizens! I'm willing—let the old devil sell us his soul!'

Their laughter relaxed them all. The russet earth laughed too, in its own way, perceptible to them alone; the horizon swayed a little, a comical cloud drifted across the sky.

The meeting was held in the administration farmyard at twilight, at the hour when the gnats become a torment. Many came, for the kolkhoze felt that it was in danger; the women were pleased that Father Guerassim was going to speak. Benches were set out for the women, the men listened standing. President Vaniuchkin spoke first, frightened to the depths of his soul by two hundred indistinct and murmuring faces. Someone shouted to him from the back: 'Why did you have the Kibotkins arrested? Anathema!' He pretended not to have heard. Duty—Plan—the honour of the kolkhoze—the powers demand— children—hunger this winter—he rolled out the great cloudy words towards the red ball which was sinking to the dark horizon through a threatening haze. 'I now give the floor to Citizen Guerassim!' Compact as a single obscure creature, the crowd stirred. Father Guerassim hoisted himself onto the table.

Since the Great Democratic Constitution had been granted by the Chief to the federated peoples, the priest no longer camouflaged himself but had let his hair and beard grow in the old fashion, although he belonged to the new Church. He held services in an abandoned isba, which he had rebuilt with his own hands and on which he had set up a wooden cross planed, nailed, and gilded with his own hands too . . . A good carpenter, a tolerable gardener (crafts which he had learned at the Special Camp for Rehabilitation through Work in the White Sea Islands), he knew the Gospel thoroughly, and also the laws, regulations, and circulars promulgated by the Agricultural Commissariat and the Central Kolkhoze Bureau. His blood boiled with hatred for

enemies of the people, conspirators, saboteurs, traitors, foreign agents
—in short, for the Fascist-Trotskyists, whose extermination he had
preached from the pulpit—that is, from the top of a ladder leaned
against the isba stove. The district authorities thought well of him.
All in all, he was simply a hairy *mujik*, a little taller than the rest,
married to a placid dairywoman. Abounding in a malicious common
sense, speaking softly in a low voice, on great occasions he could utter
vehement words which breathed inspiration. Then all his hearers
turned to him, gripped and moved, even the Young Communists back
from military service. 'Christian brothers! Decent citizens! Folk of
the Russian soil!' In his confused but often vivid periods he mingled
our great fatherland, old Russia, our mother, the beloved Chief who
considers the lowly, our infallible pilot (may the Lord bless him!),
God who sees us, our Lord Jesus Christ who cursed the idle and the
parasites, drove the chafferers from the temple, promised heaven to
those who did their work well, St. Paul who cried to the world: 'He
that will not work shall not eat!' He brandished a crumpled sheet of
paper: 'People of the soil, the battle for wheat is our battle . . . A hellish
brood still crawls under our feet! Our glorious people's power has just
struck down three more assassins with its sword of fire, three more of
Satan's hirelings, three more cowards who were trying to stab the
Party in the back! May they burn in eternal flames while we set to
work to save our harvest!'

Kostia and Maria applauded together. They had met in one of the
last rows, from where they could see only the priest's bushy hair
against a background of gloomy bluish sky. Here and there, people
crossed themselves. Kostia put his supple hand around Maria's neck
and braids. Firm cheek-bones, slightly snub nose. The girl warmed
him. When he was near her, he seemed to feel the blood pulsing faster
through his veins. Her mouth was big and so were her eyes. There were
in her both a vigorous animality and a luminous happiness. 'He's a
man of the Middle Ages, Maria, but he speaks well, the old devil! It's
as good as done now, he has got it started . . .' He felt her hard,
pointed breast graze his arm, he smelled the strong odour of her armpits, her eyes made his head swim. 'Some definite decision must be
reached, Kostia; otherwise our people may still drift away.'

Father Guerassim was saying:

'Comrades! Christians! We will go ourselves! Seed, tools, supplies
—we will carry them on our own backs, in the sweat of our brows,

slaves of God that we are, free citizens! And the Evil One, who wants the Plan to fail, who wants us to be treated as saboteurs by the government, who wants us to go hungry—we will shove his wickedness down his putrid throat!'

A woman's voice, tense and high-pitched, cried: 'Forward, Father!' And immediately teams were made up to collect sacks. They would start that very night, under the moon, with God, for the Plan, for the soil!

A hundred and sixty-five bearers, capable of carrying sixty loads by relieving one another, set out through the night, walking in single file, plunging into the dark fields. The moon was rising, huge and bright on the horizon—towards it Kostia led the first team, made up of young men who sang in chorus, until they were exhausted:

> 'If war comes,
> If war comes,
> O our strong land,
> —Let us be strong!
> Little girl, little girl,
> How I love your little eyes!'

Father Guerassim and Agronomist Kostiukin brought up the rear so that they could keep the laggards moving by telling them stories. They bivouacked on the bank of the Syeroglazaya, the Grey-eyed River, more milky than grey; a soft, continuous rustling rose from the reeds. The cold dew of dawn chilled them to the bone. Kostia and Maria slept side by side for several hours, rolled in the same blanket for warmth, too tense to talk to each other, although the moon was magical, ringed with a circle of pale light as big as the world. They set off again at daybreak, slept again in the forest through the noonday heat, reached the high road, trudged along it in a cloud of dust, and reached the township before the offices closed. The Party Committee provided a good meal for them—fish soup and groats; the truck drivers' orchestra played as they started off, some bent under their sacks and bundles, others singing, and the red flag of the Communist Youth preceded them as far as the first turn in the road. Yet Kostiukin, Kostia, and Father Guerassim had spoken bitter words to the Committee. 'Your transport section has been making fools of us—neither trucks, nor tractors, nor carts—the devil take you!' Kostiukin's face contracted furiously, reddish and wrinkled like the head of some old bird of prey. 'People are not made to be beasts of burden! We can manage it for once—but the kolkhozes that are sixty miles and more away—what are they to do?'—'Very true, comrades!' the township secretary answered with a conclusive gesture towards one of his committee: 'That means you!' Father Guerassim said nothing until almost the end, then he spoke in a veiled voice, full of implications: 'Are you quite sure, Citizen Secretary, that there is no sabotage at the bottom of this?'

Nettled, the secretary answered:

'I guarantee it, Citizen Administering the Cult! Gasolene deliveries are behind, that is all.'

'In your place, I would not guarantee it, Citizen Secretary, for God alone probes men's consciences and hearts.'

His repartee roused a hearty laugh. 'Isn't he getting to be a little too influential?' the representative of Security whispered, uncomfortably caught between two directives, one of which prescribed that the clergy should be permitted to acquire no political influence, the other ordering the cessation of religious persecution. 'Judge for yourself,' answered the Party secretary, also in a whisper. Kostia increased their embarrassment by emphatically stating: 'The Comrade Administering the Cult is our real organizer to-day.'

Every hour counted, since they had lost at least seven days on the work schedule after having lost many more waiting for transportation, and since the rains were now to be feared. The one hundred and sixty-five trudged on to the point of exhaustion, bent under their loads, sweating, groaning, swearing, praying. The roads were abominable—there were soft clods that melted underfoot, or stones that made you stumble. Now they were staggering along a sunken road, through mud and pebbles. The moon rose, huge and russet and cynical. Kostia and Maria were taking turns on the same seventy-pound sack, Kostia carrying it as much as possible, yet husbanding his strength so that he should hold out longer than Maria. Dripping with sweat, the young woman trudged on in a steamy odour of flesh. The burden-bearers emerged into a silvery plain. The moon, risen to the zenith and now white, hung over them; their shadows moved beneath them over the phosphorescent ground. The groups straggled out. Maria was carrying the sack on her head, steadying it with both hands; her armpits were bare; her shoulders, her breasts, the tense line of her throat, resisting the force of gravity, caught the light. Her lips were open, baring her teeth to the night. Kostia had stopped joking many hours ago, had almost stopped speaking. 'We are nothing now but muscles operating . . . muscles and will . . . That's what men are . . . That's what the masses are . . .' Suddenly it was as if the mauve and milky sky, the moonlit night, had begun singing in him: 'I love you, I love you, I love you, I love you . . .' unwearyingly, endlessly, with stubborn enthusiasm. 'Give me the sack, Maria!'—'Not yet; when we get to those trees there. Don't talk to me, Kostia.' She was panting softly. He went on in silence: 'I love you, I love you . . .' and his tiredness vanished, the moonlight marvellously unburdened him.

When the hundred and sixty-five bivouacked by the Grey-eyed River, the Syeroglazaya, to sleep a few hours before dawn, Kostia and Maria lay down beside their sack, facing the sky. The grass was soft and cold and damp. 'All right, Marussia?' Kostia asked, in a tone which was indifferent at the beginning of the short sentence but which suddenly became caressing upon the diminutive which closed it. 'Falling asleep?'—'Not yet,' she said. 'I'm fine. How simple everything is—the sky, the earth, and us . . .'

Lying on their backs side by side, their shoulders touching, infinitely close to each other, infinitely detached from each other, they gazed up into space.

Without moving, smiling up into the faintly luminous sky, Kostia said:

'Maria, listen to me, Maria, it's really true. Maria, I love you.'

She did not move, her hands were crossed under her head. He heard her regular breathing. She said nothing for a time, then answered calmly:

'That's fine, Kostia. We can make a good solid couple.'

A sort of anguish seized him, he overcame it and swallowed his saliva. He did not know what to say or to do. A moment passed. The sky was magnificently bright. Kostia said:

'I knew a Maria in Moscow; she worked underground, building the subway. She came to a sad end, which she didn't deserve. Her nerves weren't strong enough. When I remember her, I think of her as Maria the Unhappy. I want you to be Maria the Happy. You shall be.'

'I don't believe in happiness during transition periods,' said Maria. 'We will work together. We will see life. We will fight. That is enough.'

He thought: 'Strange, here we are husband and wife, and we talk like two old friends; I was longing to take her in my arms, and now I only want to make this moment last . . .'

There was a silence, then Maria said:

'I knew another Kostia. He belonged to the Communist Youth, like you, he was almost as good-looking as you are, but he was a fool and a skunk . . .'

'What did he do to you?'

'He made me pregnant, and left me because I am a believer.'

'You are a believer, Maria?'

Kostia put his arm around her shoulders, he sought her eyes and found them, with their look that was as dark and as luminous as the night.

'I do not believe in ecclesiastical mumble-jumble, Kostia, try to understand me. I believe in everything that is. Look around us, look!'

Her face, her clear-cut lips turned impulsively towards him to show him the universe: that simple sky, the plains, the invisible river among the reeds, space.

'I can't say what I believe in, Kostia, but I believe. Perhaps it's just in reality. You must understand me.'

Ideas flooded through Kostia: he perceived them in his heart and his loins as he did in his mind. Reality, embraced by a single motion of the whole universe. We are inseparable from the stars; from the authentic magic of this night in which there is no miracle; from the waiting earth; from all the confused power that lies within us . . . Joy filled him. 'You are right, Maria, I believe as you do, I see . . .' The earth, the sky, the very night, in which there were no shadows, brought them inexpressibly together, forehead against forehead, their hair mingling, eyes to eyes, mouth to mouth, their teeth meeting with a little shock. 'Maria, I love you . . .' The words were only tiny gilded crystals which he dropped into deep, dark, sluggish, turbulent, enrapturing waters . . . Maria answered with restrained violence: 'But I've already told you I love you, Kostia.' Maria said: 'I feel as if I were throwing little white pebbles at the sky and they turn into meteors, I see them disappear but I know they will never fall, that's how I love you . . .' Then, 'What is rocking us,' she murmured, 'I think I'm going to sleep . . .' She fell asleep with her cheek on the sack, smelling the odour of wheat. Kostia watched her for a moment. His joy was so great that it became like grief. Then the same rocking put him to sleep too.

The last stretch, which had to be covered first through the morning fog, then under the sun, was the hardest. The line of staggering bearers reached from horizon to horizon. The president of the kolkhoze, Vaniuchkin, came to meet them with carts. Kostia dropped his sack over Vaniuchkin's head and shoulders. 'Your turn, President!' The whole landscape was calm and bright.

'The sowing is safe, brother. You are going to sign me two two-week leaves right away, for Maria and myself. We're getting married.'

'Congratulations,' said the president.

He clicked his tongue to hurry on the horses.

Romachkin's life had recently become more dignified. Though he was still in the same office, on the sixth floor of the Moscow Clothing Trust, and though he was not yet a member of the Party, he felt that he had increased in stature. An official announcement, posted in the hall one evening, had said that 'the assistant clerk in the salaries bureau, Romachkin, a punctual and zealous worker, has been promoted to first assistant with an increase in salary of fifty roubles per month and citation on the Board of Honour.' From his ink-stained and glue-smeared desk in insignificance, Romachkin moved to the varnished desk which stood opposite to the similar but larger desk of the Trust's Director of Tariffs and Salaries. Romachkin was provided with an inter-office telephone, which was rather a nuisance than otherwise, because the calls interrupted him in his calculations, but which was a symbol of unhoped-for authority. The president of the Trust himself sometimes called him on this telephone to ask for information. Those were solemn moments. Romachkin found it somewhat difficult to answer sitting down, and without bowing and smiling amiably. If he had been alone, he would certainly have stood up, the better to assume an air of deference as he promised: 'At once, Comrade Nikolkin; you shall have the exact figures in fifteen minutes . . .' Having promised, Romachkin straightened up until his back touched the back of his swivel chair, looked importantly around at the five desks in the office, and beckoned to the sad-faced Antochkin, whose liver was always giving him trouble and who had replaced him at the desk in insignificance. 'Comrade Antochkin, I am looking up some information for the President of the Trust. I need the file on the last conference on prices and wages and also the message from the Textile Syndicate concerning the application of the C.C. directives. You have seven minutes.' Spoken with simple firmness from which there was no appeal. Assistant Clerk Antochkin looked at the clock as a donkey looks at his driver's whip; his fingers flew through the files; he seemed to be chewing on something . . . Before the end of the seventh minute, Romachkin received the papers from him and thanked him amiably. From the other side of the room the old typist and the office boy looked at Romachkin with evident respect. (That they were both thinking: 'Oh, that worn-out rat, who does he think he is! I hope you get your bellyful of it, Citizen Bootlicker!' Romachkin, who was always well disposed towards everyone, could not suspect.) The head of the office, though he went on signing letters, rounded his shoulders approvingly. Romachkin was discovering authority, which enlarges the individual, cements organization, fecundates work, saves time, reduces overhead . . . 'I thought I was nobody and only knew how to obey, and here I am, able to give orders. What is this principle which bestows a value on a man who had no value before? The principle of hierarchy.' But is hierarchy just? Romachkin thought about it for several days before he answered himself in the affirmative. What better government than a hierarchy of just men?

His promotion had brought him yet another reward: the window was at his right, he had only to turn his head to see trees in courtyards, washing drying on wires, the roofs of old houses, the pinnacles of a church, washed with yellow and old rose, humbly surviving beside a modern building—almost too much space, almost too many astonishing things, for him to concentrate properly on his work. Why does man have such a need for dreams? Romachkin thought that it would be a sensible idea to put opaque glass in office windows, so that the sight of the outside world should not be a distraction which might reduce the quantity of work accomplished. Five small, almost round pinnacles, surmounted by tottering crosses, survived amid a forgotten garden and a group of ill-assorted houses a century and a half old. They were an invitation to meditate, like forest paths leading to unknown clearings which perhaps did not exist . . . Romachkin felt slightly afraid of them even as he loved them. Perhaps people still prayed under those meaningless and almost colourless pinnacles, in the heart of the new city mathematically laid out in straight lines drawn by steel, concrete, glass, and stone.

'It is strange,' Romachkin said to himself. 'How can anyone pray?' To keep himself in good working trim, Romachkin allowed himself a

few minutes between one job and the next. These minutes he devoted
to dreaming—without letting it be apparent, of course, pencil in hand,
brows knit . . . What alley through which I have never walked leads to
that fantastically surviving church?

Romachkin went to see, and the result was a new accomplishment in
his life—a friendship. He had to go down a blind alley, pass through a
carriage gateway, cross a courtyard lined with workshops; thus he
arrived at a small, ancient square, shut off from the rest of the world.
Children were playing marbles; and there was the church, with its
three beggars on the steps and its three praying women kneeling in the
solitude of the nave. Pleasant to read the nearby signboards—they
made up a poem studded with harmonious and meaningless words and
names: *Filatov, Teaseler and Mattressmaker, Oleandra, Shoemakers'
Craft Co-operative, Tikhonova, Midwife, Kindergarten No. 4, The
First Joy*. Romachkin met Filatov, teaseler and mattressmaker, a childless widower, a prudent man who no longer drank, no longer smoked,
no longer believed, and who, at fifty-five, was taking free night courses
at the Higher Technical School to learn mechanics and astrophysics.
'And what have I left now but science? I have lived half a century,
Citizen Romachkin, without suspecting that science existed, like a
blind man.' Filatov wore an old-fashioned leather apron and a proletarian cap, unchanged for fifteen years. His room was only nine feet
by five, a converted vestibule, but in the back of it he had cut a window
which gave onto the church garden; and on the window-sill he had a
hanging garden of his own, constructed of old boxes. A copying stand
in front of his flowers gave him a place to copy out Eddington's *Stars
and Atoms*, with annotations of his own . . . This unexpected friendship
occupied an exalted place in Romachkin's life. At first the two men
had not understood each other very well. Filatov said:

'Mechanics rules technique, technique is the base of production,
that is, of society. Celestial mechanics is the law of the universe.
Everything is physical. If I could begin my life over again, I would be
an engineer or an astronomer; I believe that the real engineer must be
an astronomer if he is to understand the world. But I was born the
grandson of a serf, under the Tsarist oppression. I was illiterate until I
reached thirty, a drunkard until I reached forty, I lived without understanding the universe until my poor Natassia died. When she was
buried at Vagankovskoye, I had a small red cross set up on her grave,
because she was a Believer herself, being ignorant; and because we live

in the Socialist age, I said: Let the cross of a proletarian be red! And
I was left all alone in the cemetery, Comrade Romachkin, I paid the
watchman fifty copecks so that I could stay after closing time until the
stars came out. And I thought: What is man on this earth? A wretched
speck of dust which thinks, works, and suffers. What does he leave
behind him? Work, the mechanisms of work. What is the earth? A
speck of dust which revolves in the sky with the work and sufferings
of man, and the silence of plants, and everything. And what makes it
revolve? The iron law of stellar mechanics. "Natassia," I said over
her grave, "you can no longer hear me because you no longer exist,
because we have no souls, but you will always be in the soil, the plants,
the air, the energy of nature, and I ask you to forgive me for having
hurt you by getting drunk, and I promise you I will stop drinking, and
I promise you I will study so that I may understand the great mechanism of creation." I have kept my word because I am strong, with
proletarian strength, and perhaps I shall marry again one day, when I
have finished my second year of study, for I should not have money to
buy books if I were to take a wife now. Such is my life, comrade. I am
at peace, I know that it is man's duty to understand and I am beginning
to understand.'

They were sitting side by side on a little bench at the door of
Filatov's workshop, late in the afternoon—Romachkin pale and worn,
not yet old, but with all his youth and vigour gone, if he had ever had
either; and Filatov, beardless and with shaven skull, his face lined with
symmetrical wrinkles, solid as an old tree. From the 'Oleandra' Co-
operative came the sound of hammers on leather, the chestnut trees
were beginning to loom larger in the twilight. Had it not been for the
muffled noise of the city, they could have thought they were in an old-
time village square, not far from a river on the other side of which was
a forest . . . Romachkin answered:

'I have not had time to think about the universe, Comrade Filatov,
because I have been tortured by injustice.'

'The causes of injustice,' Filatov answered, 'lie in the social mechanism.'

Romachkin feebly wrung his hands, then put them on his knees.
They lay there, flat and without strength.

'Listen, Filatov, and tell me if I have done wrong. I am almost a
Party member, I go to meetings, I am trusted. At yesterday's meeting,
the rationalization of work was discussed. And the Secretary read us a

newspaper paragraph on the execution of three enemies of the people, who assassinated Comrade Tulayev, of the C.C. and the Moscow Committee. It is all proven, the criminals confessed, I don't remember their names, and what do their names matter to us? They are dead, they were murderers, they were miserable creatures, they died the death of criminals. The Secretary explained it all to us: that the Party defends the country, that war is at hand, that we must kill the mad dogs for love of mankind . . . It is all true, very true. Then he said: "Those in favour raise their hands!" I understood that we were to thank the C.C. and Security for the execution of these men, I suffered, I thought: And pity, pity—does no one think of pity? But I did not dare not to raise my hand. Should I be the only one to remember pity, I who am nothing? And I raised my hand with the rest. Did I betray pity? Should I have betrayed the Party if I had not raised my hand? What is your answer, Filatov, you who are upright, you who are a true proletarian?'

Filatov reflected. Darkness fell. Romachkin's face, turned towards his companion, became beseeching.

'The machine,' said Filatov, 'must operate irreproachably. That it crushes those who stand in its way is inhuman, but it is the universal law. The workman must know the insides of the machine. Later there will be luminous and transparent machines which men's eyes can see through without hindrance. They will be machines in a state of innocence, comparable to the innocence of the heavens. Human law will be as innocent as astrophysical law. No one will be crushed. No one will any longer need pity. But to-day, Comrade Romachkin, pity is still needed. Machines are full of darkness, we never know what goes on inside them. I do not like secret sentences, executions in cellars, the mechanism of plots. You understand: there are always two plots, the positive and the negative—how is one to know which is the plot of the just, which the plot of the guilty? How is one to know whether to feel pity, whether to be pitiless? How should we know, when the men in power themselves lose their heads, as there is no doubt that they do? In your case, Romachkin, you had to vote Yes, otherwise things would have turned out badly for you, and there was nothing you could do about it, was there? You voted with pity—well and good. I did the same thing, last year. What else could we do?'

Romachkin had the impression that his hands were becoming lighter. Filatov invited him in, they drank a glass of tea and ate pickled cucumbers with black bread. The room was so small that they touched each other. Their proximity gave birth to an increased intimacy. Filatov opened Eddington's book and held it under the light. And:

'Do you know what an electron is?'

'No.'

Romachkin read more compassion than reproach in the mattress-maker's eyes. That a man should have a long life behind him and not know what an electron was!

'Let me explain it to you. Every atom of matter is a sidereal system . . .'

The universe and man are made of stars, some infinitely little, others infinitely great, Figure 17 on page 45 showed it clearly. Romachkin had difficulty in following the admirable demonstration because he was thinking of the three executed criminals, of his hand raised in favour of their death, of his hand which had felt so heavy then, which had now—strangely—become light again because he had set pity against machines and stars.

A child cried in the next courtyard, the lights in the shoemaker's shop went out, a couple embraced, almost invisible, against the church railing. Filatov came as far as the end of the square with his friend. Romachkin walked on towards the railing. Before going into his room, Filatov stopped for no reason and looked at the black ground. What have we done with pity in this human mechanism? Three more men executed . . . They are more numerous than the stars, since there are only three thousand stars visible in the northern hemisphere. If those three men killed, did they not have profound reasons for killing, reasons connected with the eternal laws of motion? Who weighed those reasons? Weighed them without hatred? Filatov felt pity for the judges: the judges must suffer most of all . . . The sight of the couple embracing in the shadows, making but a single being by force of the eternal law of attraction, consoled him. It is good to see the young live, when one is at the sunset of life oneself. They have half a century before them, by the law of averages: perhaps they will see true justice, in the days of transparent machines. It takes a great deal of fertilizer to feed exhausted soil. Who knows how many more men must be executed to feed the soil of Russia? We thought we could see ahead so clearly in the days of the Revolution, and now we are in the dark again; perhaps it is the punishment for our pride. Filatov went in, put the iron bar across his door, and undressed. He slept on a narrow mattress spread out on boxes, and kept a night light burning. The spiders began their nocturnal travels over the ceiling: the little black creatures, with legs like rays, moved slowly, and it was absolutely impossible to understand the meaning of their movements. Filatov thought of the judges and the executed men. Who is to judge the judges? Who will pardon them? Need they be pardoned? Who will shoot them if they were unjust? Everything will come in its time, inexorably. Under the ground, everywhere, under the city, under the fields, under the little black square where the lovers were no doubt still continuing their caresses and endearments, a multitude of eyes shone for Filatov, on the edge of visibility, like stars of the seventh magnitude. 'They wait, they wait,' Filatov murmured; 'eyes without number, forgive us.'

Romachkin's anxiety returned when he found himself once more in the poverty-stricken whiteness of his room. The noise of the collective apartment smote ceaselessly at his bastion of silence: telephones, music from the radio, children's voices, toilets being flushed, hissing of kerosene pressure stoves ... The couple next door, from whom he was separated only by a plank partition, were arguing feverishly over a deal in second-hand cloth. Romachkin put on his nightshirt: undressed, he felt even more puny than dressed; his bare feet showed wretched toes, absurdly far apart. The human body is ugly—and if man has only his body, if thought is only a product of the body, how can it be anything but doubtful and inadequate? He lay down between cold sheets, shivered for a moment, reached out to his bookshelf, took a book by a poet whose name he did not know, for the first pages were missing— but the others still kept all their magical charm. Romachkin read where the book opened.

> *Divine revolving planet*
> *thy Eurasias thy singing seas*
> *simple scorn for the headsmen*
> *and behold o merciful thought we are*
> *almost like unto heroes.*

Why was there no punctuation? Perhaps because thought, which embraces and connects by invisible threads (but do such threads exist?) planets, seas, continents, headsmen, victims, and ourselves, is fluid, never rests, stops only in appearance? Why, precisely to-night, the reference to headsmen, the reference to heroes? Who should reproach me, who despise nothing but myself? And why, if there are men who have this ardour for life and this scorn for the headsmen, am I so different from them? Are not the poets ashamed of themselves when they see themselves in their solitude and their nakedness? Romachkin put away the book and returned to the papers of the last few days. At the foot of a Page 3, under the heading *Miscellaneous Information*, the government daily described the preparations for an athletic festival in which three hundred parachutists, members of school sports clubs, would take part . . . Huge bright flowers float down from the sky, each bearing a brave human head whose eyes intently watch the approach of the alluring and threatening earth . . . The next item, which had no heading and was set in small type, read:

The case of the assassins of Comrade Tulayev, member of the Central Committee.—Having confessed that they were guilty of treason, plotting, and assassination, M. A. Erchov, A. A. Makeyev, and K. K. Rublev, sentenced to capital punishment by the special session of the Supreme Tribunal sitting in camera, have been executed.

The Chess-Players' Association, affiliated with the All-Union Sports Federation, plans to organize a series of elimination games in the Federated Republics preparatory to the forthcoming Tournament of Nationalities.

The chess-men had human faces, unfamiliar but grave-eyed. They moved of themselves. Someone aimed at them from a long way off: suddenly they jumped into the air, their heads bursting open, and vanished inexplicably. Three accurate shots, one after the other, instantaneously demolished three heads on the chess-board. Numb and half asleep, Romachkin felt fear: someone was knocking at the door.

'Who's there?'

'I, I,' answered a radiant voice.

Romachkin went to the door. The floor was rough and cold under his bare feet. Before drawing the bolt he waited a moment to master his panic. Kostia came rushing in so impulsively that he picked Romachkin up like a child.

'Good old neighbour! Romachkin! Half-thinker, half-Hero of Toil, shut up in your half-room and your half-pint destiny! Glad to see you again! Everything all right? Why don't you say something? Ultimatum: Everything all right? Answer yes or no!'

'Everything's all right, Kostia. Good of you to come. I am fond of you, you know.'

'In that case I order you to stop looking at me like a man who's just been pulled out from under a bus! . . . The earth is revolving magnificently, the devil take you! Can you see it revolving, our green globe inhabited by toiling monkeys?'

Back in the warmth of his bed, Romachkin saw the little room enlarge, the light burn ten times brighter.

'I was just falling asleep, Kostia, over this hodge-podge in the papers: parachutists, executions, chess tournaments, planets . . . Absolute madness. Life, I suppose. How handsome and healthy you look, Kostia. It's wonderful to see you . . . As for me, things are going extremely well. I've had a promotion at the Trust, I go to Party meetings, I have a friend, a remarkable proletarian with the brain of a physicist . . . We discuss the structure of the universe.'

'The structure of the universe,' Kostia repeated in a singsong voice. Too big for the cramped little room, he kept turning round and round.

'You haven't changed a bit, Romachkin. I bet the same anæmic fleas feed on you at night.'

'You're right,' said Romachkin, with a happy little laugh.

Kostia pushed him back against the wall and sat down on the bed. His tousled hair, in which the chestnut lights looked russet, his aggressive dark eyes, his big, slightly asymmetrical mouth, bent over Romachkin.

'I don't know where I'm going, but I'm going somewhere. If the coming war doesn't change us all into carrion, old man, I don't know what we are going to do, but it will be fabulous. If we die, we'll make the earth bear such a crop as was never heard of. I haven't a copeck, of course; my soles are worn through and more, of course . . . And so on. But I am happy.'

'Love?'

'Of course.'

Kostia's laughter shook the bed, shook Romachkin from his toes to his eyebrows, made the wall tremble, echoed through the room in golden waves.

'Don't let it frighten you, old brother, if I seem drunk. I'm drunker yet when I haven't had anything to eat, but then I sometimes go mad . . .

'You remember, I gave up working on the subway like an industrialized mole under the streets of Moscow, between the Morgue and the Young Communist Bureau. I wanted air. I was fed up with their discipline. I have discipline enough of my own to set up shop with, it's inside me, my discipline. I got out. At Gorki I worked in the automobile factory: seven hours in front of a machine. I was willing to become a beast in the long run, to give the country trucks. I was going to see fine cars come out, all shiny and new—it's prettier and cleaner than the birth of a human being, I assure you. When I told myself that we had built them with our own hands and that perhaps they would eat up the roads in Mongolia bringing cigarettes and rifles to oppressed peoples, I felt proud, I was glad to be alive. Good. Dispute with a technician, who wanted to make me clean my tools after hours. "What do you think?" I said to him. "That the wage earner doesn't exist? The worker's nerves and muscles have to be kept up just as much as the machines do. So long." I took the train, they were going to accuse me of Trotskyism, the idiots, but you know what that means: three years in the Karaganda mines, no thank you! Have you ever seen the Volga, old man? I worked on board a tug, fireman first, then mechanic. We towed barges as far as the Kama. There the rivers are full, you forget cities, the moon rises over steep forests, an immense vegetable army stands guard day and night, and you hear it calling to you insidiously: Ours is the true life—if you do not drink a cup of silence with the beasts of the forest, you will never know what a man ought to know. I found a substitute in a Komi village and went to work for the regional Forest Trust. "I'll do anything, as far away as possible, in the most out-of-the-way forests," I said to the provincial bureaucrats. It pleased them. They put me to inspecting foresters' posts, and the militia took me on for the fight against banditry. In a forest at the end of the earth, between the Kama and the Vychegda, I discovered a village of Old Believers and sorcerers who had fled from statistics. They had taken the great census for a diabolic manœuvre, they had convinced themselves that their lands were going to be taken from them once more, their men sent to war, their old women forced to learn to read and then to study the science of the Evil One. They recited the Apocalypse at night. They also proclaimed that everything on earth was corrupt and that nothing remained for the pure in heart except patience—and that their patience would soon be exhausted! "And then what will happen?" I asked them. "It will be the return of the millennium." They offered to let me live with them, I was tempted to on account of a beautiful girl, she was as vigorous as a tree, exciting and pure as forest air, but she told me that what she most wanted was a child, that I had seen too much of machines to live long with her, and that she did not trust me . . . I left there, Romachkin, to get away before their Last Judgment arrived, or I became a complete imbecile . . . Through brothers of theirs in the city, the Elders asked me to send them recent papers, a treatise on agronomy, and to write and tell them if "the census had gone by" without wars, floods, or plunder . . . Shall we go and live with them, Romachkin? I am the only man who knows the paths through the forests along the Sysola. The forest animals don't harm me, I've learned to rob wild bees' hives for honey, I know how to set traps for hares, to set traps in rivers . . . Come on, Romachkin, you will never think of your books again and when someone asks you what a tram is you will explain to the little children and the white-haired old men that it is a long yellow box on wheels which carries men and is made to move by a mysterious force that comes out of the bowels of the earth over wires. And if they ask you why, you will find yourself hard put to it for an answer . . .'

'I am willing,' said Romachkin weakly. Kostia's story had enchanted him like a fairy tale.

Kostia jerked him out of his dream:

'Too late, old man. There are no more Holy Scriptures or Apocalypses for you and me. If the millennium is ahead of us, we cannot know it. We belong to the age of reinforced concrete.'

'And your love affair?' asked Romachkin, feeling strangely at ease.

'I got married at the kolkhoze,' Kostia answered. 'She is . . .'

His two hands began a gesture intended to express enthusiasm. But they remained suspended for a fraction of a second, then dropped inertly. Even as he spoke, Kostia's eyes had fallen on Romachkin's long, feeble hand, spread out on a page of a newspaper. The middle finger seemed to be pointing to an impossible paragraph:

The case of the assassins of Comrade Tulayev, member of the C.C. Having confessed that they were guilty . . . Erchov, Makeyev, Rublev . . . have been executed . . .

'What is she like, Kostia?'

Kostia's eyes narrowed.

'Do you remember the revolver, Romachkin?'

'I remember it.'

'Do you remember that you were looking for justice?'

'I remember. But I have thought a great deal since then, Kostia. I have become aware of my own weakness. I have come to understand that it is too early for justice. What we have to do is work, believe in the Party, feel pity. Since we cannot be just, we must feel pity for men . . .'

A fear of which he did not dare to think would not let his lips utter the question: 'What did you do with the revolver?' Kostia spoke angrily:

'As for me, pity exasperates me. Here you are'—Kostia pointed to the paragraph in the paper—'take pity on those three, if that makes you feel any better, Romachkin—they are beyond needing anything now. As for me, I have no use for your pity, and I have no wish to pity you— you don't deserve it. Perhaps you are guilty of their crime. Perhaps I am the author of your crime, but you will never understand it or anything about it. You are innocent, they were innocent . . .'

With an effort, he managed to shrug his shoulders. 'I am innocent . . . But who is guilty?'

'I believe that they were guilty,' Romachkin murmured, 'since they were found guilty.'

Kostia gave a leap that shook the floor and the walls. His hard laugh rattled against things.

'Romachkin, you win all prizes! Let me explain to you what I guess. They were certainly guilty, they confessed, because they understood what you and I do not understand. Do you see?'

'It must be true,' said Romachkin gravely.

Kostia paced nervously between the door and the window. 'I am stifling,' he said. 'Air! What is wanting here? Everything!

'Well, my old friend Romachkin, good-bye. Life is a sort of delirium, don't you think?'

'Yes, yes . . .'

Romachkin was going to be left there alone, he had a wretched, worn face, wrinkled eyelids, white hairs around his mouth, so little vigour in his eyes! Kostia thought aloud: 'The guilty are the millions of Romachkins on this earth . . .'

'What did you say?'

'Nothing, old man, I'm just maundering.'

There was empty space between them.

'Romachkin, this place of yours is too gloomy. Here!'

From his inside blouse pocket Kostia drew a rectangular object wrapped in an India print. 'Take it. It's what I loved the most in the world when I was alone.' Romachkin's hand held a miniature framed in ebony. In the black circle appeared a woman's face—magically real, all sanity, intelligence, radiance, silence. With a sort of amazed terror, Romachkin said: 'Is it possible? Do you really believe, Kostia, that there are faces like this?'

Kostia flared up:

'Living faces are much more beautiful . . . Good-bye, old man.'

As he hurried down the stairs Kostia had a blissful sensation: He seemed to be falling, the material world dissolved before him, things became aerial. He followed the streets with the light step of a runner. But in his mind anxiety loosed a sort of thunder. 'It was I who . . . I . . .' He began running as he approached the house where Maria lay sleeping—running as he had run one night long ago, that Arctic night, when the thing had suddenly exploded at the end of his hand, making a black flower fringed with flame, and he had heard the police whistles all around him . . . The dark staircase was aerial too. Apartment No. 12 housed three families and three couples in seven rooms. A 25-candle-power bulb burned in the hall, looped up close to the ceiling so that it could not easily be unscrewed. The walls were sooty. A sewing machine, fastened to a heavy chest by a chain and padlock, was reflected in the cracked mirror of the coat stand. Irregular snores filled the half-darkness with a bestial vibration. The door of the toilet opened, the figure of a man in pyjamas hovered indistinctly at the end of the hall and suddenly stumbled noisily into something metallic. The drunken man bounced back against the opposite wall, striking his head against a door. Angry voices came through the darkness—a low voice saying 'Shhhhh,' and a high voice showering insults: '. . . gutter rat . . .' Kostia went to the drunken man and caught him by the collar of his swaying pyjamas.

'Quiet, citizen. My wife is asleep next door. Which is your room?'

'Number 4,' said the drunk. 'Who're you?'

'Nobody. Stay on your feet! Don't make any noise or I'll give you a friendly poke in the jaw.'

'Good of you . . . Have a drink?'

Kostia pushed the door of No. 4 open with his elbow and flung the drunk inside, where he gently collapsed among overturned chairs. Something made of glass rolled across the floor before breaking with a crystalline tinkle. Kostia groped his way to the door of No. 7, a triangular closet with a low slanting ceiling in which there was a round dormer. The electric bulb, at the end of a long cord, lay on the floor between a pile of books and an enamel basin in which a pink chemise was soaking. The only furniture was a chair with the seat broken and an iron bed, on which Maria lay sleeping, stretched out straight on her back, her forehead lifted, vaguely smiling. Kostia looked at her. Her cheeks were pink and hot, she had wide nostrils, eyebrows like the outline of a pair of slim wings, adorable eyelashes. One shoulder and one bare breast were uncovered; on the amber-coloured flesh of the breast lay a black braid with coppery lights. Kostia kissed her bare breast. Maria opened her eyes. 'You!'

He knelt beside the bed, took both her hands.

'Maria, wake up, Maria, look at me, Maria, think of me . . .'

No smile came to her lips, but her whole being smiled.

'I am thinking of you, Kostia.'

'Maria, answer me. If I had killed a man, ages ago or a few days or a few months ago, on a night of unbelievable snow, without knowing him, without a thought of killing him, without having wanted to, but voluntarily just the same, with my eyes wide open, my hand steady, because he was doing evil in the name of ideas that are right, because I was full of the sufferings of others, because, without knowing it, I had pronounced judgment in a few seconds—I for many others, I who am unknown, for others who are unknown and nameless, for all who have no names, no will, no luck, not even my rag of a conscience, Maria, what would you say to me?'

'I would tell you, Kostia, that you ought to keep your nerves under better control, know exactly what you're doing, and not wake me up to tell me your bad dreams . . . Kiss me.'

He went on in an imploring voice:

'But if it was true, Maria?'

She looked at him very hard. The chimes on the Kremlin rang the hour. The first notes of the 'International,' airy and solemn, drifted for a moment over the sleeping city.

'Kostia, I have seen enough peasants die by the roadside . . . I know what it is to struggle desperately. I know how much harm is done involuntarily when the struggle is desperate . . . Just the same, we are going forward, aren't we? There is a great and pure force in you. Don't worry.'

Her two hands plunged into his hair, she drew the vigorous and tormented head towards her.

Comrade Fleischman spent the day finding their final places in the files for the dossiers in the Tulayev case. There were thousands of pages, gathered into several volumes. Human life was reflected in them just as the earth's fauna and flora are to be found, in tenuous and monstrous forms, in a drop of stagnant water observed through a microscope. Certain documents were to go to the Party Archives, others to complete dossiers in the files of Security, the C.C., the General Secretariat, the foreign branch of Secret Service. A few were to be burned in the presence of a representative of the C.C. and Comrade Gordeyev, Deputy High Commissar for Security. Fleischman shut himself up alone with the papers, about which there hung an odour of death. The memorandum from the Special Operations Service on the execution of the three convicted criminals gave only one precise detail, the time: 12.01, 12.15, 12.18 a.m. The great case had culminated at the zero hour of night.

Among the unimportant documents added to the Tulayev dossier since the end of the investigation (reports on conversations in public places, during the course of which Tulayev's name was alleged to have been mentioned; denunciations concerning the murder of a certain Butayev, an engineer at the waterworks in Krasnoyarsk; communications from the criminal police concerning the assassination of a certain Mutayev at Leninakan; and other documents which flood, wind, or the stupidity and uninspired folly of the law of averages seemed to have swept together), Fleischman found a grey envelope, postmarked 'Moscow-Yaroslavl Station' and merely addressed: 'To the Citizen Examining Magistrate conducting the Tulayev case investigation.' An attached memorandum read: 'Transmitted to Comrade Zvyeryeva.' Another memorandum added: '*Zvyeryeva: under strict arrest until further order. Transmit to Comrade Popov.*' Administrative perfection would, at this point, have demanded a third memorandum concerning the as yet unsettled fate of Comrade Popov. Some prudent person had merely written on the envelope, in red ink: '*Unclassified.*' 'That's myself—unclassified,' thought Fleischman with a shade of self-contempt. He nonchalantly cut open the envelope. It contained a letter, written by hand on a folded sheet of school notebook paper and unsigned.

'Citizen! I write to you from compulsion of conscience and out of regard for the truth . . .'

Ah!—somebody else denouncing his neighbour or happily giving himself up to his idiotic little private delusion . . . Fleischman skipped the middle of the letter and began again towards the end, not without noticing that the writing was firm and young, as of an educated peasant, that there was no attempt at style, and very little punctuation. The tone was direct, and the Security official found himself gripped.

'I shall not sign this. Innocent men having inexplicably paid for me, there is no way left for me to make amends. Believe me if I had known of this miscarriage of justice in time I would have brought you my innocent and guilty head. I belong body and soul to our great country, to our magnificent Socialist future. If I have committed a crime almost without knowing it which I am not sure of because we live in a period where the murder of man by man is an ordinary thing and no doubt it is a necessity of the dialectics of history and no doubt the rule of the workers which sheds so much blood, sheds it for the good of mankind and I myself have been only the less than half-conscious instrument of that historical necessity, if I have led into error judges better educated and more conscientious than myself who have committed an even greater crime while believing that they too were serving justice, I can now only live and work freely with all my powers for the greatness of our Soviet fatherland . . .'

Fleischman went back to the middle of the letter:

'Alone, unknown to the world, not even knowing myself the moment before what I was going to do I fired at Comrade Tulayev whom I detested without knowing him since the purge of the higher schools. I assure you that he had done immeasurable harm to our sincere young generation, that he had lied to us incessantly, that he had basely outraged the best thing we possess our faith in the Party, that he had brought us to the brink of despair . . .'

Fleischman bent over the open letter and sweat bathed his forehead, his eyes blurred, his double chin sagged, an expression of utter defeat twisted and ravaged his fat face, the innumerable pages of the dossier floated before him in a choking fog. He muttered: 'I knew it,' annoyed because he found himself having to restrain an idiotic impulse to burst into tears or to flee, no matter where, instantly, irrevocably—but nothing was possible any more. He slumped over the letter, every word of which bore the stamp of truth. There was a mouselike scratching at the door, then the voice of his maid asked: 'Would you like some tea, Comrade Chief?'—'Yes, yes, Lisa—make it strong . . .' He walked up and down the room for a little, read the unsigned letter over again, standing this time, the better to confront it. Impossible to show it to anyone, anyone. He half opened the door to take the tray on which stood two glasses of tea. And, within himself, he talked to the unknown man whom he glimpsed behind the folded sheet of ruled paper. 'Well, young man, well, your letter is not bad at all . . . Never fear, I am not going to start a hunt for you at this point. We of the older generation, you see, we don't need your erratic and self-intoxicated strength to stand condemned . . . It is beyond us all, it carries us all off . . .'

He lit the candle which he used to soften sealing wax. The stearine was encrusted with red streaks like coagulated blood. In the flame of the bloodstained candle Fleischman burned the letter, collected the ashes in the ash-tray, and crushed them under his thumb. He drank his two glasses of tea and felt better. Half aloud, with as much relief as gloomy sarcasm, he said:

'The Tulayev case is closed.'

Fleischman decided to hurry through the rest of the filing, so that he could get away earlier. The notebooks which Kiril Rublev had filled in his cell had been put with a sheaf of letters 'Held for the inquiry'—they were Dora Rublev's letters, written from a small settlement in Kazakstan. Sent from the depths of solitude and anguish to be read only by Comrade Zvyeryeva, they made him furious. 'What a bitch! If I can lay my hands on her, I'll see that she gets her fill of steppes and snow and sand . . .'

Fleischman leafed through the notebooks. The writing remained regular throughout, the forms of certain letters suggested artistic interests (very early in his life, and long outgrown), the straightness of the lines recalled the man, the way he squared his shoulders when he talked, the long bony face, the intellectual forehead, the particular way he had of looking at you with a smile which was only in his eyes, as he expounded a train of reasoning as rigorous and as subtle as an arabesque in metal . . . 'We are all dying without knowing why we have killed so many men in whom lay our highest strength . . .' Fleischman realized that he thought as Kiril Rublev had written a few days or a few hours before his death.

The notebooks interested him . . . He ran through the economic deductions based on the decrease in the rate of profit resulting from the continuous increase of constant capital (whence the capitalist stagnation?) on the increase of the production of electrical power in the world, on the development of metallurgy, on the gold crisis, on the changes in character, functions, interests, and structure of social classes and more particularly of the working class . . . Several times Fleischman murmured: 'Right, absolutely right . . . questionable, but . . . worth considering . . . true on the whole or in trend . . .' He made notes of data which he wanted to check in books by specialists. Next came pages of enthusiastic or severe opinions on Trotsky. Kiril Rublev praised his revolutionary intuition, his sense of Russian reality, his 'sense of victory,' his reasoned intrepidity; and deplored his 'pride as a great historic figure,' his 'too self-conscious superiority,' his 'inability to make the mediocre follow him,' his 'offence tactics in the worst moments of defeat,' his 'high revolutionary algebra perpetually cast before swine, when the swine alone held the front of the stage . . .'

'Obviously, obviously,' Fleischman murmured, making no effort to overcome his uneasiness.

Rublev must have been very sure that he was going to be shot, or he would never have written such things? . . .

The tone of the writing changed, but the same inner conviction gave it even more detachment. 'We were an exceptional human accomplishment, and that is why we are going under. A half century unique in history was required to form our generation. Just as a great creative mind is a unique biological and social accomplishment, caused by innumerable interferences, the formation of our few thousand minds is to be explained by interferences that were unique. Capitalism at its apogee, rich with all the powers of industrial civilization, was planted in a great peasant country, a country of ancient culture, while a senile despotism moved year by year towards its end. Neither the old castes nor the new classes could be strong, neither the one nor the other could feel sure of the future. We grew up amid struggle, escaping two profound captivities, that of the old "Holy Russia," and that of the *bourgeois* West, at the same time that we borrowed from those two worlds their most living elements: the spirit of inquiry, the transforming audacity, the faith in progress of the nineteenth-century West; a peasant people's direct feeling for truth and for action, and its spirit of revolt, formed by centuries of despotism. We never had a sense of the stability of the social world; we never had a belief in wealth; we were never the puppets of *bourgeois* individualism, dedicated to the struggle for money; we perpetually questioned ourselves about the meaning of life and we worked to transform the world . . .

'We acquired a degree of lucidity and disinterestedness which made both the old and the new interests uneasy. It was impossible for us to adapt ourselves to a phase of reaction; and as we were in power, surrounded by a legend that was true, born of our deeds, we were so dangerous that we had to be destroyed beyond physical destruction, our corpses had to be surrounded by a legend of treachery . . .

'The weight of the world is upon us, we are crushed by it. All those who want neither drive nor uncertainty in the successful revolution overwhelm us; and behind them they have all those whom the fear of revolution blinds and saps . . .' Rublev was of the opinion that the implacable cruelty of our period is explained by its feeling of insecurity: fear of the future . . . 'What is going to happen in history tomorrow will be comparable only to the great geological catastrophes which change the face of the planet . . .'—'We alone, in this universe in transformation, had the courage to see clearly. It is more a matter of courage than of intelligence. We saw that, to save man, what was needed was the attitude of the surgeon. To the outside world, hungry for stability to the point of shutting its eyes to the ever-darkening horizon, we were the intolerable evil prophets of social cataclysms; to those who were comfortably established inside our own revolution, we represented venturesomeness and risk. Neither on one side nor the other did anyone see that the worst venture, the hopeless venture, is to seek for immobility at a time when continents are splitting up and breaking adrift. It would be so comforting to say to oneself that the days of creation are over: "Let us rest! We are sure of all tomorrows!" '—'An immense rage of reprobation and incomprehension rose up against us. But what sort of wild conspirators were we? We demanded the courage to continue our exploit, and people wanted nothing but more security, rest, to forget the effort and the blood—on the eve of rains of blood!'—'Upon one point we lacked clarity and daring: we were unable to perceive what the evil was which was sapping our country and for which for a time there was no remedy. We ourselves denounced as traitors and men of little faith those among us who revealed it to us . . . Because we loved our work blindly, we too . . .'

Rublev refuted the executed Nicolas Ivanovich Bukharin who, during the trial of March 1938, exclaimed: 'We were before a dark abyss . . .' (And now it became only a dialogue of the dead.) Rublev wrote: 'On the eve of our disappearance we do not reckon up the balance sheet of a disaster, we bear witness to the fullness of a victory which encroached too far upon the future and asked too much of men. We have not lived on the brink of a dark abyss, as Nicolas Ivanovich said, for he was subject to attacks of nervous depression—we are on the eve of a new cycle of storms and that is what darkens our consciences. The compass needle goes wild at the approach of magnetic storms . . .'—'We are terribly disquieting because we might soon become terribly powerful again . . .'

'You thought well, Rublev,' said Fleischman, and it made him feel a sort of pride.

He shut the notebook gently. So he would have closed the eyes of a dead man. He heated the sealing wax and slowly let drops of it, like burning blood, fall on the envelope which contained the notebooks. On the wax he pressed the great seal of the Archives of the Commissariat of the Interior: the proletarian emblem stood deeply printed.

About five o'clock Comrade Fleischman had himself driven to the stadium where the Athletic Festival was in progress. He took a seat on the official stand, among the decorated uniforms of the hierarchy. On his left breast there were two medals: the Order of Lenin and the Order of the Red Flag. The high, flat military cap increased the size of his fat face, which with the passing years had come to look much like the face of a huge frog. He felt emptied, anonymous, important: a general identical with any general of any army, feeling the first touch of old age, his flesh flabby, his spirit preoccupied by administrative details. Battalions of athletes, the young women with their arching breasts preceding the young men, marched past, necks straight, faces turned towards the stands—where they recognized no one, since the Chief, whose colossal effigy dominated the entire stadium, had not come. But they smiled at the uniforms with cheerful confidence. Their footsteps on the ground were like a rhythmic rain of hail. Tanks passed, covered with green branches and flowers. Standing in the turrets, the machine-gunners in their black leather headgear waved bouquets tied with red ribbons. High banks of cloud, gilded by the setting sun, deployed powerfully over the sky.

Paris (Pré-St.-Gervais),
Agen, Marseille,
Ciudad Trujillo (Dominican Republic).
Mexico 1940–42.